"Another stellar effort from Taylor."
—Booklist

"Satisfies from start to finish."
—Kirkus Reviews (Starred Review)

"Action-packed....Those who prize
authentic military action will be rewarded."
—Publishers Weekly

P9-EGL-598

Praise for the Novels
of Brad Taylor

Enemy of Mine

"The story moves along at a rapid clip . . . satisfies from start to finish."　　*—Kirkus Reviews* (starred review)

"Few authors write about espionage, terrorism, and clandestine hit squads as well as Taylor does, and with good reason: He spent more than twenty years in the army before retiring as a Special Forces lieutenant colonel. His boots-on-the-ground insight into the situation in the Middle East and special skills in 'irregular warfare' and 'asymmetric threats' give his writing a realistic, graphic tone."　　　　　　　　　　　　*—Houston Press*

"Taylor gets exponentially better with each book, and if someone is hunting for a literary franchise to turn into a film, they need to be looking at this series."

—Bookreporter.com

"Action-packed. . . . Those who prize authentic military action will be rewarded."　　　*—Publishers Weekly*

"Pike Logan returns in another stellar effort from Taylor, a retired Delta Force commander. . . . Readers of novels set in the world of Special Forces have many choices, but Taylor is one of the best. His obvious insider knowledge, combined with a well-constructed narrative, make all his work—and this novel in particular—a delight for fans of the subgenre. The added female viewpoint here provides a fascinating perspective on a primarily male-dominated world."　　　　　　　　　　　　　　*—Booklist*

All Necessary Force

"Fresh plot, great action, and Taylor clearly knows what he is writing about. . . . When it comes to tactics and hardware, he is spot-on."　　　　　—Vince Flynn

continued . . .

"A fast and furious tale with a boots-on-the-ground realism that could only have been evoked by someone who intimately knows combat. Brad Taylor spent decades fighting America's enemies in the dark corners where they live, and his experience shows. Pike Logan is a tough, appealing hero you're sure to root for."
—*New York Times* bestselling author Joseph Finder

"Anyone who admires America's fighting forces and appreciates a page-turning read as much as I do is sure to find Lieutenant Colonel (ret.) Brad Taylor's debut thriller exciting. *One Rough Man* is authentic and gripping."
—Newt Gingrich, *New York Times* bestselling author and former Speaker of the U.S. House of Representatives

"The deadly duel between Pike and the terrorists is both cerebral and graphically violent. . . . [Taylor] brings such incredible realism and authenticity that readers feel like they are looking over the shoulders of a real antiterrorist operation. This will appeal to Brad Thor and Vince Flynn fans."
—*Library Journal*

"*One Rough Man* has a level of authenticity unrivaled in thriller fiction, and that's because of the author. . . . To say that this is going to be an exciting series is an understatement."
—*The Chattooga Press*

"This is one wild, fun, and unforgettable ride."
—Bookreporter.com

"Taylor has created a true heroine in plucky college student Jennifer. While she's not in Logan's league, she knows how to hold her own."
—*Mystery Scene*

"Brad Taylor provides an exciting thriller that grips the audience from the opening mission in Georgia and never slows down for a nanosecond. Action-packed."
—Genre Go Round Reviews

ALSO BY BRAD TAYLOR

One Rough Man
All Necessary Force

ENEMY OF MINE

A PIKE LOGAN THRILLER

BRAD TAYLOR

A SIGNET BOOK

SIGNET
Published by the Penguin Group
Penguin Group (USA) LLC, 375 Hudson Street,
New York, New York 10014

USA | Canada | UK | Ireland | Australia | New Zealand | India | South Africa | China
penguin.com
A Penguin Random House Company

Published by Signet, an imprint of New American Library, a division of Penguin
Group (USA) LLC. Previously published in a Dutton edition.

First Signet Printing, January 2014

Ⓟ REGISTERED TRADEMARK—MARCA REGISTRADA

ISBN 978-0-451-41993-4

Printed in the United States of America
10 9 8 7 6 5 4 3 2

To my mother and father,
for teaching me the art of the possible

Certainly there is no hunting like the hunting of man and those who have hunted armed men long enough and liked it, never really care for anything else thereafter.

Ernest Hemingway

The enemy of my enemy is my friend.

Arabic Proverb

PROLOGUE

Two months ago

The time to start recording came and went, and I hesitated still. I studied the screen, searching for whatever was causing my reticence. I saw nothing out of the ordinary. Nothing I hadn't seen a hundred times before. A simple room, ten feet by twenty feet, with only a beat-up desk and chair. No place to hide. No weapons of any kind. A room tailor-made for a takedown.

Yet a vague unease made me pause, like the fleeting stench of something rotten under the floor. Made me believe that perhaps I wouldn't want anyone in the future to see what I was about to witness.

The camera was located just above the single door to the room, allowing me full view of its entire length. The image it fed to the screen was grainy and harsh as it strained to work in the dim light of the single fluorescent bulb. The corners were hidden in shadows, but the desk was clearly illuminated. Good enough to trigger the assault when the time came.

I caught movement, and saw the top edge of the door swing open. I quickly dialed my phone, alerting the team. "Stand by."

A figure entered the frame. It was a woman. Not the target. She moved to the desk, then turned around, giving me a clear shot of her face. I knew her.

What the hell is she doing here? Why didn't she stay home?

I said, "We have an innocent on the X. I'm calling an abort."

A voice I didn't recognize answered. "Mission takes priority. No abort."

A small girl entered the screen, running to the woman.

"You've now got two innocents. One child. Abort. My call."

"It's not your call. It's a Taskforce call, and the mission takes priority."

The decision made no sense. We had plenty of other opportunities to get this guy, and the noncombatants had the potential to turn the hit into a fiasco. At the very least, it would be impossible to keep the operation from leaking out.

"Who the hell is this? Put on the team leader."

All I heard was "Mission takes priority." Then a click as he hung up. I was redialing when another figure entered the room. A man, but not the target. The man didn't turn around, but I knew who it was. The woman's face showed fear, and the child darted behind her back. The man advanced toward them both and I saw he was holding a club.

The phone connected and I said, "The innocents are in trouble. Execute, execute, execute."

The mechanical voice said, "Trouble from the target? Is the target there?"

"No. It's someone else, but he's bad. I know he's bad. Get in there!"

"The mission takes priority. We wait for the target."

The man jabbed with the club like he was holding a sword, hitting the woman in the stomach. She doubled over.

"Dammit, get your ass in there, now!"

The phone was dead.

The man swung the club upward, catching the woman in the jaw. The impact split her jaw sideways in a spray of blood, the stark white of bone punching through the red flesh of her cheek.

I screamed at the flickering image and grabbed the edges of the monitor, desperately trying to will myself to the scene.

The woman fell backward onto the desk, exposing the girl. She cowered at the man's feet, tears running down her face, her mouth open in a shriek I couldn't hear. The man grabbed her by the head and lifted her off the ground. He rocked to the left once, then violently swung to the right, whipsawing the small child into the wall by her head. She crumpled in an unnatural heap. The man withdrew a knife from his jacket and held it up high. In full view of the camera. For me to see. Then he began to slowly turn toward the lens . . .

. . . And I woke up, drawing in great gulps of air. I was disoriented and bathed in sweat, the feeble light from the outside parking lot finally showing me the corners of the hotel room. I felt an echo, and wondered if I'd screamed for real. I began to sit up when the nausea hit. I scrambled for the toilet through the dim light, reaching it a second before spewing out everything I had eaten in the last six hours.

The heaves subsided and I curled next to the toilet, still trembling at the aftershocks of the dream.

The man had returned, and now he was bringing my family with him.

I should have never looked at the pictures.

It had been four years since the murder of my wife and daughter, and I had never had a dream of the crime. I had dreamed of the man plenty. He stalked me like a Freddy Krueger, popping up in all sorts of weird ways, but never with my family. Never. I had been blessed with nothing but good dreams of them. Dreams that brought melancholy when I awoke, but good nonetheless. Ephemeral moments I tried hard to remember, but which faded away like fog hit by the morning sun. Unlike this one. Acid wouldn't remove the etching it had left in my soul, I knew.

Why did I look?

I had come back to Fayetteville, North Carolina, to check on any progress in solving the crime, like I had done about every three months since the murders, as if my presence would cause something to break free. It never did. The case was as cold as Jimmy Hoffa, and the police barely tolerated me now. They were nice enough, but they knew it was going nowhere, and looked at me with pity.

This time I had decided to study the crime-scene photos to see if there was a clue they were missing, something I'd never done before. Something others had warned me against. Four years ago the officers had said the pictures were brutal, and because of it, at every visit, I had never asked. This time I did. And they were right.

Now the pictures had brought the stalker to my family. Had allowed him unfettered access to torture me every night, a faceless mass of evil that would never leave me in peace.

In all the dreams I saw him from the back. He never turned around. Never showed me his true nature, content to simply taunt me, like he had tonight with the knife. Deep inside, a part of me begged for him to show himself. A corner of my soul that lived in blackness and craved escape. Craved relief. It believed that if I could see him, I could kill him.

And it desperately wanted to do that.

1

When she saw her suitcase come up first on the conveyor belt, the investigator's face broke into a smile. The flight from Beirut had been a long one, and she was ready to get home. Had she known how little time she had left, she most definitely would have preferred it to come out last—or not at all.

Across the baggage claim area, a man caught her expression, and grinned to himself at the irony: He knew the airport luggage tag that had proved so efficient in delivering her suitcase would also be the cause of her death. All he needed to do was make sure she didn't rip it off and throw it in the trash before she left the airport.

He watched her intently until she had exited, suitcase in tow, traitorous baggage tag flapping in the breeze. In her right hand, she held a briefcase, and in the swing of her arm the man caught a glimpse of the handcuff that attached it to her wrist. That was his target. Along with destroying the information in her brain.

She exited in the direction of the shuttle bus that ferried passengers to the Rotterdam train station, but she could just as easily be hiring a car to her destination. Either way, he knew where she was going: Leidschendam, home of the Special Tribunal for Lebanon.

Established in 2009, the tribunal was tasked with investigating the 2005 assassination of Rafic Hariri, the former prime minister of Lebanon. Amid rumors that high-ranking officials in the Syrian government and their terrorist proxy Hezbollah had a hand in the murder, massive protests had rocked the country demanding the removal of Syrian occupation forces from Lebanon. Called the Cedar Revolution, it proved to be the catalyst for a Syrian withdrawal from the country later that year. It could have ended with that—a Syrian retreat and rumors—but the tribunal was now investigating in earnest, turning over stones that should have been left untouched. Four Hezbollah foot soldiers had already been indicted, with the inquiry climbing ever higher into the ranks.

The woman was an investigator for the prosecution, and had finally managed to find a well-placed person who would talk: a disgruntled former Syrian intelligence asset with an axe to grind and some inside knowledge. He had spent an hour and a half with the investigator. Hezbollah had done what it could to prevent the meeting, but failed, managing only to make an example of the man after the fact to dissuade others who might think about talking.

The information she had discovered was extremely volatile. Knowing Hezbollah's reach, she had chosen not to file a report electronically, and certainly wasn't going to discuss it on a phone system run by the very terrorists she was investigating. She flew straight back from Beirut to the tribunal's office in the Netherlands to report in person. Which is where the man hunting her came in.

Unlike the bloodbath that could be perpetrated in Lebanon against Lebanese civilians, the investigator would have to be handled with care. Her death could in no way be attributed to her work. It *had* to appear innocent.

At first, the man thought about simply mugging her and stealing the briefcase, leaving her as a victim of random street crime. After conducting a site survey, he realized that wouldn't work. Unlike his hometown of Chicago, there wasn't a whole lot of violent crime in the Netherlands, and certainly none in the middle of the day in Leidschendam. Not to mention he'd probably have to cut off her hand to get to the contents of the briefcase, which would raise an eyebrow. He'd have to be more subtle.

After giving the investigator some time to clear the area, the man left baggage claim and returned to his car. He didn't necessarily need to beat her to her residence in Leidschendam—he had already prepared the reception— but he wanted to see the results in real time. If she traveled her usual route, she'd take the train and then walk home. That meant a three-stage movement: shuttle to the Rotterdam train station, train to the Leidschendam station, then a little over a quarter of a mile trip remaining to her house. If she followed her pattern, she'd walk it instead of getting a cab. He should be there in plenty of time to enjoy his work.

He was quite proud of his scheme, and wished his new career allowed him to converse with others like him. If there were any others, that is. He hadn't run into any with his professional skills. Just pipe-swingers with no imagination. He'd only conducted four missions where the objective had been targeted killing, but he'd found he had a talent for it. Three had been flawless. One had been an unmitigated disaster, causing him to flee the United States for good, and landing him in his current position working with Syrian intelligence. Or Hezbollah. With the spasms rocking Syria in the wake of the Arab Spring, he wasn't sure who was footing the bills anymore.

He was a meticulous planner, something that had facilitated his success in his new career field, just as it had facilitated his success in the U.S. Navy SEALs while fighting in Iraq and Afghanistan. Using that skill, he had found his method of execution.

While there was little street crime, one thing the Netherlands did have in abundance was natural gas. The country was the second largest exporter in the European Union, and almost every house used it.

Preparing the home in the investigator's absence had been easy. Figuring out how to trigger it had been hard. He had to *know* she was home, and had to execute fast enough to prevent her from discovering the trap he had prepared, which meant a surveillance team.

In no way did he want to involve anyone else in the

operation, especially not a bunch of swarthy Hezbollah gunmen who would stick out like charcoal in the snow. Being blond-haired and fair-skinned allowed him to move invisibly throughout the country, but he had no other contacts like himself. No one that could blend in. Still, he also knew that singleton surveillance efforts were a recipe for failure, which left him in a little bit of a catch-22. Until he stumbled upon the baggage tag idea.

The airline she used had invested in radio frequency identification, or RFID, for their baggage control. A small transmitter was embedded into the destination tag given at check-in. Unlike a bar code, it didn't have to be seen to be read, and would register from a much greater distance. In use by everyone from Walmart to the U.S. Department of Defense for tracking merchandise and end-items, RFID was now being used to track passenger baggage in order to prevent the huge expense airlines paid recovering and delivering lost luggage.

The tag itself simply transmitted the name of the owner of the luggage and the destination, read by machines tucked strategically around the baggage control areas of airports. Nothing sinister or evil. Just a unique identifier for each bag. You couldn't gather any more information from the RFID than that which was printed on the outside of the tag in the first place, but if you wanted to trigger an explosion exactly when a certain person entered a kill zone, the tag was ideal. It just required a slightly different kind of signal receiver. The primary risk was someone else carrying the luggage. Luckily, the investigator traveled alone.

Using his Hezbollah contacts, he had gleaned the investigator's RFID signature assigned by the airline in Beirut, fed it into a reader located in her apartment, then daisy-chained it to the initiation device. He now had no need to keep eyes on her at all. Sooner or later she'd arrive home with her luggage, and she—along with her briefcase—would be incinerated.

He took the A13 away from Rotterdam, and twenty minutes later he was boxing Sytwendepark in Voorburg, the town adjacent to Leidschendam. He passed through a traffic circle and took a left, then pulled into a parking space for a series of modern flats. Checking his rearview, he confirmed he could see the investigator's small one-story house on the parallel street, across an expanse of grass and sidewalks. He settled in to wait.

After thirty minutes, he began to grow antsy, wondering if maybe he should have mounted a surveillance effort. Wondering if she hadn't gone straight to the tribunal without stopping at home to drop off her luggage. Killing her after she'd delivered her report would be futile.

She should have been here by now.

He considered his options, toying with a kitchen magnet that housed a picture of the investigator with a man. He always collected something from each mission, and had taken the magnet while setting up his trap. It wasn't strange, like some Hannibal Lecter serial killer. He wasn't commemorating anyone's death, simply the mission it-self, like the platoon sergeant in *Saving Private Ryan* scraping sand into a can for each beach landing. At least that's what he told himself, even though everything he collected was something personal from the victims them-selves.

He glanced up the street, hoping to catch a glimpse of his prey. He was rewarded with the sight of a person dragging luggage down the promenade between his road and hers, about three hundred meters away. He couldn't be sure it was his target, but the odds of two people with luggage at this time, on this street, were pretty slim. He sank back into his seat and waited, checking his rearview for the front of the house. What he saw caused him to sit back up.

A man was stapling something above her front door. The same man from the kitchen magnet picture.

What the hell?

He looked out his window and saw the investigator still walking, closing the distance. She'd be at home in a matter of minutes.

He turned around completely, facing the residence. The man was hanging some sort of sign over the door, like one of those happy-birthday stringers purchased at a grocery store. The sign was in Dutch, but he knew in-stinctively what it said. *Welcome Home.*

Shit. It's a booty call.

During the entire time he had cased the place, he had never seen anyone pay any attention to the house, which, of course, made sense now, since the investigator was in Beirut. He cursed his stupidity.

The boyfriend used a key and entered the home. If allowed to continue, he would find the trap the assassin had laid, and raise the alarm—before the RFID tag triggered.

Reacting without thought, the assassin exited his car and sprinted to the door. He saw the target in the distance, now close enough to identify. He had about thirty seconds. Maybe a minute if he locked the door behind him. A minute to kill the man and exit out the back of the house before the investigator inadvertently blew them all to pieces.

He entered, slammed the door, and locked it. He found the boyfriend next to the RFID reader on the kitchen counter, a bag of rose petals in one hand and a bottle of wine in the other.

The boyfriend shouted something in Dutch, then pointed to the RFID reader, saying something else. The assassin closed on him, grabbing the back of his head and slamming it into the counter in a blow that should have killed him outright. If not, it most certainly should have stopped the fight. Miraculously, the boyfriend rose, blinded by the blood in his face but screaming at the top of his lungs and swinging wildly.

The assassin danced back, out of reach, and picked up a vase, hearing the investigator outside. He flung the vase full-force into the head of the boyfriend. Unable to see to block the missile, the vase cracked him above the bridge of his nose and dropped him like a stone.

The assassin heard more shouting and turned to find the investigator in the foyer, raising her luggage as a weapon with both hands, the briefcase dangling off her wrist. He prepared to deflect it and continue the assault when he realized what was about to happen.

She's going to kill us all.

He had no firm idea of the RFID's reading range, but clearly, since he was still alive, it didn't extend to the foyer. He was positive, though, that if she threw the luggage at him, it would turn into a much greater weapon than she planned.

He saw her wind up to heave the bag, and began running. He glanced back and saw the bag turning in the air in slow motion, the tag fluttering like confetti from the handle. He hit the large plate-glass window at the back of the room full-force, oblivious to the pain as he punched through. He crashed beyond the brick protection of the walls as he heard the initiation of his clever kill-box: a small *wump*, followed by a blast of fire out of the window like the late ignition of a gas grill.

He rolled around on the ground for a second, ensuring he wasn't on fire, then rose and surveyed the damage. The outside of the house had contained the blast, but the inside, through the window, was an inferno.

No way will they be able to find anything through forensics.

He circled around to his car, milling in with the multitudes that had come to help or just watch the show. He fled the neighborhood at a leisurely pace, driving randomly for five miles before stopping and pulling out an international cell phone.

"This is Infidel. It's done."

2

Colonel Kurt Hale finished his briefing, knowing that the detailed information was overkill. The target, who they'd nicknamed "Crusty" because his hair reminded everyone of the *Simpsons* cartoon character Krusty the Clown, had been chosen for Omega authority on two other occasions. Nothing in Kurt's briefing had changed from those other two attempts at taking him off the board. In fact, Crusty had become *more* involved in terrorist financing—and maybe stepped into an operational role. The only thing that had changed was the Oversight Council's membership roster after the presidential election. Not a complete shuffle, but five of the thirteen members were new. It shouldn't matter—the information should stand on its own—but Kurt had learned the hard way that individual personalities meant a great deal in Washington, DC.

As the commander of the Taskforce—a counterterrorist organization made up of the best operators from the special mission units of the Department of Defense and the National Clandestine Services of the CIA—Kurt wasn't a voting member of the Council. Since the Task-force operated outside the bounds of U.S. law, everything they did was incredibly sensitive, and his position was seen as too much of a conflict of interest. He agreed with the sentiment, but in this case he was afraid the Council would balk simply because they were new. Well, new and the fact that the last Taskforce action had occurred on U.S. soil—directly against their charter—and had almost made front-page news. If it had, the entire Council would have ended up in jail, their lives destroyed.

Kurt could tell they were skittish about granting him Omega, the last mission's close call fresh in their minds. Luckily, President Warren had decided to attend this up-date. Theoretically, his vote carried no more weight than anyone else's, but realistically, everyone knew it did, if for no other reason than he'd appointed everyone else on the Council.

He knows how critical this vote is. I'm giving them a softball. If they say no here, we might as well disband, because the next one will be worse.

Kurt waited for the first question. It came from President Warren, setting the tone. "So this is the same guy we were chasing when we diverted to Bosnia two years ago? The financier?"

"Yes, sir. No change to his operational profile. Still in Tunisia, and still doing bad things. The only difference is that he's moved from Tunis to Sousse, farther down the coast."

"And no change to *our* operational profile?"

"No, sir. We've been at Sigma for the last three years. Never changed. Same cover organization, same planning considerations."

The Taskforce called each stage of an operation a different Greek letter, starting with Alpha for the initial introduction of forces. Sigma was the last phase before Omega—authority for a takedown. The end for a terrorist.

"How can you say nothing's changed? Tunisia went through a seizure two years ago. The government was overthrown. Another one has taken its place. Surely that matters."

Kurt was momentarily taken aback at the attack, expecting the president to support him. Then he realized that's exactly what the president was doing, giving him a platform to short-circuit any reason for the Council to say no.

"Well, yes, that's a consideration, but truthfully the change of government has made this easier, not harder. Besides finding a target, the biggest problem in doing an operation in another sovereign country is penetrating that country's own security apparatus. In this case, it's in disarray. The public distrusts anyone in the old intelligence agencies."

The new secretary of state, Jonathan Billings, tentatively snaked his hand in the air like he was in grade school. He'd never been in an Oversight Council meeting, and Kurt could tell he was intimidated. Maybe wishing he'd never agreed to sign the nondisclosure statement and seal his fate should something go wrong. After the troubles he'd had with the previous SECSTATE, Kurt dreaded what was going to come out of his mouth.

President Warren said, "John, you don't need to raise your hand. What do you have?"

"Uhh . . . I know I'm new to the Oversight Council, but I'm wondering why we're wasting so much time on this. Seems like an easy decision to me. Unless I'm missing something. From what I was briefed, this profile is the perfect mission. *Am* I missing something?"

Kurt fought to control his facial expression, keeping it neutral, waiting on a council member to confirm or refute the statement. It came from the secretary of defense, a man who'd lived through every Omega operation conducted. Not an enemy, but someone who understood the repercussions.

"Hang on, here," the SECDEF said. "Yeah, it's the perfect profile, but so is a takedown of just about a thousand other people. We can do the mission, I don't question that. But is this guy still worth the effort? After the death of bin Laden and all the other leadership in the old AQ hierarchy? Is he still a player, or is this a Taskforce vendetta based on the fact you've never managed to get him?"

Kurt said, "Yeah, he's worth the effort. Besides continuing to be a conduit of funds for various terrorist groups, we now have indications he's stepped into an operational role. It's not something we can pin for sure, but he's apparently funding an assassination attempt in Lebanon, refusing to provide money unless he gets to pick the target. It's not a direct threat against U.S. interests, but given the unrest over there, pulling him now can only be beneficial."

The director of the CIA said, "How sound is that intel? From what I'm seeing, about half is just guessing at what's going on in the Levant."

Kurt said, "Honestly, not that good. We've got a case officer in Lebanon with greater penetration than any of your assets—no offense—but it's still iffy. We're putting a team into Syria in the next few days to see if we can regain a handle there, but that's not a determining factor here. Forget I mentioned the Lebanon assassination angle. Crusty still needs to go. He's a threat to U.S. national interests. Always has been."

The SECDEF and DCI sat back, satisfied. President Warren called the vote, and before Kurt knew, it was over. Omega authority. For a target the Taskforce had hunted since its inception. He didn't want his emotions to show earlier, maybe clouding the vote, but this *was* personal.

Finally. He wanted to flee the room right there and send the message to the team.

President Warren interrupted his thoughts. "Okay, on to other business. Who's going to Syria, and when?"

Kurt smiled. "Pike. Well, Pike's company."

"I thought his 'company employees' were in Tunisia? Taking down Crusty?"

"They are. It should have taken five months to get a visa for Syria, but the Syrian government pushed it through. Pike's going with Jennifer. The team will catch up. We can't waste the opportunity. We don't know when the government will shut down our entry. Nobody else in the U.S. can get in, but Pike's cover business worked out perfectly. The government itself is actually helping us penetrate."

"When's he leave?"

"Uhh . . . as soon as possible. We got the visas back today. But he doesn't know he's deploying yet."

3

I heard Jennifer enter the front door of the office and I rapidly began stroking keys, desperately trying to shut down the first-person shooter I was playing and bring up the boring archeology research I was supposed to be assimilating. I wasn't quick enough, which was about par for the course in the game itself.

Getting my ass kicked by a bunch of thirteen-year-olds, now about to get my ass kicked by Jennifer.

"What are you doing? Are you playing that stupid game?"

Show apparent innocence . . . no proof . . . give up nothing.

"What? What do you mean? I'm studying. Just like when you left."

Jennifer leaned against the door and shook her head, giving me her "disapproving teacher" face. I would never tell her this, because it would only encourage her, but the look really worked. I felt a little ashamed before she even opened her mouth.

"Pike, come on. This is our one shot at a real archeological expedition. You *need* to know this stuff, if for no other reason than to protect the cover. There won't be any Taskforce oversight helping us out here. You need to look and sound like you know what you're doing on this dig."

Jennifer and I were partners in a cover company called Grolier Recovery Services, which camouflaged Taskforce activity. Ostensibly, we specialized in facilitating archeological work around the world. In reality, we used the company to let us penetrate denied areas so we could put some terrorist's head on a spike. The cover had worked well so far, because it gave us a plausible reason to travel anywhere that had something of historical significance, which was basically any place on the planet with solid ground—and a few places underwater.

The difference was that we'd really been hired for this job. No Taskforce paycheck on this one, although it was the Taskforce that had linked up our company with the project. Jennifer was really, *really* looking forward to the trip, because she was a pencil-neck at heart. A scientist torn between being a plant-eater and a meat-eater.

I said, "Jennifer, we aren't leaving for at least three months. The Syrians aren't going to approve a visa for either of us until they're convinced we aren't some secret James Bond organization. I've got plenty of time to study this boring shit."

I saw her eyes cloud and knew I'd blurted too much from the heart.

"Wait . . . wait . . . that didn't come out right—"

"Boring shit? Is that what you think? Well how about you do it because *I* asked for a change? I've done *everything* you've asked for the Taskforce. Don't mess this up for me. All you have to do is a little studying. I promise, you'll like it. Bloodshed and death. Right up your alley."

We'd been asked by an American university to help reestablish archeological work at a place called Hamoukar in northern Syria, right near the border with Iraq. The site had been discovered in 1999, with digs conducted every year since then. In 2011, with the upheavals in Syria, the digs had been discontinued. Now, the university was headed back to reopen the dig and had hired us to provide the coordination and on-site security for the work.

The find was apparently one of the oldest cities ever discovered, a treasure trove of artifacts that sent shivers down my spine. I couldn't *wait* to see the broken pottery shards and old bricks. Okay, that's a little uncharitable, I suppose. There was one cool thing about the place: The city itself had apparently been destroyed in the first recorded occurrence of urban warfare.

I spread my hands, attempting to salvage the night. "Okay, okay. I'll study it. I promise. I get it's important. We still going out tonight? Or am I grounded?"

She squinted for a second, then said, "Maybe I should have you take a test. If you pass, we'll go out."

I smiled. "Fire away. I know more than you think."

"Oh, please. You'll just make up something and claim I'm wrong. Let's go. Where'd you decide?"

Tonight was the one-year anniversary of the establishment of our business. We'd tossed a coin to see who'd get to pick and I had won. Which meant we weren't going to some wine bar.

"Blind Tiger. On Broad Street."

"Do they serve anything besides hamburgers?"

"Yeah. You'll like it. I promise."

4

I dropped Jennifer off out front and found a parking spot a block and a half away on Church Street. The Charleston weather was perfect, with a warm breeze and the will-o'-the-wisp smell of pluff mud hanging faintly in the air. I passed a wedding reception and had my short walk marred by a rowdy group breaking free and following me down Broad Street. As luck would have it, they came right into the pub with me, apparently deciding that paying for their liquor was more fun than drinking for free.

I scanned the inside of the pub for Jennifer, came up empty, and moved to the backyard patio. I spotted her at a table at the rear of the deck, two drafts of Guinness in front of her. I couldn't fault her taste.

I pulled out a chair. "Great choice on the beer. Did I sit at the right table?"

She grinned. "I keep my word. You won the bet, so it's your beer."

She snaked a hand across the table. "How was last night?"

I knew why she asked, and was a little embarrassed at the attention.

"Fine. He didn't come."

Jennifer knew exactly who I meant. She knew everything that had occurred with my family, and I'd poured out my soul about the dream when I'd returned back to Charleston two months ago. The stalker had shown up a few times since, but only once with my family. Jennifer prodded me every day about it, and I was sure she was going to recommend some psychobabble therapy if it happened again. She stared at me like she was surveying my conscious for a lie, as if I was a chick who needed to vomit my feelings in a social group, which did nothing but piss me off.

"Quit that. You're going to ruin the night. Can we talk about something else?"

She considered me for a moment, squinting her eyes. I waited her out until she finally shook her head. She held up her phone. "Our contact with the university called," meaning the Taskforce. "Our visas have been approved. We can go as soon as we're ready."

Before I could answer, one of the drunk groomsmen rammed into the back of my chair, knocking me forward. I whirled around to see him standing with his hands in the air.

" 'Scuze me. Sorry."

His four other buddies and the two women with them were all laughing like they were watching a stand-up routine, drinking out of plastic cups that had been decorated for the wedding reception. I felt Jennifer grab my wrist, getting my attention.

"Let it go. They're just having fun."

I told the guy it was no problem, and sat back down.

"What did Kurt say?"

"Apparently the Syrian government is keen to get this dig going again. Prove to the world that they're returning to normal. The Ministry of Culture pushed through the visas. The university isn't prepared to deploy yet, but they want us to go over and do a site survey. If we say it's good, they'll follow."

Site survey. Right. Chickenshits are afraid. Kurt must be laughing his ass off at the Syrian government helping the Taskforce penetrate their state.

"What about Knuckles and the crew? They're supposed to go with us."

Before she could answer, another drunk groomsman was standing by our table, swaying slightly.

"Hey, I want to apologize for my friend there. Let me buy you guys a beer."

I smiled at him, "That's okay. We're fine. Thanks."

"I want to. I really want to." He listed forward, spilling some of the beer from his ridiculous pink cup onto our table.

I stood up. "I said it's all right. Please leave us alone."

My tone was nice, but my glare wasn't. Jennifer saw the challenge going out and stepped between us, looking at me.

"Let's go somewhere else."

Why the hell should we leave? I thought about it. About the trouble we'd get in. About our trip coming up and the unwanted attention I'd draw if I mopped up the deck with all five of these assholes. And about the fact that Jennifer had asked—which meant more than the other considerations combined.

"All right. You get to pick this time, but walking distance from here."

She took my hand and led us through the throng of the drunken wedding party. We were on the far side of the group when one of the men reached out and pinched her ass, then ducked back into the protection of the pack, giggling.

I couldn't believe the audacity. Jennifer and I still didn't know where we stood with each other, whether we were business partners, friends, or something more. One thing was for sure, though: Our relationship had gone way beyond my letting anyone treat her like that.

I plowed into the group and snatched the culprit by the front of his shirt, ready to rip him apart. Before I could do anything, Jennifer was on us.

"Pike! Don't! It's not that big of a deal. Let it go. He's drunk."

I stared into his eyes. "You're fucking lucky. If you apologize I won't ruin the fun you're having tonight."

His friends closed in around us. Jennifer, having seen in the past where situations like this would end up, pulled me, saying, "I don't need an apology. Come on. Let's go."

I hesitated, then pushed the man back, putting a cap on the anger and shame I felt at walking away. I knew they thought I was afraid of their numbers. That they'd won. I turned without a word and walked away. Jennifer took my hand again and grinned. "Thanks. You're getting better at asshole control."

Her smile took some of the sting out of my humiliation. I started to reply when one of the drunks groped Jennifer's ass again. The ending was not exactly what he expected. Before he could withdraw his arm and get away, Jennifer had locked it up, causing instant compliance. She swept his legs out from underneath him and he hit the ground hard, cracking his head. She fell with him, rotating around and stretching out his arm with her legs over his body. He began to scream like a child at the pain she was giving him.

Now who needs some control?

I could hear the wedding girls shrieking at what Jennifer had done. Probably wondering how they could learn to do it too. One of them began dialing a phone.

The problem with Jennifer's choice of submission was she couldn't do anything to defend herself without letting go of the man on the ground. But she knew she didn't need to.

She shouted, "Pike!" as one of the men reached for her hair. He got a handful before I landed a perfect uppercut. He was bent slightly at the waist, his chin forward. I felt his jaw slam shut as his head snapped straight back. He collapsed onto the deck, unconscious.

I spun around and faced the group, Jennifer's tussle to my back.

"Anyone else want a piece of us?"

The women just stared slack-jawed, but I could tell the men realized they had tangled with more than they had bargained for. Even in their drunken state. They were all looking for something interesting on the ground or in the trees. Anywhere but at me.

I caught flashing lights in my peripheral vision. The bridesmaid must have called the police. *Out of time.*

I slapped Jennifer's hands, shouting, "Time to go!"

She released his arm and I jerked her to her feet, saying, "Can't go out the front door."

Jennifer looked at the ten-foot brick wall at the back of the patio and started sprinting.

Great . . . acting like a monkey to evade the law. No damn dignity whatsoever.

I sprinted after her and we hit the wall at the same time, me coming off a table and her running straight up it in a toe-kip. We landed in the parking lot behind it and kept going, Jennifer laughing like we had just thrown water balloons at a car.

Driving back over the Ravenel Bridge to Mt. Pleasant, I said, "You talk about me losing control, what the hell was that back there?"

She looked a little embarrassed, then indignant.

"Enough was enough. I didn't try to hurt him. I was just subduing him. If it had been you he'd be in the hospital."

She tried to show how serious she was, but a grin leaked out.

"Well, what were you going to do after you subdued him?" I said. "With all those other guys around?"

She didn't respond, because we both knew the answer. *I* was going to step in.

"Look, I'm good with it. Those assholes deserved it, but if there's a learning point here it's that you can't go around doing that sort of stuff."

"*What?* That's what I'm always telling *you*."

"No, no, I don't mean because I think it's wrong. I mean because you're a woman. I can run around kicking ass all day and it won't raise an eyebrow."

She started to wind up and I rushed out, "It may be chauvinistic, but that's just the truth. Word's going to get out about that little scuffle, and people are going to wonder how a pencil-neck anthropologist managed to kick someone's ass that was twice her size. You have the skills now, and you need to protect them. Protect what we really do. Sorry, but that's just the way it is."

I expected her to blow up, but instead I saw her reflecting on what I had said. I decided to drop it.

"Hey, in the end I'm just glad you'll only take so much shit before you blow your top. I was beginning to wonder if you had to have a gun at your head before you'd defend yourself."

She grinned again, and I knew we were beyond it, lesson learned.

"You never finished about Knuckles. Is he coming with us, or not?"

"Not. Apparently he has his hands full doing something else."

5

Knuckles felt the heat radiating off the black pavement like an open oven, the sweat rolling down his face in a perpetual drivel, forcing him to wipe his nose every few seconds to keep the salty liquid from hitting the screen in his lap. For the first time, he began to wonder if the sensitive equipment could withstand the punishment. After all, almost all of it was specially constructed—without the military specifications that made the equipment look, well, military.

Taskforce spends bazillions on kit and I'm in a van with no AC. Blending in is one thing, but this is ridiculous. Johnny's going to pay.

Johnny was the team leader of the Taskforce element that Knuckles was replacing, and as such, he was the one who'd coordinated all of the in-country assets. Not that Knuckles couldn't have done so in his sleep. He'd been to Tunisia chasing Crusty on and off for damn near eight years, always waiting on Omega.

In truth, the rotations had grown boring, with only one bit of adventure when Crusty had moved from Tunis, the capital, to Sousse, farther down the coast, after the uprisings that brought down the government in the initial salvos of the Arab Spring. Crusty didn't know it, but the move actually fit in better for the Taskforce cover. His desire to remain anonymous to whatever new government took over had inadvertently helped them out.

A couple of years ago, Knuckles had actually gotten Omega authority while he was on rotation—on the X and ready to go—when he'd been diverted to another mission, sparing the terrorist yet again. He had begun to think that Crusty would never go. That he had some lucky charm allowing him to evade the U.S. net, even though he stomped around in plain sight. Knuckles had deployed to Sousse with his team three days ago, and while transitioning with Johnny's team, prepping for yet another collection mission, the mythical Omega call came from Colonel Hale.

The Bluetooth in his ear chirped, the voice coming through sounding sterile because of the encryption. "Knuckles, this is Decoy. We're in."

"Good to go . . . break, break, Johnny, you got eyes on Crusty?"

"Still at the office. No issues."

Lieutenant Colonel Blaine Alexander, the element leader for Omega operations, had decided to continue with the collection mission first, before taking Crusty down. Knuckles had fought it, wanting to do the mission and get the hell out of Tunisia, but there'd been some chatter about an assassination attempt, and while an interrogation would collect invaluable data, there was the option to simply monitor Crusty for a few days. See what he said and who he talked to. So they were planting clandestine cameras inside his residence, imaging his hard drive, and wiring the place for sound. If it didn't provide any benefit, they'd take him down.

Knuckles couldn't fault Blaine's logic, especially since Crusty had evaded capture for damn near ten years. Interrogations were fine, and Crusty would get plenty of them, but you never really knew if the subject wasn't just stringing you along, telling you a bald-faced lie to protect himself. As Blaine had said about the cameras, "one-eye don't lie."

A few more days won't hurt . . . if I don't melt.

He looked at his watch and called Johnny again, wondering why Crusty was breaking his pattern, today of all days.

"Johnny, this is Knuckles, what's his status? He should have broken the box ten minutes ago."

"Easy. I've got the place locked down, and a beacon on his moped. He's still inside. If it changes, I'll call you."

Knuckles paused, wanting to remind Johnny who was in charge out here on the ground. He took the high road.

"Roger. Standing by."

The call aggravated him. The light admonishment of "easy" was a direct slap in his face. Made more glaring because everyone on the net knew that he'd just spent the last eight months in physical therapy from a catastrophic wound sustained on a mission similar to this one. It was an unspoken question of whether he was still capable. *Like I'm about to panic or something.*

In truth, Johnny's team should have been headed home right now, but with the additional mission tasked by Blaine, they'd stayed behind, their whole purpose to keep eyes on Crusty while Knuckles's team did the breaking and entering. It made sense, because Johnny's men had the most recent pattern of life on the target, but the call still grated.

His earpiece crackled, bringing him back to the mission. "Cameras and mikes in place. Going to image the hard drive now."

"Roger. No movement on the target. Plenty of time."

Johnny cut in, "Crusty's on the move. Got a trigger on the moped."

What?

"Say again? The moped's moving? Who was the trigger on the office? Did you get positive ID that he left the building?"

"Uhh . . . no. No PID. But the moped's leaving now. I've got the beacon track. I'm getting someone on it. I'll have a visual ASAP."

"How'd he get out without you triggering?"

He got no response and knew there'd been a screwup. He saw no reason to drive the blade home a second time, and simply waited. He was in a position to react, should he have to.

Still plenty of time. Let it play out.

Knuckles called Blaine in the Ops Center, giving an update and letting him know they were in motion.

Retro, the other operator with him, analyzed the beacon track and said, "He's doing the usual pattern. No issues there, but how the hell did he get out of the building without Johnny seeing him? Something's not kosher."

"I don't know, and I don't trust this tech surveillance bullshit. All we know is that his moped is moving. No idea if he's on it or not." Knuckles thought about it for a second, then said, "We're still good. He's either in the building or on the moped. We got that track, and he's still a good twenty minutes away from his house."

Knuckles was about to check in with Decoy, when he was beaten to the punch. "We got an intruder. I say again, we got an intruder."

What the hell? In all the time they'd tracked Crusty, he'd gone to this apartment alone.

"Say again?"

Decoy's breath came in pants as he sprinted somewhere Knuckles couldn't see. "His mistress just entered the building. We're moving to the roof. We've got the cameras operational on Wi-Fi. She's on the ground floor, and searching. I don't know what she's searching for, but it had better not be us."

"Get out of sight. Get gone."

Seconds later, Decoy came back, no longer out of breath. "She's packing up. She's got some luggage and she's shoving things in."

"What do you mean? She's packing *his* clothes? How's she acting? Is she taking a trip with a friend, or running from the law?"

"She's definitely running from the law. She's packing like someone's going to kick the door in. And it's all of his shit. There isn't any women's stuff in here. She's on the second floor now, and ripping his laptop apart from the docking station."

Knuckles remembered the mission. "Did you image it?"

"No time. She came in before we could."

It took a moment for the full ramifications to hit home. *He knows he's being hunted. He's going to run.*

He called Blaine and gave a SITREP, getting authority for an in-extremis takedown of a fleeting target. It was risky, because they weren't set for a perfect hit, but they *did* know his habitual route. Knuckles was positioned to intercept if necessary. The only problem was that Crusty was now going to pick the kill zone. Not optimal.

Retro gave him a location of the beacon track, and he saw it was only a few blocks away, on a street headed to the P12 highway. Still inside the residential area where the roads were no more than alleys, ribbons that wandered aimlessly, hemmed in by wall-to-wall buildings on either side.

Got to get to him before he hits the thoroughfare.

He gunned their van, swinging it around the narrow street, ignoring the bleating horn from the vehicle behind him as he hopped the curb to complete the U-turn.

"Retro, give me a lock-on."

"Two blocks back. He's on a one-lane road right now. Take a left, and we'll intersect his line of march behind him. What's the play?"

Knuckles thought for a moment, driving like a madman, then said, "Push his ass over with the van. If anyone's on the road, let him go."

"Vehicles aren't the only threat. You can't predict who'll see this from the buildings. You sure?"

"No. But he's running, which means we've been blown somehow. We need to get his ass for that as much as anything else."

They made the left and entered a narrow one-way road with barely enough room for the van, the uneven cobblestone surface rattling Knuckles's teeth. In front of them was a moped, the man on it having a bald top with a ring of ragged hair blowing in the wind, a Bluetooth headset in his ear.

Crusty.

Knuckles looked down the street and saw nothing but the occasional garbage bin. No vehicles or pedestrians. He inched the van forward, saying, "Check our six. Anything?"

Retro said, "Nothing I can see, but that don't mean shit."

"Good enough for government work."

Knuckles floored the van, closing in behind the moped. He brought the nose adjacent to its rear tire, then gently swung the bumper over, just enough to kiss the rubber. The contact caused Crusty to panic, jerking the handlebars in an overreaction. The moped skipped onto a pile of trash, he hammered the front brake, and the front wheel locked up. The moped swung sideways, launching the terrorist out of the saddle. They both skittered to a halt twenty feet in front of the van.

Retro was already out of the door before the bike stopped its slide, Taser at the ready. He hit the juice as Knuckles pulled abreast, the door of the vehicle open and waiting.

Retro threw him in the van, slamming the door shut and giving Knuckles a look of utter amazement. Knuckles floored the gas, getting out of the area, feeling physically sick.

He called Blaine in the Ops Center.

"We took down the moped. But it isn't Crusty."

6

His true name was Abdul Rahman, but he had not heard it uttered aloud in years. Sometimes, lying on his crude pallet adjacent to the remains of the Nahr al-Bared refugee camp, surrounded in darkness feebly attacked by a lone candle, he would say the name over and over, as if to prove it still existed.

He was known by many, many different names. So many that even he had trouble remembering which one to use for a given mission. He took pleasure in knowing that the Lebanese authorities, along with the Zionist dogs in Israel, believed they were tracking four or five different men.

Another time, another place, and he would have been an educated man. A scholar, perhaps. Or an engineer. He certainly looked the part. He was only five feet four inches tall, and slight of build. His vision was so weak that he was forced to wear glasses with lenses thick enough to distort his eyes when seen from the front.

Although bordering on physical frailty, he'd been blessed with one thing that had allowed him to survive in the refugee camps as a child, and to thrive as a soldier of

God: His intelligence outmatched that of just about any-one he came across. He had never been formally evalu-ated, but even as a child he had known that he was smarter than everyone else. Not in a smug or superior way. It was just a fact, like the boys who were stronger. Truth be told, he used to play stupid as a child so as to better fit in with the other boys in the camp, and had found this talent to be helpful when he wanted to be underestimated as a grown man.

His intelligence had facilitated many successes in the long struggle, but it was his strength of will that set him apart from the average fighter, no matter their skills. He simply would not quit.

In 2007, the Lebanese Armed Forces captured him in a massive sweep when they invaded the Nahr al-Bared refu-gee camp to root out the Palestinian terrorist group Fatah al-Islam. He was not a member of that group, and consid-ered it to be just one of many with more brawn and rage than brains. He went to prison anyway, with a dozen oth-ers, and was beaten for weeks, but he never gave up any of the aliases he had used in the past. Names that would have sealed his death. Eventually convinced they held a nobody, he was released, and he returned to the camp only to find it had been utterly destroyed in the fighting. A wasteland of shattered concrete and bent metal.

Infuriated at what had become of his home, he had finished the job of the LAF. Using his Palestinian connec-tions, he hunted down the remaining Fatah al-Islam members who had evaded the Lebanese net. In his mind, they did not understand the struggle, and had brought untold suffering on the Palestinian people in the camp for nothing more than a bank robbery. A simple crime that garnered nothing.

His actions spawned a plethora of myths: Hezbollah assassins had infiltrated the camps to blunt the growth of Sunni extremism; Israeli Mossad agents were using a secret weapon that killed from a distance; or a Jack the Ripper–type bogeyman was on the loose. The last was closest to the truth, with Palestinian mothers using his acts to keep rowdy children in line. He didn't bother to correct them. He became known as *Ash'abah*, or the Ghost.

He didn't associate himself with any specific group, but he'd worked for them all at one time or another. The Palestinian Liberation Organization, the Popular Front for the Liberation of Palestine, Palestinian Islamic Jihad, and many more. At the least, even with the politics and infighting, they'd all been driven by the same desires he had: pushing Israel into the sea and reclaiming Palestinian land. Recent history around the Middle East had changed that equation, frightening him to his core.

Libya was gone as a supporter, and Syria, once a staunch ally in the struggle, providing funding, equipment, and protection, was now struggling with its own survival. Osama bin Laden was dead. And the once vaunted Palestinian Liberation Organization, which had evolved into the Palestinian Authority, was on the slippery slope of capitulation, eschewing terrorism and even discussing whether to overtly affirm Israel's right to exist.

It made him physically ill, and forced him into bed with organizations whose goals he did not embrace and to whom he never would have given the time of day. Which was why he was searching for a coffee shop in south Beirut, in the heart of Hezbollah territory. Far from the protection of his Palestinian brethren.

It was only a two-hour journey by time, but seemed much farther as he left the area controlled by his people and entered Beirut, a free-for-all of sectarian feelings. The civil war had ended over ten years ago, but the scars from it still existed. It was a risk just entering Hezbollah's domain, regardless of the fact that they'd asked him to come.

He traveled through the city proper, following the old green line from the war. Reaching the south of the city, he began traveling west, toward the suburb officially known as Haret Hreik, but called the *Dahiyeh* by everyone else. The home of Hezbollah.

The Beirut he knew was left behind. More and more propaganda began littering the streets, with images of Hassan Nasrallah, the leader of Hezbollah, plastered everywhere, along with pictures of suicide bomber "martyrs." Green-and-yellow flags with a fist holding an AK-47 emblazoned on them fluttered in the breeze. Sullen men were on every street corner, armed with assault rifles, glaring at him. Begging him to do something that would allow them to stop him.

He had believed that Hezbollah was but one militia among many, and that the Sunni groups were just as powerful. He now saw he was wrong. There would be no

Lebanese incursion here, like his home had suffered in 2007, because of one crucial fact that made all the difference: Hezbollah was armed better than anyone else in the country, including the military. And men on the street corners were proud to show that off.

It aggravated him to see it, because no other group or sect was allowed to bear arms in Lebanon. Actually, by a United Nations resolution, neither was Hezbollah, but nobody seemed to question this fact. Nobody but the Zionists, that is.

He parked his car on a side street and got out to walk. He knew he was close, and circling the block was getting him nowhere.

No sooner had he stepped away from his vehicle than an enforcer carrying a radio approached him. The usual young jihadi with something to prove, a strong beard, and a stronger attitude. The Ghost knew the type, and, although it disgusted him, he also knew he was at the man's mercy. This was the last place on earth he, a Palestinian Sunni, should raise a ruckus if he wanted to live.

"What do you want?"

The Ghost went into supplication mode, knowing his frail-looking physique would help.

"I'm supposed to meet someone at a coffee shop, but I'm having trouble finding it."

He gave the name of the shop, along with the names of the men he was to meet. Immediately, the man's posture changed. He turned and barked into a radio. When he returned, he was polite.

"This way. They are waiting."

The guard led him through an alley, glancing back to make sure the Ghost followed. Possibly trying to figure out why this frail Palestinian was meeting the top tier of Hezbollah's military wing. He didn't care. He'd long since given up on posturing, letting his actions speak for him.

There was no doubt in his mind that, should things get dangerous, he had an even chance of living to see tomorrow, and a fifty-fifty chance was better than most of the odds he had faced. It would mean he would have to kill this man-boy, but he'd be able to do it.

Unlike the schoolyard fights he'd lost as a kid, where the ultimate victory was the bully shoving his face into some offal, this would mean death, and every human, no matter how tough in a simple fistfight, was at heart a frail beast when the object was killing. No armor, no fangs, no poison. A pathetic sack of flesh with a multitude of vulnerable points. If one knew where to strike.

As in the past, his physique gave his Hezbollah guide enough confidence to let down his guard, which would be his undoing, should it be necessary. Unlike the toughs on the street, he'd been in the cauldron. Killed with all manner of weapons, including none at all.

7

Knuckles gunned the engine to get out of the kill zone, ignoring the questions coming through his earpiece. When there was a break in the radio traffic from Blaine, he simply said, "Stand by," and switched from the command to the operational net, giving everyone else the situation as he knew it, and further instructions. "Johnny, collapse on the house. The girl's the new target. Decoy, set up a trigger for Johnny's team. Follow the girl. She's going to meet up with Crusty."

Retro had his knee in the back of the guy they'd ripped off the moped, going through his pockets. He pulled out a cell phone, and rapidly found the last-called number, reading it out to Knuckles.

Back on command net, Knuckles gave an abbreviated SITREP. Before Blaine could ask a question, Knuckles said, "Got a number I need a lock on. And I mean *now*."

Knuckles waited, knowing that Blaine was pulling his hair out, wanting to cut the whole mission, but also knowing he wouldn't do it with a chance of success. Although that success was now looking pretty damn slim.

After a pause, Blaine said, "Give it to me."

Yes. Knuckles read it off and gave his location.

While it was being run, Blaine said, "What's your heat state?"

"Probably pretty bad, but nothing overt as far as I can see. Why?"

"I'm thinking we don't push this. We pull back and wait for him to surface."

"Sir, he *knew* he was being hunted. It was a pretty elaborate ruse. We need to get him *now,* and not just because he's a terrorist. We can't let him talk to anyone else. We still have a thread in the girl, and maybe the phone."

"You know he tossed that phone the minute the moped guy said he was going down."

"Maybe. Maybe not. And we have the girl. Get Birdseye in the air."

The entire force was in Tunisia ostensibly conducting geographic surveys in the El Borma oil fields near the border with Algeria. As such, they had a Piper Navajo aircraft with them equipped for "aerial photography" to "facilitate" follow-on seismic surveys. In reality, the bird was specially equipped for man hunting, and included unique optics that might be needed now.

"Save that bullet. If I launch the bird, he's going to do one lap around the city, then fly to the fields. I can't have him overhead for any length of time without questions."

Knuckles silently cursed the restrictions of working

under the elaborate covers created by the Taskforce. It made them as inefficient as the terrorists they chased.

Blaine said, "Just sent you the grid for the phone. It's off now, but last location looks to be right outside the Medina."

Well, almost as inefficient.

"Roger. We're on the move."

"Watch yourself. You hear me? I don't want you pulling any Pike shit."

Retro climbed into the front seat, a grin on his face at the reference to his old team leader. He brought up the computer map as Knuckles intersected the P12 highway.

"What're we doing?"

"We're going to get that guy one way or the other."

"So we're winging shit now?"

"No. Amateurs wing shit. We're working under pressure."

Johnny came on the net. "The woman has just entered the Medina. Gonna be tough staying on her in here."

Match.

The Medina was an ancient shopping area that had been built and rebuilt countless times for more than a thousand years. Surrounded by stone walls that gave it the image of a fortress, it housed a ton of cheap souvenir shops, museums, and mosques, and was literally a maze of cobblestone streets that ran seemingly at random. It was the perfect place to avoid detection. Or pick up on surveillance, since the gate to the Medina was a choke-point everyone would have to use.

"Stick with her. His last location was just outside. They're going to meet inside. Does she still have his luggage and computer?"

"Yep. And she's moving fast."

"Which gate?"

"The big one. The martyr gate."

"Watch for countersurveillance through the chokepoint. I don't think he'll have any, but so far everything I've thought has been wrong."

"I've already got men inside ahead of her. Figured it was prudent."

Smart man. Making up for the moped mistake. Knuckles pulled into a restaurant parking lot off of the road that paralleled the port and killed the engine. "Good to go. We'll be about five minutes behind. Coming in through the Jedid gate south of you."

Retro said, "What about Crusty Two?"

Knuckles glanced back at the man, now flex-cuffed and gagged. "Put him to sleep."

He waited while Retro cinched the man's collar into his carotid arteries, causing him to pass out. Knuckles knew he would only remain unconscious for a few minutes, and he hated the thought of leaving the terrorist to his own devices while they were gone. He'd done that once before, and the guy they had captured had escaped.

He didn't see a choice.

8

They were through the Jedid gate and into the maze, a small knapsack filled with equipment bouncing against Retro's back, when the next call came in.

"She's stopped in a courtyard, sitting on a bench next to a mosque. It looks like a women-only mosque. We're sticking out big time."

Shit. Crusty was proving to be pretty damn smart after all. "Clear out. Can you send a guy through the courtyard every few minutes? Does it naturally lead somewhere else?"

"Yeah, it does, but I'm going to run out of people in three minutes. We can't park our ass here."

"I've got two more. Start the rotation and we'll follow up. We can start back the other way one by one if we have to. Where are you?"

Instead of directions, Knuckles heard, "I have no idea. Sending a picture."

Knuckles pulled out his phone, got the SMS text with the picture, and saw the mosque, a small one hemmed in by the usual stone-and-stucco buildings left and right, separated by less than four feet. Knowing the photograph was geo-tagged with its location, he initiated the GPS feature of the phone and loaded the picture. Within seconds, he had an arrow directing him to Johnny's location, along with a distance scale showing three hundred meters.

"Got it. On the way."

By the time Knuckles reached the courtyard, Johnny had used up all of his men, one after the other slowly walking through the open space and continuing on. Knuckles knew the individual walks of thirtysomething males would look out of place to anyone on the hunt, regardless of whether they did anything suspicious. He began calculating how to camouflage what they were doing and saw it was impossible. They'd get one pass each on the mosque. Maybe two at the most, but no more than that.

We need Jennifer for this bullshit.

The thought came unbidden and surprised him.

There had been a lot of discussion about females in the Taskforce after Jennifer and Pike had stopped a terrorist strike the year before. Knuckles, along with everyone else in the Taskforce, had argued against the idea. There had never been a female on the sharp end of the spear, and he, along with plenty of other operators, was determined to see that didn't change. There was no way a female could do what they did. Sure, Jennifer had risen to the occasion, but she was different. It wasn't like they all would.

During the debate inside Taskforce headquarters, Pike

had said nothing. He'd simply looked at Knuckles with disappointment.

Now Knuckles realized why. Pike had never argued the point at the time because he knew words alone would do no good. The men would have to realize what Jennifer brought to the table on their own. *Like now. A man and woman together could spend all day in that courtyard and not draw attention.*

He stopped short of the entrance to the courtyard, inside a cobblestone alley with brick-and-stucco residences built hundreds of years ago hemming him in. He sent Retro in first and backtracked out of the alley. While wandering through a meat market, waiting on Retro's call of being off target, he got their first indication of movement.

"All elements, she's off the bench and standing on the steps to the mosque. There's a woman in a burqa walking toward her."

Burqa? The full-length dress that covered a woman from head to toe was not unheard of in Tunisia, but it certainly wasn't competing as a lead in Tunisian women's fashion. Knuckles had seen very few in his multiple tours here.

He said, "Keep eyes on. Keep eyes on."

"She's eyeballing me. I can't. I'm off target."

Knuckles broke protocol and sprinted to the entrance of the courtyard, slowing down to a walking pace when he came within view of the mosque. He saw the burqa take a bag from the mistress as they both walked up the steps and entered the mosque. The gait of the covered woman triggered a memory in Knuckles's mind, gleaned from countless hours of surveillance.

Crusty.

If it *was* Crusty, his plan was pretty ingenious, since there was no way a Western male would be able to penetrate a female-only mosque. Crusty didn't have to run any countersurveillance on his mistress, as they'd be able to lose whoever was on them just by entering. *Except we have some tricks as well.*

He called Blaine, sending him the geo-tagged picture of their location. "Get Birdseye up. Crusty's got some plan of escape out of that mosque, and I'm betting it's the roof."

Blaine said, "He's already airborne, doing a 'pipeline survey' north to south. He'll be on team net, ETA thirty seconds."

Knuckles smiled at Blaine's bending his own rules, and poked him in the eye. "What happened to one shot with the bird?"

"He's circling north of the city. You'll still only get one pass. Don't push it."

"Roger that." Knuckles switched back to the team net. "Johnny, do some research on the buildings adjacent to the mosque. If he were going to jump, which one would he go to?"

Birdseye came on. "Knuckles, on station. You get about five minutes on target before I deviate from my flight plan. After that, it's a thirty-minute turnaround from the oil fields."

"Roger. You got eyes on the roof?"

"Clean shot. Can see it clearly through optics."

"Retro, you getting the feed?" He knew that Retro had stopped what he was doing as soon as he heard the Birdseye call, locating a concealed position that would allow him to set up his downlink and handheld video screen.

"Roger. Nothing moving right now."

Johnny said, "Looks like the buildings left and right are apartments. The one to the rear is a small hotel. It also has an alley that leads to the Medina wall."

That's it. He gave instructions to Johnny, setting his team up in a box around the hotel. He left Retro in place and called Decoy to meet him in the alley as the assault element. Before Decoy arrived, Retro said, "Got movement on the roof. Burqa woman and the mistress just exited."

"Decoy, what's your status?" Knuckles said, "If that's Crusty, we'll know shortly. He can't jump from roof to roof wearing that sack."

"Two minutes. Brett and I'll be there in two minutes."

Retro said, "Mistress went to the left/east wall and looked across to the adjacent building."

East? That's not the hotel.

"Say again? Which wall?"

"She's running. She's across. East building. I say again, east building."

Shit.

"Burqa's off. It's Crusty. He's throwing the luggage across."

"Roger all. Johnny, box the east building now. We're on the way."

Knuckles took off, running into Decoy and his other teammate when he rounded the corner. They said nothing, just falling into step behind him.

Johnny came on. "We're set. Only way in and out is the north and south."

"Which one will he use? Where should we stage?"

"North. Stage north in the alley. South fronts some shops. He'll probably want to stay out of sight this close to the mosque."

Yeah. Why would he come out so close? Risky.

Retro came on. "They're still going. They didn't enter the building. They're going to the next building to the east. I say again, the mistress just jumped to the next building to the east. Crusty's throwing luggage."

Jesus Christ! Johnny came on before he issued a command. "Moving. This building makes more sense. Exits north, south, and east. East exit is just a walkway, but it leads to the Medina wall. It's hemmed in on both sides by buildings."

"Roger." Knuckles knew they were falling behind Crusty because they had to run about twice as far around the buildings as he did straight across them. If Crusty sprinted down the stairs and out the door, they might miss him. It was going to be close.

"Knuckles, this is Birdseye. We're out of space. I've got to continue on."

Knuckles couldn't believe what he'd just heard. At a dead sprint, panting into his Bluetooth earpiece, he said, "Negative. Do not leave. I say again, do not leave."

"Not my call. Can't risk the cover and I've already deviated wide from my flight plan. I'll give you optics as long as I can, but it's going to be a rear view from a distance."

Knuckles swore, but knew he was right. If they managed to get Crusty, and someone mentioned strange aircraft orbits that tied it to his disappearance, the ensuing investigation would be catastrophic. They'd already raised their signature by running all over the place like a Laurel and Hardy movie.

He reached the corner of the third building and held up, pulling out his smartphone. He initiated the moving map and saw Johnny's team setting up, each man a glowing green icon. "Johnny, I'm coming in now. I'll be passing your south team shortly."

"Roger. I got you."

"Knuckles, this is Retro. The camera angle's off. They're across the building, but they disappeared behind the roof access. I don't know if they went in or not."

"Can't you see if they break out? Onto another roof?"

"Stand by. . . . Feed's breaking up. Birdseye's out of range."

Dammit. "Wonderful. Since you're free, start working exfil procedures. Figure out how we're going to get out of here with up to two extra. Johnny, your guys see anything?"

"We can't see past the parapet, but nobody's looked down, I'll tell you that."

"We'll take the east side of this building, in the alley. Move the guys there to the next building. Are they prepared to assault?"

"Negative. They're equipped for surveillance only."

Spread too thin. "Okay, tell 'em just to trigger. If Crusty keeps going, we'll fall back into surveillance mode. Try to track 'em to a bed-down site."

Knuckles and his men rounded the corner to the small alley, a cobblestone path with barely enough room to walk two-abreast. He slowed his pace, looking left and right for exits or Peeping Toms from adjacent buildings. He saw none. Just litter here and there. He located the doorway from the building thirty feet ahead, noticing that it was actually an alcove that sank inward a few feet. He motioned Decoy to the other side, mimicking working a pistol. He was drawing his own Taser when the recessed door swung open, taking him by surprise.

A man, exiting in a hurry and looking backward, smashed into him. The man whirled around, and Knuckles smiled.

"Hello, Crusty."

9

The Ghost followed the Hezbollah tough through a maze of alleys, moving deeper into the neighborhood and farther from his car. Eventually, the man pointed to a shop that was no more than a hallway, hacked off at one end with plywood. Four tables lined the length of the place, one with two men sitting, drinking out of small espresso cups no bigger than shot glasses.

They had to be aware of his arrival, but paid no attention. Another power play. One more than the Ghost was willing to endure. He strode right to the table and sat down, letting them say the first words.

Nothing happened for a pregnant second, the two taken aback. Then the older one, with a gray-flecked beard, looked from him to the tough and said, "You wish to disappear?"

"I wish to dispense with the posturing and get to the business of why I'm here. It has been a long drive from Tripoli and a longer time to find this shop. If you have nothing for me, I'll leave. If you try to stop me, I'll still leave, only a little more winded."

The bearded man sized him up, saying nothing. Then he smiled. "You don't look it, but you are who they said you'd be." He held out his hand. "I am Abdul Majid. This is Ja'far Hussein. Thank you for coming."

The Ghost shook both their hands without giving a name, then waited.

Majid said, "We believe that the Palestinian cause— your cause—is being hijacked. The Palestinian Authority has agreed to a peace overture from the United States and Israel. A meeting is being set up in Qatar, where money will change hands. Money that will kill the Palestinians' right of return. We have contacts in Hamas who would like this meeting to be stopped."

The Ghost bristled. "Hamas? Why on earth would I care about them? At one time they would never have agreed to anything short of Zionist annihilation. Now, they've joined in a unity government with the Palestinian Authority. They are like everyone else. Giving in when it suits them."

"Not all in Hamas agree with the unity government. But you're right about one thing: They have political concerns and won't do this themselves. Neither will we, which is why we've contacted you. We can put you in touch with some men here who are not Hamas or the Resistance. They have contacts with a financier in al Qaeda who uses a bank here in Lebanon. A bank that we control. This group will give you further instructions, if you are willing."

"Willing to do what? You haven't said."

"Kill the American envoy. The Palestinian Authority is almost bankrupt. They cannot continue because of the sanctions the West has placed on them due to their political reconciliation with Hamas and their bid for statehood with the United Nations. They have asked for covert funding, saying the moderate Palestinian elements are in danger of being swept away. The West has agreed, and the envoy is bringing it. Kill him, and the peace falls apart. Hamas gains political control of the Palestinian Authority, and your goal of the return is still within reach."

Of course, he thought, *Hezbollah—or Hamas—needn't worry about funding as long as the Shia dogs in Iran keep them in baksheesh.* He knew these men cared not a whit about the return of Palestinian refugees to their historic homeland. They only wanted the discord with Israel to continue to give them a reason to maintain their arms. As a "self-defense" force.

Ja'far spoke for the first time. "One thing: You cannot kill the man here, in Lebanon, no matter what this other group says. The al Qaeda financier has said he preferred it here, but we have told him no. They may push you that way. Do you understand?"

The Ghost said, "No, I don't. If that's the easiest, that's what I will do."

"You don't need to understand why, but you will not kill the American here. It will produce repercussions that will ultimately affect our goals."

"Our" goals? Or your goals?

"I understand. If I can get the funding and infrastructure to travel somewhere else, I agree. It will require much more in the way of intelligence, though, because I won't be able to do my own work."

"They will provide the funding. We can provide whatever infrastructure you need. We have assets all over the world. We're also able to penetrate the Palestinian Authority. You will know what they know."

"Where do I meet this other group?"

"The meeting is in four days, in the Ain al-Hilweh camp." Ja'far smiled. "You won't have to come back here." He read out an address, then said, "What shall we call you, should we need to communicate?"

The Ghost thought for a moment, then said, "*Ash'abah*."

He saw the change in the men's demeanor and twisted the knife a little more. "It's what everyone calls me back home."

10

For the thirtieth time, Jennifer said, "I can't believe this. Are you sure there's a message?"

"Yeah, I am. Can you quit asking that? We'll know soon enough. If you can get me to an open area."

I had my GPS out, but it wasn't picking up a satellite signal due to the enclosure of the buildings left and right. We were in the Old Town of Damascus, doing a little "sightseeing," after the fiasco of getting through immigration the previous night.

The trip itself was falling apart, and Jennifer wasn't pleased. We'd run into trouble as soon as we'd landed. The official from the Ministry of Culture who'd expedited our visas was now persona non grata inside the government of Syria. No telling why, but with Syria in such a mess I was sure he was now getting the rubber-hose treatment. And he'd painted a bull's-eye on Jennifer and me, since the government thought we were connected with him.

Our contact at the State Department had been no help. He wasn't expecting us to travel for another three to five months, and with the U.S. Embassy shuttered in Syria due to the troubles, we had no one local to help. Jennifer had fumed, really pissed that her scientific expedition was slipping away. I tried to calm her down, then simply left her alone to grump in her room. When I got to mine, I'd found our mission had changed.

This morning we'd gone for breakfast, where I'd finally gotten the courage to tell Jennifer we had to collect a message from the Taskforce. I couldn't talk about it in the hotel, because after our experiences at immigration and customs, I was sure that place was wired for sound, so I'd just gone to sleep after logging out of my Yahoo account.

The e-mail, ostensibly from the university, complete with a university address, simply inquired about our flight. That would have been fine, except it also asked for a status of camera equipment we didn't have with us. The word "camera" was a prearranged code letting me know we had a message from the Taskforce. I didn't want to know how they'd hacked a legitimate university e-mail address.

Probably twenty laws broken just by opening the message . . .

At breakfast, Jennifer's face had fallen the minute I had mentioned it, which actually hurt a little, but she knew the priority and knew the physical requirements for collecting the message. I left it up to her to find the area.

The Taskforce had multiple ways to transmit covert messages, depending on the security of the host country.

The easiest method was a simple VPN back to our "company," but some countries—such as Syria—controlled their Internet and prevented VPNs from working. The next easiest way was an encrypted e-mail, but once again, foreign intelligence services usually owned their Internet, and while they couldn't read the e-mail, they knew it had been sent. Best case, they knew you were doing something secret and would amp up the scrutiny to find out what that was. For a real businessman, that was no issue, since they were doing what they said they'd be doing. For the Taskforce, it could mean mission failure.

We'd tried carrying our own satellite equipment for a cut-out. Strictly commercial, off-the-shelf stuff like M3 or Thrane to blend in, which would allow us to have an Internet connection that bypassed the host country. That had worked until a team, traveling as cellular technicians, had had the equipment confiscated at customs. They'd been told that the country in question "had robust Internet," and thus the communications gear wasn't needed. Between the lines they heard, "We don't want you talking where we can't listen."

The Taskforce realized they needed a no-fail way to get messages out while operating within denied areas, such as Syria. Some fifty-pound head in the communications section had come up with the solution.

The first Global Positioning Satellite was launched by the U.S. military in 1978. Since then, a broadening constellation of satellites has been continually launching signals to earth in an ever-increasing refinement of geolocation capability. Now, the little GPS receiver you bought at Walmart would triangulate your position to the meter. All over the globe.

The genius idea was embedding the message traffic into the GPS signal. A customs official would confiscate just about any other piece of communications gear before a GPS, especially if it worked as advertised when checked.

Ordinary GPS wouldn't even realize the signal was there, but our special GPS would receive it, decode it, and display it. Since the U.S. government owned the entire technology, it was nothing to get the necessary tech stuff done to make it happen. The only downside was the weakness of every GPS signal, which had a hard time working in dense areas. Embed some data within it, and you really needed to have a wide-open area and some time for the GPS to lock on to the satellite and receive the more complicated signal.

We were currently in the al-Hamidiyah Souk, which was about as good for getting a GPS signal as being in a coal mine. Crowded on all sides by vendors selling goods ranging from kids' toys to perfume, it had an old tin roof that blocked everything, including sunlight. I was beginning to think Jennifer was purposely making this hard.

"Are you sure you know where you're going? Isn't there a park or soccer field around that doesn't require us to go this deep into the city?"

"Keep your pants on. The Umayyad Mosque is right at the end of the souk."

"Mosque? Seriously?"

She stopped and turned around. "You really didn't do any studying, did you? This has all been some joke. You knew we weren't going to get up north."

Her expression wasn't angry. It was resigned, like she'd just realized that all her exertions and studying had been nothing but a pale jest at her expense. It hurt again.

"Jennifer . . . I had no idea. I really wanted to do this trip. I know I've made fun of the research, but that's because I thought we *would* do the trip. If I'd known this was going to happen, I wouldn't have been acting like a jackass."

After a moment of silence, she said, "Whatever this message is, it's not going to be good. I can feel it. You're going to make me do something bad."

Jennifer had already been forced to do things in the name of the United States that the average citizen would consider horrific, and she'd understood the why, but she wanted me to say it wasn't so this time. Wanted me to make good on my promise of letting her do something purely for the joy of scientific discovery instead of the bloody self-defense of the United States.

I didn't know what the incoming message would say, but I knew I couldn't promise Jennifer anything. Like a coward I changed the subject.

"How's a mosque going to help us? We can't even get in."

She started walking again. "The Umayyad Mosque is one of the holiest shrines of Islam. It's a huge tourist at-traction. Yeah, we can't get into the inner workings, but we can get to the courtyard, which is enormous. Big enough to get the signal we need with a plausible reason for being there."

She looked back at me. "Unlike a simple soccer field."

The comment was meant to convey she understood the mission and was thinking about how to do it given our operational cover.

We reached the end of the souk and circled around to the tourist gate entrance of the mosque. After buying our tickets, we went through a doorway labeled "putting on special clothes room." We were given hooded cloaks to wear, me because short-sleeved shirts were frowned upon and Jennifer because, well, she was a woman.

"What's up with this place?"

"It's the first great mosque."

"Great is right. It looks like a crib from MTV with all the marble and gold."

She was scowling at my verbal history slight when I saw a mausoleum off to the right, a small, white building with a red roof.

She said, "Saladin's last resting place."

"Saladin? *The* Saladin? For real?"

I saw a little grin seep out because I was enjoying the same thing she did. Old dead people and pottery shards.

"Come on," she said. "Let's get to the courtyard and get this God-almighty-important message."

"Hey, let's look around a little bit. Work the cover some. We're tourists."

She smiled for real. "If it's got something to do with

bloodshed, you get interested. Okay, you want me to tell you about Saladin?"

Jennifer was famous in the Taskforce for her history lessons. Not in a bad way, as if she was always spouting off, but in a good way, because she knew more about the history of the world than any knuckle-dragger in the command. In this case, I didn't need the lesson. Saladin was a Kurd who'd smoked the European crusaders, giving them fits with his military skills. A leader of the first order. I knew all about him, but had no idea he'd been entombed in Syria.

"I'm good on this one. I'll just go take a peek. Why don't you take the GPS into the courtyard? I'll catch up."

She disappeared through a door, and I entered the mausoleum. There wasn't much to see inside, and I realized that I was itching to know what the Taskforce wanted. I wished I hadn't given the GPS to Jennifer, allowing her to see the message first. I glanced around for a few seconds, then took off at a fast walk to find her. I entered into the courtyard, which was as large as Jennifer said it would be. I saw her sitting down, looking at the screen.

"Did you get it?"

"Yeah," she said. "I did."

Her demeanor gave me no clue if it was going to be good or bad. "Well?"

She stood up and dusted off her pants. "It's instructions for a PM."

Whew. PM stood for personal meet and was spy-talk

for a clandestine meeting between a controller and his asset, which in this case would be us. Nothing more than an hour out of our life.

"See. All that crying over nothing. We'll do the meet and continue on once this visa mess gets sorted out. Kurt probably just wants to pass us instructions to check something out here in Damascus before we head north. More than likely it was just too much data to send using the GPS."

"I don't think so."

"Why?"

She handed me the GPS, the smile from earlier long gone.

"The PM's in Beirut."

11

Two days later, Jennifer walked into a café in the Hamra section of western Beirut, just down the street from the American University. She saw a hodgepodge of tourists and students, with the right wall lined by twenty-somethings smoking water pipes and discussing political opinions. It was one of the few areas where such discussion wouldn't end in gunfire.

She crossed the threshold at precisely twelve minutes past one o'clock, as the GPS message had stipulated. She was wearing a shirt that buttoned in the front and was carrying a map in her right hand, per the instructions.

She knew she was being watched, but made no attempt to look around. Instead, she went to the hostess and asked for a menu, getting redirected to the menu on the wall.

While pretending to look at it, she sensed someone gazing over her shoulder.

A man said, "This place is supposed to have the best breakfast in town, but I don't know about lunch."

She turned and saw a fiftysomething executive in a

business suit, swarthy, maybe Mediterranean, maybe Latino, with a large gut protruding over his belt.

She said, "Lunch is probably just as good."

The man smiled at the correct response. "Join me, if you want."

She followed him to the back of the café, beyond the prying ears of the students and tourists, sitting at the last small table in the restaurant.

He immediately began giving her instructions, a mad minute of information on why they were meeting and what they were discussing, should she be asked later. A facade to cover the conversation and protect both of them.

She said nothing, memorizing everything that came out of his mouth. When he stopped, his serious demeanor left, replaced by a cocky smile.

"My name is Louis Britt, and I guess I'm supposed to help you out."

"Louis Britt? You're kidding. Not 'Abdullah Moham-med'?"

"Unfortunately, no. Trust me, this damn name has caused nothing but trouble over here. I'm sure the idiot who gave me my documents is laughing."

He picked up the menu and said, "I thought they would be sending me an operator. No offense."

She smiled back, taking a liking to him for some reason. "They did."

"No, I don't mean another case officer, I mean a Task-force operator. Someone who can act on my information.

Kurt contacted me and gave me a dump on a hit in Tunisia, then directed this meeting. I've been deep so long, I was shocked when it happened. I thought the world was ending. And now I'm meeting you. You CIA? DIA?"

"Look, I'm just an overeager anthropologist with a liking for Middle Eastern historical sights. I'm supposed to be in Syria on a dig. Unfortunately for me, I also have some other unique skills. So does the man who watched you enter the restaurant. I don't know what a true 'operator' is, since I've never been in the military, and it seems like everyone who's ever held a gun says that's what they are nowadays, but I do know I'm the one they sent for this meeting. What do you have?"

He leaned back. "Wow. I *have* been gone too long. The world is just not right." He said it with a smile, breaking off when the waitress approached to take their order. Watching her walk back to the kitchen, he said, "Man, to be young again. These Lebanese women are friggin' *hot*." He winked. "Not that my age has stopped me any."

Jennifer gave a tentative smile, wondering where this was going. *Is he coming on to me? Really?*

She'd never done an operational linkup with a deep asset and was unsure what to make of the guy. On the one hand, when they'd met, he was as professional as anyone in the Taskforce, executing the operating procedures like a robot. Now, he was acting like a drunk businessman who'd come to Beirut for a convention.

He saw her draw back and took her hand. The act sent

her instincts into the red zone, until she felt something in her palm.

"Don't worry. I'm not trying to get in your pants. Unless you'd like it, that is."

He grinned again and pulled his hand away.

"That's an SD card with a complete rundown on a hit that happened in Tunisia three days ago. Taskforce took down a guy that was financing an assassination here in Lebanon. Originally, we didn't care because all the indicators pointed to a simple sectarian hit against some other faction in this fucked-up country. Taskforce now thinks it may be directed against Western interests. Meaning the U.S."

"So what are we supposed to do? Get this card to someone else? Why were we pulled from Syria?"

He snickered, then saw she was serious. "They didn't tell you why you were sent?"

"No. All we got were the PM instructions."

"Well, *operator*," he said, "you're here to save the day. Get the assassin. Protect American interests and all that bullshit. Same thing we always do."

Jennifer said nothing for a moment, doing the wasted mental calculations of how the mission would affect her trip to Syria. Like a child who'd let go of a balloon, seeing it float inexorably skyward, she tried to find a way to get back what she wanted. She realized Syria was lost for good.

"All right. What can you offer me besides this SD card?"

"Well, for one there's a very big discrepancy between the information found in Tunisia and what I know. I've been hearing about a hit for a few months, but it was always against internal Lebanese interests. Now, the intel weenies think the guy from Tunisia was financing a hit specifically against a U.S. government official. I think they're wrong."

"Why? If it's single-source intel from the mission, it seems prudent. Not something to ignore."

"It came from the hit, but there wasn't any smoking gun. You'll see when you boot up that SD card. The target hasn't talked yet. The Taskforce intel folks went through his hard drive and pieced it together. They're keying on the words 'infidel' and 'American,' and made a leap of logic. It's prudent if taken by itself, but I've been working here for over seven years, feeding the beast quality intel. Those analysts go through one hit and all of a sudden everything I've said is discounted. I've been hearing those same words used in reference to plenty of assassination attempts, but not as the target."

"You mean they're going to kill a foreign national in the *presence* of an American? At an American-sponsored conference or something?"

"No. In this case, 'infidel' has a very specific meaning to these guys. I'm telling you the assassin *is* an American."

12

Back in our hotel room, Jennifer gave me a rundown of what she'd learned while I went through the SD card the agent had passed. I hated hearing the briefing secondhand, but I'd had to make a hard call on who went into the café and had decided that I'd do more good outside, ready to react should something go wrong. Jennifer possessed a steel-trap mind and would draw much less attention to the meeting than I would. Hot little hammer meeting a businessman was better than a roughed-up expat.

The case officer's story certainly matched up; the SD card had a clinical report, with all primary references being the thoughts of some analyst with a fifty-pound head. No concrete information on the target or the timing, with every statement preceded by "appears to be" or "suggests." Not a lot of help in our decidedly fluid mission statement. I decided to do my own investigation.

"Come on. Let's go see a guy I know."

"Who?"

"A soldier I met a long time ago on a training package

here. Before the Taskforce. Before Nine-Eleven. He's a Special Forces guy I trust."

We left our fancy hotel, a five-star treat that tried hard to make you forget the deadly terrain it was parked within, but failed because of the metal detectors and physical searches at the door.

Heading to the coast road, we passed the destroyed Holiday Inn, a mocking, bullet-ridden reminder of the animosity simmering just below the surface of Beirut. A testament to both the potential and the reality of the country.

Going generally south along the coast, we left the city behind us. About forty minutes later, we turned east and entered the foothills of the Chouf Mountains, home of the Druze sect.

One of the eighteen recognized sects in Lebanon, it was a monotheistic religion that was neither Christian nor Muslim. Primarily found in the Levant, the Druze were known for their fighting prowess and staunch loyalty.

Driving along winding mountain roads, full of switch-backs, we reached the small town of Deir Al Qamar. I cut north, finally stopping at a modest stone house carved straight into the side of the mountain, with a view that would command millions in the United States.

I killed the engine and said, "Hope he still lives here."

"Really?" Jennifer said, "That's the best you can do? How long has it been? Ten, fifteen years?"

"Yeah, but all these homes are family owned. This isn't like America. The sects tend to stick together for survival, and none more so than the Druze. If he's not here, whoever is will know where he lives now, and it'll be somewhere close."

The door of the house swung open before we were out of the car, an attractive girl of about thirteen on the stoop. She said something in Arabic back into the house, then, in heavily accented English, said, "Can I help you?"

I stopped at the base of the steps. "We're looking for an old friend of mine. I met him when I was in the Army a long time ago. His name's Samir al-Atrash."

Before she could answer, Samir himself came onto the stoop. He looked exactly the same, a tall, rangy guy with jet-black hair and a bushy mustache. He stared at me without recognition for a second or two, and as I waited to see if he would remember me, I realized I was wrong. He wasn't exactly the same.

My memory of him had been frozen decades before, and like holding an old photo to your reflection in a mirror, I saw the changes. He had some gray coming through and a few more wrinkles. Crow's-feet around his eyes where there'd been none before.

He said, "Pike?"

I grinned. "I was beginning to think I hadn't left an impression on you, what with all the money we wasted on your training."

His face split into a smile. "Impression? No, you didn't. At least not in any good way."

I introduced Jennifer, and he led the way into his

house. We settled into a small, comfortable den, the girl from earlier now teamed with a younger boy, both clinging to the armchair Samir was sitting in.

"You've been busy," I said. "You were single the last time we talked."

"Times change. Sooner or later, you realize what's truly important. You don't have a wife? Children?"

"No." *Not anymore.*

He laughed and said, "You're going to die a greasy, dirty old man. You should try it, Pike. I think you'd like the lifestyle."

I barked a fake laugh and awkwardly changed the subject, not wanting to make him feel bad. His brow furrowed at the abrupt shift, but I pressed on, talking about our business interests instead. How we loved the travel and adventure. Jennifer helped out by asking questions about the Druze. As usual, she knew more than I did and had never even been to the country.

At a natural pause in the conversation, he whispered to his kids, then watched them scamper away and disappear into the back of the house.

"What can I help you with?" he asked, "Surely you didn't drive into the mountains just to banter about your lack of commitment or your love of travel."

About time.

"Well, I was hoping to run something by you. Your unit, actually. See if that intelligence fusion cell you always bragged about can corroborate anything. Surely that thing is wired throughout the country by now. Pride of the Lebanese Armed Forces. Isn't that what you said it would be?"

He glanced at the floor, then said, "I'm not in Special Forces anymore."

"Oh . . . well, can you still get access? As a regular grunt?"

"Pike, I'm not in the Army. I quit after the 2006 war."

"Really? You would be the last guy I thought would leave the Army. What happened?"

His demeanor shifted, and not in a good way. "Israel invaded us and the Lebanese Armed Forces did nothing, letting Hezbollah do all the fighting that should have been done by the LAF. We didn't even react when the Israelis blew up one of our convoys, killing a general. It was disgusting. Even my Special Forces unit sat on the sidelines and watched the civilians get slaughtered. If it hadn't been for Hezbollah, many, many more would have been killed."

The answer surprised me, not the least because of his vociferousness about the subject. This wasn't the soldier I had left. A man all about unity and Lebanese solidarity, about a true armed force that had no sectarian leanings. Now he was siding with Hezbollah, the "militia" that started the fight in the first place by kidnapping two Israeli soldiers. And it was Hezbollah that Israel went after. Not the LAF. I wasn't looking to get into a political argument, realizing more things had changed than the crow's-feet.

"I'm sorry to hear that. It was good seeing you again. We'll get out of your hair."

He sat up. "Don't look at me like that. I don't need your pity, and I'm not confused. I'm the one who lives here. I saw it happen. Thousands of Lebanese *civilians* killed, compared against *maybe* one hundred and fifty Israelis. All soldiers."

He was gripping the armchair hard and breathing heavy, daring me to say something against him. I recognized the signs. We were skating over a sore that I had opened, and he was about to do something we'd both regret.

I said, "I'm not looking for a fight. We'll just leave."

He stood up, mocking me. "Not looking for a fight? That's not what you used to say. All that training to protect something and all you were doing was helping out the Israelis. You in the West are all alike. Train the stupid locals then leave when the hostilities get to a level you don't like. You don't know what suffering is."

That was enough. Very few had suffered as I had, and the fact that he had two children walking the earth told me he wasn't one of them. I balled up my fists, ready to go as far as he wanted to take it. I saw Jennifer jump up, probably wondering what she should do. I was wrong.

She stepped between us, looked Samir in the eye and said, "Pike's family was murdered. Both his wife and child. For nothing. That's why he changed the subject when you started talking about marriage. Don't push his buttons about suffering. I promise you won't like the results."

I whipped my head to her. Samir's mouth fell open.

She continued. "He has the same rage you do. He looks just like you when he gets worked up. He didn't invade Lebanon; so don't take it out on us."

Samir looked from her to me. I said nothing, but my expression told him it was true. He sagged back into his chair. When he spoke, he was back to being the Samir I knew.

"I am sorry. Sorry for the both of us."

I exhaled and sat down as well.

"That's okay," I said. "The rage is mostly gone now." I smiled. "Jennifer was just trying to scare you."

He scraped something off of his knee and said, "Maybe I can help anyway. I have sources. I can ask around."

"No, no. This is like what we used to investigate. I'm not going to ask you about the price of bread in Tripoli. Don't worry about it. It was good just seeing you. Let's leave it at that."

"Wait. I'm telling you I have sources. Just like I used to have. Let me help."

I paused and looked at Jennifer; she shrugged, saying, *What's the harm?*

"Okay. My government has heard about an assassination attempt here in Lebanon. The sticky point is that we can't figure out the target. Some analysts say it's Lebanese, and some say it's American. With the new United States envoy to the Middle East doing his first tour, coupled with the peace process in Qatar, people are getting antsy. I just figured I'd see if you could help neck it down. See what you've heard."

Surprised by the question, he said nothing for a moment, sizing me up as if for the first time, seeing things that should remain in the shadows.

"Because it would help in your archeological business?" he said. "Help you find sites? You and Jennifer?"

I held his eye for a moment, then said, "Because I was asked to check while I was here. Nothing more. A favor for friends in the government. Can you get that to the fusion cell?"

"No. My sources aren't military ones."

"Druze?"

He said nothing, simply looking at me, and it clicked. He'd gone completely over.

"Tell me you're not with Hezbollah. You can't possibly be with those murdering thugs."

He grew indignant. "I am Druze, and will always be, but Hezbollah is a power. We have connected with them. They aren't the murderers you say they are. They are the majority in our government now. I'm not with them, but I don't fight them."

"How on earth can you—a Druze—say that? They want an Islamic state, for God's sake. They started the damn 2006 war! They've got a fucking theme park celebrating the destruction of your country. And you blame Israel . . ."

I stomped to the door, Jennifer right behind me. I opened it, turned around, and said, "They are your road to ruin, and you don't even see it."

"Pike, wait. No matter what you think of them, they can help. After the Hariri assassination they've become very sensitive to killings in Lebanon. They get blamed for them all. If what you say is true, they'll want to stop it just as much as you do. And me. They have connections like nobody else in this country. They'll be able to find out if it's true or not. I promise they won't want an American getting killed here. They want to consolidate political power, and that would only hurt them."

"I can't believe I just heard that come out of your mouth. They kill Hariri, the man putting your country back together, and now I should use their help because they got caught and don't want to get blamed again. Do you hear yourself?"

"They didn't kill Hariri. You can believe that. No way. That's just what the Zionists want the world to believe. Either way, you have the same interests here."

I didn't like the stench of it, but he was right. Feed this to Hezbollah, and they'd get to the bottom of it. Unlike us, they'd just cut off some heads. The end-state was fine by me. The only question was whether they weren't behind it in the first place. Odds were what he said was true. Hezbollah didn't do a lot of kidnapping and killings of foreigners anymore, since they'd gotten hammered for the suspicions of killing Hariri—and since they'd assumed a majority in the government.

I decided I was willing to risk it . . . with some caveats.

"If you go to them, you'd better make damn sure you don't mention me or Jennifer. Nothing about us, understand? You might trust those torturing Islamic fascists, but I sure as shit don't."

I gave him our cell number and walked out to the car, Jennifer in tow. To my back, Samir said, "I'll call tomorrow."

When I didn't respond, he said, "Pike. I'm still Samir. I wouldn't join a group of terrorists. Hezbollah doesn't run around killing anymore. The civil war is long over. They don't hire assassins."

13

Infidel felt comfortable following the Druze. He had stuck to main thoroughfares and was now walking on foot down the Corniche, the long stretch of western coastline along Avenue de Paris. Full of fishermen and tourists, it was easy for the assassin to blend in. The only reason anyone came to the Corniche was to walk, so no destination was expected. He could follow all day long without arousing suspicion. Not that it mattered. The Druze seemed relaxed in the environment and showed no signs of attempting to sort out any surveillance efforts.

Yesterday, the assassin had met his contacts in Hezbollah at the same coffee shop they always used, in the heart of the *Dahiyeh*, surrounded by thugs. He was not a timid man, but he greatly feared being killed by mistake inside the stronghold. After all, he looked exactly like someone a paranoid foot soldier for Hezbollah would think was a U.S. spy. Someone to torture purely for the pleasure of it. He was thankful for the iron hold Hezbollah's hierarchy had over their men. It was cultlike in its efficiency.

The meeting was strained, with a vibe that was different from that of previous encounters. He'd been paid and congratulated for his successful killing of the investigator, then told about a rumor of an attack in Lebanon, possibly against U.S. interests. A walk-in, a Druze no less, had brought information from an unknown source.

Ja'far and Majid had both professed innocence, but had heard of a meeting between Palestinian freedom fighters that they wanted to check out. The meeting was supposed to be a simple strategy session, but Hezbollah now wondered if it was something more. They wanted him to provide the Druze with equipment to record the meeting. Which was definitely strange.

Why waste effort on a recording? Why not just hammer them? Hezbollah certainly had the ability—and the will—if this meeting had a snowball's chance in hell of stopping their political agenda. Killing Palestinians wouldn't affect Hezbollah at all, unlike killing an investigator of the tribunal—and they'd paid him for that easily.

He was sure there was something more going on, and he thought he knew what it was.

They've set something in motion and are afraid of losing control.

The meeting was in the port city of Sidon, a little less than an hour south of Beirut, but outside of Hezbollah-land. If he was right, it meant they were using Sunnis for the job—whatever it was—but the Sunni groups had nowhere near the discipline of Hezbollah. All rage and jihadist fervor.

And that's why I'm being asked to help. They wanted him to provide the means to ensure that the Palestinian radicals weren't just taking the money and about to screw up Hezbollah's plans.

The one thing that confused him was the Druze connection. Why make up the story about an unknown source and a possible assassination attempt? Why not just say they'd heard about something strange going on and have him provide the equipment, like every other transaction they had done? The story held a ring of truth, and an unknown source providing information to Hezbollah scared him.

Doing some digging, he'd learned that the Druze had been an operator in a very elite section of the Lebanese Armed Forces. A counterterrorist expert who'd cut his teeth on the operational side, then proven just as valuable on the analytic side, creating an intelligence fusion cell that had grown to be a thorn in Hezbollah's side. Actually, a thorn in everyone's side, from the Sunnis to the Israelis. Very, very effective—and nonpartisan. Why the soldier was now working with Hezbollah was a mystery. It raised the hair on his neck. His paymasters may not care, but he wanted to know what he was getting into.

The Druze finally left Avenue de Paris, cutting down to the Riviera Hotel, then hanging a left, going into the tunnel underneath the highway to the hotel's beach club, a popular tourist attraction on the coast, with multiple bars, pools, and beachfront property.

He wandered around for a moment as if looking for something, then settled onto a stool at a bar, with a view of the entrance to the resort. He ordered a drink and seemed to be just killing time.

Infidel took a seat behind him, on a chair underneath an umbrella, his back to the ocean. He settled down to wait, but it didn't take long before he saw activity.

A Caucasian came through the entrance and scanned the area. The assassin recognized him immediately, not believing what he was seeing. His stomach clenched in unfamiliar fear.

What the fuck is he doing here?

I ENTERED THE RIVIERA BEACH CLUB thirty-five minutes before the meeting I'd set with Samir. I wanted some time to check out the area, find any vantage points or entrances I'd missed to locate any surveillance that might be following him. I'd given Samir a specific route, then dropped Jennifer off at the tunnel on the Corniche, a chokepoint that was ideal to see if someone was on his tail. Her location would give a good five minutes before he came within view. If she called me, I'd simply disappear.

I glanced around the area, then did a double take. Samir was sitting at the bar.

I stalked over to him, fuming.

"What the fuck are you doing here? *I* come in first. *You* follow. Did you forget that?"

He held his hands up. "Whoa. Calm down. I was in

the area early and didn't feel like sitting on a park bench downtown. You're paranoid. Nobody's following me. This isn't the civil war."

I sat down on the barstool next to him. "You'd better hope not, or we're both getting our heads cut off." I then looked into his eyes. "Unless you're protected and serving me up."

"Pike, trust me, I'm the one on the inside. This is my country, and I would never put you in jeopardy. I did what you asked and got some information. You were right. You want to hear it, or walk away?"

I grimaced, wanting to punch him, but said, "Give it to me."

"There's a meeting planned in Sidon. It's between a couple of Sunni Palestinian groups and supposedly about the financing of Palestinian efforts with no specific targets. The same stuff that goes on all the time. My contacts have heard that they're going to talk about a general planning of attacks inside Israel. They're now worried that they're discussing an attack against the envoy from America, here in Beirut. They want to stop it, if that's the case."

"Okay. Great. Go stop it."

"Come on, Pike. How many gunfights have you heard since you've been here? You think we can just run in and shoot everyone like it's the Old West? They can't simply 'stop' it, like you say. It's just a meeting between men, and we still have some semblance of law here."

"Okay, fine. What can you help me with? Where's the meeting?"

"I don't have the address yet, but it's coming. I do know it's not in the camps. The meeting is being held in neutral territory in the city proper. Apparently, the two groups don't trust each other, and, as you know, any territory in the camps is owned by some militia. Even given that, more than likely none of my contacts will be able to get close. It's a Sunni area, and you'd be surprised at how quickly they can sniff out another sect."

"Including Druze, I suppose."

"Uhh . . . well . . . yeah. That's where I'm going."

"Why can I get in and you cannot?"

"I don't know you can, but you have a greater chance than me or my contacts do. We smell, look, and act Lebanese, but we don't belong in Sidon. The city is not like Beirut. It's much, much more conservative, but if they want to meet in neutral territory, it probably means in an area full of people like you to prevent any overt attack. You don't belong in Sidon either, but you have a reason for it, as a tourist. You have a good shot at getting what we want."

I considered what he said, knowing it would be very, very dangerous. He saw me thinking and thought my resolve was faltering.

"We can't get into the site, but we'll be there on the outside. Providing security."

That didn't give me any confidence.

"Who? A bunch of lunatics who would just as soon cut off my head?"

He smiled. "No, no. My men. Druze. They have no other allegiance than to me. They will do what I say."

"Are they any good?"

"Just as good as me. I trained them. And you trained me."

I threw down the toothpick I was playing with.

"Well, that doesn't give me any assurance. Today, you fucking ignored all of that training."

He held his arms out and smiled. "Today there was no threat."

14

Twenty-four hours later I was walking north along a tight little street in the port town of Sidon, about forty minutes south of Beirut. I carried an ancient laptop in a shoulder bag like an itinerant poet looking for the perfect setting to get in touch with my feelings.

The meeting was scheduled in thirty minutes, at eight p.m., and I was scoping the area before setting up in the chosen meet site, a large khan set next to the ocean. I reached the coast road and could see an ancient stone castle out in the water, at the end of a causeway, an old relic from the Crusades. Pretending to take in the view, I analyzed the daily rhythms of life. Nothing stood out. I knew that Jennifer, along with Samir's little posse, was establishing surveillance positions around the café and would warn me if something looked dirty. I didn't trust Samir's crew, but I sure as shit trusted Jennifer.

I walked across the coast road, seeing my destination, a large café with both inside and outside seating. From Samir's sources, the meeting would take place at the northeast corner, at the farthest table inside. I would set up early at the next table, happily typing away on my laptop, the hippie backpacker engrossed in the simple life of Sidon, sucking down espresso.

The laptop was actually nothing more than a camera housed in the shell of a computer. It had video capability both on the front and back of the screen, which meant I could set up facing the table or with my back to the meeting.

Samir had gotten the camera from his contacts and shown me how to use it, proud of his ability to get such equipment and eager to prove his contacts wanted to help. I'd stressed to him that after this was all said and done, *I* was the one walking away with the intel. He could take the computer/camera back to Hezbollah, but not before I had a complete copy of what was on it. Giving Hezbollah the chance to do the dirty work was fine, but if they failed to take action, I wanted the Taskforce to be able to protect American lives. He'd said Hezbollah would have no issue with that—like they were a bunch of schoolmarms simply out to help the illiteracy rate instead of a pack of bloodthirsty, backstabbing murderers.

All in all, the camera itself was pretty simple. A couple of keystrokes to boot up the software, then a couple more to start the recording. The hardest part was aiming the lens, since I wouldn't have the luxury of seeing what I was taping at crunch time. After about an hour of practice, I was pretty good at it. The worst thing about the system wasn't the skill required. It was the weight. The damn laptop felt like I was hiking around with an anchor on my shoulder. Hezbollah might be a powerhouse here, but they were still third-world when it came to covert equipment.

I set up in the café, taking note of the patrons around me. Some of them, without a doubt, were security for the meeting. It didn't require any special skill to pick them out. Twentysomething tough guys at every corner, holding drinks they didn't touch and glaring around. No training whatsoever.

I, on the other hand, looked like a sissy-boy. Fake glasses in place, Birkenstocks, and a hippy shirt with long sleeves. They sized me up and ignored me in the same glance.

The café itself contrasted starkly with the cinder-block houses and businesses jammed together just across the coast road. It was elegant and clearly old, with vaulted ceilings, wood moldings, and pillars scattered throughout the room. It reminded me of a Disney set for *Aladdin*. It wasn't particularly crowded, but had enough people to keep the waiter busy. One man, at the opposite corner, caught my eye. Seated by himself, he was doing nothing overtly suspicious, and I wondered why I had keyed on him. Frail and skinny, he looked more like a pussy than I did, but I had learned to trust my instincts, and for some reason, he had pinged.

I surreptitiously watched him for thirty seconds, then went back to the room. He had done nothing but sip his coffee, showing no interest in anything going on. Certainly not at my end of the café.

Getting paranoid.

I had decided to put the meeting table to my back and use the camera on the screen side of the computer. Samir's intel said the meeting would last no more than five minutes, and it would make me look less conspicuous. The position also afforded me the ability to watch the entrance without turning around every few minutes. I'd let them get seated, then hit record, leaving the computer running while I went to the men's room.

Five minutes before hit-time I got movement around me. More men came inside, taking the tables to the left and right. Hard-looking guys, who spent all their time peering out from the table instead of focusing in and talking to one another.

The hit-time came, and a couple of older men entered and took a seat at the target table. They ordered something to drink and waited. My pulse started to pick up.

Here we go.

So far, I appeared to be good, with nobody paying me a second glance. Two minutes after hit-time, a large Arabic man came through the entrance, oozing outward machismo. The only thing stopping the effect was the set of Coke-bottle glasses he wore. They made him look ridiculous, like a demented Mr. Magoo. He swaggered in and settled his eyes on the target table.

That's him. All bluster and bad attitude.

My heart rate began to hum, but I showed no outward sign. I stroked the keys, waiting on the last one, and focused on my screen, running through the mission in my head. I began to second-guess my camera angle, my distance, and everything else. We would only get one shot, and if I screwed this up there'd be nobody to blame but myself.

The man settled himself directly to my back, facing away from me, which sort of sucked because I wouldn't get a facial recognition shot of him, but I knew the embedded microphones would pick up the conversation.

They did the usual Arabic greeting, and I hit the final key, standing up quickly to avoid spoiling the view. I slowly walked toward the restrooms, pretending I didn't know where they were. I flagged a waiter and asked. Given directions, I made my way at a leisurely pace. I entered the bathroom and looked around, dismayed to see there wasn't a stall I could hide behind for a time.

I was pondering how I could kill five minutes when an explosion rocked the place, sending plaster from the ceiling.

What the hell?

I raced back to the main room and saw my little corner table was on fire, with torn bodies from the meeting lying all over the place. The explosion had been small, but forcefully directed against the target table. Coming from my table, where the computer had been vaporized. Coming from a screen I should have been facing. The rage came instantly.

Those fuckers . . .

That's why the damn computer weighed so much. It hadn't been old-school technology. It had been ball-bearings and explosives. And Samir, my *friend*, had given it to me.

I had time later to sort it out. What I needed to do first was get out of the area before anyone remembered I was the one at that table.

I fled outside and saw I was too late. Seven of the toughs providing security earlier closed on me before I could react. Two grabbed me, and one swung a club at my head.

SITTING ON A PARK BENCH DOWN THE STREET, Jennifer heard the explosion and stood up, trying to vector the specific location. When she saw smoke rush from the target café, she took off at a sprint.

On the opposite side of the street, she reached the front in time to see Pike exit. She shouted his name, but was drowned out. She watched helplessly as he was viciously clubbed around his head and body, a group of men kicking and punching him on the ground until a van pulled alongside. He was unceremoniously thrown in the back, and the van raced away.

She was at a momentary loss, trying to piece together the chain of events. She pushed through the crowd and caught a glimpse of the carnage at the target table, realizing what had happened. Realizing they had been used.

She knew that Pike had very little time before he was killed, and the clock was ticking. Now. She exited the café, getting free of the crowds, and saw Samir across the street. She sprinted right at him.

Samir saw her coming and shouted, "Jennifer! What happened? Where's Pike?"

Before he could react, she wrapped one arm around his waist and grabbed his elbow with the other. She rotated around, levered her hip against his groin, and whipped his body up and over hers through the air.

He thumped the ground hard, and she straddled his waist. "Where did you take him?"

When he shouted nonsense, she began striking, just like a training day, blocking his ineffectual attempts to stop her and hammering his face over and over again, each blow bouncing his head off the concrete. One of his men arrived and grabbed her forearm, halting the assault. She rotated her arm in a quick circle, breaking it free at the same time she trapped his wrist. She violently twisted against the joint, hearing a rewarding crack as the wrist shattered and the man went to his knees.

She returned to Samir, who had now put his arms across his face, shouting, "Stop, stop! I didn't do anything!"

"Where is he?"

When he said nothing, she began striking him again, this time with less effect as his arms prevented her from direct contact. Two other Druze arrived and began to battle her. It took three before she was pulled off of Samir.

15

The Ghost's ears were ringing from the blast. Having lived his entire life in Beirut, his body had reacted instantly, hitting the floor even before his conscious mind knew why.

The initial shock over, he peeked from underneath his table, seeing the carnage across the café. So far, nobody in the restaurant had reacted. Still shocked, they simply cowered and whimpered. He saw the briefcase the men had brought lying underneath a body, apparently intact.

When initially given the meeting location, inside the Ain al-Hilweh Palestinian refugee camp, he'd been happy with the choice. Reflecting on the location after he'd left the *Dahiyeh*, the Ghost had balked, telling the Hezbollah leadership he'd meet, but on neutral terrain. They'd come up with this café, but he still wasn't completely satisfied.

He'd decided to send someone else to the meeting. Someone with the physical characteristics the men would be expecting. A tough guy with a swagger. He knew the main identification method would be the glasses his bad genetics forced on him. It had been very little effort to find someone in the camp who met the specifications and needed money. He'd given him instructions and paid him up front, sending him into the meeting wearing glasses with thick lenses.

He didn't worry about missing out on any discussions, because he'd specified that all information was to be passed to him in hard form. Initially, before he'd come up with his doppelgänger plan, it was simply because he didn't want to spend a single second more than he had to with these men. He trusted them about as much as he would the Mossad. It looked like that mistrust had just saved his life.

He'd think about the whys of the attack later, but knew one thing: There was a leak somewhere. He was willing to bet it was with the Sunnis and not Hezbollah. In Lebanon the fragmented Palestinian groups had always tended to fire before aiming. He could well imagine how many people knew about this meeting because of their bragging.

Seeing the waitstaff starting to recover, he duckwalked over to the table, screaming for someone to help him and beginning to conduct triage on the shattered bodies in the blast. He rolled one man over, ostensibly checking for signs of life, but in reality exposing the briefcase. He waited for the crowd to gather, as he knew it would.

Seconds later, he was surrounded by a plethora of people all shouting instructions, one splashing water from an ice bucket on the small fire, another throwing chairs and tables out of the way to clear the area.

He leaned over and closed his hands on the briefcase, the handle slick with the blood from the man who had been lying on it.

Someone tapped him on the shoulder, asking if the meat he was leaning over was alive. He said no and stood up.

He pushed through the crowd and reached the street, gripping the briefcase tightly in his hands.

16

The men continued to pummel me inside the van, shouting in Arabic. I protested in English, demanding to know what I had done, setting my innocence as soon as possible. I knew it would matter little, and I was in serious, serious trouble.

The van careened down the narrow roads, eventually driving without swerving left and right, which meant we were out of town. There weren't any windows to see out of, even if they'd given me a chance to look, but I knew we were headed to the Ain al-Hilweh Palestinian refugee camp. Once past that barrier, I knew my chances of survival would be close to zero.

One of the men began shouting into a cell phone in Arabic. Seeing me watch, another shoved a coarse burlap sack on my head, blocking out the light.

Here we go. If they bring out a video camera and a knife, it's last-chance time.

The men weren't professional, because they'd left me with both my watch and cell phone. That was good on the surface, but could prove deadly. No training equaled no discipline, which meant I could be killed out of rage without them thinking about the consequences. I hoped these guys would want to question me at length—extending my life, as it were—and prayed that's what the shouting on the phone had been about. Someone with a cool head giving orders instead of leaving me to my fate with these Neanderthals.

Eventually, we stopped. I was cuffed on the head and dragged out of the van, the hood still on.

Without any concern for my well-being, we speed-walked up a flight of concrete steps. I kept slipping, banging my shins and trying to break my fall with my arms. Every time it happened, I was slapped and punched for a couple of seconds before being jerked to my feet.

I was thrown through a doorway, slamming into a wall. Two men jerked me through another door and forced me into a chair. I was rapidly tied around all of my limbs, then left alone for a minute or two.

I heard footsteps, and the hood was ripped off of my head. I faced one of the men who'd lumped me up to begin with. They still hadn't taken my cell phone, which was good. The longer I had it, the better.

"Who do you work for?"

Here it comes.

In the movies, this is when I would spit in the guy's face and tell him to fuck off. Because I'm so tough. In real life, I knew aggravating this man was the last thing I should do. My survival rested on my ability to convince them they'd made a mistake.

"I work for myself. I own a business. If it's a ransom you want, my partner will pay, but we don't have a lot of money."

He slapped my head.

"Who do you work for in the U.S. government? The CIA? Or maybe Mossad?"

"CIA? Is that what you think? You've made a terrible mistake. I'm just a businessman here on vacation. I don't work for any government, I swear. I'm not even religious, and certainly not Jewish!"

Before I could answer, another man entered. Older, and much more self-assured, with an eight-inch salt-and-pepper beard just like Osama bin Laden used to have.

The boss.

He said something in Arabic, and the tough said something back. The boss screamed at the man, and immediately he was ripping through my pockets. He found the cell phone and passed it over. They both left the room, and I prayed the phone stayed in the building. It was my last bit of hope.

I went through strategies for prolonging the inevitable, but my mind was having trouble staying focused. I felt a deep sense of fear, a pathological phobia of what was about to happen, and it was blotting out logical thought. I knew that sooner or later they were going to get rough, and I had seen what that entailed.

In 1984, the CIA chief of station in Beirut, William Buckley, was kidnapped by Hezbollah. Months later, an unmarked videotape arrived at the U.S. Embassy in Athens. In it, a nude William Buckley was being gruesomely tortured. Another tape arrived every few months, until one came simply showing him dead, the skin puckered all over his naked body from repeated abuse.

The tapes were classified, but I had seen them. They had left a mark on my soul, grainy images branded in my brain and guttural screams haunting my dreams, made all the more visceral because they were real. The pain, shrieks, and agony weren't from a screenplay, but a living man. The tapes had left a disquieting mark on my sub-conscious that had never gone away. I hadn't ever told anyone, but Buckley's fate was my singular fear. And now I was going to live it. Buckley had managed to survive for more than a year of inhumane captivity. If it came to it, I hoped my demise would be much, much quicker.

Rescue wasn't going to happen. An enormous effort had been made to locate Buckley, using the entire powers of the Central Intelligence Agency, along with help from a multitude of Western intelligence agencies and Mossad. He was, after all, the Beirut chief of station. None of it had mattered.

I had no such luxury. Nobody even knew I was miss-ing. There would be no grand struggle to locate and re-cover me.

All I had was Jennifer.

JENNIFER FOUGHT WITH ALL OF HER MIGHT to prevent be-ing thrown into the van, but it was wasted effort. With four men holding her writhing form, she made them work, but that was all. They heaved her through the sliding door hard enough to slam against the other side.

She sprang to her knees and turned to fight, striking the first man who tried to enter with two quick jabs. The back doors opened, and two men piled in. She lashed out with her feet, connecting with one and trying to slip past the other out the back, to freedom.

He slammed her above the ear with a straight right punch, causing stars. She continued to spin toward the rear, getting her hands outside the van. She pulled, and felt her legs grabbed. She was ripped inside and set upon by both men. They began to punch her all over, forcing her to curl to protect herself. She felt the van move and heard someone shouting in Arabic. The punching stopped, followed by the men simply holding her down.

She heard her name called over and over. She looked to the voice and saw Samir staring at her in concern, his lip split, nose bleeding, and the left side of his face swollen.

"Have you gone mad? What in the world happened?" he said.

She began to buck, trying to get out of the men's grasp, spittle flying from her mouth.

"Jennifer, stop it! Look at me."

She relaxed, her eyes on the ceiling of the van. "Looks like you got us both, you son of a bitch."

"I had nothing to do with that bomb. I still don't know what happened. Where's Pike?"

She looked at him, trying to sense deception. "The

computer you gave Pike didn't only have a camera. It had a bomb."

He said nothing, his mouth dropping open.

"I get that you have a vendetta. I heard you talk in your house, but why use us? Use Pike? He said you were his friend, and that means a lot to him. He doesn't have many, and you used that against him."

"I did no such thing. I would never do that. I'm not a terrorist. You are wrong about the computer."

"Then let me go. Right now. I need to use my phone. Pike's in real trouble."

He turned to the men and said a sentence or two in Arabic. They released her. She pulled out her phone and called the Taskforce, knowing she was breaking every rule there was by using an open line.

A receptionist answered. "Blaisdell Consulting, how may I help you?"

"I'd like to speak to Kurt Hale, please."

"I'm sorry, there's no one here by that name."

She mentally crossed her fingers and said, "Prairie Fire. I say again, Prairie Fire."

The receptionist hesitated, then said, "Please hold."

After a wait, a voice she recognized came on. "Whom am I speaking with?"

"Kurt, it's Jennifer. I don't have time to explain, but I need a lock on Pike's phone. Right now."

There was a pause, then, "Who is this? I'm not sure you have the right number. We're a consulting firm."

They're going to blow me off. Even after the code word. They're going to sacrifice Pike to protect the Taskforce.

"Kurt! Listen to me! Pike's in serious trouble. Send me the grid. Please!"

"Good-bye. Please don't call back."

The line went dead. She was stunned. She couldn't believe they would sacrifice one of their own to protect themselves. She noticed the men staring at her, waiting for her to talk. She said nothing, sagging against the metal of the van, her mind trying to find a solution that didn't exist.

Her phone vibrated with a text message. When she looked at it, she saw a latitude and longitude displayed, along with the note "call secure immediately."

Jesus Christ. Damn Taskforce subterfuge. Kurt's going to pay for that.

Back in business, she barked, "Take me to the U.S. Embassy. Drop me off as fast as you can."

"Why? The Embassy can't help. We can. Tell me what you know."

"Like I would trust you as far as I can throw you. Take me to the damn Embassy. Where's my bag?"

One of the men tossed her knapsack to her. She pulled out a tablet PC and began working it.

Samir said, "I had nothing to do with that bomb. Maybe someone else sent it. This is Lebanon, you know."

She didn't look up, still working the tablet, saying, "And that's why the security detail we saw before the explosion immediately singled out Pike, huh? They knew it was his computer because they saw him inside with it. *They* knew who put the bomb in there, and so do I."

"Even if that's true, it wasn't me. I was used just like you were. Let me help. Where is Pike?"

She turned the tablet to him. "Here. Take me to the consulate right now. We're running out of time."

He looked at the map and said, "That's the Palestinian refugee camp. Your consulate will be no help there. It'll take forty-eight hours to even get permission to enter, and that permission will reach the men holding Pike long before you do. Let us help. The gates of the camp are guarded by Lebanese Armed Forces. I can get you in."

"For what? So you can kill both Pike and me and prevent embarrassment to Hezbollah with our story? We wouldn't want it to get out that they were behind the killing, would we?"

He said nothing for a moment, then turned and spoke in Arabic to the men in the van. The conversation lasted a couple of minutes.

In English, he said, "If you are correct, they used me just as they used you. I'm not convinced they did, but I know that Pike has been captured, and I will give my life to free him. My men as well. Is that enough?"

She knew what he said about the consulate was correct. The damn State Department weenies would pee their pants when she came running in with her story. Pike's location was growing colder by the second, and it would take forever to get them to react. By then, his cell phone could be in the hands of a fourteen-year-old who'd purchased it on the black market.

"How good are you and your men?"

"Very, very good. Pike trained me, and I trained them. We don't look like much, but we can get the job done."

"Weapons?"

Samir turned to a man in the back. He unzipped a duffel, showing the worn bluing of a beat-up folding stock AK-47.

"They aren't fancy, but they'll shoot."

"We do this, and I'm in charge, understand? You follow my orders. You don't, and I'm going to start shooting in both directions assuming you're a threat."

He looked like he'd swallowed curdled milk. "You? You think you're going on the assault? Have you lost your mind? You're an anthropologist. Leave this to us. We know how to fight. I understand your lack of trust, but this is something for professionals. You need certain skills to win."

She pulled out the AK and began a functions check. Satisfied it would work as advertised, she seated a magazine and racked a round.

Seeing the surprise on Samir's pummeled face, she bared her teeth in a predator's smile.

"You looked in a mirror lately? I've got the skills, and I'm in charge."

17

Kurt Hale slammed his handset into the cradle. "Mike! Get your ass in here."

The duty officer, hearing the tone, stuck his head in the door in seconds.

"Yes, sir?"

"Geolocate Pike's cell phone ASAP. Text the grid to this number." He looked at the last-called display on his desk phone and scribbled the number on a sticky note.

"Got it. Commo section has Pike's handset selectors already?"

"Yeah. They've got something. IMEI, IMSI, or some other tech shit. I don't care what they're executing right now, they drop it. This is a Prairie Fire. Send the grid as soon as you get it, and include in the text for them to call secure immediately."

George Wolffe, the Taskforce deputy commander, was entering the office just as Mike raced away.

"Whoa, must be free beer somewhere."

Mike said nothing, disappearing down the hall with a purpose.

George said, "What's that all about? What's up?"

"I don't know. Pike's in trouble. Jennifer called on an open line asking for the location of Pike's cell phone. She triggered a Prairie Fire."

George said, "You're shitting me."

Prairie Fire was the code word for a catastrophic event. It meant the overt compromise of a Taskforce team or the impending death of a Taskforce operator. When used, everything in the Taskforce came to a stop, with all assets that could react dedicated to that team. In all the years of Taskforce existence, the words had never been uttered.

"Not shitting at all. I don't know what it's about, but it looks like you finally get to see your plan in motion."

Before accepting the position of DCO of the Taskforce, George had spent decades inside the CIA's National Clandestine Services, most of that time in the Special Activities Division conducting covert operations on every continent but the Antarctic. Some of the missions had been just short of suicidal, with no way to call for help should the worst occur. Unlike the military, when SAD hung it out there, it was absolutely for keeps. No reserves, no cavalry, no rescue.

George understood when that attitude was truly necessary, but on several occasions, when he'd come close to dying on a mission that was a little ill-conceived, he was convinced it was simply because of a lack of forethought. The CIA leadership was so used to the mission profile that they just took it on faith that nothing could—or should—be done if things went bad. After working with select Department of Defense Special Mission Units, and seeing the care they put into contingency planning for operations, his mind-set changed. When he helped form the mission profile for the Taskforce, he had implemented a panic button should a Taskforce operator find himself in dire straits. Kurt had picked the code words—the same code words used by his father on top secret cross-border missions in Vietnam.

Kurt said, "What can we leverage for Lebanon?"

"Mostly tech stuff, which you're doing now. Nothing in the AO, team-wise."

"What about Knuckles in Tunisia?"

George paused, thinking. "Yeah. Crusty's done, and they're just doing cover development now, but you pull them officially and it's a risk."

George was reminding him that one of the key ways to blow an operation was to flee too soon after it was over. The police would naturally look at who immediately left following a mission, searching for leads. Because of this, Taskforce teams would stay in the area of operations for as long as necessary, ostensibly doing whatever their cover said they should be doing. Knuckles's team was now servicing the oil fields in Tunisia, finishing out their "contract."

"The black hole's still off the coast of Tunisia, right?"

"Yeah."

"Knuckles is a SEAL. So's Decoy. Anyone else dive qualified on that team?"

"Yeah. Brett, the new guy I brought over from Special Activities Division. He was a Force Recon Marine in an earlier life. Probably hasn't done any scuba action in years, but he could figure it out. What are you thinking?"

"Swim 'em into Beirut. Unofficial. Get 'em on Pike, then get 'em back to Tunisia, before anyone knows they're gone."

"I don't know. . . . Who'll pick 'em up? Who's doing the advanced force work? They can't just walk out of the ocean."

"One step at a time. Find out who's dive qualified on that team and give 'em a warning order. It may go nowhere, but I want 'em ready. I'll be out of the net for a few hours. I have to alert the Oversight Council. They'll need to approve any movement of Knuckles's team."

AN HOUR LATER, walking down the hall to the Taskforce conference room of the Old Executive Office Building, Kurt caught a glimpse of the West Wing of the White House out a window. As he neared the room, he could hear muted chatter spilling into the hallway, the members who were available for this quick meeting guessing as to what it was about.

He stepped through the door and the buzz of conversation dropped away, as one by one they realized he had entered. A quick survey showed that only eight of the thirteen members were present, something that could be expected given the duties of the people appointed to the Council. He was surprised to see President Warren in the room, figuring if anyone had been unable to attend, it would have been the president.

He went to the small podium at the front of the room and cleared his throat, unsure how to proceed.

"You're probably wondering why I've called you here" flashed through his mind. Instead, when he had everyone's full attention, he just laid it out.

"Today, at thirteen-forty-eight DC time, we had a Prairie Fire alert from Lebanon. One of our Taskforce operators is in jeopardy, quite possibly lethal. I'm looking to move a team into the country as soon as I can, and I need your approval to do so, because it's not without risk."

All eyes were riveted on him. He continued with the specifics of what he knew, and his best guess as to the nature of the trouble. When he finished, President Warren spoke first.

"So you don't know he's captured. You're just worst-casing it?"

"That's correct, sir, although I can't see what else it could be. Jennifer wouldn't call over an open line for a lock-on, invoking Prairie Fire, if she'd simply lost him at a souk somewhere. She said he was in trouble. That, coupled with the phone grid, tells me he's in bad-guy hands and she needed his location."

"What are the odds it's the Lebanese authorities and not terrorists?"

"I'd hate to guess. LAF would be best case, but if that happened I don't think she'd call Prairie Fire, and his phone grid wouldn't be in a Palestinian refugee camp notorious for hiding terrorists."

The national security advisor, Alexander Palmer, spoke up. "What's this mean? Worst case? I get Pike getting killed, but that's not worst case."

He saw Kurt bristle and said, "Calm down. I'm not being callous, and we don't have time for emotions. I want him back as much as you, but what's it mean the longer he's in custody?"

"Catastrophic. He's been in the Taskforce since its inception. He knows just about every cover and front company we use, along with every tactic, technique, and procedure. We can't do anything operational until we get him back and determine what he was forced to divulge. If we don't get him back, we have to assume everything's compromised. The Taskforce is finished."

He saw a few eyes widen and realized they were thinking he meant the Taskforce would become public knowledge, along with their involvement.

"I'm not talking about an exposé in the *Post*. If he's been captured by Hezbollah or one of the Palestinian groups, they're not going to brag about the intel bonanza. They're going to use it to penetrate our counterterrorist capability so they can thwart it. That's why I'm saying the Taskforce is finished. We'll have to assume they know every method we utilize. It'll be like us operating thinking we're wearing camouflage when the enemy sees blaze orange."

Palmer said, "Didn't we already have an indication

that there'd been a penetration from the operation in Tunisia? Didn't he know he was being hunted? Isn't that why you guys took him down as a fleeting target?"

Kurt said, "Yes, sir, we thought that, but we were wrong. Turns out Crusty was convinced he was being followed by the new Tunisian government for some heinous things he'd done in support of the old regime. It had nothing to do with terrorism. Just a coincidence. This, on the other hand, is the real deal."

"How long to get a team in there?"

"I've got a warning order to Knuckles in Tunisia. He's the closest one, but because he's covered under the oil company, he can't just pick up his team and fly to Lebanon without risking the exposure of the Crusty operation. Best case, I can get him in-country in forty-eight hours."

"How long do you think Pike can last?"

"What do you mean by *last*? You mean live, or keep his mouth shut?"

Palmer grimaced, then said, "I mean keep his mouth shut."

"I honestly don't know. Pike's as tough a man as I've ever seen, but if they're using extreme pressure, forty-eight hours is a long, long time."

18

The old man shouted at the toughs to stop the ineffectual slapping and punching, seeing it was getting them nowhere. In fact, they were moving backward because I was now having trouble talking through my swollen face.

They sat back and studied me, waiting. Another man entered the room, middle-aged and carrying an old-fashioned leather doctor's bag. With a chill, I realized that the punching had simply been for pleasure. They had no serious interest in my protests of innocence. They had been waiting on this man.

He talked to the old man for a moment, then opened the satchel, pulling out a scalpel. He sliced my shirt off of my body, exposing my chest.

Here we go. Need to focus. Need something to focus on.

In surprisingly good English, he said, "You know, we can keep you alive forever. In a state of perpetual pain. I have worked on many men and have gotten very, very good at walking the balance. Do you know of William

Buckley? Hmmm? Of course, you wouldn't admit it—not yet anyway—but he was one of my first patients."

The statement made me physically nauseated, searing my core in fear.

He put down the scalpel and pulled out a handheld set of pruning shears.

"I like it when you know that death is coming. I'm humane that way. I don't want you wondering each day if that day will be the last. I can't imagine the mental pressure that would cause, so I've come up with a system. I cut off your fingers and toes as time goes on. Not in any systematic way, of course. You won't wake up knowing today will be the day you'll lose your pinky toe, for instance. You'll just know that when you run out of fingers and toes, we have no more use for you.

"Today is your first one."

He approached with the shears, and I began to struggle, mightily trying to break my bonds. The two toughs clamped down on me, preventing what little wiggle room I had in my restraints. One shoved a piece of my shredded shirt in my mouth while the other held my hand steady.

The doctor took my left pinky finger and placed it in the shears. I began to thrash like a shark on a line, to no avail. He looked me in the eye and clamped the shears closed.

I screamed until my vocal cords felt shredded, the sweat pouring off of my face and the blood jetting out of my hand.

He held me by my hair, shaking my head.

"Look at me. See where this is going. You will talk; there's no doubt about that. But you can die with nineteen fingers and toes, quickly and cleanly."

His words penetrated my pain, and I realized he was right. I needed to die right fucking now, before I started spilling my guts. In my thrashing, I had felt my right leg not as tight as my left. I thought I could slip it down far enough to stand up and throw myself backward. If I could break the chair, I could make a run for the door and get killed quickly.

Before I break.

I couldn't do it right now, with the two toughs on me. I would need to last until I didn't pose a threat. That meant I needed to focus for what was to come. I ignored the words coming out of the man's mouth, knowing it was just more fear talk, and tried to find something to anchor against.

I thought about Jennifer, about living to see her again, and felt nothing but despair.

They got her too. Because of Samir. That son of a bitch.

The fact that I wouldn't get to punish him for his treachery made me see red, made me want to scream at the injustice. And I found my anchor.

Jennifer had told Samir that I held a rage like he did, but that had been a little bit of an exaggeration to make him feel good. When my family had been murdered, my rage had been much, much worse. A blackness that wanted to destroy everything it touched. And Samir's betrayal caused it to stir. A feeling I had spent years fighting, I now stoked until it was white-hot.

Live long enough to kill Samir. Live to see him die.

The man with the doctor's bag had put down the shears and picked the scalpel back up. He saw the emotion flit across my face.

"Oh? A tough one. I guess you don't want to die with nineteen fingers and toes. We'll see about that."

DEEP INSIDE THE AIN AL-HILWEH CAMP, Jennifer stayed underneath a moldy wool blanket, hidden from view. It was now past eight o'clock at night, but there was still enough light out to make her worry should someone look inside the van while they were stopped.

True to his word, Samir had managed to talk to the Lebanese Army guards outside the camp and had gained access. She didn't know what he had said and didn't really care. All she cared about was Pike, and her imagination was running wild with the thoughts of what was happening to him. Every second was precious.

She heard Samir say something and stuck her head out. He held her tablet in the passenger seat, directing the driver. He turned around.

"That's it. At least, that's where his phone was today when you called."

She saw a three-story building that looked like an apartment complex, with two men standing at the entrance holding AKs.

Jesus. We can't go door-to-door in that place. We'll last thirty seconds.

"What is it? A housing area? Where do you think they'd have Pike?"

He got the driver moving again and said, "It's not housing. It's one of their headquarters. There are no friendlies inside. Pike will be up high. On the second or third floor. It gives them time to hide him if anyone comes inside that shouldn't."

By the time they had circled through the maze of alleys and buildings, a germ of an idea had begun to form. The darkening gloom gave her courage.

"Can you guys climb buildings? Did Pike show you that?"

"No. Not specifically, but we learned to climb mountains and rock walls with ropes."

Dammit.

"If you had a rope coming down, could you climb the back of that building?"

Now parked to the rear, in a lot for an abandoned restaurant, Samir scanned the building, seeing the crude cinder-block walls and pipes jutting out.

Watching him thinking about it, she said, "It's only three floors. Surely you can do that."

"Yes. We can."

She touched a cheap yellow nylon towrope inside the van. It was a half-inch in diameter, and appeared to be long enough. "Tie in some knots. Every three feet. We're running out of time."

"Who's going to get it up there?"

"I am. We can't get in from the front. We'll get in a gunfight right off the bat, and they'll kill Pike before we reach him. We climb the back to the top balcony. I'll lay in the rope, you guys follow. When we're ready, we assault from top to bottom until we find Pike."

Samir said nothing for a moment, looking at the building. When he returned to her, he said, "Are you really an anthropologist?"

"Yes. As a matter of fact I am. But not tonight."

One of the men finished with the rope, and Jennifer took the last AK-47 out of the duffel, locking in a full magazine and slinging it over her shoulder.

"What's that for?"

"Pike. I imagine he'll be wanting to kill someone by the time we reach him."

They exited the van and moved silently to the rear of the building, the adjacent walls blocking out the last stabs of the sun, covering them in shadow. Nobody challenged them in the alley, the Palestinians' confidence in their superiority this far into the camp overweighing their security.

Reaching the base, Jennifer's concern became the myriad of electrical cables coming out of the building. There must have been a hundred, all haphazardly strewn out of the building and across the alley. It would make the climb hard, as anyone following her would have to thread them without the freedom she would have to move left and right, because they'd be using a rope.

She said, "Is this building up to code?"

Samir gave her a questioning look, and she said, "Nothing," bending down to remove her shoes. She slung her AK across her back, above the extra one, and draped her shoes around her neck.

"Okay. Here we go. I go up first, place the rope, and two follow behind one by one. When we get three at the top, we assault. Have your remaining two men take out the goons at the front door, assaulting that way, but they wait for us to initiate. We go as far as we can until contact is made, then you hit them." She looked at Samir. "Don't translate that unless you're absolutely sure what I mean. Repeat it back to me."

When she was satisfied, he turned and rattled off about five minutes of Arabic, then pointed at one other man. The remaining two faded from view down the alley, getting a bead on the front door.

She looked at the wall, a ragged affair slapped together with torn brick, broken windows, and stray cables. She knew she could climb it with ease, but wondered if she should. If it was smart attacking a terrorist stronghold with men she didn't even trust. All to try and find a man who may not even be here, based on a phone grid from hours ago.

Pike, you'd better be inside.

She picked up the rope and draped it over her shoulders, her hands shaking.

Samir said, "You all right?"

"No," she said. "But I'll be better when you break the sill of that balcony. Don't let me down."

He simply nodded, kneeling down to pull security for her climb.

She took one deep breath, then lightly jumped up and grabbed a protruding pipe. From there, she scampered up the side of the building like a lizard, finding finger- and toeholds out of instinct. She threaded her way through the cables, avoided the second-floor balcony, and reached the third. She hung on it for a second, then did a chin-up until her eyes were level with the edge.

She was happy to see a crude pipe railing to anchor the rope. Beyond it, she saw a sliding glass door partially cracked open, and a man sitting in an old and torn over-stuffed chair watching a flickering thirteen-inch television, an AK leaning against the TV stand.

19

Jennifer lowered herself until she was simply hanging, thinking about her options. She'd seen no other men in the small room, although there was an open doorway leading out. She could probably take him quietly. The TV should mask the noise she made getting over the railing.

But she knew she'd better be prepared to assault on her own. If he reacted before she could close on him, it would be a gunfight, and it would mean game-on. She wouldn't be able to wait for Samir and his men. She'd have to assault by herself to keep the element of speed and find Pike before they killed him.

She went back and forth in her mind, thinking maybe she should climb back down and talk to Samir about other options.

To hell with it. Pike's probably getting beat up while you sit here wasting time.

She went hand-over-hand to her left, getting to the farthest point away from the open door. She pulled herself up slowly, making sure the two AK-47s were away from the metal of the railing. She hooked a leg over and used it to torque her body, spinning over the railing and landing softly on her feet.

She flipped one AK off her shoulder and waited, aiming at the door entrance. When nothing happened, she duckwalked to the open door, the TV now bright and flickering in the gathering darkness.

The man was still there, still watching, although his body had shifted.

So he's awake.

She saw that she could squeeze through the door, but not with the rope and weapons on her back. She could lead with one weapon in a hand, then squeeze through, but she'd be in trouble if he turned around when she was halfway across.

No other option.

She set down Pike's weapon and the bundle of rope, her shoes still draped around her neck.

Like playing the old game "Operation," she threaded the AK through the door, then followed it, going as slowly as possible so nothing clanked against the door frame.

After an eternity of inches, she reached the far side. She silently reslung the AK across her back and moved up behind the chair in a crouch. She studied the position of the man's head for a moment, then struck, wrapping a forearm around his neck.

He became animated instantly, trying to leap to his feet and swinging his arms wildly, but instantly was still too late. She clamped her hands together and used her shoulder to press his head down. Within seconds he had slumped back into the chair, unconscious from the lack of blood to his brain.

She kept the guillotine hold in place for a second longer just to make sure, then released him, springing back and rotating the AK into the ready position. He didn't move. She rolled him out of the chair and hog-tied his feet to his hands, bending his body backward in an arc. She finished by stuffing a dirty rag in his mouth. Satisfied he was secure, she slid open the door and rapidly tied the nylon rope to the railing, then lowered it to Samir.

She felt it tug twice, letting her know he was on the way. She went back into the room, aiming her AK at the open door behind the television. She heard him reach the balcony, but didn't turn around.

He entered the room and saw the guard.

"Who's that?"

"No threat."

Samir said nothing for a moment, sizing her up yet again. When he saw the rise and fall of the man's chest, he said, "You didn't kill him?"

"No need."

Samir shook his head. "You have real skill, but are naïve. Kill him now, save a life later."

He took a pillow and pushed it into the man's face, holding it in place until the chest failed to move. Jennifer said nothing.

They heard a clank from outside, as if someone was kicking the wall. She motioned for Samir to investigate.

He moved to the balcony and jerked the rope for several minutes before coming back inside.

"The next man is hung up in the mess of electrical wiring. It will be a little longer."

Jesus. What else can happen?

"How long? We can't sit in this room forever. This guy was someone's guard relief, and they're going to come looking for him."

Before he could answer, gunfire shattered the night, first a few rounds, then a major firefight, with AK-47s rocking on full automatic.

Samir said, "That's from the men at the front. They've made contact."

"Just you and me now," Jennifer said. "We can't wait for your partner on the rope. You ready?"

He checked to make sure a round was loaded, smiled, and said, "You going to lead the way, anthropologist?"

20

My torturer moved the scalpel to my bare chest, and I began screaming into the gag, shaking my head to let them know I wanted to talk. Anything to draw out the time.

He pulled out the rag of my shirt and waited.

"You guys have made a mistake. If you look at my past travel and what I've been doing, you'll see I'm who I say I am. I swear. I just came from Syria, where I'm working with the Ministry of Culture on an archeological site. . . . Please . . . check it out before you do this."

He shook his head. "You and I both know that's not true. If you want the pain to stop, you need to give me something more. Don't waste my time with your contrived story. Nobody in this room believes it, including you. I will ask you a question, though. How many archeological firms carry laptops full of explosives?"

The question caved in my courage, because there was no way on earth to counter it. No way for me to convince them they held the wrong man, nothing I could say that would alter the cold, hard facts of the café bombing.

They were going to break me. The fear swept through me, my mind racing for a way out. A way to get them to kill me, but there was nothing I could do with the two toughs to my left and right. They'd just capture me before I made it out of the room.

He leaned in again, and I prepared for the pain, channeling my rage to hang on.

A single gunshot rang out, giving him pause. After a moment of silence, another one boomed, then another, until at least four weapons were firing on full automatic.

He pulled back and looked at the old man for instructions. The boss barked something in Arabic, and the two toughs to my left and right ran out of the room.

It was just me against the two remaining men, with no weapons in sight.

Big mistake.

I sprang up on my loose right foot, throwing myself backward. I got about two feet in the air and landed hard on my back, shattering the chair.

I stood up with pieces of chair still tied to me, both wrists strapped to lengths of wood that used to be the arms.

I grabbed the old man by his pristine bin Laden–wannabe beard and whirled around, like an Olympian conducting a hammer throw. I did a full circle, generating as much velocity as I could, and released his head straight into the rock wall of the room, seeing it cave in with a satisfyingly meaty thud.

I turned on the torturer, who had backed up and started waving the scalpel. I stared into his eyes and smiled.

I worked the pieces of chair loose from my wrists, giving me a stout, ironwood club for each hand. I noticed nails sticking out of each end and turned them to the rear, mimicking his voice.

"Don't worry, I won't use the nails. I don't want you to die too soon."

I moved in on him, bringing the first club down on the forearm that held the scalpel, shattering it.

He screamed, a guttural sound from deep inside. The clubs became a blur, beating him all over his body, striking any available spot. Whenever he tried to protect himself, I moved somewhere else. I broke his jaw, both cheeks, his nose, ribs, clavicles, and anything else I could harm, the clubs working like a Japanese Taiko drummer.

He fell to the ground with pink, bubbly froth coming out of his mouth. I continued on like some demented gorilla, trying mightily to burst his internal organs, the rage flowing through me and into him.

Eventually, I slowed out of sheer exhaustion and saw I was now drumming a lifeless bag of meat. The rage evaporated, and I realized I had wasted precious seconds. The gunfight was still going on, and I felt a glimmer of hope that I might not need to simply die. Maybe I could escape alive.

I ran to the back of the room, to a door that hadn't been used, hoping it led to a back hallway out of the building, away from the gunfire. I ratcheted the knob and found it locked.

I heard shouting behind me and whirled around, raising my clubs in a ridiculous attempt at defense.

The two toughs came back through the door, flabbergasted at the carnage. One ran to the old man while another took aim at my head.

I threw a club as hard as I could, causing him to raise his weapon to block the missile. The wood ricocheted off of the AK and hit him in the head. It exploded open in a mist of blood.

What the hell?

He fell over as my brain registered a gunshot. Two other individuals had entered behind him, both armed and shooting. The second tough whirled at the gunfire and brought his weapon up, but never got off a round before his head exploded as well.

The two swept the room for additional threats. Seeing none, one went to the bin Laden wannabe I'd cratered into the wall, and the other focused on me.

It was Jennifer. Walking toward me barefoot and holding an AK, her shoes draped incongruously around her neck. I was at a loss for words.

My little protégé.

She was staring at me with a crooked grin.

I said, "I'm never going to live this down."

The smile reached her eyes, and she said, "Yeah, must be tough getting to actually live."

She pulled an AK from her back and tossed it to me.

When I caught it she saw the damage to my left hand. I quickly wrapped the wound with a remnant from my torn shirt. Through the shock on her face, I knew she understood what had happened. I changed the subject before she could even ask.

"I'm not being nitpicky," I said, "but usually an operator puts his shoes on *before* the gunfight."

She looked down and saw I was right. She blushed and took the shoes from around her neck, bending down to put them on, saying, "I never got the chance . . ."

Over her kneeling form I saw the other man who had come in with her, checking on the vital signs of the bin Laden wannabe.

I recognized who it was, the rage flooding back.

Samir's back was turned to me as he searched the man on the ground. I racked a round into the AK and strode right at him. I came abreast of Jennifer, and she leapt up, trying to push me back.

"Pike, stop. It's not what you think. Samir didn't do anything."

I swept her aside and knocked Samir to the ground, putting a foot on his head.

"You miserable fuck. If I had the time, I'd carve you up like your buddies did to me."

His eyes were wide and rolling left and right. He tried to talk but couldn't because of the pressure I was putting on his head. I jammed the barrel of the AK right behind his ear and put my finger on the trigger.

Jennifer, who'd been jerking on me in an attempt to

get me off of Samir, saw the move and stopped her attempts lest they caused me to fire.

She pleaded with me. "Pike, don't do this. He saved your life. He and his men assaulted this place. Move your finger off the trigger."

I didn't hear a word. All I felt was the ultimate betrayal of the man at my feet and the terror of the last few hours. I itched to squeeze. Seven foot-pounds of pressure, and it would all be over.

Jennifer leaned in, no longer pleading. She whispered into my ear, her voice steel. "Pike. Stop right now. Back off. We still have to get out of here, and you're screwing up the mission. You're going to get us all killed. We need him to get out of here. We need his weapon and his men."

The words penetrated my rage, snapping me back to the present.

"Kill him later. After we get out."

She was absolutely right. *Get the mission done.* I removed my foot and pulled back the AK, but I kept the barrel pointed at his head. "What's the plan?"

"Get out through the top, away from the fight downstairs."

"What about site exploitation?"

Samir sat up and spoke for the first time. "Pike, I had nothing to do with that bomb. I was used just like—"

I snarled, "Shut the fuck up. Don't open your mouth. You can keep the weapon, but if that barrel goes anywhere close to Jennifer or me, I'm gutting you."

I returned to Jennifer. "What about SSE?"

"Have you lost your mind? We came here to get you. Mission accomplished. Now we're getting the hell out. We don't have the time to search this place. Even if we did, we don't have the manpower to clear it first. You think I came in here with a Taskforce element? I've got a bunch of guys I just met who claim you trained them. Let's get out of here while we still can."

I went to the door, listening to the rhythms of the firefight a floor below. "You guys clear the upper floors?"

Jennifer snorted and stomped to the back of the room, ratcheting on the same door I had tried, looking for another way out. Samir said, "Yeah. Upstairs is clear."

Jennifer came back over. "Jesus, Pike, stop what you're thinking. We're lucky to be standing here talking. Get your ass moving up those stairs."

"Jennifer, I'm not leaving without some intel. I'm cleaning this place out of computers, passports, and anything else I can find."

She tried to appeal to my sense of mission again. "Pike, think about it. We'll have to clear and secure the entire building for site exploitation. We'll have to kill everyone here first."

I wiped the blood seeping out beneath the makeshift bandage on my left hand.

"Yeah. That's a definite fringe benefit."

21

Infidel chose to park the car on the outskirts of the *Da-hiyeh* and walk in. He had some equipment within the vehicle that he'd more than likely be leaving behind, and he'd prefer that nobody in Hezbollah saw how he'd arrived.

His summons had been uniquely brusque, and he was fairly certain his Hezbollah paymasters were a little upset at the computer bomb. He hadn't bothered to ask their permission, but since they were so paranoid anyway, he was sure they'd applaud his initiative. Well, almost sure.

He turned the corner to the café and saw three men standing at the entrance—where there was usually one. *Not a good sign.* He continued on, the only indication of his concern being a subtle caress of a carbon-fiber push dagger hidden parallel to the leather on the inside of his belt. A subconscious reassurance that he wasn't without some means of self-defense.

He reached the men and smiled, holding out his backpack to be searched. Instead, the men motioned for him to raise his arms. He did so and was subjected to a thorough pat-down, while his backpack was ripped apart.

That had never happened before either. He assumed that he was being punished for his little handiwork and not yet actively suspected of anything. Although with Hezbollah, you never knew. They were as paranoid as the Nazi faithful at the end of World War II, seeing assassins in the shadows everywhere. Being paid as an assassin probably didn't help his image. Especially with the call sign Infidel.

The search finished, he entered the coffee shop, finding it empty. A man followed him in and nudged him forward with the barrel of a rifle. He thought about resisting, but didn't. It crossed his mind that he might remain compliant right up until they put a bullet in his head. How far was too far? Where was the line when he would need to fight back? Impossible to know. Seeing a stairwell at the back of the café, he wondered if he'd already crossed it.

He paused for a second, knowing if he entered the stairwell there was really no turning back. He'd be trapped by a man with a gun inside a shooting funnel. The man nudged him again, and he started to climb.

Reaching the top, he saw Majid and Ja'far at a table, both looking at him sternly. Almost comically. He inwardly breathed a sigh of relief.

"You two upset about something? What's with all the new security?"

Majid motioned to a chair. "Please. Sit down. We have something to discuss with you about your latest assignment. And the one before."

He sat, the tension coming back at the last statement. *The one before? Something go bad with the investigator?* He knew the rules of the game. He'd seen what happened to people who were no longer useful. In 2005, the head of Syrian intelligence in Lebanon had committed "suicide" right after speaking with the U.N. about the Hariri assassination. A valuable asset had become a potential liability overnight, and Syria had liquidated him. The assassin knew he was only as good as his last job. The minute he was a threat, he would be gone.

He decided on the confused approach. "Okay. You'll have to start, since I have no idea what this is about."

Majid smiled. "Really? Infidel, we use you because of your skills, not your judgment. We tell you what to do, and you do it. That's why you're paid. To do things that we cannot accomplish on our own. Don't tell me you have no idea. Tell me why."

He held his hands up in a gesture of surrender. "Hey, you can't be mad about the bombing in Sidon. Is that it? You guys pay me to take care of problems, and that's exactly what I did. You told me to provide a covert camera to the Druze contact, but you didn't do any investigation on the asset he was using, did you?"

When Majid and Ja'far said nothing, he felt on more solid ground. He continued. "The asset wasn't some garbage man. He was a United States intelligence operative.

He was setting you up. I recognized him and took him out. Like you pay me to do."

Majid said, "We didn't tell you to kill anyone. We wanted to see the outcome of that meeting. Make sure they weren't doing anything that could harm us. Now, you've very likely set us into a fight with the Palestinians in the camps, something we have tried to avoid. You blunder around like every other American, without any understanding of the consequences."

"Hand me my bag," he said. Majid nodded to the guard who held it, and the assassin pulled out a digital camera. He flipped to a series of photos and held the camera out. Ja'far took it.

"That man you see with the Druze is Nephilim Logan. He was a U.S. counterterrorist commando. One of the best they had. I know this because he almost killed me a couple of years ago. Now, I'm sure he's working with the United States against you. That's why I sent in the bomb. Trust me, he is not your friend, and he deserves to be dead. I'm sorry if the other deaths might cause you issues, but it wasn't your meeting. You never said protect it. What I did was protect you. Like you pay me to do."

Majid and Ja'far flipped through the digital stills of the camera, absently looking at the pictures. When they were done, Ja'far spoke. "You have your uses, Infidel, but only so many. You have done us a service until today. Now, the killing of the investigator is gathering interest, and you have compounded that by killing an American intelligence operative. What are we to do with you?"

The assassin blinked. *Gathering interest?* "What the hell does that mean? The tribunal hit was magic. No way can anyone connect anything with you guys."

"No. Not magic. Close, but there were two bodies in the wreckage. The investigator and her boyfriend."

"Yeah? So fucking what?"

"The boyfriend's face was fractured. Like he'd been beaten."

He snorted. "Who gives a shit? They died in a gas explosion. Maybe he was hit by some flying debris. What's the difference?"

"The difference is that people are digging now. Because of who the investigator was. We hired you for no fingerprints, and now there are questions."

"You don't have any directed at you. There is *no* connection to you. You're clean."

"You're wrong. There *is* a connection. We worry about the future. What will the Sidon attack cause? Who will question that? The Americans?"

The assassin stood, edging toward the door. He knew what that meant: *He* was the connection. "That group was Palestinian, from the camps. At least that's what you told me they were. I operated on your intelligence and cut off a threat to your operations. The Americans will look no further than the camps and chalk this up to rival groups. In the end, if there was an assassination plot, it's dead now. Right? Isn't that what you were afraid of anyway?"

Ja'far stiffened. "We don't tell you the details. Only

what we want done. And in this case, we wanted a *recording*. Not death. You may have—"

Majid cut him off with a look, and Infidel knew something more was going on. He now worried about getting out of the room alive. He backed toward the door.

"I'm sorry if I did anything to harm your interests. You know that's not what I do. I've shown you my skill. I understand you're upset, so let's call the last payment you owe me null and void. We're even. Okay?"

Majid laughed. "You Americans. It's always about the money. We don't care about that. If we wanted to kill you, we would do so right now—regardless of the money."

Infidel waited, ready to pull the carbon-fiber blade. Now was the go or no-go moment.

"Don't look so worried. You can go. We just want you to be aware of our concerns. If we are to continue, you need to be more attuned to our needs."

Ja'far smiled. "Or more attuned to your final wishes."

Infidel smiled back, a weak grin that made him feel foolish. The guard at the door with the AK-47 saw his trepidation and grinned as well, enjoying the feeling of superiority. The bully in the room liking his torment.

He left down the stairwell in controlled haste. When he reached the bottom, he was followed by the two men who had remained in the café. He paid them no outward mind, but caressed his carbon-fiber lucky charm again.

They followed him all the way out of the *Dahiyeh*.

When he hailed a cab, they showed no sign that it was anything other than what they expected. When the cab pulled away, guaranteeing his freedom, he initiated the electronic collection device he'd installed in the wheel well of the vehicle he was leaving behind.

22

The Ghost checked the security of his hotel room door, deciding it was good enough. If someone wanted to come through the hard way, it would take more than one blow, and that would leave plenty of time to get him out on the balcony, and away.

He'd managed to slip out of Sidon in the chaos of the bombing and had elected not to drive all the way home to Tripoli. He wanted to open the briefcase as soon as possible, but he needed a secure area to analyze the information. He'd stopped in Beirut and rented a room in the Hamra area, next to the university.

He placed the briefcase on the chipped table in front of the television and stared at it for a second. He went into the bathroom, blotted a washcloth in the sink, and returned. He righted the briefcase and cleansed the dried blood from the handle. He wasn't sure why he did it, but it felt like the right thing.

He placed it back down flat and opened it. Inside was a sheaf of papers, a wallet, a thumb drive, and a passport.

He picked up the passport and wallet first. Credit

cards and Saudi Arabian identification for a man named Ahmed al-Rashid. One more name for his record books. He was pleased to see it was a Gulf Cooperation Council country. Being in the GCC would make it much easier to pass across borders of any member state. The passport itself looked official, but was in pieces, with the picture missing. He assumed he would have received instructions on final assembly, but that was obviously not going to happen now.

The credit cards were in the same name, as was the international driver's license. In the sheaf of papers he found a bank statement, with a balance of fifty thousand dollars. He assumed one of the cards was a debit card from the bank. The money was fine to get started, but he wouldn't be using the identity of Ahmed for very long. If he decided to continue.

He continued flipping through the papers and found the biography of the United States Middle Eastern envoy. A man named Jeffrey McMasters. Fifty-seven years old, with the face of a distinguished patrician. Gray around the temples and a hint of a smile around the eyes. A professional diplomat with over thirty-five years of service. He noted he was a former ambassador to the United Arab Emirates and had worked in the Jordanian Embassy, but had done nothing with the state of Israel. That stood to reason because the United States would be looking for someone who understood the area, but who could never be accused of having a bias.

He flipped to the next page and saw the itinerary of

McMasters's Middle East trip. The envoy was hitting quite a few countries over the next seven days. Most stops simply stated the city and duration, but some actually listed the events of the day and the lodging arrangements. The Ghost guessed that the Hamas offshoot group had greater penetration of some countries than others.

He saw the envoy was due to land in Lebanon tomorrow, but would be spending only about eight hours on the ground before leaving again and flying to Turkey. He would visit at least four other countries before his final stop in Doha, Qatar, for the peace talks. The stop before that was Dubai, UAE.

Dubai was one of the few places with a complete itinerary, and the chosen hotel caught his eye. The Al Bustan Rotana, a premier five-star establishment in a city known for five-star establishments. But this hotel had a little extra notoriety, beyond the luxury. It was the same one where the Mossad had assassinated Mahmoud al-Mabhouh, chief of Hamas's military wing, in 2010. A spectacular killing by the Zionists that made the Palestinians look weak.

Using fake passports from at least four different European countries, the hit team had conducted surveillance on Mahmoud for days, penetrated his room in the hotel, waited on him to return, then suffocated him to death.

The irony of the envoy's choosing this hotel bit deep. Maybe he *would* take on the assignment. To kill McMasters in the same hotel as the Hamas operative would send a clear signal—especially if done in the same manner. No giant car bomb. No random slaughter of civilians. A targeted killing in a special place.

He shuffled through the rest of the paperwork, seeing more credit receipts and other useful information, but nothing substantial. In truth, he only half focused on it, his brain turning over the nuances of the attack.

He knew that neither Hamas nor Hezbollah would acknowledge any role in the killing, which left him alone. Breaking up the peace process might be good enough for those factions, but he wanted the world to know why. He'd have to create a group out of whole cloth and begin seeding jihadist Web sites with some statements. Get them ready for the claim of credit after the attack. Luckily, in this day and age, all it took was an Internet connection to be an instant jihadi. He knew he would have the name of his "group" on the world stage should he succeed. More important, he'd have the Palestinian plight on the world stage as well, just like Black September had at the Munich Olympics in 1972.

He kicked around the idea. He knew if he chose to do it, he'd have to get rid of the Saudi identity within forty-eight hours after using it. Someone had leaked the information of the meeting in Sidon, and he had to assume that whoever that was had all the information he had. Including the target. Thus, he couldn't use it to attack. He would need to get another, without Hezbollah help.

He reflected on the explosion in Sidon yet again, at a loss as to who had perpetrated the attack. It couldn't be Hezbollah, because the set-up was way more complicated than necessary. Why go through the trouble of bringing him down to Beirut, convincing him to attend the meeting, then agree to the change in venue if they only wanted to kill him? And if the targets were the other men, why bring him in at all? Simply do it.

In the end, he decided it didn't matter. Someone had attacked the meeting, and he'd probably never find out the who or why, since everyone had an agenda. The only decision that mattered was whether he wanted to continue on or disappear. If he wanted to continue, he needed to make sure that Hezbollah knew he was alive. Give them confidence that he was working for them and prevent them from shutting off the credit cards and bank accounts for the Saudi identity. In fact, have them complete the passport and other identity papers. He was sure they could point him to a forger.

He made his decision and picked up the phone. He would continue on, initially as their man, on their puppet strings. Lull them a little bit, before cutting the strings and becoming *Ash'abah*.

The Ghost.

23

The man called Infidel saw his Hezbollah contact take a seat along the Corniche, eating a cup of gelato just like he'd been instructed. He dialed the contact's number, watching him pick up the phone.

"I'm across the street from you, inside the park. See me?"

He saw the kid look left, then right, finally fixating on his park bench.

"Come on. You can finish the ice cream over here. I have another assignment."

The boy raced across a break in traffic and slid into the park bench next to him. He gave the assassin his goofy smile and said, "A lot of work lately. That's good, huh?"

The assassin handed him an MP3 player, saying, "I need you to listen to this and translate what's said."

The boy eagerly took the device, wanting to be a part of an operation, loving the feeling of being a Hezbollah foot soldier. He was no more than sixteen or seventeen and could have been a merchant or an aspiring businessman, something Lebanon used to be known for. Instead, he was an aspiring terrorist in an organization that was cultlike in its brainwashing. He'd never had a chance to live, and now, because of his affiliation, the assassin would see to it that he never did.

The boy was his conduit into Hezbollah for mundane matters, when he didn't need to see the hierarchy. He was the person who had provided the computer camera/ bomb to the Druze. Whenever simple instructions, money, or equipment needed to be passed, it came through the boy. He was smart and loyal to a fault, convinced that the assassin was some super-secret Hezbollah weapon who had the ear of Nasrallah himself. The name Infidel meant a great deal in the boy's circle of friends, and the fact that he was the conduit gave him special status and envy.

"I had a meeting today with some people on behalf of the party. It went a little strange, and I implanted a technical device to record what was said after I left. That's what I want you to translate. It's a couple of hours of tape, but not all of it is dialogue."

It was no accident that he'd left the Hezbollah meeting without asking for his backpack or other equipment. The digital camera he had shown the Hezbollah members cloaked a remote recording device with a wireless transmitting capability. It would pick up all conversation for two hours of continuous use and transmit that recording in bursts to a special collection device. The range was limited, so the assassin had been forced to embed the collection capability in the frame of his car, which he could access via the cell network.

He'd waited three hours after his meeting before conducting the download. He hadn't wasted the time, going straight back to his apartment, packing up, and moving to a small, nondescript hotel. He'd taken precautions to never let Hezbollah know where he lived, but was under no illusions about their reach. Luckily, everything he owned fit into a large duffel bag and two Pelican cases.

The boy pulled out a notebook. Before hitting play, he said, "Does this have something to do with the computer I'm picking up from the Druze contact?"

Taken aback, the assassin showed no emotion. "Yeah, it does. How'd you get roped into getting the computer back? I thought that was a one-way deal."

"It's not your computer. I think that one is destroyed. The meeting the Druze attended was attacked, and he left with someone else's computer. He called the party, and I'm supposed to pick it up in a few hours near the university."

The assassin simply nodded, his brain working in overdrive. "Well, we don't have a lot of time then. Listen to this, and you'll be on your way."

The boy put in the earphones and hit play, listening and scribbling on his pad. The assassin left him to it, trying to puzzle out this latest bit of intel. What was this about a computer? And why would the Druze contact Hezbollah? Surely Nephilim Logan was now dead, and the Druze would suspect Hezbollah had killed him. Something was not right.

He watched the boy for any signs of what was being said, but nothing registered in his body language until about an hour into the tape. Then, the boy stopped writing and looked at him, his eyes wide. When the assassin did nothing but give him a hard look in return, he went back to the page, scribbling furiously. Soon enough, the tape was done.

"Well, what do you have?"

"Abu Infidel, it's not good. You need to stay away from these people. Tell the Resistance what they're doing."

"Spit it out. What's on the tape?"

"Well, there's apparently an assassination being planned, but not here in Lebanon. Somewhere else. The assassin was at the meeting with your computer. Someone attacked the meeting, and there's something about an American intelligence agent, who's now dead. There's a lot of the talk that I couldn't understand because it was garbled, but the assassin lived. He called the person on this tape, and he's going forward with his plan. He asked for help."

"Who is it? What's his name? What's his target?"

The Infidel quietly seethed. *He* was the chosen one for this work, the professional used when it was something delicate with strategic implications, and they'd hired someone else. The fuckers had actually gone to another player when he had a *perfect* record.

"They didn't say. They seemed pleased that he was continuing, but didn't say anything specific, except the target was bringing money and they wanted that money to go away."

"Money? For what? Who's bringing money?"

"I don't know." The boy put his hand on the assassin's forearm. "Your name came up. They said they were going to kill you to keep you from affecting the operation because of something else you'd done."

The news didn't really upset him. Deep inside, he knew his time here was coming to a close. Hezbollah was just too damn paranoid to let him run around forever. He knew they'd try to kill him sooner or later. The issue now was stopping that order before it got out to the Hezbollah chain of command. He'd last five seconds in Beirut if that happened, looking over his shoulder at everyone who walked behind him.

The second issue was this new assassin. *Kill me, huh? How about I kill your whole fucking plan?* It was a matter of pride now.

He didn't know the man's name, but he knew where to find it. And he'd need the computer the boy was supposed to pick up. He looked at his watch and saw he had about forty minutes before the meeting with the Druze.

"Come on. I need you to read something else."

"What? I don't have time for that. I have to meet the Druze, then pass the computer to someone else."

"Who?"

"Abu Aziz."

That computer is important. Abu Aziz was one of the guys on the inner circle protective detail of Majid and Ja'far. It would work out well that he wasn't in the *Dahiyeh*, because he was a giant of a man and the most competent. Of all the inner circle that the assassin had met, Aziz was the only one with combat experience, having earned his position through skill in the 2006 war with Israel.

"I'll pay for you to get to that meeting. I have as much interest in this as you do."

He stood up and flagged a cab. The boy mistook his irritation at what he had translated as an urgent need to inform the Resistance. He entered the cab as well. He said nothing until they entered the outskirts of the *Dahiyeh*, then said, "You have something for me to read here?"

The assassin saw his face twist in confusion, and said, "Just a quick stop. Nothing for you here. You take the cab to the meeting. When you get the computer, come back here. Don't worry about taking the computer to Aziz. Bring it right back here. I'll be upstairs with the leadership. Give me a call, and I'll let you know if it's okay to come up."

Infidel smiled. "I'll introduce you to the power brokers. The real people of the Resistance. Forget about Aziz. He's an errand boy."

The boy's eyes glowed at the thought. He nodded vigorously. "I'll come right back here. You'll tell them to call Aziz?"

"Yes."

Infidel paid the cabdriver up front, then walked to the café, glancing to make sure his car was still parked where he'd left it. He was fairly sure he'd need a rapid mode of exfiltration, and waiting on a cab wouldn't cut it.

Two men were at the entrance. Walking up to them was incredibly dangerous, but he had one card to play: He supposedly had no idea Hezbollah wanted him dead. If these guys didn't either, then he'd be allowed into the café just as he had been before. If they did know about the order, they'd be smirking behind his back, thinking they were now saved the trouble of hunting him down. Either way, they'd let him into the inner sanctum, with no idea that he knew what they'd planned for his fate. A little thing, this bit of information, but something potentially decisive for a man of his skills.

He allowed himself to be frisked, telling them he'd simply come back for his camera and backpack. The two guards radioed into the inner sanctum. He hoped that Majid and Ja'far would be upstairs and not inside the café. Killing everyone there would be difficult. He needn't have worried. The radio call came back, and a conversation ensued, with both guards surreptitiously stealing glances at him. They finally told him he could enter, and led him through the café to the stairs, one in front and one behind.

So it's option number two. Good. Rather have them know why I'm killing them.

The guard in front opened the door to the office and stepped inside. The assassin caught a glimpse of Majid and Ja'far inside, both with insincere smiles. The door swung outward, toward him. In one fluid move, he swung the door closed on the lead man and pulled the carbon-fiber push dagger from his belt, the blade sticking out between the second and third finger of his clenched fist.

Four inches of plastic in the shape of an arrowhead with a handle perpendicular to the blade, it looked like the T-bone of a porterhouse steak, with four ridges that ran from the handle down to the tip. None of the ridges held much of an edge, but that didn't matter. It wasn't made to cut, but to stab.

The assassin turned to the guard behind him, tied up the hand holding the pistol grip of his AK, and punched the man three times in the neck with the push dagger. He grunted twice, and a fountain of blood jetted out of his neck, spraying the walls like a garden hose dropped by a child.

The assassin let him fall to the ground and swung open the door. As expected, the first guard was coming through it to find out what had happened. His eyes went wide at the slaughter, but his brain wasn't quick enough to react.

The assassin punched him three times in the fold where his neck met his shoulders, and another fountain of blood erupted, spraying the hallway in an obscene amount of crimson liquid.

The assassin let him drop, picked up his AK-47, and entered the room.

24

Like some bloody apparition from a horror movie, the Hezbollah leadership watched Infidel close the door.

"I understand you guys have some issues with my work."

To their credit, they showed no fear. *Because they still think they're in control.*

Majid spoke first. "Abu Infidel, I have no idea why you chose to seal your fate, but you are done now. Your choice is how you die. Put down the gun, and it will be quick."

"Shut the fuck up. I have no time for bullshit Arabic bravado. You hired another assassin, and I want to know who. There's also the matter of money going out. A great deal of money. I want to know where."

Ja'far said, "The other killer is none of your concern. It isn't Hezbollah business. Leave us now and we may reconsider your fate."

The assassin walked over to Ja'far, grabbed a fistful of hair, pulled his head back, and punched him deep with the push-blade. Ja'far's arms swung wildly. He leapt to his feet, clamped his hands over the wound to his carotid artery, and ran in a circle like a decapitated chicken, finally slamming into a wall and sliding to the floor, the blood still pumping out of his destroyed neck.

The assassin looked at Majid. "I understand you plan on killing the Druze like you were planning on killing me. You guys just don't give a shit who you fuck over, huh?"

Majid's eyes were wide, but he said nothing.

"You'd better start talking, you raghead piece of shit. You wanted me dead, and now you reap what you sow."

Majid said, "Abu Aziz will be here any time. You can kill me, but he will kill you. Make no mistake, you are dead."

"Abu Aziz? The guy bringing the computer from the Druze? Is that who you mean? Actually, I don't think he's going to show up. At least not anytime soon. Maybe a little later. With a fucking mop to clean this place up."

Majid showed his first sign of fear. "What do you want?"

"I want to know who the killer is. That's it."

"I don't know his name. He calls himself the Ghost. That's all I know."

"Really. What alias did you give him? How's he traveling?"

"I don't know. He got his identity from a Palestinian group. We had nothing to do with it."

"Bullshit. You gave him something." He saw a computer at the back of the room, and went to it.

"Is it in here? The information?"

"That computer is nothing. Just a desktop work machine for the coffee shop."

"Really? Okay, then type in the password. Now."

Majid did as he asked, and the screen filled with Arabic.

"Can you read that, Infidel?"

The assassin felt his phone vibrate. He smiled. "No, but I think I know someone who can."

He spoke briefly into the phone, then turned to Majid. "That's the Druze computer coming up. Last chance. You help me now, and you live. You don't, and you die."

Majid closed his eyes and began rocking slightly, chanting in Arabic. The assassin shook his head. *Fatalistic sons of bitches, that's for sure.*

He walked around the chair until he was behind the chanting man. He circled Majid's neck with his forearm, cinched it tight, and twisted harshly. He let go and watched the body hit the floor, the right foot twitching.

He went quickly to the door and dragged inside the bloody body he'd killed on the threshold. He placed both of the dead guards' bodies against the near wall, hiding them from first view. He was moving to the dead Hezbollah leadership, intent on hiding them as well, when he heard a knock at the door. He cursed, took one look around, then walked over and pushed it open.

The boy stood on the threshold, looking wide-eyed.

"Abu Infidel, what is all of this blood? What's going on?"

The assassin smiled. "Nothing now. We had some issues. But it's taken care of. I told you I'd get you in to
meet the party faithful. Come on in and say hello."

The boy nodded hesitantly and crossed the threshold.
When he saw the massacre inside, he balked, attempting
to back up and escape through the door.

The assassin stopped him, trapping his elbow joint in
a come-along and forcing him to drop the computer he'd
brought.

"I didn't say they'd talk back. Be happy you get to see
them at all."

When the boy calmed down enough to assimilate his
surroundings, the assassin continued.

"What I need you to do is go through these computers and tell me the identity of the target and the identity
of the forger helping out the assassin. Do that, and I'll let
you live."

25

I pulled up the geolocation software suite one more time and was rewarded yet again with a null ping. I began to think we'd made a mistake giving the computer back to the enemy.

Probably not any free Wi-Fi in this whole damn country.

We'd made it out of the Ain al-Hilweh camp surprisingly easily. It had turned out that the building wasn't heavily occupied, and since Jennifer and Samir had killed everyone above us, we had only a small contingent below, which had been effortlessly sandwiched between us and Samir's men out front. No issues whatsoever, except I would have liked to have made them suffer a little more.

We had split up and searched, with me giving guidance to focus on computer equipment. I knew we had plenty of time, since the "police" wouldn't respond to a firefight here in the camps until they were sure it was over, but I didn't want to push my luck by digging through terrorist sock drawers. We'd come away with a single laptop and some thumb drives.

We'd fled to Samir's house in the Chouf Mountains. I

had wanted to gut every single one of the Druze militia-men in the back of the van, but Jennifer held me back. Eventually, Samir had managed to convince me that he wasn't Dr. Evil and hadn't set me up. Which meant that someone else had an agenda. It remained to be seen who.

Going through the computer, we'd found the itiner-ary for Jeffrey McMasters, the new Middle Eastern envoy from the United States, along with a bunch of tangential information about the meeting that occurred today, in-cluding the bona fides for the two sides.

What caught my eye was the description of the assas-sin. It was nothing like the guy I had seen, with the ex-ception of the Coke-bottle eyeglasses. The person who was supposed to be at that table was a small, frail man. Instead, the man gutted by my computer bomb was a six-foot-three-inch bruiser. Which left a huge gap in our knowledge of what the hell was going on. McMasters was targeted for assassination, that much I was sure of, but we had no idea by whom. Forget the specific individual, we didn't even know which ideological group, which was a necessary precursor to stopping the attack.

The first order of business had been to contact the Taskforce and feed them everything we had. Unlike Syria, Lebanon was still a free-for-all of Internet access, so we managed to get our "company" VPN up and running fairly easily, using the Internet from Samir's house. I made Samir wait in another room and got Kurt on the line. Samir didn't fight it, knowing full well by now that we did a little bit more than archeological work.

I gave Kurt a very succinct account of what had occurred. I let him know that Jennifer's call of Prairie Fire was a good one, but downplayed my time in captivity, sticking to the mission. I didn't mention what had happened to me, or the fear that still lingered, a rotting sore I pretended not to notice.

Jennifer had watched me closely on the ride back and on the VPN. I could feel her eyes on me, sensing my trauma like some rabbit detecting a coming earthquake.

We had never spoken about it, but we had a connection that was a little strange. Some sort of innate bond that defied explanation. From the very first time we had met, I had been able to intuit her pain, plugged into her being in some visceral, subliminal way.

In the past, it had been helpful because it had always been *me* bringing *her* through some traumatic event. Serious combat actions she had been exposed to for the first time, death and destruction the average person could only imagine that almost crushed her ability to continue. I had sensed when she was on the edge and had pulled her through every event, then patted myself on the back when it was done. After all, I was the commando.

Now, I was subconsciously hurting. I didn't want to admit it to myself, but I was undergoing an unhealthy dose of post-traumatic stress, and she could smell it as well as I could. The connection apparently worked both ways, which did nothing but piss me off. I could handle the issue and didn't need her starting in on some self-help bullshit.

I'd ignored her stare and gotten Kurt on the line through the VPN. I told him what we had and demanded a team.

He said, "I've got one moving now. Well, not a full team, but I can get you Knuckles, Decoy, and a new guy named Brett."

I was surprised to hear he'd alerted anyone at all, but when I heard it was Knuckles and Decoy, I didn't give a damn about anything else. Those two were worth an entire Taskforce team as far as I was concerned.

I said, "Perfect. What's the story on the new guy?"

"Just came over from the Special Activities Division. I'm going to swim them in after launching them from Tunis by rotary wing. He was the only other guy who had subsurface infiltration experience. Don't worry, he's solid. He's a former Force Recon guy."

"Great. A jarhead. No issues here, as long as he knows who's in charge. Which is something I need to know as well."

I was a civilian, and Knuckles was still active duty. Technically, he should be in command, but I was the man on the ground who understood the situation.

Kurt smiled and said, "You're ground force commander. Like you would have it any other way. I'll let Knuckles know."

I knew Knuckles wouldn't care, but would have to make sure this new guy from SAD—which always had a tendency to push things—understood the chain of command.

Kurt had finished by giving me PM instructions for another meeting with the case officer, telling me to be prepared to pass off linkup instructions with the team.

After feeding the Taskforce everything we could intel-wise, including an image of the hard drive from the laptop, I decided to download and install a free software program called "Prey," and give the laptop back to Hezbollah. Made to track stolen laptops and cell phones, the program would allow us to track the computer's location, let us voice-record anybody within range, get screenshots of the Web sites they were on, and get a webcam picture of whoever was using it. In short, get us more intel than we had now. Of course, we'd scrubbed the laptop first, deleting anything that could be potentially useful to the terrorists.

The software package wasn't nearly as good as some of the custom applications the Taskforce could implant, but hey, you worked with what you had. The problem with my grand idea was that in order to initiate any of its features, the computer had to be within range of a Wi-Fi hot spot, and so far we'd been out of luck. We had no idea where the computer had been taken after Samir met his Hezbollah contact and passed it off.

I pinged it again and was surprised to get a response.

"Hey, we're in business! The computer's stopped, and it's sending a signal."

Jennifer and Samir gathered around me as I initiated the geolocation feature. When a map came up, with an icon representing our computer, Samir said, "That's the heart of the *Dahiyeh*. Headquarters for Hezbollah."

"No surprise there."

I initiated the webcam, and we got a shaky image of a young Arabic man. The pictures came in once every second, so it was like watching a herky-jerky old-fashioned movie. He was banging away on the keyboard and talking to someone out of range of the camera. Samir said, "That's my contact."

I turned on the microphone, getting a tinny response with the voices sounding like they were coming from a tunnel.

"Abu Infidel, I can't find anything more on this computer. I'm not sure why the Druze gave it to me. It's like everything but the original programs have been deleted."

Jennifer became agitated. "He's speaking English and he said 'infidel'! He called that guy Infidel, just like the case officer said."

I waved my hands to get her to be quiet so we could hear. I saw a set of arms above the boy's shoulders, the head still hidden.

"Yeah, I agree. The other computer had all the information I needed anyway. You've done fine."

One snapshot the boy was facing the camera, the next he was turned facing the man. He said, "So, can I go?"

"Unfortunately, no."

And then, in stilted slow motion, an arm encircled the boy's neck. He began to thrash in the chair, drool coating his chin, then blood. The individual webcam shots were as repulsive as a pornographic snuff film, and I felt a crippling déjà vu. The boy was dying in front of my eyes while I was impotent to do anything. Just like the dream of my family. I tried to turn away, but was riveted at the death. My adrenaline began to race, and I had to physically stop myself from grabbing the monitor and screaming, setting the dream free from the imagined world. The sliver of darkness in me stirred, straining for the face of the killer, as if it would provide the answer to my own demons.

One second we were looking at the eyes of the boy bugging out of his head, his mouth open in a silent scream, then the screenshot simply showed an empty chair.

Nobody said anything. A shadow passed over the screen as the killer sat down, taking the boy's place.

It took a moment, but I recognized the figure.

"Oh my God," Jennifer said. "That's Lucas Kane."

26

Kurt Hale watched the cloud of cigar smoke drift to the ceiling and was secretly sure President Warren had turned off the smoke detectors. The accumulated haze made it hard to see the ceiling of the Oval Office. The president didn't seem concerned, puffing away and staring out the window behind his desk.

"So Pike's okay? Out of enemy hands so to speak?"

Kurt said, "Yes, sir. He got dinged up a little, but he's safe."

The president spun his chair around. "Dinged up? That's what you guys call it? I'd say he was tortured. And for nothing. This little Taskforce adventure was off the charts in stupidity. What on earth was Pike thinking? Who were the Lebanese he used? Without authority, I might add."

Kurt grimaced. "They were some Druze that used to be in the LAF Special Forces. Pike trained them before the Taskforce existed. If he trusts them, so do I."

"Some trust. They had him smuggle in a damn IED

without his knowledge. Then he gets captured because of it. It's loose as shit, even for Pike."

"Sir, he's just trying to get the mission done, and speaking of that, we have some indicators of—"

President Warren flipped open a folder on his desk and cut him off. "Get 'em home. Now. I've given orders for McMasters to skip Lebanon on his trip. I don't care how much Pike trusts those men. That place is an absolute snake pit, and there's no sense tempting fate, even if Pike says he blew up the assassin."

"Sir, that's what I wanted to talk to you about. We're not so sure the threat's gone."

President Warren closed the folder. "What do you mean?"

"Remember the reports I showed you about an American assassin code-named Infidel?"

"Yeah. As I recall that theory was discounted by the intelligence from the Tunisian hit. What about it?"

"Pike took a computer from the site where he was held. We bled it dry of information, then he inserted it back into the extremist network using some software that allowed him to access it remotely."

"And?"

"And we got a clear screenshot of an American from inside a Hezbollah headquarters building, along with McMasters's entire itinerary on the computer. Infidel is real, and skipping Lebanon doesn't mean McMasters is safe."

"So you found a Westerner working for Hezbollah,

and the official itinerary of a U.S. envoy. Why's that a big deal? Every government he's visiting will have the itinerary, and a white guy inside Hezbollah doesn't equate to some badass assassin."

"It was more than the official itinerary. It had specific hotels, events, and dates of stay. Much more than we ordinarily include in official message traffic. And it was in Hezbollah's hands, not some friendly government."

Kurt pulled out a laser-printed photo from his briefcase. "As for the white guy, we know who he is, and it's not good."

"Who?"

"Remember the hired gun Harold Standish used a couple of years ago? Tried to wipe out a Taskforce team in Bosnia?"

"Yeah. Lucas Kane, right? Got his own team wiped out instead and then killed Standish as payback. I thought you guys were hunting him."

"We were, but after he disappeared in Bosnia, his trail went absolutely cold. We heard rumors and ran them to ground, but always came up empty. I quit focusing on it because it was a drain on resources. He wasn't a threat to U.S. interests, and I figured he'd turn up on his own sooner or later." Kurt stood and tossed the screenshot photo on the president's desk. "Looks like he has."

The president stared at the grainy image for a moment. "So you think Lucas Kane is on the hunt here? That McMasters's trip is in jeopardy anyway, even if we avoid Lebanon?"

"Yes."

"And what would you have me do? Call it off completely? I can't do that. It's the first time in years we've been able to get the peace process rolling again."

"No, sir. Of course not. Even if it were just a sightseeing trip, I wouldn't advocate turning it off. We can't be held hostage to threats. It gives the bastards exactly what they want. I'm just saying mix it up a little bit. Alter the itinerary so it's different from what we found. Increase the security posture around him."

He paused. President Warren said, "And?"

"And let me launch the Taskforce guys from Tunisia."

The president leaned back, a half smile on his face. Kurt continued. "The Oversight Council has already approved it. The only difference is our purpose for going. It's the same country, same threats, same method of infiltration."

"Kurt, please. The only thing 'different' is the primary reason for the approval. Now that Pike's safe, there's no justification to launch. We should go back to the Council."

"Sir, they're going to say no, and we're going to lose the one lead we have. Lucas Kane is a proven killer, and we have no idea what identity he's traveling under. If we don't get on this quickly, he'll disappear again. Best case, we simply lose an opportunity to bring him to justice. Worst case, we're standing over the body of a dead Mideast envoy. And your peace process is in the gutter."

"My, my, how attitudes change. I remember when *you*

used to be the one demanding Oversight Council approval on everything. Now, you want to duck them."

Kurt shook his head. "No, sir. Not duck. They've already given approval for the three members to deploy, so I'm just stretching it a little bit. They don't have to know Pike's safe until after the launch. Then, they're already on the ground. I want oversight, but by a competent body. Let the Taskforce get something done in Lebanon, and it will give the Council a little confidence in our abilities. Right now, they're a bunch of handwringers."

President Warren considered for a second, then nodded. "Okay. Get 'em into Lebanon and see if you can get a handle on Lucas. But they don't do anything else without Council approval, understood?"

Kurt said, "Yes, sir," and waited to be dismissed. Instead, the president rotated around in his chair and gazed out the Oval Office window again.

"You think this cash giveaway is doing anything for the peace process? You think it's a good idea?"

A couple of years ago Kurt would have been completely taken aback by the question, but he'd grown accustomed to the president's asking him things that had nothing to do with the Taskforce. While they both understood their respective positions, the truth was the president liked bouncing ideas off of Kurt. Trusted him as a man outside the political machine, and thus a person who could give an opinion that wasn't tainted by whatever poll was in vogue at the time.

Kurt didn't want to admit it, but he enjoyed the role

of trusted confidant, even when the questions were out-side his expertise. He had learned to caveat his answers if he felt he was leading the administration down a road about which he had no knowledge. Something else he knew the president respected. In this case, achieving peace within the Levant, he had more knowledge on the topic than ninety percent of the "experts" out there.

"I think any attempt at a reconciliation between the Palestinians and the Israelis is a good thing. Solve that problem, and you put a damper on every other issue in the region. Long-term, that is. In the short term, it will cause more violence. There are just too many groups who have specific agendas that cannot be met with compro-mise. And I mean both on the Israeli and the Palestinian side."

The president returned his attention to Kurt. "That's not my question. Do you think it's a good idea to give the Palestinian Authority twenty million dollars? Am I funding terrorism? We have no idea who's going to get that money."

Kurt said nothing for a moment, realizing his answer would not be the usual pontification, but instead possibly alter the course of national security. He'd seen it before. A small comment in a roomful of people, then on the news the next day. It had always amazed him how na-tional strategy was often formed more on the words of trusted advisors than the opinions of experts.

"Sir, I don't think I can judge that. If your folks say it's a good idea, then I'd go with it."

"Really? That's your answer? I could get that from my secretary. I'm not going to change course based on what you say alone. I just want your opinion. Am I about to give twenty million dollars to a terrorist group?"

"Sir . . . honestly, I don't think so. Hamas is a terrorist group, and they've been funded by Iran for years. A limitless pocket book. They're in competition with the Palestinian Authority for the support of the people. If Hamas wins that fight, there will be no peace. No way will Israel deal with a group that has a stated goal of the eradication of their country."

"But if word gets out, I'll be castrated. How can I overtly state we won't support any organization that does business with Hamas, then covertly give that same group money?"

Kurt smiled. "That's why you're the president, and I'm just a talking head."

President Warren dropped his pen and shook his head. "Great. Okay. Thanks for that vote of confidence. Getting back to Lebanon, what's the next course of action?"

"Uhhh . . ." Kurt said. "Well, I figured you'd be agreeable to the team deploying, so I infiltrated some documents and equipment to Beirut. Pike's linking up with it as we speak."

President Warren gave him an incredulous look. "And if I'd said no?"

"Then Pike would have had some passports he would never use. I had to prep early to make this work." He saw the president's face darken and raised his hands in a gesture of surrender.

"Hey, all I'm trying to do is protect your peace process. What good is the money if the man holding it is slaughtered?"

27

Jennifer saw a newspaper in Louis Britt's right hand, the signal that the meeting was safe. She moved straight past the hostess and took a seat at the case officer's table. Now that they could recognize each other, there was no need for the verbal dance to prove who they were. He went through the mad minute again, ensuring they both understood what to say should they be asked about the meeting at a later date, then passed her a key across the table.

"That's to a locker at the Charles Helou Bus Station. Inside are the documents and other equipment you asked for."

"How much equipment? Will I need to bring luggage to conceal it?"

"No, it's in a backpack already." He took a drink of water and surprised her with his next statement. "You people have been busy. Taking the fight to the military wing of Hezbollah isn't the smartest thing I've seen, but it *is* gutsy."

"Hezbollah? I didn't think they worked in the refugee camps."

His turn to be surprised, he said, "Palestinian camp? I'm talking about the killing of the Martyrs Battalion leadership. Hezbollah's little covert assassination cell."

"That wasn't us, but it *is* something we hope you can help with." She pulled out the screenshot of Lucas Kane. "We think it was this guy. Your Infidel assassin. Ever seen him before?"

He studied the grainy screenshot, then said, "Nope. Where was it taken?"

She pulled a tablet PC out of her bag and showed him a Google map with the location marked.

He said, "Heart of the *Dahiyeh*. Headquarters for Hezbollah. If he's on the Martyrs Battalion payroll, he's in very, very deep. Nobody will know his name but the top leadership. And like I said, they're dead now."

"Yeah. Like *I* said, we think he killed them."

He scoffed. "Well, then forget about finding him. He's already smoked."

"I'd like to think so, but this guy has a survival instinct that's on steroids. If anyone could get out of there alive, it would be him. Before things went bad between him and this Martyrs Battalion, they had to be helping him out. Whatever passports or IDs he's using, they had to have gotten it for him. He's not traveling on his true passport, we know that."

"How?"

"His name's Lucas Kane. The Taskforce has had a run-in with him in the past, and he's been on a watch list for at least two years. Never once has that name spiked. We've also scrubbed the database here in Lebanon. That name never entered or left the country."

He said nothing for a moment, thinking. "Let me see that map again." He studied it, saying, "Hezbollah has built their own communications infrastructure inside Lebanon. A parallel system with the help of Iran. They claim it's to help them defend the country against Israel, but it's really just one more step to them becoming a shadow government. I've passed the nodes of that network to the Taskforce should we need to target them in the future." He pointed at a building a few blocks away from the geotag of the Lucas screenshot. "That's the central junction for the fiber-optic grid and a server farm for the network."

"Okay. How does that help? You think we should hack the network? You think his information will be in there?"

"No. The network itself is pretty secure. So much so that the Lebanese government went to war with Hezbollah over it in 2008. The LAF pretty much lost, and the communications grid is bigger than ever. Even so, the Martyrs Battalion information won't be on it. Hezbollah's fairly open now that they hold a majority in the government. Even its military runs around flaunting weapons. But they have to hide the assassination cell, especially after Hariri. There *is* a database, but it will be air-gapped. It won't be on any network."

"So?"

"It's in this building. I was trying to get access to it to

prove my Infidel theory, but had no luck. You get a pipe into that, and you'll know everything about Infidel." He leaned back in his chair. "But good luck with that."

"You don't think we can get access?"

"No way. Like I said, it'll be air-gapped, with no contact to the World Wide Web. No Wi-Fi, no Internet, nothing that can be exploited, so you'll have to physically get hands on a computer that's in the network. And that computer is in this building, in the heart of Hezbollah-land."

"Can you get us greater fidelity on where this computer would be located in the building? So we don't have to run around trying every system we see? Can your source network figure that out?"

"Yeah. I already have that information. I just couldn't get anyone willing to risk gaining access because they were convinced it was suicide. Add to that the fact that Hezbollah's entire infrastructure is now on red alert because of the Martyrs Battalion leadership killings, and it's certainly suicide now. And I mean suicide for a source of mine who's Arabic with access to the building."

"Well, we'll see. Get me the information on the computers and let us worry about access."

"I'll get it to you, along with whatever security information I have, but a piece of advice."

"What?"

"You white boys go in that building, make sure you save one bullet for yourself. No way do you want to get taken alive."

28

Knuckles watched the deck of the ship grow smaller as the Bell 427 picked up forward speed. He keyed the mike on his headset.

"Say good-bye to the *QE Two*. I don't think we're going to see the black hole again."

In the dim light of the helo he saw Decoy's teeth flash above the dive mask around his neck.

"Fine by me. That damn boat is the smelliest thing I've ever had the misfortune to sleep on."

The *QE II* was the sarcastic nickname of a salvage boat that plied its cover all over the Mediterranean, picking up scrap metal at various ports and transporting it elsewhere. The company that owned it was located in Tangier, Morocco, and was ostensibly a Moroccan entity. It paid Moroccan taxes, flew the Moroccan flag, and employed ethnically diverse individuals, without a Caucasian among them. It was completely outside all suspicion to the Arab states it operated within. It was another thread in the web of the Taskforce, a profitable, multimillion-dollar corporation that existed for one purpose. In between its journeys,

the boat acted as a floating transfer point, allowing terrorists who were snatched to be flown out of country and
dropped off. The men would return back to the original
country, continuing with their cover activities without anyone realizing what had happened. In a perfect mission, the
terrorist simply disappeared into a "black hole," hence the
code name for the vessel.

In this case, Knuckles had transferred Crusty, then returned to Tunisia only to be recalled two days later on an
alert from Taskforce headquarters. The ship had begun
steaming east, getting in range of the Levant coastline
when the mission had been scrubbed. Eight hours later,
it was back on.

Having spent the majority of his military time inside a
SEAL team, he was used to the on-again, off-again nature
of the work, but this time the mission caused him some
concern.

Ordinarily, Taskforce planning worked from the
ground up, with Knuckles being told the objective, but
left to his own devices to determine how it would be executed. In this case, all planning had been conducted by
someone else, and he was about to exit a moving aircraft
into the Mediterranean Sea, then swim for two hours for
a linkup with another boat.

All the parameters had been provided to him. The grid
for the boat, the signals for the beacons, the helicopter's
flight path, and the release point had been handed to him
complete. He knew it was because of time sensitivity and
the lack of ability to directly communicate with his link-

up, but it did nothing to ease his fears. Once in the water, they were on their own. If they moved to the linkup, and nobody was home, they'd still be two hours off the coast of a hostile country.

Pike, you'd better be waiting.

His other concern was Brett, the third man on the team. There was no doubt the guy was handy in a gunfight, and plenty smart, but he'd spent the past twelve years in the Special Activities Division of the CIA's National Clandestine Service. He hadn't done any subsurface work since he was in the Marines, a long, long time ago, and they were swimming the Draeger LAR V rebreather.

A closed circuit underwater breathing apparatus, the Draeger recirculated the exhaled gas from the swimmer, and thus no telltale bubbles escaped as with an ordinary scuba system. It was perfect for clandestine infiltration, but the gas mixture was also very deadly. Make a mistake in using it, and it would kill quickly.

He patted Brett on the knee. "You sure you're good on this system? I don't want to be towing a dead body after thirty minutes."

Brett smiled, his teeth stark white against his ebony skin. "Yeah. Quit worrying about me. A few different buckles and switches, but it's basically the same thing I trained with. Besides, I'm just along for the ride."

The crew chief tapped his shoulder, holding up five fingers.

Knuckles echoed the command, shouting, "Five minutes!"

All three began preparing for the cast off of the helicopter, Brett working the waterproofed equipment bundle to the door while Knuckles and Decoy prepped their diver propulsion vehicles.

Knuckles checked his GPS and was relieved to see the release point he'd programmed approaching. *At least that will go correctly.* He shut off the GPS and zipped it into a waterproof bag. Hopefully, it would be the last time he looked at it, since it wouldn't pick up a signal underwater. If he needed a GPS again, it meant the linkup had failed, and they'd had to surface to get a reading on where they were in relation to the shore.

The helicopter slowed and dropped down to the deck of the ocean, so close that Knuckles could see the white foam of the rotor wash in the moonlight. The crew chief gave the two-minute call and tossed his headset onto the floor of the helo. He positioned his mask on his face and placed the Draeger mouthpiece in, opening the dive surface valve to allow the flow of oxygen. He purged the system, then turned to help Brett.

At the one-minute call, he edged to the open door, holding his diver propulsion vehicle in his lap, then assisted Brett with the bundle of equipment. He would be first out, followed by Brett and the bundle, then Decoy with the second DPV.

He was so intent on making sure Brett was stable and ready with the bundle that he missed the thirty-second call. He felt the crew chief slap him on the shoulder and heard, "Go!"

He turned in confusion only to find the crew chief wildly pointing out the door and shouting "Go, go, go!"

Without hesitation, he chucked the DPV out the door and followed suit, before the towline attached to it yanked him out anyway.

He hit the water with a hand on his dive mask and went under, cursing himself for jumping before he was ready. *Dumbass crew chief thinks an extra second or two matters?*

He broke the surface, followed his towline to the floating DPV, and popped a ChemLight, holding it in the air. Only then did he do a three-sixty survey of the water, the roar of the helicopter fading, leaving a ringing in his ears and a deep quiet all around.

He saw two other ChemLights and stroked to them. Decoy was already prepping his underwater scooter for the ride, while Brett was slowly treading water, holding on to the neutrally buoyant bundle.

He got an "A-OK" hand signal from both.

He attached his towrope to the plate on the DPV to his front, then attached a separate towrope to Brett's harness behind him. Decoy did the same, hooking his secondary towrope to the bundle.

He secured his attack board onto the DPV, checked to make sure the compass and depth gauge functioned, then got a final A-OK hand signal, the constraints of using the Draeger preventing them from removing the mouthpiece to talk. Once in place, the body itself became part of the system, a symbiotic relationship that couldn't be broken until the dive was complete.

The restrictions of the LAR V rebreather were a trade-off, but worth it. While it allowed them to swim underwater without telltale bubbles, its true value was in the length of time it could stay under. At thirty feet of depth, they could swim for four hours without surfacing, which, if his calculations were correct, would be enough to make it to the coast should the linkup fail. What was waiting for them there would be the new problem.

Knuckles triggered the DPV and dove, reaching twenty-five feet. He lined up his compass, set the pitch of the propeller on two-thirds, and began moving through the water at a rapid clip. The light attached underneath his DPV gave him enough illumination to see about five feet ahead of him, reminding him of the movies from submersibles at the ocean floor. A thin reed of illumination swallowed by infinite blackness. It was disconcerting and claustrophobic, but something he was used to after hundreds of night dives. He simply watched the compass needle, checking off to his left occasionally to make sure Decoy's ChemLight was still with him.

Finding a boat in the middle of the ocean was literally worse than finding a pinhole in a field of snow. Using just a compass, with the variable currents underwater and the probability of error of the release point, would guarantee failure, but they had a little help inside their DPVs.

Made by Gavin Water Sports, they were a commercial, off-the-shelf item that looked a little like a torpedo, with a long cylinder up front attached to a propeller. Unlike with the ones Knuckles had trained with in the Navy, he was connected to the device by a towrope instead of riding it as a passenger. Although DPVs were ordinarily used for cave diving and shipwreck exploration, the Taskforce had modified them for clandestine infiltration. In the nose of each was a transducer that would pick up the signals from a sonic beacon. Once it made an encrypted handshake, a computer would take over the steering, guiding them directly to the boat. All Knuckles had to do was get within eight hundred meters—the range of the beacon. A whole lot more room for error with the compass, but still easy to screw up. Miss the bubble by fifty meters and they'd never know it.

Passing the one-and-a-half-hour mark, Knuckles began to feel the adrenaline pick up. One hour and fifty minutes into the dive, Knuckles felt sweat form in his wetsuit, and not from the exertion. By the calculations he had made from the release point, they should hit the boat in two hours. Which meant, traveling at two hundred feet per minute, they should now have been within range of the beacon.

Here we go. Fucking plan B.

If he reached two hours, he was going to conduct a grid pattern, traveling north for five minutes, then repeating the move south for ten minutes. Two racetracks like that, and he would be at a decision point: Continue searching, or use the remaining battery power of the DPV to reach shore.

The two-hour mark passed, and he waved his Chem-Light, bringing the DPV to a halt. Decoy waved his as well, and cut by him to the south. *What the hell is he doing?*

He watched the bundle go by, a shadowy blob miraculously following Decoy as if it could swim on its own. He made sure Brett was ready to move, then turned and followed suit, getting a little aggravated at Decoy for not following the plan. He increased his speed to overtake the rapidly disappearing glow from Decoy's DPV, intent on knocking some sense into the man, when his transducer pinged. He felt a subtle shift in the direction of the DPV and knew the computer was locking on.

Two minutes later, he no longer worried about the compass, the DPV driving on autopilot. They were on the outer edge of the bubble, and for whatever reason, Decoy's transducer had picked up the signal first.

He gave a mental sigh of relief and began focusing on the next problem: how to survive a gunfight on the open water if it wasn't Pike in the boat.

29

Sitting out under the stars, with the waves gently rocking the boat, I felt a sense of calm I hadn't experienced in a long time. It was very pleasant. Something I wouldn't mind doing at another time with Jennifer, only with a case of beer and some fishing poles. Not like the ones we'd brought when we'd rented the boat, which were simple props used to convince total strangers we were actually going fishing and not conducting secret missions in their sovereign country. Truth be told, if I did get out on a boat alone with Jennifer, I probably wouldn't want to spend the time trying to catch some smelly, slimy animal with a brain the size of a pea. Although that would ultimately be her decision. I felt the boat rise again and glanced her way. She was giving me the look again, a painful *I'm going to ask about it, but maybe not* expression.

She'd come back from her PM with the sonic beacon and a host of different passports, looking a little grim about the information she'd received. I'd listened to her, then told her not to worry about it just yet. If we could penetrate the place, we would, but I wasn't going to do it in a frontal assault. There's always a solution. The trick is finding it.

I'd flipped through the documents, recognizing Decoy and Knuckles from their photos, but not their names, which stood to reason, since officially they were still in Tunisia. The third passport belonged to the new guy, Brett, and I was surprised to see he was black. I don't know why, I just had a different mental image. He was short, at five feet seven inches, but either fat or full of muscle, because he weighed 185 pounds. Given our line of work, I was betting on muscle. He had an open face, with a smile in the photo, like he was enjoying a secret joke. That told me a lot about him. Usually, guys who think they're some sort of badass try to project power in official photos. Very few will smile. I figured we'd get along fine.

Jennifer checked the GPS to make sure our little sea anchor hadn't let us drift too far off, then said, "How much longer?"

"Should be here within thirty minutes, if Knuckles doesn't screw up and head to Egypt."

She nodded and sat back down, staring at me. *Here it comes. She's been working up the courage.*

"You didn't sleep last night."

We'd stayed at Samir's house, sleeping on the floor of his living room, which meant she'd had plenty of time to analyze me.

"I slept fine. I'm okay."

Which wasn't true. I had some bad dreams reliving the capture, but nothing that was making me catatonic.

"I heard you moaning. . . . It's okay to talk about it."

"Jesus! I'm fucking fine! Let it go. I know you want to play Florence Nightingale, but I don't need it."

I saw her snap back at my tone and felt like an ass. She turned to check the GPS again, and I said, "Hey. Sorry. I didn't mean to yell at you."

She said, "Remember Cairo? What I did?"

"Yeah." She'd been forced to kill a guy with a lamp, literally beating his brains out.

She took my hand in hers. "Well, I had issues with it like you said I would. And you helped me through it. I'm just returning the favor. I know you. Your capture was more than just a firefight. It hurt. I can tell."

I was thinking up a witty comeback, something to deflect this little probe into my psyche, when I caught sight of my other hand. The one with less than a full deck of fingers. I realized I just didn't have the energy.

"Okay. It was more than a firefight. Much more. It's probably a phobia I've had since I joined the Army."

Her mouth dropped open. I continued. "The problem is I've had years to worry about that situation because of my job, building it up in my head, petrified of it ever coming to pass. It did, but truthfully, now that it's over, my time was less than what Daniel Pearl experienced. Or William Buckley. I'll be okay."

She searched my face, trying to ascertain if I was being genuine or just placating her. Her eyes reached mine, and I held fast, daring her to question the veracity of what I had said. We spent a second in silence, then she smiled and patted my hand, apparently convinced we'd turned some corner in our relationship, which confused the shit out of me because I didn't know what our relationship was.

She said, "I know you'll be okay. I just wanted to let you know I'm here."

Please. Stop this before my manhood flees. I decided to turn it up a notch.

"Here for what? As my therapist, or something else? We never did have that big talk you kept threatening."

The smile was replaced by confusion, then embarrassment. Before she could say anything, the beacon squawked.

I grinned. "Saved by the bell. Get ready to pull in some tired swimmers."

She said, "Pike . . . I'm not trying to hide anything."

I checked the sonar echo on the little display attached by wire to the beacon thirty feet below. Two blobs were about five hundred meters out and closing fast.

"Seriously, this'll have to wait. Get out the clothes and blankets."

She did nothing for a moment, then turned to a duffel bag at the stern of the boat. I opened up the giant cooler we'd brought, now full of lead weights and a fishnet.

I laid the fishnet on the deck, attaching the weights to the corners. I checked the sonar again and saw the blobs were fairly close. When I was operational, I hated using the sonic beacon because nobody could tell me its effect on marine life. Yeah, it worked fine guiding in clandestine infils, but I wasn't convinced it didn't sound like a dinner bell to sharks. *Glad I'm in the boat.*

I saw the blobs were right underneath us now. As anal as Knuckles was, I knew he would be concerned about surfacing. He didn't get to plan any of this, and I'm sure he was convinced during the whole damn trip that he was doomed. Now he'd be positive I was some hajji itching to blow his head off. I toyed with the idea of playing a joke on him, but figured he wouldn't take it the right way.

I suppose I should have passed along some final bona fides when I'd provided the grid to the linkup, like flashing a light six times followed by two or some other method to prove we were who we said we were, but I always figured that sort of stuff was overkill. I mean, really, if there was a boat out here with a top secret beacon mated to a Taskforce DPV, didn't that pretty much say it all? Keep making up signals, and it just creates more chances for screwups when someone makes a mistake. Of course, Knuckles didn't see it that way. We were complete opposites, with me being all about free-flow and him being the guy who organized his sock drawer alphabetically.

Jennifer came up next to me, saw the sonar, and said, "What are they doing?"

"Probably playing rock-paper-scissors to see who gets to poke their head up first. This is ridiculous." I decided a joke wasn't off the table—and to give Knuckles the bona fides he was looking for. "Take off your bra."

"What?"

"Take it off. You can do it underneath your shirt. I've

seen you. Wrap it in one of those fishing weights and drop it overboard."

She caught why I had asked and gave me her disapproving teacher look, but with the hint of a smile. She reached underneath her shirt. I turned and faced the bow until I heard a splash, then looked overboard. Ten seconds later a head broke the surface, followed by two others. One held her bra in the air.

I said, "Man, you guys are careless. Anybody could have known you were meeting a woman out here and brought an American bra to drop overboard."

One head said, "Fuck you, Pike. Hello, Jennifer. Help me with the bundle."

I recognized Knuckles's voice and kicked over the ladder. Within thirty minutes we had the DPVs broken down and the wetsuits shredded, all now lying in the fishnet. While the men got warm under dry clothes and a blanket, Jennifer and I transferred the kit from the bundle to the fish cooler that had held the net.

Most of the equipment in the bundle was the usual weapons and tech gear. Cameras, H&K UMPs, Glocks, beacons, and assorted other stuff Knuckles thought we'd need. We reached the bottom, and Jennifer held up an item I'd never seen, saying "What's this?"

It appeared to be one of those gun-type mounts that held an SLR camera with a long telephoto lens. It had a shoulder stock and a trigger grip with a rail extending out. On top of the rail was a cylinder a foot and a half long with four metal rods running parallel to its length.

Hanging to the left side was an offset scope. At the base was a square box with a host of buttons and dials.

I took it and held it up to Knuckles. "What the hell is this thing?"

"It's an EMP gun. You sight through the scope, pull the trigger, and it'll knock out electrical components. At least it's supposed to. It's worked fine in testing, but had some issues on our predeployment training. I didn't use it in Tunisia, but figured it might come in handy here."

"Who'd we steal this from? Microsoft?"

"Actually, the Department of Defense. They have a request for proposal to develop an EMP gun that can disable a car. You know, so instead of using snipers with anti-armor rounds or spike strips, they simply zap the car with the EMP and cause it to shut down. Electronic fuel injection, computers, all that shit that's in a car nowadays is vulnerable."

"This thing will stop a car?"

"Hell no. We just stole the technology. The one they're working on right now is about the same size as a car. They're still trying to make it small enough to be useful. Ours is much less powerful. It'll only take out small electrical components, like a computer, alarm switch, or a radio. It's pinpoint and limited to about fifty feet, but might be useful."

I held it up to the light of the cockpit for a better look, and Decoy noticed the bandage on my left hand. More precisely, he noticed the length of the bandage.

"Jesus," he said. "Somebody shot off your pinky?"

I raised my hand so they could all see it. "Didn't shoot it off, but it's not as bad as it looks. They only took the first joint. Most of it's still there."

The boat grew quiet, the truth of my statement sinking in. Nobody was sure how to respond. I saw Jennifer wanting to say something to help, but I shook my head. Brett broke the silence.

"You should put some Monkey's Blood on it. That'll fix it."

Everyone looked at him incredulously. I said, "What the hell are you talking about?"

"You know. Monkey's Blood. Didn't your mom put that on every single boo-boo you ever got? You don't see it much anymore, but man, that stuff was a miracle worker. At least that's what my mom says."

"You mean Mercurochrome? The red shit they put on kids' scabs?"

"Yeah. That's it. Monkey's Blood. It works on everything."

At first, I was wondering how such an idiot could have reached the Taskforce. Then I saw the same inside-joke smile from his passport photo, and I started laughing. Before I knew it, everyone was giggling and snickering, even Jennifer. Brett had managed to defuse the entire discussion, without making an overt attempt. I was right. We'd get along fine.

I stood up and tied the fishnet closed, attaching a final twelve-pound anchor in addition to the other lead weights. Decoy and I shoved the net overboard, watching to make sure it sank with the evidence of the infiltration.

I said, "Come on. Let's get back to Lebanon. We've wasted enough time on mothers' remedies."

Jennifer fired up the engine and got on a heading back to the Beirut marina. Knuckles said, "Well, now that you mention it, I have no idea why we're here. Originally it was to rescue you. What is it now?"

"Somebody's trying to kill the new Middle Eastern envoy, and we're going to stop it."

"Any leads, or are we working from scratch?"

"You remember that guy who tried to kill us in Bosnia two years ago? The one that got away?"

Knuckles's face turned grim. "Oh yeah. I remember him. I wish I'd put a bullet in his head when I had the chance."

I pulled out the screen capture we'd taken in Samir's house.

"How'd you like a second shot?"

30

Lucas Kane took notice of the atmosphere surrounding him as he walked toward the photography shop. It was located in south Beirut, still in a prominently Shia area, but outside the hard-core Hezbollah state-within-a-state. Nasrallah posters adorned every other street corner, but that was it. No paranoid gunmen or street toughs with radios. Still, he was generating interest. He could feel the eyes on him from every direction, all wondering what this infidel wanted here. Wondering if maybe he was lost.

He wasn't. The photo studio was the location of the Hezbollah asset that had helped the Palestinian assassin with his documents. Probably the same one that had built Lucas's own. He didn't know. All he'd done was provide passport photos to Majid, and Hezbollah had done the rest.

He'd driven by earlier in the day on a reconnaissance, noting the business hours. He wanted to ensure that nobody else was in the studio when he entered, so he'd waited until just before closing. For what he had to do, he couldn't afford anyone else being present. Well, he could, but it would just make things messier.

The killing of the Martyrs Battalion leadership was on the street, and Lucas knew his time in Beirut was done. Luckily, from what he'd heard, nobody knew who had done it and the routinely paranoid Hezbollah immediately began ranting about Zionist infiltrators. It would only be a matter of time, though, before he was questioned. He had no illusions about how that would go, having watched the interrogation of loyal Shia who were suspected of working with the CIA. In November of 2011, Hezbollah had rolled up the entire CIA network inside Beirut. In so doing, they hammered any and all they thought were working with the enemy. Hezbollah didn't care if they killed thirty innocents if it meant getting one guilty party.

He'd already been called twice on his private cell phone from a number he didn't recognize. Since the phone only worked on the parallel Hezbollah communications architecture, he knew it wasn't good and had ignored both calls. He figured he had twenty-four hours at best before Hezbollah made a concerted effort to find him. The only thing going for him was the fact that the Martyrs Battalion was so secretive, not many in Hezbollah even knew he existed. Not many, but enough to cause him concern. One in particular worried him: Abu Aziz, the head of security for the Battalion. The man had never trusted Lucas and was probably the person who'd found the bodies.

He entered the studio, a small bell tinkling above the

door. He heard someone shuffling from the rear and waited.

An old man of about seventy rounded the corner and came up short when he saw Lucas, a spark of recognition in his eyes.

He's seen my passport photos. He's the same forger.

"Can I help you?" the man said in English.

"I'm looking for Abu Bari." Lucas used the Hezbollah *kunya* of the forger, letting him know he was in on the secret.

The proprietor shifted uncomfortably and looked out the window, whether to ensure nobody was about to enter or hoping someone would, Lucas was unclear.

"There's no one here by that name."

"Yes, there is, and I'm looking at him. Perhaps we should talk in the back."

The man considered the request, then shuffled by Lucas. "Let me lock up."

Instead of producing a key, he reached for the door handle, and Lucas knew he was about to run. If he made it to the street, he would be free. No way could Lucas take him down in this neighborhood.

Lucas slammed his body against the door, feeling nothing but skin and bones. The storeowner wailed.

"I'm here on Hezbollah business. Don't make me report you."

He nodded over and over again, then said, "I am Abu Bari."

"Lock up."

He did so, and Lucas followed him to the back. He positioned a chair to block the door and took a seat.

"Anyone else here?"

"No."

"Good. I'm sure you've heard of the deaths of Majid and Ja'far, correct?"

Bari nodded, his eyes growing more fearful.

"Well, I'm trying to find out who killed them, and I believe you helped that man flee the country."

"No! In no way would I have done this!"

"Did you not provide documents for a Palestinian known as the Ghost?"

Bari became more agitated. "Yes, but Majid told me explicitly to do so. He gave the order."

"Well, that's going to be a little hard to prove, since he's got a hole in his neck the size of a dog's head."

"He did! You must tell them that!"

"I will, depending on how much you help me. If you really didn't mean to assist the murderer, then you should want me to find this Ghost."

"I will, I will."

Bari turned to a computer and rapidly began typing passwords. In seconds, the Ghost was on the screen.

"Here. Here is the man Majid sent."

The computer showed a Saudi Arabian passport for a person named Ahmed al-Rashid, complete with the picture of a stone-faced Arab wearing thick glasses.

Lucas inwardly smiled. "Print that. What else did you do to help him?"

"He had me make a visa for Yemen and a visa for the United Arab Emirates."

"A visa for UAE? Why? The Kingdom is a member of the Gulf Cooperation Council. He doesn't need a visa to go there."

"He had me make the stamp, but I didn't use it in the passport. He took the stamp with him."

Lucas considered this twist. Forging the Yemen visa made sense, because, while a Saudi citizen could obtain one free of charge upon entering the country, it would mean a greater paper trail, as the Ghost would have to make up a Saudi Arabian address and where he would be staying in Yemen. The UAE visa, on the other hand, was confusing. Why take a stamp?

Because he's not going to keep that passport. He's going to get another one, and he doesn't know which country it will be from.

The Ghost was proving to be pretty damn smart.

"What else did you help him with?"

"Nothing. I swear. Wait, he did ask me for the names of two *hawaladars*, one for Yemen and one for Dubai."

Lucas absorbed the information, realizing that the Ghost was laundering whatever money Hezbollah had provided him before they could change their mind and shut off the funding.

Hawala was an ancient banking method still used in the Arab world to transfer money across the globe. Completely outside traditional banking, it simply consisted of two trusted agents in each of the countries in question.

One went to the first agent, said he wished to transfer money, and gave the funds to be transferred. The first agent took a commission, gave a code for the second agent, and all that remained was to travel to the second country, meet the agent, present the code, and pick up the money.

The key component was that both agents of the *hawala* exchange trusted and knew each other. No records were kept on who transferred the money, only on the balance between the two agents. Thus, in order to receive the money, a personal meeting would have to occur, where the code would be presented. A meeting that Lucas could intercept.

"Write down the names and addresses of the agents here in Beirut. Both for Yemen and Dubai."

When Abu Bari had finished, Lucas asked, "Can you make me a new passport? Either United States or a Canadian one?"

"Yes, but it will take time. Both Canada and the United States use electronic chips in their passports now. Impossible for me to forge. The only way to create a new passport now is to use an old one that is still valid, and they are few and far between."

Shit. Damn antiterror methods are making it hard to earn a decent living.

Lucas knew all about the electronic chips. They were RFID tags like the one he had used to kill the investigator; each included all relevant information on the passport, including the picture. He knew the United States had gone to them, but didn't realize that Canada had as well.

The only document he currently possessed, outside of his authentic personal papers, was the Canadian passport he had used in the Netherlands—and he certainly wasn't going to hang around to get another.

"All right. I think I'm done here. All I need you to do is write down a sentence on a piece of paper."

Bari's eyebrows scrunched together. "What sentence?"

"Just a statement saying you didn't know you were helping the murderer and want to prove it to the leadership. Write, 'It was the Ghost. I didn't know before he came,' then any other Islamic crap after that you would like, begging forgiveness. I'll pass it to the leadership and maybe they'll leave you alone."

Bari's hands trembled as he wrote. *Perfect. Looks like a dying hand.*

Lucas circled around behind him, pulled out his carbon-fiber punch-blade, and patiently waited for him to finish.

When Bari set the pen down, Lucas said, "Move the paper to the shelf in front of you."

Bari did so, asking, "Why?"

Lucas punched him in the neck with the blade and watched the man writhe on the ground, bleeding out. "Because I didn't want to get blood on it."

After the body had quit twitching, Lucas positioned it on the floor with an arm outstretched, holding the pen. He then placed the paper under the hand. He left the computer as it was, with the Ghost's Saudi passport prominently displayed on the screen.

He knew that any competent forensics team would ascertain in seconds that it was staged, but counted on the bumbling paranoia of Hezbollah not to have the skills or desire to check. With any luck, they'd be chasing the Ghost and save him the effort, freeing him up to secure his retirement.

His security work in this section of the world was done, he knew. No way could he continue anywhere that had the potential for Hezbollah reach. Unfortunately, the Middle East was the last place left. Working anywhere in Europe or South America would put him inside the radar of the United States, which wanted him badly. Africa remained an option, but the thought disgusted him. In truth, he wanted an out, and Hezbollah had provided it.

Inside the Martyrs' headquarters, before he'd killed the boy, he'd found out everything he could on the Ghost and had learned something very, very interesting. The Middle East envoy was bringing a large sum of money to the peace talks. Money that was black and completely in cash. Money that would set him up for the rest of his life, sitting on a beach without an extradition treaty. All he had to do was prevent the Ghost from killing the envoy before the meeting.

So he could do it.

31

The Ghost picked up his battered suitcase and entered the bustling flow of people headed to customs. The Sanaa airport overflowed with people of all types, including a surprising number of Westerners, most likely journalists trying to figure out the latest spasm that would rock the turbulent country.

The airport was on the verge of being decrepit, with grimy walls and listless guards who apparently were paid to simply stare at the floor.

He approached the immigration desk, worried that his dialect would give him away. He had no real knowledge of how someone from Saudi Arabia spoke and hoped the man at the counter didn't either.

His fears were unfounded, as the official took a cursory glance at his visa, stamped his passport, and waved him through.

He exited the airport and was accosted by a swarm of taxi drivers standing next to a smorgasbord of different vehicles, all with white bodies and orange quarter panels. He selected one and asked the driver to take him to the old city.

His first task was to retrieve his money from the *hawaladar* before the man's business closed for the day. After that, he would need to find a suitable replacement passport.

He ignored the bleating horns and the maniacal swerving of the cabdriver, lost in his own thoughts. He had a lot of preparations and fewer than four days to accomplish them.

He hadn't realized the cab had pulled over until the driver rotated completely around and pointed to a massive stone archway crossing the road. "Bab Al-Yemen."

He paid with his dwindling reserve of money, took his suitcase, and gave the name of a travel agency, asking where it was. All he had been told was it was near the gate to the old city. The driver shrugged, saying he had no idea.

On his third attempt, he found someone who knew the location, and was happy to see it was less than a hundred meters away, across the square.

The *hawala* system was usually no more than a form of extra income. A way to make a commission in conjunction with a primary business. In this case, the *hawaladar* owned a travel agency. The Ghost entered and ignored the proprietor's efforts at conversation. He showed his passport, recited the six-digit code, and walked away with a thick wad of Yemeni rials. No signature, no paperwork of any kind.

He entered the old city through the great stone gate and found a hotel, a rundown affair that catered to the lower income. The room consisted of nothing more than a mattress on the floor, a dangling lightbulb, and a mirror on the wall, but it was clean. He left his luggage and began to wander the old city, looking for a suitable target.

His criteria were simple: First and foremost, the target needed to bear a fairly close resemblance to himself. Other than that, the target needed to be traveling alone and not necessarily here on business. Someone who wouldn't be missed for a few days at least. He had decided on Sanaa's old city for this reason, as most of the people here would be tourists, although he knew the pickings would be slim given the upheavals Yemen had been going through.

He wandered the souks in the darkening gloom, beginning to think this mission might need to wait until after he'd conducted his business. Using Hezbollah's contacts, he had established a meeting with Khalid al-Asiri, a technical bomb-maker. A member of al Qaeda in the Arabian Peninsula, the man was reputed to be a master at camouflaging explosives and was responsible for constructing the ingenious printer-cartridge bombs that almost brought down two cargo aircraft in 2010, along with underwear-bomb devices splashed all over the news. The meeting was the following day, in Zabid on the coast of Yemen, and not something he could miss.

If he found nobody tonight, he would have to spend an extra day in Sanaa after his meeting, a day he couldn't afford. The alternative was to use the tainted Saudi passport. A passport that too many people knew about.

As he stopped in the middle of a spice souk, the smells made his stomach rumble. He was about to leave and search out a restaurant when he noticed a man haggling over a bag of spices. He was younger than the Ghost and didn't wear glasses, but was slight of build with the same facial characteristics. Unlike the locals in the souk, he was wearing a full-length dishdasha without the ubiquitous sport coat over the top. The Ghost edged closer until he could hear snippets of conversation. His interest picked up when the man, attempting a harder bargain, stated he was leaving in two days and couldn't come back tomorrow. *Not from Sanaa. Good sign.* When he heard the man say he wished to mail the spice to his mother in Jordan, he backed off and waited, ignoring his stomach.

He followed the target for another three hours, until it was completely dark. Finally, carrying all of his purchases, the Jordanian entered a hotel, an economic step above his own, but still on the cheap side. The Ghost stopped short in the small lobby and surveyed the establishment. It had a few chairs, a table, and one lone staircase. If he went up, the clerk at the counter would surely see him. Difficult to do what he needed and get away.

The hotel maintained an old-fashioned keyboard behind the counter, and the Ghost took note of the key number handed across, debating his next steps.

He went back outside and surveyed the street. He circled the hotel, looking for a side entrance he could use, but found none. He did find a group of young boys playing in the dirt and came up with an idea.

He approached them and said, "I'll give you each two hundred rials if you'll play a joke on my friend inside the hotel."

The boys were skeptical, but when he produced the money, they eagerly stepped forward.

"All you have to do is tease him until he chases you out. Get him to chase you down the street. I'm going to slip in and surprise him on his birthday."

Now all smiles, they took the money and began jabbering among themselves, coming up with a plan as they circled around to the front. When they entered, the Ghost waited to the side.

In short order, he heard a commotion, followed by the desk clerk shouting. Something rattled to the floor, bringing on more shouting. Seconds later, the boys came flying out of the doorway, laughing and shouting. The clerk was a few steps behind them, but a lifetime of tobacco ensured he'd never catch up.

As soon as his back was turned, trotting down the street, the Ghost slipped inside and bounded up the stairwell. He quickly looked at doors, finding the one that matched the key he had seen. Not wasting any time on an elaborate ruse, he simply knocked. When it was opened, he pushed the target back, entered, and closed the door.

The man got out one exclamation of surprise before the Ghost hammered his windpipe with the knife-edge of his hand. The target collapsed to his knees, holding his throat. The Ghost threw him on his back, straddled his body, and trapped his arms to his side.

He placed a hand over the man's mouth and nose, and rode the bucking body until it quit moving. The Ghost held on for an additional minute, then checked for a pulse. Finding none, he searched the body, pulling out the man's travel documents from a pocket. He opened the passport and was relieved to see the man was indeed from Jordan. The picture looked passable as well.

He slowly stood, feeling shame at what he had done. He glanced at the corpse and consoled himself by remembering the cause he was serving. The fact that the target was Jordanian helped, as the Hashemite Kingdom had a long history of persecuting Palestinians.

He was about to place the passport into his own pocket, when he noticed something that made him feel ill. There was no Jordanian national identification number. The target lived in Jordan, but wasn't a citizen. Which meant one thing: He was a Palestinian, from the West Bank or somewhere else.

The Ghost had killed one of his own.

LUCAS FINISHED PACKING HIS POSSESSIONS, deciding what he would take and what he would be leaving behind forever. He got it all down to a backpack and one duffel bag. It left him no room for any specialized equipment, but with any luck he'd be able to get that in Dubai.

He had a list of Hezbollah contacts all over the world, and routinely used them as cutouts to get hotel rooms and operational equipment. He'd have to be careful setting up any meetings, but with the secrecy of the Martyrs

Battalion and his little ploy with the forger, he was fairly confident he could leverage assets outside of Lebanon without them turning on him. It wasn't like Hezbollah sent daily updates around the globe, and most of the contacts were simply part-time help with a specific skill-set. Hezbollah wannabes, as it were.

He was sure the Ghost had gone to Yemen, but was equally confident he was headed to Dubai next, and he had the location of the *hawaladar* there, giving him a handle. At first, he'd worried that the assassin would attempt his attack in Yemen, but a review of the envoy's itinerary showed Yemen wasn't on the agenda. No, the Ghost was going to attack in Dubai, and that's where Lucas would stop him. He was pleased at the Yemen delay, as it would give him time to travel to Qatar and begin building his own trap, before the inevitable clampdown in security for the peace conference.

Finished packing, he toyed with the idea of going out on the town. He was leaving Beirut tomorrow, never to return, and hadn't ever sampled the nightlife here. He'd seen it, of course, the loose women and brash men partying the night away, but had never entered that realm due to the secrecy of his job. In no way could he be entangled with a female inside Beirut. Although he'd often dreamed about it. Snooty little bitches from rich sugar-daddy Lebanese. He would have loved to show one a good time instead of the whores he'd had to pay while on assignment outside of the country.

Why not tonight? It's not like you'll be here in the morn-

ing to worry about the consequences. And Hezbollah stays so far removed from the discos they're no threat.

Fuck it. He left the hotel and headed to Rue Monot in the Ashrafieh district. He looked for a disco that was dimly lit and not too loud. Dim, because he'd been told time and time again that his eyes were a deal breaker, and he didn't want to scare away any potential partners on first glance. Years ago, a date had said they reminded her of a bruise—purple and rotting.

He returned two hours later, a statuesque young Lebanese woman in tow. He'd convinced her to have a nightcap of coffee, although she'd said she didn't have time to stay long.

As soon as the door closed, he leaned in and kissed her. When she tried to pull away, he clamped a hand on the back of her neck. She broke free and slapped him hard across the face.

He rubbed his red cheek, getting aroused at the exchange. Wanting to push it further. "That'll cost you a little foreplay. Fuck the coffee. Take off your clothes."

She attacked him in fury, using her nails as claws. He blocked her amateurish attempts and slapped her hard enough to knock her down.

From the floor, her anger dissolved into abject fear.

"A fighter," he said. "I like that in a woman."

32

Jennifer flipped through the channels on the ancient television, but without cable all she picked up were local Beirut stations speaking Arabic. She turned it off and glanced at her watch for the umpteenth time. *Still a half hour before hit-time.*

Footsteps in the hallway outside her door caused her to quit breathing. She glanced at the *abaya* dress she'd carelessly thrown on the bed, calculating how long it would take her to get it back on. When the footsteps receded without a knock on her door, she exhaled, wondering yet again how she had been talked into this. Pike had said there was no way they'd do a frontal assault into the Hezbollah communications node, but he hadn't mentioned that the alternative was Jennifer infiltrating the place by herself.

After getting picked up at the marina by Samir, they'd conducted a complete mission analysis of the communications facility from his house. Using all of the data the case officer could supply, which was considerable, they searched for a weakness.

Situated above an electronics store that took up the whole bottom floor, there was only one way to access the top three floors: a stairwell in the back. The store operated as a legitimate business, but all of the people working there were Hezbollah, and half were armed.

The computer in question was in an office on the third floor, surrounded by other offices. The server farm occupied the second floor, and the case officer was unsure what was on the fourth floor.

The building had a small alley on the left and right that ran about seventy meters deep before dead-ending into a wall. The case officer had assured them that there was no secondary entrance. The building to the left was an apartment complex, the one to the right some sort of mix of residences and offices.

Initially, it had looked like there was simply no way to infiltrate the place. Anyone entering the electronics store would be under immediate scrutiny and completely unable to enter the offices in the back that accessed the stairs. Trying to skip the first floor and enter through the second, using a ladder in the alley, was out as well, since the server-farm windows were all heavily barred. They kicked around the idea of bringing a ladder in that would reach the third floor, then realized they were talking insanity.

They toyed with a concept of coming through the roof, but since the asset could give no information on the fourth floor, they tossed it aside. That option would simply be blind.

In the end, it was Pike who'd made the connection.

Jennifer remembered his question, and the chill it gave her. *What about going from building to building? Work your way around the ledge on the third floor?*

The men had all started analyzing the photos of the exterior, seeing the six-inch shelf that went from the buildings to the left and right, around through the alley wall, and across the target. She had known where this was going. With her acrobatic skills, they would expect her to make the climb. She silently waited for someone to say this idea was also insanity. Instead, Samir read a sign in Arabic on the apartment building and stated they were advertising openings.

Pike had looked at her then, a question on his face he didn't need to verbalize. She said, "I can't get in an apartment there! Come on, I'm a Caucasian female."

Samir said, "Nobody would know if you wore an *abaya* with a *niqab* veil covering your face. Just keep your eyes downcast to hide their color. You'll look like every other pious Muslim woman."

"Who'll get me in? What if someone asks me a question?"

Pike said, "One step at a time. Let's contact the case officer and see if his asset can rent an apartment on the third floor facing the building."

She felt sick to her stomach at the thought of the mission, but the pieces had rolled relentlessly into place. The asset had managed to rent a suitable space, had given the key to the case officer, who had passed it to the team at a hastily established dead-drop. From there, she'd dressed from head to toe in a black *abaya*, hidden her face with a *niqab*, and walked into the building behind Samir, moving straight up to the apartment.

They'd passed another male on the stairs, and staring at the steps as she walked, she was certain the man could hear her heart thumping like a bass drum.

Samir had left her there, waiting on nightfall, and had loaded Pike and the others into a panel van, parking it on the street outside the target. They were her only means of rescue should things go wrong.

She looked out the window at the target building, dimly lit by streetlights, running through her mind the thousands of things that could go wrong and how she would counter them. She felt her cell phone vibrate and saw a text from Pike.

How's it going?

She'd sent a status report every ten minutes, per their plan, but knew Pike was worried about her. *As he should be. Asshole.*

She replied, *Fine*.

PIKE: Hot as hell in van. No AC. Should have planned for that.

JENNIFER: Serves right. Ur not doing any work.

PIKE: Let's f'ing hope not. If I am, things have gotten bad.

She really didn't need that reminder, and simply sent back *K*.

Soon, much, much too soon, it was time to go. She texted that she was going off cell and onto radio comms, then prepped for the mission.

Dressed in a black Under Armour second-skin top and bottom, she cinched her hair into a tight ponytail, affixing the covert earplug into her ear canal and the small transmitter/receiver to a nylon belt around her waist. After getting a communications check with Pike, she did one final scrub of the cloning device and mini-computer she would use to crack the system in the target, getting a green light. She placed it, two flashbang grenades, a lockpick kit, and a thermal imaging device into a backpack. Once she was satisfied at how the equipment was weighted in the backpack, she strapped on a shoulder holster with a suppressed Glock 30, her only means of defense. The last thing she did was place a circular glass cutter inside the neckline of her Under Armour shirt, trapped against her chest by the material.

She shrugged into the backpack, took a deep breath, and said, "Exiting the building."

She heard a "Roger" as she was maneuvering the backpack through the small window opening. Standing on the thin shelf, she ran her hands up the rough wall, reaching for the shelf on the fourth floor. Once she made contact, she called, "Moving," and began a slide-shuffle down the ledge toward the wall of the alley.

The trip went smoothly until she made the final corner

from the alley wall to the target building. Sliding her hand forward, she hit empty air as the ledge above her disappeared.

She slipped backward and teetered for an eternity, held on to the wall by just two fingers of her left hand that still had contact with the upper ledge.

She regained her balance and closed her eyes, getting her breathing under control. She looked up, trying to determine where the ledge began again. She knew it did from studying the target window during the day. The gap had to be small. Something that had just crumbled through time.

She strained to see through the gloom, wishing she'd worn night-vision goggles. She had decided against them because of their lack of depth perception, but she could have used them now.

A passing car spilled enough light for her to see the ledge, a mere foot away. But it might as well have been a mile.

She took several deep breaths, working up her courage. When she was ready, she turned her feet left and right until they were flush with the wall, then dropped her left hand from the ledge. Spread-eagled, sliding directly against the rough brick, she inched across the gap. When she felt she had gone far enough, she slid her hands above her head and felt relief flood through her when they made contact.

Minutes later, she reached the target window. Leaving one hand on the ledge, she pulled out the glass cutter and sliced a circle directly above the window latch. Popping it free, she reached inside to twist the latch. She hesitated. The asset had said the building wasn't alarmed beyond the first floor, but she knew she was now betting her life on that information.

So what are you going to do? Go back?

She twisted the latch and popped the window an inch, holding her breath. Nothing outward happened. She rapidly raised the window, wanting to be on the inside if a silent alarm had been triggered. In one fluid move, she squatted, rotated around, and fell backward into the room.

She rose in a crouch, drawing her Glock. When nothing happened, she reported, "Inside."

Pike came back on, "Jesus Christ, Koko. Took you long enough. We're out here having a heart attack. How about some SITREPs?"

She grinned at the stupid call sign she'd earned on their last mission, but said nothing, settling for a double-click of the transmission button.

She moved to the door of the office and drew the thermal imaging device, placing it directly on the wood. She turned it on, hearing the soft whine as it warmed up. Within seconds, she could pick up any heat source in the hallway on the other side. And she saw at least two. Moving.

Not good. According to the asset, there were no guards in the building after nightfall. Just one lone sentry in the electronics store downstairs.

Maybe that's him. Maybe he'll move back downstairs in a little bit.

She pulled back to the far corner of the room and gave Pike an update.

He replied, "You said two? There shouldn't be two. If that's the sentry, it should just be one."

She said, "Yeah, I know. Let me give it a few minutes and see what happens."

Pike came back again, repeating himself, "Koko, you copy? There shouldn't be two."

She replied again, only to hear, "Koko, Koko, this is Pike, you copy?"

She keyed the mike again, but didn't get through. She realized her radio was dead.

She heard a squeak and saw the door opening inward.

33

I tried one more time to contact Jennifer, then hammered the floor of the van.

Knuckles said, "Easy. She didn't say she was in trouble. She sounded calm. It's just a radio issue."

"Maybe. Decoy, get up in the front. Get eyes out and see if there's any sort of reaction coming."

My imagination was taking on a life of its own, spurred by the thoughts of what I had been through in the Palestinian refugee camp.

Decoy said, "No reaction yet. Dead as a cemetery out there."

I picked up my suppressed H&K UMP and turned on the holosight, checking the reticle.

Knuckles said, "Hold on. Stick with the plan. Don't jump the gun here."

Brett read my expression and started working his UMP.

I tried to reach her again and failed. My mind flashed to the pruning shears, the absolute terror of captivity, superimposing Jennifer in the hands of those monsters. *No fucking way.*

I dialed her cell phone and got voice mail. That was the last straw. I said, "Kit up. We're going in."

Decoy scrambled into the back, strapping the EMP gun to his side while Knuckles said, "Pike, you sure about this?"

I powered up my night-vision goggles and said, "You don't know what they'll do to her. I've been there."

He stared at me for a second more, then started kitting up. When everyone was ready, I said, "No change to the plan. Brett leads the way. Any questions?" Nobody said a word, and I slid open the van door. We hit the ground running, reaching the front door in seconds.

Decoy, Knuckles, and I pulled security outward while Brett went to work on the lock of the wrought-iron gate covering the glass door. Within seconds he had it open, swinging it out of the way. He turned back to me, his NODs looking like cat's eyes caught in a flashlight. I tapped Decoy, and they switched places, Decoy handing his UMP, radio, and NODs to me. He swung the EMP gun around while the remainder of us moved out in a semicircle about ten feet away.

Knuckles had said the EMP worked fine, but it had a tendency to backsplash, and the last thing I wanted was to short-circuit all of our electronics while we destroyed the alarm leads.

There was a short hum, then nothing. Decoy whirled back around, pumping his fist up and down. I tossed him his kit as we collapsed back onto the glass door.

Brett went to work on the lock just as I noticed movement inside. A flashlight hit us full on, lighting up the alcove and blinding our NODS. Decoy fired over Brett's shoulder through the door, and the light dropped.

Brett quit working the lock and simply kicked the bullet holes, shattering the pane of glass and rushing through the gap. We all followed suit, fanning out to cover the room.

JENNIFER ROLLED TO THE RIGHT, in the direction the door opened, using it to block the view of the person entering. She heard a man speaking Arabic, answered by another. She leveled her Glock at the opening, wanting to wait until the man fully entered before pulling the trigger. She hoped that the darkness and the fact that her pistol was suppressed would allow her an element of surprise, letting her get the jump on the second man before he realized what had occurred to the first.

Nothing happened. All she heard was a slight slapping of the wall. Then the lights blazed on in the room.

Oh shit.

She coiled her legs underneath her, preparing to close the gap and shorten her trigger time between targets. She rose into a crouch, focusing on her front sight post, when the sharp sound of breaking glass cratered the silence.

The two men began yammering, then she heard the sound of running feet. She waited a minute, then inched toward the entry and peeked out. The hallway was empty.

She raced to the door the asset had described, ripped out her lockpick set, and went to work. Not nearly as experienced as the rest of the team, it took her several minutes to break the lock free, the time beating her down as she reflexively looked over her shoulder for the two men to return.

She felt the tumblers click and slipped inside the office, snicking the door closed behind her. She surveyed the room in the soft glow of her flashlight and saw three desktop computers.

Which one? She didn't have time to do all three, and the damn asset hadn't mentioned more than one system.

She went to the back of the computers, finding their Ethernet ports. Two had CAT 5 cables running out. The one on the left had nothing. *Gotta be it. Unless the damn asset was wrong about the air gap too.*

She powered down the system, plugged the automated cloning device into a USB port, and fired the computer back up. When the screen reappeared, she followed the prompts to clone the hard drive. After hitting YES to the question about proceeding, she got an hourglass with a digital bar showing twenty minutes remaining.

She moved to the opposite side of the door, Glock at the ready, and pulled out her cell phone to call Pike. She saw the missed call from him and relaxed for the first time.

That explains the broken glass. All hell's breaking loose now.

WITH NO IMMEDIATE THREATS on the bottom floor, we began flip-flopping toward the stairwell in back. No longer concerned with stealth, we simply mule-kicked every door that was locked.

Speed was my primary goal. I knew if they had Jennifer and realized we were coming for her, they'd evacuate and I might never see her again.

I entered the final office and saw the stairway to my front, fully illuminated from the inside. I heard feet pounding down the stairs and slammed up against the wall on the edge of the door, Knuckles on the other side. I heard Decoy and Brett still kicking doors one office over and so did the men coming down. Their chatter ceased, and I heard the distinct sound of rounds being chambered. They began a half-assed stealthy descent.

I raised my NODs to my forehead and caught Knuckles's eyes. I did the universal finger across the throat, meaning take them without any noise. I had no idea who was above them and wanted to maintain at least some element of surprise. The suppressed UMPs were certainly quiet enough, but I didn't want to risk an AK going off when the bodies hit the floor. Knuckles nodded and raised his NODs as well.

The two men stopped inside the stairwell, softly chattering. Eventually, they worked up enough courage to exit, but paid absolutely no attention to their rear security. They walked out with AK-47s at their shoulders, staring straight ahead.

When they cleared the frame and were about two steps into the room, I glanced at Knuckles. He nodded, and we pounced, breaking both of their necks in sequence like a macabre synchronized drill team, then softly lowered the bodies.

I called Brett and Decoy, getting them to our location. Knuckles and I positioned at the base and we flip-flopped up the stairs, two men pulling security while two went up a landing.

We reached the second floor and heard a racket down below, several men shouting and yelling in Arabic.

Knuckles said, "Looks like our exit's fucked."

With a single focus, I replied, "We're moving too damn slow. Get up the stairs."

We hit the third floor landing and exited, guns going left and right looking for a threat. I raced down the hall to the room Jennifer had used to enter and found an open window. Nothing else. *Shit*.

Knuckles entered behind me, saw my face, and returned to the hallway, an urgency in his expression for the first time. I followed in time to see Decoy and Brett close on the target door. Right behind them, we slid into the stack.

Across the frame, Decoy nodded and flung open the door. Brett entered first and went right. I went left, the muzzle tracking everything my eyes came across. I focused on a figure and centered the red dot on the eye orbit. And recognized Jennifer aiming a Glock at me. She immediately raised her hands, but didn't say a word. I was almost catatonic with relief. The rest of the men piled in, saw it was clear, then got guns back out into the hallway.

Knuckles said, "Okay. What's the play now?"

I didn't respond, still savoring the fact that Jennifer

was alive and out of the torturers' hands. He repeated the question, and Jennifer said, "My radio went dead. I didn't have time to call on the cell."

Knuckles said, "Not your fault. Blame lover-boy here for not trusting you."

It hit home that I'd made a mistake. Possibly a catastrophic one given the men downstairs. Jennifer rubbed a little salve into my wounds.

"It worked out for the best. If you hadn't come in, we wouldn't have gotten the clone. I was about to be in a gunfight when they went to chase you, leaving the door open for me to penetrate."

Brett said, "Still ten minutes on this download. What do you want to do?"

I put the mistake aside, getting back to the mission.

"Shut it down," I said. "Take what we have and move up to the fourth floor. Find a roof exit and get out of here while those guys search."

We were on the roof in short order, making our way past clotheslines and air-conditioning units to the apartment building adjacent to the target. We reached the access to the floor below, and Decoy said, "What now? How are we going to exit here?"

I could feel the tension in the men, all knowing they would last a millisecond on the street as American infiltrators. I looked around the roof, hoping for some answer to jump out at me.

Jennifer smiled, more calm now that she was in our hands, and said, "Time for a little Pike miracle action."

I realized she didn't think coming in had been a mistake.

I said, "You're the miracle. We need to get you back into the apartment so you can get the van. We'll keep doing the roof hop until we're a safe distance away, then get to the street."

Decoy said, "How the hell is she going to do that? Dressed like Catwoman?"

"Brett's going to the apartment to get her costume. He'll come back, she'll change and exit. We'll keep moving north."

Brett said, "What? I don't speak a lick of Arabic, and I'm dressed like a damn commando."

"You're black. It'll give you an edge. Best we can do. Besides, you look like an *Arabic* commando with those clothes. Leave your NODs and UMP. Just take the pistol. You hit trouble, and we'll be right behind you guns blazing."

Brett muttered, "Always about the black man," and turned to the roof access. Jennifer passed him the key and gave him directions.

We waited for eight minutes, watching car after car arrive at the target building. When he returned, he had Jennifer's *abaya* and *niqab*.

She walked a short distance to put them on, pulling me out of earshot of the other men. "You know you screwed up here tonight. I was okay."

She affixed the veil until all I saw were her gray eyes. She winked. "The after-action review is going to be murder. But I'm glad you came. No matter what they say tomorrow, I'm not sure I would have gotten the drop on both of those guys. I probably would have ended up calling you—trying to use a cell phone in the middle of a gunfight. You made the right decision for the wrong reasons."

They shouldn't have, because I was the man with all the experience, but her comments meant a great deal. I winked back and said, "I'm just glad you're okay. Let's get the hell out of here."

34

The Ghost scraped down the alley in a dented and rusted rental he'd picked up in Sanaa, seeing the minaret for the grand mosque, but unable to find the entrance in the maze of side streets.

One of the oldest cities on earth, and once the capital of Yemen, Zabid had declined to a state of abject poverty, with the entire town reminding him of the refugee camps back home. Full of crumbling buildings constructed of homemade brick and mortar, all jammed together with little forethought to any overarching plan.

The drive west had been rapid on the arid desert road, with only two stops at checkpoints manned by hard men armed with AKs. He had no idea whether they were government, opposition, or simply bandits, but they let him pass. He had given himself an extra hour just for such difficulties and was pleased he had met so few. It gave him enough time to conduct a reconnaissance on the Al-Asha'ir Mosque, the location where he was told to meet the AQAP contact.

Squeezing through a gap that might or might not have

been meant for vehicles, he saw the entrance to the mosque to his front. He killed the engine and waited, surveying the area. Nothing suspicious stood out. A man swatting a donkey pulling a cart, a couple of kids playing in the dirt, a lone woman clad in black carrying a bucket of water. The usual ebb and flow expected from such a town.

The mosque showed no activity. Eventually, a boy of eighteen or nineteen walked up the steps. Dressed in Western clothes consisting of jeans and a T-shirt, he held a newspaper in his right hand. *The signal.*

The Ghost gave him a few minutes, then followed. He found the boy in the large entrance hall, now deserted. The teennager saw him approach and waited, nervously shuffling from one foot to the other. The Ghost gave him the verbal bona fides and saw the boy visibly relax.

He said, "Khalid sends his regards and wishes to help in any way he can."

"Good. I haven't much time and am in need of his expertise. I require enough explosives to fit inside two shoeboxes, and I need it packaged in such a manner that I can place them in baggage for aircraft. Like the printer-cartridge bombs he made."

"Carry-on baggage?"

"No. I'll check the luggage holding the material."

The boy nodded, considering, then said, "It can be done fairly easily. That is not much explosive. When do you need them? How soon are you flying?"

"I wish to leave tomorrow, but I am at your mercy."

"It can be done." The boy passed him a cell phone.

"I'll call you on this to tell you where to meet. It will be tonight."

"One more thing: I require the explosives to be initiated wirelessly. Can you construct such detonators so that they will not draw attention?"

"You mean Wi-Fi through the Internet, or by radio signal?"

"Internet. I will need at least five."

"Easy. I can make them look like simple Western garage-door opener parts."

"You? You will make the explosives and detonators? I thought Khalid was the expert."

The boy smiled. "He is, but he has been teaching others. He was almost killed last year with Anwar al-Awlaki and knows he will eventually be found. I am your contact and will build your request. Don't worry. Your detonators are simple, and you only require camouflage for the explosives, no complicated barometric timing devices or other things."

"Fine. Build them as fast as you can. I'll be awaiting your call. I want to drive back to Sanaa tonight."

EIGHT HOURS LATER the Ghost sat in the shade of a dilapidated café, drinking tea and staring at the phone he had been given, willing it to ring. He was startled when it did, then surprised when the voice on the other end wasn't his contact. He wrote down the instructions provided, paying particular attention to the directions he would need to navigate the maze of the town.

35

Captain Brian Wilcox watched the men loading the back of the old Yemeni army truck and realized he still had time to back out. To let the Yemenis handle the mission without him. To follow the orders he had been given.

He was an operational detachment commander from the Fifth Special Forces group, and his team was on loan to the CIA with the mission of training a special counterterrorist unit of the Yemeni police. Paid for with CIA dollars, the unit was arguably the best in the country. Wilcox should have been proud of what he and his team had accomplished, and he was, but he was sick of hiding on post training while the men he taught went into harm's way. But that was the deal made with the Yemeni government. No Western face on any assault. Training only.

In his heart, he knew it was prudent. With the troubles wracking Yemen, and the accusations made that the government was nothing more than a Western puppet—especially given the devastation of U.S. drone strikes on

AQAP for the past few years—it would do more harm than good for a U.S. Special Forces team to be seen on an assault, giving the terrorists a propaganda coup. In truth, he knew he should feel lucky they were still operational at all, since every other unit had completely lost focus on al Qaeda in the Arabian Peninsula and become nothing more than regime protection against the opposition and protests rocking the country.

Still, Wilcox felt the unit had reached a plateau and that the only way to increase the effectiveness of the training was to see how the men operated on a live mission. Relying on what the Yemenis said after the fact, knowing their predisposition to whitewash mistakes and glorify every little success, was not efficient. It was like teaching all the plays on the practice field, then never seeing the team play a game. Being forced to only listen to the team tell him they'd won, when about fifty percent of the time the predator feed he watched in the JOC showed a different score.

To take them to the next level, he needed to at least see a couple of operations from the ground. So, he'd decided to go on this one. Just him and his team sergeant, not the entire team. And not to lead it. To simply observe.

His team sergeant saw his reticence and said, "Sure you want to do this? We'll be crucified if word gets out."

"Yeah. It's the right thing to do. Just be sure you stay out of the fight. No running to the gunfire."

The team sergeant smiled. "Shit. You know this'll be

another dry hole. Khalid's not stupid enough to advertise his location like their intel says he did."

Wilcox cinched the Velcro on his body armor. "Let's hope so. No way do I want to get in a gunfight. A dry hole will show us plenty about how they operate, and there's enough intel indicators to say the place is bad."

THE GHOST READ THE ARABIC PHRASE spray-painted on the brick wall and stopped his vehicle. *Right house.* Larger than most, with a second story, it had a courtyard out front but was still dilapidated, with the courtyard walls crumbling in places.

As soon as he entered, he knew he was in trouble. Four men with AK-47s faced him, showing no sign that they were friendly. His contact was not in sight. To their rear several chains hung from the ceiling, and piles of soiled clothing lay about the room. What disturbed him most were the maroon stains on the walls and floor.

He said, "Is one of you Khalid al-Asiri?"

The first man spoke. "No, but Khalid sent us. It seems you might not be who you say you are, and we're going to find out what's true."

"What do you mean? I was sent here by the Resistance. By a man named Majid. Surely you know this. Why do you not trust me now, after sending your contact to meet me?"

"Majid's dead, and the Resistance says you might have killed him, after you killed our friends with a bomb. Maybe you're an infiltrator for the far enemy."

"What? That's insane! They came to me. I didn't seek them out. How could I be an infiltrator?"

"We'll know soon enough."

The Ghost didn't bother to try running, knowing they would simply kill him. He raised his hands in the air. In short order, he was hanging from one of the chains, naked from the waist up. One of the men wheeled over what looked like a battery charger for a car.

CAPTAIN WILCOX FELT THE EYES of Lieutenant Bashir on him and said, "Wishing I'd stayed behind?"

Bashir said, "As long as you stay in back, I don't mind."

"Don't worry. You're in charge. I won't do anything but watch."

Unless things get ugly. Bashir was a good man and a good commander, but Wilcox knew he wouldn't follow the Yemeni's orders if they became engaged in a serious firefight. Something Bashir knew as well. The unit was about as good as any force he had trained, with every man hand-selected from the counterterrorist police force, but they were still junior varsity. Still at the level where they could do something stupid in a firefight, and if it came down to it, Wilcox and his team sergeant would take over the operation, their lives superseding the orders to stay hidden.

Wilcox felt the truck jerk to a halt and peeked out the corner of the tarp covering the bed while the men quietly deployed. He saw them fan out in a security perimeter while the breacher placed a charge on the front door. *Swift and silent. Pretty good.*

He was patting himself on the back when a wrenching scream punctured the air. Coming from inside the house. Then all hell broke loose.

36

Too late, the Ghost realized there was no convincing the men of his innocence. They weren't looking for the truth. They were looking for a confession, and he feared soon they would get it. His body was racked in pain, his skin slick with sweat. He barely had the strength to raise his head, and they had just started.

One of the men applied the battery charger to his naked chest again, and his frame locked up in a rictus of agony, a screeching wail torn from his throat filling the air. As quickly as it came, the pain left.

"Tell us what you did. Who you are. My friend is losing patience and wants to start working below the waist."

The Ghost looked at the man with his eyes barely open, blood trickling from the corner of his mouth where the electricity had caused him to bite his tongue.

Allah, deliver me from this pit. Help me on my path.

The torturer said, "Your choice. So you know, when we tire of the electricity, we begin with the real pain. With knives."

He bent down and began yanking on a pant leg, giving the Ghost a clear view of the front door so far, far away. Freedom he would never see again. He was staring at the portal, transfixed at the thought of escape, when it shredded inward in a blinding flash.

The shockwave from the detonation flattened the torturer to his front and disoriented the others. Before they had even comprehended there had been an explosion, multiple men entered the room, firing wildly.

The man on the floor bear-crawled down a hallway while the other three began firing back. Caught in the middle, the Ghost simply hung like a rack of meat, praying he wouldn't be hit.

He saw two men in uniform go down, but more poured through the doorway, while still others fired through the windows. The three torturers continued to shoot, until one by one they were silenced. After about a minute, all that he heard was the stomping of feet and the shouting of commands. Eventually, one of the men focused on him.

When questioned, he lied, saying he was a Saudi Arabian citizen who had been kidnapped. He stated it must have been for ransom. One of the police cut him free from the chains. As he was gathering his clothes he saw them bring in the primary torturer. Alive.

He knows the truth. The Ghost couldn't allow the man to be taken for questioning, especially if it was questioning like he had just endured. The man would give him up in a heartbeat.

Only half-feigning rage, he screamed and raced across

the room, picking up the broken iron hinge of the door as he went. Using it like a dull axe, he feverishly hammered the torturer in the skull, getting in three solid blows before he was pulled off and thrown to the floor, with all gun barrels now trained on him.

He screeched that the man had tortured him, then began to wail as if he was traumatized. A heated argument began about his fate. As he had hoped, some of the men sympathized with his actions. The commander looked at him with pity and ended the discussion. He was left alone, but the barrels all remained on him constantly now. He stared at his torturer, trying to catch a rise and fall of the man's chest. He saw none. He watched the commander leave the room to the outside. He knew his mission was done, but was feeling some comfort in his ability to escape to fight another day.

He collected his *dishdasha* and felt the weight of the traitorous cell phone his contact had given him, along with his Saudi passport. He gave a silent prayer of thanks that he had left the Jordanian passport in the car. Having two passports of two different men would have been hard to explain. He then remembered where he had gotten the phone and felt a stab of fear. There was no telling who or what that cell had contacted, and eventually these men would take the phone from him and scan it. At the very least he needed to delete the call history. He pulled the phone out as surreptitiously as possible. And saw he had two missed calls and a text message.

Where are you? Call me soon. Your package is ready.

It was from the contact, and he'd called while the Ghost was being tortured. The boy didn't know what had transpired. Didn't realize the Ghost was now viewed as an enemy. *And he's built the explosives.*

ON THE FAR SIDE OF HIS TRUCK, Wilcox was nervously fidgeting with his weapon, trying to determine if the fight was over or just paused. He was in constant communications with his team sergeant in the truck to his rear, but neither could see anything except shadows moving through the windows.

It had taken all of his self-control not to run to the breach and begin coordinating the assault, especially when he saw the men he had trained wildly shooting through the windows from the outside. He had settled for simply taking cover behind his vehicle. His team sergeant had actually made it to the left side of the breach before being ordered back. Now, they waited in the silence. He knew he should hide in the truck again, but there was no way he would, given the danger.

Eventually, he saw Bashir exit the building, and he waved his team sergeant over.

Bashir said, "It's a torture house. Inside are about fifteen men, all showing signs of terrible abuse. One was being tortured while we assaulted."

Both Americans had witnessed plenty of such houses in Iraq and had no desire to enter this one. Seeing a circle of hell like this would live a long, long time in their dreams.

Wilcox said, "What about Khalid?"

"Not here. There were four men, all dead. One killed by a prisoner."

Serves that bastard right.

"Well, let's get 'em back, get 'em medical attention and question them. They're all the intel we're going to get."

"We don't have the space for that. We had planned on a maximum of five detainees. Not fifteen."

"Call for transport. Get a bunch of trucks out here."

Bashir said nothing for a moment.

"What? Why's that a bad idea?"

"Because you are here. I'll have to call an ordinary army unit, and they can't see you. They don't even know you're in the country, and the word will spread rapidly."

Bashir saw his expression and continued. "It doesn't matter. They will have no information. I have seen this before. Most will be unable to describe much because of the torture, and the few that can will have nothing to offer. We have what we came for in the cell phones we found inside."

Wilcox considered the information, trying to find a way around. Eventually, he acquiesced, with a caveat. "Okay. Here's what we do. Go get a biometric profile of every one of them. See if any ping. If they do, we bring them along. If not, we add them to the database. When you're done, call for the transport. Leave a team of guys here to guard them while the trucks are on the way."

"I cannot leave a team here, in this town, without protection. It's too dangerous. The insurgents may attack for revenge. Either we all stay, or none stay."

Wilcox knew what he said was true, with insurgents attacking anyone in uniform throughout this area of Yemen. What went unsaid was that Bashir had no leadership beyond himself. There was no noncommissioned officer corps to speak of. Unlike Wilcox, he had no team sergeant to rely on to accomplish the mission.

He said, "All right, all right. Get the profiles, then leave as much food and water as you can, and tell them medical help is on the way. That'll get 'em to stay until the army trucks get here. If they're as beat up as you say, they'll probably just sit for a while anyway."

Bashir waited a beat, then nodded and began issuing commands.

The team sergeant spat in the dirt and said, "Guess we'd have been better off staying in the rear, huh?"

Wilcox looked at the sky. "No. I don't think so. Bashir wants nothing to do with these guys. At least we'll get the bio data. If we hadn't been here, we wouldn't even have gotten that."

37

"So you're telling me we risked all of this for nothing? The Taskforce couldn't get anything off of the computers that will give us a handle on Lucas?"

Kurt read my expression from the VPN and said, "No, no, it wasn't for nothing. We did get an incredible treasure trove of information related to Hezbollah operations, including apparently a possible operation in the Netherlands. We just didn't get anything specific for Lucas. There were over a thousand names in the system you hacked."

"Run the names through all the airline databases leaving Lebanon in the last three days. He's in there somewhere. We get a match, and we'll follow up."

I knew I was grasping at straws, but didn't want to let it go. We'd barely made it out of the *Dahiyeh* last night, with several more bits of high adventure before we had linked up with Jennifer and the van, including Jennifer's having to subdue a civilian in the apartment stairwell. I didn't want to believe all of that work had been for nothing. Bringing the team in, attacking the heart of Hezbollah, and getting out by the skin of our teeth. It made me seethe.

"Pike, the names are in Arabic. We can't run them *all* against *every* database. We'd end up with a hundred false positives. We did scrub the list for phonetic spellings of English names, but that list is still in the hundreds. We don't even know why they're in the database. They could be targets or on the payroll. There's just no way to tell. Give the analysts more time. They'll come up with something."

"We don't have time. The envoy's only got a few more days before he reaches Qatar, and he's in very real danger if Lucas is after him. What about infidel? Any of those names cross-checked with the term *infidel?*"

"Unfortunately, no. Infidel is in there, but the cross-check wasn't on the data you brought back."

Dammit. Should have stayed until we had everything from the hard drive. I knew that was just twenty-twenty hindsight talking, and I'd made the right call. Then I remembered what he had said earlier.

"What was that about a hit in the Netherlands?"

"Nothing much. Something to do with the Special Tribunal for Lebanon. Apparently, Hezbollah was looking at an operation against the STL, but they've been talking about that for years. We did a scrub, and the only thing remotely related is the death of an investigator in a gas explosion. The police have already closed the books on that one, though. They did a thorough investigation because of the nature of her work and some strange forensics they discovered, but they found absolutely no linkage to anyone related to Hezbollah. None."

Because they're looking for the wrong race and religion.

I said, "The case officer here thinks Lucas was a hired gun for outside work precisely because he wasn't tied to Hezbollah by ideology and he was Caucasian. Run those phonetic names against the flight records leaving Amsterdam to Beirut for three days after the death of the investigator. Is that necked down enough? There can't be more than a couple dozen flights, and no way would Lucas have hung around. If he had anything to do with the explosion, and he's in that list of names, he'll pop."

I saw Kurt turn and yell at someone behind him. He wrote instructions on a piece of paper, handed it to a man outside of camera range, then returned.

"That won't take but a few minutes. But you're really grasping at straws."

I smiled. "Better than nothing. We got a team here ready to go."

"Don't get ahead of yourself. Even if this does pan out, I need to get Council approval before you guys go hot-rodding after Lucas."

"I know, I know, but we need to prep now. We're going to need equipment because we're flying commercial. Can you get a bundle ready to drop? If we don't get anything on Lucas, it won't go anywhere. We don't need Council approval for that."

Kurt said nothing. I could tell he thought the entire thing was wasted effort and that I was just wishing for a break. Getting a bundle operational was a lot of work, much more than simply building it. In addition to the equipment, Kurt would have to start planning flights to a bunch of tentative drop areas, including both the United Arab Emirates and Qatar, which meant diverting aircraft and building covers for their operations. I pressed him.

"Sir, I know it's a long shot, but—"

Before I could finish, he turned from the screen and took a sheet of paper. I held my breath while he read it. He said something to the analyst offscreen, pointing at the sheet. He nodded and returned to the VPN.

"I don't know how you come up with this stuff. Two names matched. Both Canadian citizens. One leaving within twelve hours of the gas explosion, one three days later."

Yes.

"Run those two names against Beirut flights for the last forty-eight hours. See if either of them were here and left."

The analyst returned in seconds, and Kurt said, "One name. Canadian. Left yesterday, headed to Dubai."

Bingo.

"Send me the data, and get me Oversight Council approval to go to Dubai."

"Wait. This is pretty thin. I'm not sure I can convince the Council to let you go. Hell, I'm not even sure *I'm* convinced. You've got your company—supposedly working in Syria—which has mysteriously acquired three new employees in Lebanon, who will now all trek to Dubai. I'm not sure the evidence is worth the risk of exposure."

"Sir, come on! Yeah, it's risky, but whether that's Lucas or not, something is going on against the envoy. You know it and I know it. There's still a couple of threads here that don't make sense, starting with the computer bomb that Lucas gave me. The guy who was killed doesn't match the description of the man that was supposed to conduct the meeting, and it still makes no sense for Lucas to kill him in the first place. We need to go with what we do know, which is that a host of people seem to want the envoy dead, with Lucas at the top of the list. And he's in Dubai. The only good thing is that he's working with the old itinerary, so we have some time to play with."

I saw Kurt wince, and said, "Right? We have time to play with before the envoy gets to Dubai?"

"No. The decision was made to keep his itinerary the same. He'll be in Abu Dhabi in three days, and Dubai the day after that."

"Who's brilliant idea was that?"

"State Department. The trip is too important, and changing the schedule would risk offending the very people he's going to see. It was carefully chosen."

"Well, that's just great. Your call, sir."

"Okay, okay. I'll brief the Council, and I'll put on a log-tech for your equipment requirements, but you still only have a name. How are you going to find Lucas?"

"I don't know. I'll figure something out."

"Don't figure anything out before I get approval, understood? No more operational activity."

"Yeah, yeah, I get it. We can't do anything more in Lebanon anyway."

While Kurt was getting a log-tech on the line, I caught movement behind me and saw Samir poking his head in the door. I quickly turned the screen blank and said, "What's up?"

His face was ashen, like he'd just been told of a death in the family.

"I need to speak with you. Urgently."

I turned the computer over to Knuckles and followed him out to the den.

"What's going on? You look spooked."

"My niece has been taken by Hezbollah. They want to talk to me about the deaths of their leadership. They suspect I had something to do with it. I told them no, and now they've captured her as leverage."

Holy shit. I could see why he looked like he was going to puke. If he went into Hezbollah-land, he wouldn't be coming back out. At least not in whole pieces. But he couldn't leave his niece to the same fate. Even so, it had nothing to do with me. He had his entire clan to help him out.

"I'm sorry to hear that. We'll be leaving soon. We can go right now if you need your house for a war council."

"That's not why I'm telling you. I'm not going to my people. They'll go berserk. Probably just capture some other Hezbollah in reprisal. They don't have the skill to help, and this could turn into a shooting war very easily."

I said nothing, his words sinking in. *He wants me to help*.

I held up my hands. "Samir, I can't do anything over here. I don't—"

"I need surgical skill. I need to get her back without unnecessary bloodshed. Your skill. This has all happened because I helped you. Please. I will turn myself in and convince them I had nothing to do with the killings, but I want you to get her back."

Kurt's last command was still echoing in my head. "Samir, I really have no authority to do what you're asking. I can't risk my men and possibly start another Lebanese civil war. I'm sorry."

"She's nineteen, Pike. A university student. She knows nothing of war."

Jennifer had entered the room and had heard the last part of the conversation. She was staring at me, waiting to hear what I would say.

38

Inching toward the desk in the Dubai immigration line, every step forward built a sense of dread within the Ghost. He had had no trouble leaving Yemen, including obtaining the necessary items for his mission, but then again, not many have particular trouble leaving a country. It's getting in that's tricky. Now, he was about to find out if his forged Dubai visa, coupled with his Jordanian passport, would withstand scrutiny.

He glanced again at the picture within the passport, mentally comparing it to his own visage. *It should be close enough.* They were both clean-shaven, and he'd purchased attire that was suitable for someone from Jordan. He closed the passport and studied the immigration desk, the people drawn toward it as if they were being sucked up by a slow vacuum.

Watching two more travelers go through the routine, he noticed each stiffen during the interview, rigidly facing the official behind the counter. He wondered what they were doing. He watched the next man, and it hit him:

They were taking a digital photo and conducting a retinal scan. Of every person in line.

He ripped open the passport again, trying to find if it had some means of digital storage. All he saw was a bar code. Surely the Jordanian's retinal scan wasn't in that, was it? The Hashemite Kingdom didn't include biometrics in their passports, did they? If so, he was doomed, because the scan of his eye wouldn't match the scan in the passport.

He looked to the rear, contemplating moving back into the terminal and claiming he had gone the wrong way. That he had a connecting flight. But he had no connecting flight. No boarding pass to present. The glaring lack of documents would invite scrutiny. Questions he couldn't answer.

While moving inexorably forward, he studied the immigration officials' actions and relaxed a little. It didn't appear as if they were comparing anything. Simply collating data, like what had happened to him yesterday with the Yemeni police.

The thought brought a bolt of adrenaline, causing his face to flush and sweat to pop on his neck. Did the Yemenis share such data? Was there a database on the Arabian Peninsula that was fed by such sweeps? It wouldn't matter that he had no reason to be suspected of anything. The scan in Yemen was for a Saudi citizen, not the Jordanian passport he held in his hand. The difference alone would get him arrested. Then, when they gave his bags a much more thorough search than normal, they would find the explosives.

He looked up again and saw there was only one more person ahead of him. *Too late to run now.* He felt queasy, like he'd eaten something rotten. He should have done more research on Dubai immigration. He had thought using the Jordanian passport was the perfect break from all that Hezbollah knew, especially now that they were hunting him out of misplaced vengeance, but he wished he had stuck with the original forged passport.

The traveler behind him gently tapped his shoulder, causing him to flinch. The man pointed, and he realized he was being waved forward. He walked woodenly to the counter and presented his passport.

The official saw the visa for Dubai, then the missing national identification number.

"You are from Jordan?"

"Yes. Well, the West Bank, but the passport and visa are from Jordan."

"What is the purpose of your stay?"

"I'm visiting a friend. I hope to find employment in Dubai."

"Who is your friend?"

He read off the name and address of a man living in the old section of Deira, near the banks of the Dubai Creek. At least this much was backstopped. The man was real, a friend, and knew he was coming. After Yemen, the Ghost would rely only on those he knew he could trust. Knew the purpose of his cause.

"What does your friend do?"

The Ghost felt a trickle of sweat track down his cheek. He wanted to wipe it away, to hide the traitorous reaction of his body, but realized the motion would only draw attention to his nervousness.

"He's a maintenance worker at the Al Bustan Rotana Hotel. He said I might join him there. They have openings."

This part was not true. The friend *did* work at the Rotana Hotel, but the Ghost had no idea about their employment status. All he cared about was the fact that the man's job would allow him to penetrate hotel security for his mission.

The official pointed to a lens on a stalk behind his chair and said, "Look here until I tell you to stop."

The Ghost did so, giving a silent prayer.

The man glanced at the screen, apparently satisfied. He stamped the passport and handed it back, already waving the next man forward.

The Ghost snatched up his passport and willed himself to walk casually to the baggage claim area, and his next challenge—getting through customs.

He found his first suitcase already circling on the baggage carousel. Two bags behind it was the large computer box, swathed in cellophane for the journey. It looked no different than a half dozen other boxes on the carousel, but contained the explosives and detonators he'd acquired in Yemen.

He placed both on a luggage cart and passed through

the door marked "Nothing to Declare." He was directed to an X-ray machine, along with four other men, all competing to get out of customs.

He waited for his luggage to be spit out on the far side, surreptitiously watching the official tasked with reviewing the screen. The man barely looked at anything coming through, and in short order, the Ghost was free, feeling the bracing heat of the Dubai afternoon.

He took three deep breaths, glancing left and right to see if anyone had followed, still not believing he had made it into the country. He heard someone shout, *"Ash'abah!"* and turned to see his friend pull up in a rusty, belching sedan.

"Hamid. It's good to see you."

Hamid exited and helped with his bags, then said, "Where to first?"

He gave out the address to his *hawaladar*, then said, "I need a place to stay. A hotel that won't be visited by anyone in authority."

"Nonsense. You will stay with me. I have a flat in the old town. It's secure, trust me."

The Ghost smiled and said, "I have one other favor."

"What? Anything to repay my debt."

"I need you to get me into the Al Bustan Rotana as an employee. I have some work to do there before they lock it down for a visit from an American."

Hamid's face fell, and the Ghost said, "What? You told me you were being promoted to a leader in the maintenance department. I won't tie you to the work. You'll be safe."

"It's not that. I would do anything for you, but I no longer work there."

At first, the Ghost didn't grasp what Hamid had said, the words too destructive to contemplate. The very idea of using the Rotana Hotel had come from his friendship with Hamid. His entire plan relied on Hamid's employment. The symmetry of attacking the United States envoy in the same hotel that Mossad had killed the Hamas operative held a poetic justice in his eyes, but it was predicated on gaining access. He'd never thought to ask if Hamid still worked there.

He considered attacking at the hotel anyway, but knew it was futile. He wanted a surgical killing. A statement that vied for publicity precisely because it duplicated the Mossad hit. Now, it would have to be a large, messy attack. And he didn't have the explosives for a car bomb.

Hamid continued. "Right after they opened the Burj Khalifa, they had a problem with the elevators. Some tourists were trapped for hours. They fired the maintenance crew, and I applied to replace them. I've worked there for over a year."

The comment tickled something in the Ghost's memory. He reached into his carry-on bag, pulling out the American's itinerary, and saw what had triggered the recollection. The Burj Khalifa was the tallest building in the world, an engineering marvel that rose like a spear out of the desert, towering over every other building in the Dubai skyline. The envoy had left his ambassadorship six months before the building opened in January 2010. He was now scheduled for a royal tour to the observation deck one hundred and twenty-four stories above the earth.

"You work at this building now?"

"Yes."

"Can you get me in there?"

39

"et me get this straight," said the director of the CIA. "You want to move a team to Dubai without any cover backstopping whatsoever? A team that's supposed to be in Tunisia and we clandestinely infiltrated into Beirut for no good reason?"

Kurt grimaced at the reaction. He'd purposely whitewashed the infiltration of Knuckles's men, blurring the line between when they'd reached the point of no return on their deployment and when Pike had been rescued.

"Yes. I know it sounds risky, but we can mitigate that as far as the Taskforce goes. The team from Tunis has clean passports that we can burn after this op."

The D/CIA pointed to the presentation Kurt had just given. "And that's the smoking gun? That's all you have?"

"Yes, it is, but the PowerPoint doesn't do justice to the man. Lucas Kane is a proven killer, and he's headed to Dubai. We've tried to capture him several times, and failed. The risk is worth it."

The secretary of defense spoke up. "I get that Kane's a threat, but you've got nothing to go on. You couldn't even find him in Dubai if you wanted. You said yourself that there was more to this that you didn't understand. That there were others involved. I think you should take some time to flesh this out, get some concrete operational information, then come back. I can't see sending a team willy-nilly to Dubai."

"Sir, you know me. Know I don't cry wolf. Yes, we don't have a handle on Lucas, and yes, there's a bunch of threads we don't understand, but we need to go with what we know. Lucas discussed finding assassins on tape, and Pike found the envoy's itinerary on a laptop computer held by Islamic extremists. An itinerary that hasn't been changed, I might add."

He saw the secretary of state bristle and hastily continued, knowing he would need the man's vote. "I'm not making a judgment on that decision, but the fact remains that Lucas is in Dubai, and the envoy's headed that way. We need to assume that Lucas has the itinerary and is going to target the envoy. We can stop it now or mop the blood up later."

By the secretary of state's expression, Kurt knew he'd hit a nerve, and was surprised at what he said next. "The itinerary was constructed with policy implications in mind. We couldn't change it at this late date without offending a great number of people and setting back the very agenda for the trip. Given that, I'm inclined to let the Taskforce continue, if they can do it without compromise. An attack on the envoy's party would be devastating to the peace process, setting us back to square one.

We can't be sure we would be able to get the people back to the table again."

The secretary of defense said, "Billings, you should sit back and watch a few of these go down before you jump so quickly to approve. Your key comment is 'without compromise,' and I don't see how that can be done." He turned back to Kurt. "How are you going to infiltrate them?"

"We'll get them in as tourists." He saw the SECDEF and D/CIA roll their eyes, and worked to mitigate the weakness in his plan. "I know that's not optimal, but tourism is one of Dubai's greatest selling points, and they don't look too hard at Westerners. We can get in and out without trouble. This is what we do."

"Seriously?" said the D/CIA. "That's what Mossad used to say. After their hit, Dubai is the last country in the Middle East I would send an operative to work without complete cover backstopping, and you're talking about sending in a shooting team with nothing."

Kurt held up his hands. "Hold on. Don't confuse what we're trying to do with that operation. The target of the Mossad hit is exactly why Dubai worked so hard to solve the crime. It humiliated them to have a bunch of Israelis come in and flagrantly kill a Hamas military commander. We're doing nothing of the sort. We're *preventing* an attack in their country, against another Westerner. As long as we don't do anything that blatantly embarrasses them, they won't look too hard, particularly given the target. They love McMasters from when he was an ambassador. They don't want harm to come to him, or to their reputation. *Especially* after the Hamas hit."

Alexander Palmer, the president's national security advisor, said, "Whoa, whoa. Aren't we getting ahead of ourselves here? Missing something? Lucas Kane is a United States citizen. Does that matter? I mean, should we discuss the implications?"

Kurt, fearing he was losing ground, said, "Lucas Kane was designated a DOA target a couple of years ago, and it's still valid. We just quit chasing him because he no longer posed a threat to national security. No longer fell into the Taskforce mandate. We don't need to plow over that ground again. We discussed the implications when he was designated."

Palmer said, "I appreciate your input, Colonel Hale, but I was speaking to the Council, not to you."

President Warren spoke for the first time. "Lucas Kane gave up any constitutional protection when he decided to attack national interests. No different than al-Awlaki. As far as I'm concerned, his citizenship has no bearing."

He waited for a rebuttal. When none came, he said, "Gentlemen, we have an unprecedented opportunity with this peace process, beyond whatever solutions we can gain at the bargaining table. The Palestinian Authority has requested certain things that, if we provide them, may very well give us great leverage in the future. I understand this deployment is risky, but damaging McMasters's mission would be catastrophic to future peace in the region."

Kurt knew the president was talking about the taste of American greenbacks he was providing to the Palestinian Authority. A carrot of money that would invariably be asked to grow, with a commensurate increase in the size of the stick behind it. He had been ambivalent before, but now was grateful for the president's decision, as it would be the deciding vote.

The secretary of defense leaned back with a resigned expression, coming to the same conclusion. "You can give assurances that they can get in and out without compromise?"

"Sir, you know I can't give absolutes, but they've done pretty good so far."

"Yeah, right. I've seen a few operations run by Pike go down. What's he doing right now? Shooting out streetlights for fun?"

Kurt smiled, knowing he had won. "No, sir. He completely understands the importance of this meeting. He's been given direct orders to stand down from anything until the Council has decided. He's just soaking up the Beirut sun right now."

40

Peeking through the small gap in the curtain behind the front seats of the van, I could see Samir inside his car three rows over, nervously fidgeting and glancing at his watch. Probably wondering if he'd made the right choice. I knew how he felt, because our plan had about a hundred different opportunities for going sideways.

Immediately after talking to Samir in the house, I'd held a war council of our own, and the team had decided that getting his niece back was the right thing to do. At first, the idea seemed suicidal, because not only did the six of us have to find the niece, but we also had to assault what was sure to be a stronghold. The only way we could see doing it successfully was to force them to come to us, then attack them while on the move. Something that was much easier said than done.

Hollywood notwithstanding, a vehicle interdiction is one of the hardest operations to successfully accomplish. By its very nature, the purpose was to stop the vehicle without harming those inside. If that wasn't the case, a simple anti-tank rocket could be used, destroying the vehicle and killing everyone aboard. The problem with a surgical interdiction was that while the team was focused on stopping the vehicle, the occupants would be focused on the team, and they usually had a very strong desire to evade capture, along with weapons they had no compunction about using. About fifty percent of the time, the operation ended in an assault anyway, with the targets getting injured in some way or another.

The difficulty was compounded here by the fact that we could in no way allow this to end in a gunfight. I couldn't be responsible for starting a shooting war between Hezbollah and the Druze. We needed to stop the vehicle and close on the men before they had a chance to react, which posed significant challenges. It was Decoy who'd come up with the idea of popping a tire with a suppressed sniper shot.

At a distance of two or three hundred meters away we could potentially disable the vehicle without the occupants knowing what had happened. The suppressor would muffle the sound of the gunshot, and while the bullet would still break the sound barrier with an audible crack, the noise was omnidirectional and would be camouflaged by the exploding tire. From there, a van driven by a Druze friend of Samir's, with Jennifer in the passenger seat dressed in her stylish black sack, would pull over to help. Once they were engaged in conversation, we'd come boiling out of the van.

That was the plan, anyway.

I saw a sedan with two men approach and said, "Get

ready." The vehicle continued on, then exited the parking lot.

Brett said, "Jesus. Where are those guys?"

The time for the meeting with Hezbollah had come and gone, and we were all getting a little antsy. You always had in your mind's eye exactly how a plan would go down, but we were attempting to take out thinking human beings with a penchant for survival, and make no mistake, they had their own ideas of what would happen.

Decoy said, "You think they've got eyes on Samir right now?"

Meaning, have they already scoped us out and were we now about to be on the receiving end of their own brilliant plan.

"I don't know. Let's give it a few more minutes, then break out. If they don't show, we'll have Samir call them from his house."

I keyed my radio. "Knuckles, you still good?"

"Yeah. It's getting hot as hell, but it won't affect my shot."

While I was most assuredly the better sniper, I'd given the task to Knuckles, wanting to be on the assault to contain whatever curveballs came our way. Of course, he'd say my assessment was most assuredly incorrect, and truthfully, he might be right. Although I would never tell him that.

Samir had come up with a beat-up Dragunov SVD, and Knuckles had test-fired it in the mountains behind Samir's house. He'd come back and said that it held a little under two minutes of angle in accuracy, meaning he could put a round just inside a two-inch circle at a hundred meters, and it would work for the operation.

The only thing that had remained was finding a place for the exchange of Samir and his niece, then the follow-on ambush. After some searching, we'd decided on the Beirut airport parking lot. The area had enough security to prevent the Hezbollah thugs from trying anything right off the bat, allowing the niece to get in Samir's car and get away, and was close enough to Hezbollah-land that they'd feel secure. It was only a half mile from the airport to the heart of their territory.

A half mile was all we had to play with. Not a whole lot of time for me to relay the description of the vehicle to Knuckles, then have him take it down from the roof of the warehouse he was lying on.

Brett said, "You still want to parlay with them?"

"Yeah. We might get something more than just rescuing Samir and his niece. Something we can use to track Lucas."

The end-state of the operation had been the biggest bone of contention, with most of the team wanting to chalk up a win once we had Samir and his niece freed. I thought that was just postponing the problem for Samir. In order to truly get him free, we needed to convince Hezbollah that he had nothing to do with the murder of their leadership, and I was fairly sure the tape we had of Lucas killing the Hezbollah courier would accomplish the goal—if I could get them to watch it. Best case, they'd lay off Samir, a civil war would be averted, and they'd give us some thread we could use to find Lucas.

Jennifer said, "White four-door sedan approaching with three men and a woman. Moving way too slow."

It took a moment, but the vehicle eventually came into my little sliver of view, stopping in front of Samir's sedan. Something verbal was exchanged, and Samir slowly raised his hands. The men exited, one holding a woman. Samir followed suit, and the woman was released, running to him. He placed his arms around her and whispered something in her ear. Only after she was safely in his car did he walk toward the men, his arms outstretched. He was roughly searched and thrown into the backseat.

"Showtime." I said.

41

Knuckles heard the call and settled in behind his weapon, staring unfocused at the rooftop to rest his eyes while waiting on the description of the vehicle. After it came, he said, "Anything unique? Any identifying characteristics?"

"Yeah," Pike said. "Front right quarter panel is dark blue or black. It's a replacement and stands out. We're going to roll in five. You ready?"

"Roger. I got the ball."

Knuckles raised his head to the scope, focusing on the exit from the airport. He'd meticulously constructed his nest to allow the weapon to rest on its own, naturally aiming into the kill zone. He wanted to take out as much human error as possible, leaving the weapon alone to work within its capabilities. Any twitch of muscle, any forcing of aim he worked to diminish. Even his heartbeat. The Dragunov wasn't the most accurate rifle to begin with, and he couldn't afford to miss by compounding the built-in error.

He saw a red vehicle exit and immediately dismissed it.

Relaxing his left hand on a sock full of sand underneath the buttstock, he raised the scope a smidgen and focused on the next vehicle. A white sedan.

He scanned for the quarter panel and saw it was dark. A different paint scheme. He felt his pulse quicken and took a long, slow breath like a yoga student, willing his adrenaline away.

"I have the target."

He heard Pike acknowledge, but wasn't listening, his mind moving to a different plane.

He squeezed the sock sandbag, forcing the barrel to drop and track on the right front tire. It was counterintuitive, but the farther away he took his shot, the better the chances of success. At this range, the vehicle was moving almost perpendicular to his line of aim, meaning he could aim at the tire head-on. The strike of the round would be a little high as the vehicle traveled forward and the tire gained ground from the time he pulled the trigger until the time the bullet struck, but he wouldn't have to worry about leading from left to right, like shooting skeet.

The longer he waited, the more the vehicle would be moving parallel to him, and the greater the chance of error. Worst case, he would have to take the shot right in front of his position, where the road curved, leaving him to actually aim ahead of the tire in order to hit it. A recipe for introducing enormous human error.

As the barrel lowered something ticked in his brain. He didn't know what it was, but he knew he couldn't ignore it. He relaxed the hand, raising the scope. He focused on the driver. And saw what it was.

"Pike, Pike, the vehicle is not correct. I have one man. A lone driver."

"Okay, okay. Stand by. Target will be exiting soon."

"No, I mean it's the *right* vehicle, but there's now only the driver. Nobody else. The vehicle fits. How many white sedans with a repaired right front quarter panel could be exiting the airport at this time?"

He heard Pike say something in his earpiece, but ignored it. He knew what had happened. They'd switched vehicles before leaving the airport to confuse any surveillance.

He tracked to the right, swinging the weapon in an arc, reaching the edge of his sandbag nest. He saw nothing but a large panel truck coming down the road, facing him head-on. *Could that be it?*

He focused on the cab, seeing two men. He knew the truck had never exited the airport. His mind working in overdrive, he sorted through the data, and remembered the flash of red he had ignored before.

He scanned back to the left and saw nothing. He swung back to the right and saw the panel truck was now in front of his position. Behind it was a red SUV that had been hidden by the panel truck, now revealed by the curve in the road.

He focused on the passengers and saw four, straining now to keep the scope centered on the vehicle as it traveled parallel to his position. *The target.*

He heard Pike requesting a SITREP, but didn't have time to give out a detailed report. The vehicle would be out of range and into the *Dahiyeh* in a matter of seconds.

Rising to a knee, he rapidly dragged a sandbag to the right and slapped the stock of the weapon on top of it, now facing ninety degrees away from where he had planned. He settled behind the weapon and lowered the scope to the rapidly diminishing vehicle, sighting in on the right rear tire.

Due to the curve in front of his position, the road going away wasn't as ideal as the road coming toward him. He would have to lead the tire some. The question was how much. The longer he waited, the less he would be forced to do so as the road began to wind perpendicular to his line of aim. But the longer he waited, the farther the vehicle moved and the greater the chance it would be outside the accuracy envelope of his beat-up Dragunov. Especially now that he would be introducing human error as he locked the scope onto the tire with muscles alone in his hastily reconstructed sniper nest.

All of these facts flitted through his mind in a nanosecond, none achieving any dominance. They were simply instinctive, like the millions of inputs a hawk receives diving at a mouse. He focused on the task, calming his body down and manipulating the rifle so he was working with it instead of forcing the shot, seating it as best he could into the sandbag.

He settled the crosshairs just inside the rear tire's rim, giving him the largest cross section to work with as a margin of error for the vehicle's forward travel. Watching it shrink with each passing second, he took a deep breath and let it out, the air escaping like a pinhole in a balloon. He was conscious of the reticle slightly bouncing in time with the pulse of his blood. Conscious of a steady breeze against his cheek. Conscious of all the outside influences on the path of his bullet, but he trusted his subconscious to adjust, minutely correcting his aim to ensure success. It was a skill cultivated over a lifetime. He caressed the trigger, lightly pulling it to the rear with a feather touch.

His eyesight slightly unfocused on the edges, the tread of the tire in stark relief in the magnification of the scope, he was startled when the weapon bucked in his hands. As he knew he would be.

He settled the scope and saw the vehicle weave, then pull to the shoulder. He squeezed his eyes shut and heard Pike shouting into the radio.

In a monotone, he said, "Break, break. Target is neutralized. I say again, target is neutralized. Past my position. Red SUV with four males inside. Original vehicle's location is unknown."

"Is it the right vehicle?"

Knuckles smiled, the question hitting home. He'd just made one of the toughest shots he had ever been called upon to do, and even he wasn't sure if he'd hit the right target.

"I have no idea. That's your part of the job."

42

Already outside the airport, I asked Jennifer if she could see the original white sedan ahead of us. The one thing we could not do was take out two separate vehicles.

"No. He's not in sight in front of us. Maybe he exited off the roundabout before he reached Knuckles."

Great. An unknown threat on the loose.

"Okay. Close on the SUV with the same plan, but keep your eyes open for that damn vehicle. Knuckles said it was only one man, but that's all it would take to turn this into a gunfight. Jennifer, you got the ball for ID. If you don't recognize Samir, we break out, no questions asked."

I keyed my radio. "Knuckles, keep an eye out for the white sedan. Give us early warning."

"Roger. He shows, what then? I can't threaten. Only shoot."

I knew the implications, but wanted the warm and fuzzy of his long reach. "You give us early warning and we'll deal with it. Just be prepared. This goes wrong, drop everyone you don't recognize."

"Roger."

I peeked between the curtains to catch a glimpse of the red SUV, but saw nothing. Jennifer was straining, leaning so far forward the veil on her face had separated, exposing the skin of her neck.

"I see it, I see it. One man out. No ID on Samir."

I started breaking out kit, along with Decoy and Brett. "Keep looking. We're almost at point of no return."

If it was Samir, he'd be in the backseat. Of that much I was sure. The rest were unknowns. Did the guy next to him have a weapon? Was it out ready to go, or holstered? Did they already have it in their mind to kill Samir? Would that make them much more prone to pull the trigger at the slightest sign of resistance? How many men would exit to check out the flat tire? One? Two? Would they be armed as well?

We hadn't seen any weapons at the airport, but then again, we hadn't seen any red SUVs either. Too many variables to plan for, but I was working with men who didn't need much planning. They could assess and execute on the fly, making correct decisions based on the variables presented. But I wasn't sure that would be enough for success. I was fine with our chances of survival, but wasn't with Samir's. I had no doubt we could close on and subdue everyone in the red SUV, killing them if it came to it, but I wasn't sure we could do it in time to save him.

He knew this, of course, when he'd agreed to the plan. He was prepared to fight for his life, and we'd planned the takedown, but there were just too many variables that we couldn't predict.

Best case, we assumed the driver would exit the vehicle and check out the tire alone. That was Decoy's target. Brett would take out the passenger up front, whether he was in the vehicle or not. That left the man in the backseat for me. Possibly wrestling with Samir over a weapon. Possibly shooting Samir outright.

Jennifer was nothing but eye candy on this one. Her whole mission was to simply lull the opposition. She'd sit in the front with her black garb on, wearing sunglasses to hide her eyes, looking like the meek Muslim woman remaining in the vehicle while Samir's friend, acting as our driver, went to help.

He would be key. While he would offer nothing in the fight, he was the trigger, which was critical for success. Go too soon, and they'd still be on edge that our vehicle was a trap. Wait too long, and they'd inevitably get suspicious about the driver's intentions. We wanted to hit a sweet spot, along with hopefully splitting the targets apart when we assaulted. To do this, the driver would attempt to get at least one of the men to our van, stating he had better equipment to help with the flat. If it worked, the trigger would be his opening the door, allowing us to assault. If that failed, and the targets waved off on any help, the driver would signal with a concealed radio, giving two clicks on the transmit button that he'd done his best and was on the verge of drawing suspicion.

I felt the van pull onto the shoulder, but still couldn't

see the SUV. Jennifer said, "One man out. The driver. Two men in the back, one in the front passenger seat. The one on the left rear looks like Samir, but I can't be sure. The sun's reflecting off the back window."

"Knuckles, you got us?" I said.

"Yeah. I got you. Clean shots right now. Tracking the driver."

"Keep your eye out for the white sedan."

"Roger."

I craned to see between the curtain, but couldn't get a glimpse of anything but the upper right rear of the SUV. Jennifer said, "Front passenger exited. Looking at the van."

I heard Arabic shouting.

"He's saying something to me. He's getting my attention. Driver is engaged with our guy."

I watched her lean out of the open window, as if she couldn't hear.

Jennifer's next words sped things up considerably.

"He's walking toward me."

I snicked the curtain shut, leaving a sliver to see through, and took my pistol in a two-handed grip.

"No change to the plan. Take your designated targets. Brett, your target's walking up to the van right now. We wait this out, until we get the signal."

I now heard the man talking, trying to engage Jennifer. I peeked between the curtains and saw her staring down, shaking her head, playing the shy wife.

The man leaned in and snatched Jennifer's sunglasses.

He said something else, and I saw his scowl sprout into amazement. *Because of the color of her eyes.*

He reached in again and yanked off Jennifer's *niqab*. Before he could remove his arms, Jennifer exploded into action, locking his elbow joint and causing him to try to climb through the window to relieve the pain.

I said, "Execute! Brett, you have my target. Right rear door. Decoy, no change."

I ripped the curtain back as I heard Brett and Decoy launch out of the van. I leaned in and hammered Jennifer's captive behind the ear with the barrel of my pistol, then raced to follow Brett. I didn't care if I'd knocked the guy out or just stunned him, knowing Jennifer would do the rest.

I could see the two men in the back of the SUV wrestling and knew it was for a weapon. We had seconds before bullets started flying and this turned into a bloodbath.

Brett reached the door and attempted to yank it open. It didn't budge. *Locked.* I reached him just as he shattered the glass with the barrel of his weapon. He unlocked the door and I ripped it open, praying Knuckles had subdued his target on the far side of the SUV.

The man held a semiauto pistol, and Samir was wrestling for control, keeping the barrel away from his body just like in a bad movie. The glass from the window glittered in the sun, sprinkled around the head and shoulders of my target. Knowing he had threats to his front and rear now, he desperately pulled the trigger, sending a bullet through the floor of the car and causing Samir to let go.

He threw his hands in front of his face, screaming as if he could ward off the coming death. Instead of shooting Samir, the gunman whirled toward me.

I parried his rotation with the gun in my right hand, a ridiculous sword fight using pistols. He put another round into the front of the SUV, and I hammered him in the face with a left cross. I controlled his gun hand and squeezed toward the cab, allowing Brett access to his body. I disarmed him, and in short order Brett had him subdued on the ground.

I scanned for other threats and saw Decoy covering a man on his knees, hands behind his head. Jennifer's target was still hanging out of the window, but wasn't moving.

"Koko, you good?"

"Yeah," she said. "He's out. No issues. Just holding him here in case he wakes up."

I leaned into the SUV. "You okay?"

Samir was ashen, but his voice was strong. "Yes. Thank you."

I wanted to take a moment to relax, but knew we had little time. Sooner or later, someone was going to report this activity, even here in Lebanon. The response would be slow, since the police would more than likely want to sweep up the brass instead of get in the middle of a sectarian fight, but they *would* be coming.

I leaned down to the man on the ground, figuring since he had the gun on Samir, he was in charge.

"What's your name?"

He said nothing. Samir said, "He's Abu Aziz. Head of security for Majid's cell."

"Okay. Aziz it is. Look, I know you don't believe this, but I don't mean you any harm whatsoever. In fact, I think we can help each other out. You think Samir had something to do with killing Majid, but he didn't. I think I know who did, and I want him as bad as you."

Aziz remained mute, his eyes filled with a hatred that radiated out like a physical thing. *Jesus. No way am I going to convince this maniac.*

I tried again. "The man is an American, but doesn't work for the government. He's tried to kill me and some friends of mine, and I want him bad."

Still no reaction. No response but the hatred.

"He worked for you. I don't know what name he gave you, but you called him Infidel."

I saw a flicker in his eyes, a crack in the facade. The name had hit a nerve.

I was carefully choosing my next words when Knuckles called, "Pike, Pike, white sedan approaching at a high rate of speed."

43

I heard the supersonic crack of Knuckles's rifle at the same time I located the sedan, about two hundred meters behind us. It swerved, but kept coming. The right front tire disintegrated, strips of rubber flung out as the driver continued on the rim alone. It screeched to a halt adjacent to the van, sparks flying from the steel rim grinding on concrete and gravel. The driver jumped out, wildly swinging an AK around, finally settling his sights on the closest target—Jennifer sitting inside the van, holding the head of his friend.

He began to scream in Arabic, which did absolutely no good. I trained my pistol on him and spoke out of the side of my mouth.

"Aziz, tell him to put the weapon down. Don't turn this into a gunfight. Tell him to quit."

Aziz said nothing. *This not being allowed to kill anyone is starting to piss me off.*

I shouted at the man, my pistol still trained on him. He swung his weapon toward me, then back at Jennifer, as if he couldn't make up his mind. In a low voice, I said, "Knuckles, you got a shot?"

"Yeah. Clean headshot."

"I mean a nonlethal hit. Can you take him down without killing him?"

"Not now. Need to get him away from the car. All I have right now is his upper body."

"All right. Got it. I'll get him to walk toward me, then knock him down."

"Your call, but no promises. It's not like I'm holding a custom long-gun here. I'll hit him, but if it rips into his femoral or tumbles somewhere else, I can't stop it."

"Yeah, yeah, I get it."

I shouted again, getting the gunman's attention, feeling like a cop trying to talk a meth addict off the ledge. The guy even looked like a meth addict. I pointed my weapon at Aziz, still subdued on the ground by Brett. The gunman followed the barrel, and recognition dawned for the first time. His eyes wide, he began screaming again. I waved him forward, then raised my hands in a gesture of surrender. My weapon was pointed harmlessly in the air, but my subconscious was screaming to split his head open. *This is why I would never have made it as a police officer.*

Feeling more confident, he walked slowly toward us, sighting down the barrel of the AK. He broke the plane of the front of the vehicle, then whipsawed onto the ground as if his thigh had been hit with an invisible sledgehammer. A split second later, the crack of the bullet reached our ears, and I was on him, first subduing, then providing first aid for the large in-and-out hole in his thigh.

WE REACHED THE FOOTHILLS of the Chouf Mountains, and I saw Aziz's eyes squint, in his mind believing I had lied, and he was now being turned over to the Druze for some incredible torture. I told Brett to signal Knuckles and Jennifer in the car to our front, then pull over.

"I wasn't lying before. I mean you no harm. We came here because it's the only safe place I know. I have no idea who's going to be looking for you in the *Dahiyeh,* but nobody here knows what's gone on. Samir specifically asked for my help because he was afraid of another civil war. I was told I couldn't harm anyone, and I tried to live up to my promise."

He looked at me with distrust, but there was a little spark of hope in his eyes that made me think he was putting on an act. *Maybe this'll work out.*

We'd fled the scene of our assault immediately after Knuckles's sniper shot, linking up with his car south of the airport. He'd hit the guy hard in the thigh, but had missed the femoral artery. We bandaged him with some QuikClot and morphine from our aid bag, checking his vitals every few minutes. He'd live but he wasn't going to a hospital anytime soon. We'd packed all of them into our van and left their two vehicles behind. I'd flex-cuffed each of their ankles and wrists, but offered water and treated them with respect.

I said, "We'll get your man to a hospital as soon as we

can, but I want you to watch something first. Will you do that?"

Aziz nodded his head, and Decoy sat him upright. I placed a computer in front of him, and explained what he was about to see, lying about how we had gotten it.

I hit play, keeping my eye on Aziz's facial expressions. The jerky image began, and I could tell immediately that Aziz recognized the surroundings, even if we didn't. That was a definite plus because he'd know we hadn't faked the film. No way could we have re-created some inner sanctum of Hezbollah. The boy entered the frame, and the truth began to solidify. Aziz began to believe. When he saw the boy die, he strained against his bonds so hard I had to hold him back. I knew at that moment that Samir was safe.

The WAV file ended with Lucas still on the screen, a grainy, bloody image that punctuated his crimes. I waited.

Aziz said, "What do you want from me?"

"Do you see?"

"Yes," he hissed, "yes, I see who is to blame. And he will pay, no matter where he goes."

"Well, then, we're on the same sheet of music. I want him to pay as well, and you people know more about him than anyone else. Did you give him anything we can track? Any cell phones or other devices? Anything at all?"

He smiled for the first time. "Why would I help the CIA? I can do this on my own. Leave us be. I understand your methods and won't seek retribution. Samir is safe."

Brett and Decoy heard him and smiled, thinking we

had mission-complete. They waited on me to say something sane, like "Okey-dokey. We're out of here." Instead, I said, "We don't work for the CIA. We don't work for the U.S. government. Infidel is personal to us. I want him, and you can help. If you get him first, so be it, but I'm still going to hunt him."

I saw Brett shake his head and scowl. I waited on Aziz. I could see his mind working over the issue, wondering about potential downsides. Wondering what he could give us that would let them go. Something harmless.

He finally said, "He had a cell phone, but he's no longer using it."

"What's the number?"

He gave it to me, and I didn't recognize it as a Lebanese number.

"What's this? Where's it from?"

Samir spoke up. "It's their internal network. An internal phone."

Shit. No good to us. It wouldn't work anywhere outside of Lebanon. I saw a small smirk on Aziz's face. He'd given what he could and knew it wouldn't help.

I said, "Watch them," and exited the van, walking to Knuckles's car.

He rolled down the window. "How's it going back there?"

"About even. Samir's okay, but I'm getting little help on Lucas."

"Well, let's call it a win."

"Maybe. You have a Taskforce phone?"

He looked at me warily. "Yeah. Why?"

I passed him the number. "See if they can track this. Get us a historical pattern. I'm looking for his bed-down site before he left. Last ninety-six hours, focusing on repeated locations."

He studied the number, then said, "Pike, they need to know the network. They can't just crack 'Lebanon phone directory.' This number doesn't even look real."

"It's Hezbollah's internal network."

"What the hell are they going to do with that?"

Jennifer spoke up. "You sure it's the internal network?"

"Yeah. No doubt."

She turned to Knuckles. "Tell 'em to look at Cedar Hill's reporting. He's already cracked the network and passed it to them. They're sitting on it right now."

"Cedar Hill? Who's that?"

"Louis Britt, the Taskforce case officer here. The one that helped us infil you and gave us the location of the computer we hit. He's already passed the information on Hezbollah's network."

Knuckles pulled out his smartphone and started typing a secure text to a number that would never be used again. I was a little concerned that the request would bounce back to Kurt in one way or another, but figured the little minions who did such work would just assume it a standard request from a deployed team. Especially since it was coming from Knuckles's phone and not mine. At least that's what I hoped. If Kurt found out we were operational without Council sanction, I was going to get roasted.

It took a couple of back-and-forths over text, but eventually, the hackers in the rear locked onto the network. In twenty minutes, Knuckles had the tower track of the phone. The last connection was more than forty-eight hours ago, but when we brought up a map, we had one location it had stayed overnight for two consecutive nights. A hotel. *The bed-down location.*

"All right. I'm going to get Samir. We'll go to the hotel and see what we can find out. I'll send Decoy and Brett up to Samir's house. They can hole up with the Hezbollah guys until we get back."

"What then?"

"We get out of here. One way or another."

44

The hotel was a small, boutique affair with less than fifteen rooms that catered to frugal travelers. It was clean, with a utilitarian lobby that was only thirty feet across. The receptionist was almost fawning at first, probably because they'd lost a ton of tourism dollars due to the upheavals in the Arab world and thought we were looking for a place to stay. As soon as we began asking questions about Lucas, using his Canadian identity, her demeanor shifted. She gave us the usual stonewall about not being able to discuss guests for privacy reasons, but she looked fearful, glancing at a door to her rear as if she hoped someone would bail her out of the conversation. *He's been here, and something happened.*

I was about to request to talk to a manager when Samir touched my arm. I thanked the woman and backed off. Samir motioned toward the exit, and we followed him. He approached a young man of about nineteen or twenty, filling up a mop bucket. The boy smiled and shook Samir's hand. They held a conversation for about three minutes in Arabic. When it was done, Samir pulled us aside.

"He's a cousin of my wife. Your Infidel was here. He checked out yesterday morning, early. He also raped a woman in his room. A university student and the daughter of a very influential businessman. The maid found her tied to the bed when she came to clean. The family has ordered the entire episode to be kept secret, to save the daughter's honor. That's why the receptionist was acting the way she was."

"Does he know who she is?"

"Yes, he goes to the university with her, that's how he knows her. He saw her leaving the hotel that morning, crying."

"Where can we find her?"

"Pike, I don't think this is something we want to dig around in. It could cause trouble. The family is a powerful Sunni one."

"Just ask him."

He stepped over and exchanged some words, then came back.

"He gave me a café she frequents during the day. He said she'll have classes starting in about an hour and might be there because the family has ordered her to act naturally, like nothing has happened. They don't want any questions that could lead to her dishonor. Her name is Fatima Ruzami."

"Okay, get us to the café and have him point her out. Only Jennifer and I will go in. She'll clam up if she has to talk in front of a Lebanese, but maybe not to some Westerners. Especially another woman."

The café was only a few minutes away, which was good, because we were now driving around like a circus car stuffed with clowns. Knuckles dropped us outside, and I had the cousin lead the way. The café had several tables lining the sidewalk left and right of the entrance, most empty. Before we reached the door, he pointed to a woman sitting alone at the farthest table outside, a small espresso in front of her.

"That's her?"

"Yes."

"Thanks for the help. You need a ride back to the hotel?"

"No thank you. I'll walk."

I waited until he disappeared, studying the woman. She was clearly attractive, with long, black hair and a trim figure. She was wearing stylish Western clothing and dark sunglasses. She remained still, not touching her espresso or looking around.

Jennifer said, "Let me start the conversation."

"My thoughts exactly. Let's go."

She didn't react to us until we'd actually sat down, me across the table and Jennifer next to her.

Jennifer gave her a warm smile and said, "Hello, Fatima. Don't be alarmed. We're friends."

Fatima started at her name and made a move to stand. Jennifer put a hand on her arm and said, "Please, Fatima, we know what happened to you. We aren't here to cause you trouble. We're here to catch the man who did it. Outside of Lebanon. Nobody will know we talked."

She sat back down, but said nothing.

"This is Pike, and I'm Jennifer."

She looked at me, then at Jennifer, but remained mute. I would have liked to read her eyes, but was prevented by her large sunglasses.

Jennifer continued, placing her hand over Fatima's on the table. "I know a little about what you're going through. I had a husband who beat me. I was able to get some payback and want to do the same for you."

Fatima sniffled, then removed her sunglasses to wipe away the beginnings of a tear. Her right eye was swollen and purple, the white inside bloodshot. *That son of a bitch.*

She said, "My family won't let me talk. They won't do anything. My *honor* is more important than catching this monster." She spat the word *honor* with disgust.

Jennifer reached out and grasped her other hand, squeezing tightly. I could see tears starting to form in her eyes as well, and I knew it wasn't an act.

"Help us. Can you tell us anything at all? Did he talk about hotels, where he had been or where he was going? Did you see any receipts, anything like that?"

"No. There was no time. I went back to his room for a cup of coffee, and he attacked me immediately. He hit me, then he tore my clothes off. I fought him, but . . . he threw me on the bed. He . . . he . . ." She broke down, sobbing with her head in her chest.

Jennifer said, "It's okay. It's okay."

I spoke for the first time. "How did you meet? Was this the only time you had seen him?"

"Yes. I was at a disco with girlfriends from the university. My phone buzzed, and there was a text. It was from him. My girlfriends had given my number to him, and I thought it was cute for him to introduce himself that way. Imaginative, unlike the usual things I see. He was handsome, so I texted back. We texted back and forth for a while, then he approached. He was charming and friendly. At first. I wish I'd forgotten my phone that night. He would have picked someone else."

I was trying to think of another line of questioning when what she said sent a bolt of adrenaline through me.

"He texted you? That night?"

His Hezbollah phone had been dead for more than forty-eight hours, which meant it was another phone.

"Yes."

I asked, "Do you still have this text?" And held my breath.

A sharp laugh escaped. "Yes. I was going to turn it over to the police, when I thought anyone cared about justice."

She pulled out her phone and showed me the text. With an international number tied to it.

Bingo.

45

"You were just here two days ago. And you're coming back?"

Lucas Kane gave his most relaxing smile, knowing that no matter what he did, it would look insincere. He just couldn't get the smile to reach his eyes, as if he actually gave a shit. Which was fine with him. He could turn the smile into something that scared hardened men if it came to it, and he had nothing to hide at Dubai immigration. Yet.

"Yes. I was called away to Qatar suddenly for business. A little emergency that turned out to be nothing. Now I'm back."

The official studied his passport as if he could glean the secrets of what Lucas had been doing the past forty-eight hours. Lucas inwardly grinned. The man was trying to find something to stop him. Some reason to harass him simply because he didn't like Lucas's shark teeth. *He would shit his pants if he knew what I've been up to. And what I'm going to do.*

Two days ago, he'd flown into Dubai just long enough

to bribe the *hawaladar*, giving him a briefcase embedded with a beacon. It had taken some work, but he'd disassembled a GPS-enabled cell phone to its bare components, concealing it in a false bottom of an old leather hardside. He'd paid the guy handsomely to use the briefcase to deliver the money to the Ghost. After that, he'd had only two hours to spare before his flight to Qatar and had used it to find a secure meeting site for his Hezbollah contact. Secure in the sense it would keep him alive.

"What business are you in?" asked the official.

"Pest control. I'm consulting with hotels here and in Qatar."

"Where are you staying?"

"The Al Bustan Rotana."

The official had him look into the camera-stalk for a picture and stamped his passport, grudgingly giving it back. *Man, they've got more photos of me than the* Enquirer *does of Angelina Jolie. Last time I'll set foot in this country.*

He passed through customs, collected his rental, and took the short drive to the Al Bustan Rotana Hotel just east of the airport. The midday sun was blistering, causing his sunglasses to fog on the brief walk from the parking garage to the lobby.

Inside, he could see the early preparations beginning for the envoy's visit. Metal detectors were in place on the front door, but not yet operational, and one bank of elevators was undergoing some sort of inspection. Checking into his suite on the fourth floor, he played stupid when the receptionist directed him to the south bank of elevators, asking why. He acted surprised when told of the arrival of the U.S. delegation, saying, "I hope it won't cause too big a disruption."

She said, "As long as you stay on the south side, you'll be fine. The delegation has the entire northeast wing of the fourth floor. Please avoid it for security reasons."

He hadn't purposely asked for a room on the same floor, but was pleased it had worked out that way. If the Ghost planned an attack here, it would be better to be closer, although he didn't see any way that could happen. The hotel would be a fortress in two days.

Inside his suite, he immediately connected to the Internet on a tablet computer, bringing up the track of his beacon. The Ghost had taken the briefcase earlier this morning, and the track showed him inside the spice souk in Deira old city, right on the banks of the Dubai Creek. The beacon had remained there for six hours. Clearly, he didn't have the briefcase with him, which was expected. All Lucas wanted was a start point. He had plenty of time to work with. The Ghost surely had a plan and would begin implementing it, but the envoy wasn't due for three days. Plenty of time to develop a pattern of life and eliminate the threat.

The souk posed a problem, though. It was a place that would prevent him from conducting surveillance for any length of time. He'd be able to blend in with the usual jerk-off tourists, but couldn't hang around without drawing attention. He knew from experience that areas like this were transitory in nature, with a constant flow of people. Tourists wouldn't get a second glance. As long as they moved on. Attempting to maintain surveillance on the stairwell of the beacon location would invite scrutiny that would be remembered by the locals manning the stalls.

He shut down the tablet and thought about his options. The kill would have to be quiet. Someplace that would allow him to escape Dubai before the body was found. Which, given the enormous number of cameras all over the damn city, meant jerking the Ghost into a van or some other vehicle. It also meant he'd need help, but that was okay. He'd already planned for that and alerted the Hezbollah contacts here. He just didn't know if they were still on his side.

He'd had no trouble in Qatar, getting explosives from a Hezbollah cell that was eager to help, but that had been more than twenty-four hours ago. No telling what had come about during that time. He had two hours before the meeting he'd established, but decided to go early to see if he could catch anyone setting up. *Better to be prepared.*

He left his rental in the garage and took a cab to the Dubai Mall, a monstrous shopping center that housed everything from high-end jewelry stores to an indoor aquarium.

In order to ensure his safety, he needed a meeting spot in a crowded location that allowed him to blend in. Some place where the preponderance of people weren't Arabic. On his reconnaissance two days ago, the Dubai Mall had fit the bill. It was frequented by tourists and expats from Europe and Asia, and he would have no trouble wandering around without drawing attention.

Finding the operational setting, he had begun to search for the tactical components he needed. A place that had a single chokepoint, allowing him to identify his contact before the meeting. He had found it in the indoor aquarium.

Like everything in Dubai, from the towering Burj Khalifa next door to the indoor ski slope a few miles away, the aquarium had its own "best" pedigree, with the largest plate of acrylic viewing-glass in the world. Lucas didn't give a shit about Dubai's endless attempts to set another record, but he had liked the entrance of the ticket counter that channeled everyone into the aquarium.

He took a seat at an ice-cream shop across from the admission counter, ordered a sundae, and waited. Thirty minutes before the meet he saw two Arab men approach the ticket booth. Both were dressed in Western clothing, like everyone else entering the aquarium. They stood out anyway, as most of the patrons were Western tourists or Arabic families with children. They didn't talk to each other in line, like the other patrons, but instead nervously swiveled their heads left and right, as if they were afraid a pickpocket was on the prowl.

Strike one.

The instructions had specifically stated the contact should come alone. The fact that two men were together didn't necessarily mean that something was amiss, since Lucas had no idea what the contact looked like, but it certainly amped things up a bit.

One of the men was rail-thin, with a long neck that showcased a large Adam's apple. The other had a pudgy gut held in by sweatpants, giving the man the appearance of a couch potato. Observing closer, Lucas saw long, powerful arms that belied the first impression, reminding him of a gorilla. Sinister and simian.

Lucas waited until the meeting was two minutes out, seeing four other possible contacts entering as singletons. It looked like he'd been wrong about the demographics, with more single Arabs entering the aquarium than he'd predicted. There was no way they were all out to get him, and one of them was the contact.

Only one way to find out.

46

Lucas entered the aquarium. Ignoring the displays to his left and right, he wound around to the back, threading through the throngs of people. He saw two of the singletons gazing at fish tanks and discounted them. Reaching the rear, he glanced at his watch, then burned thirty seconds at a souvenir kiosk, pretending to look at trinkets, but really eyeballing a stairwell. Nobody went up except kids.

Lucas's final tactical consideration for the meet had been a location that prevented anyone from closing on him while he was conducting it. A secure area that allowed him to observe those around him without announcing he was conducting any business. He'd located it in a rope bridge that traversed throughout the aquarium. Hanging just below the roof and connected to faux trees from a simulated rain forest, it facilitated unobstructed views to the pathways of the aquarium below and canalized anyone approaching by restricting them to the rope bridge itself.

At ten seconds out, he mounted the stairs, brushing past children bouncing up and down on the bridge.

Ahead, at the first anchor tree, the skinny man with the Adam's apple leaned on the ropes of the bridge, looking down. He held a metro schedule in his right hand.

Right time, right place, right bona fides. His chubby partner was nowhere to be seen. Lucas approached and said, "This mall is amazing."

The man started, then, in a stilted voice that spat out syllables like a metronome, said, "It is the largest in the world."

Lucas grinned at his pathetic delivery and held out his hand. After they shook, he said, "I'm the Infidel, and I understand you can help me."

The contact nodded nervously, and Lucas returned to watching the mass of people below. In short order, he found the chubby man simply because he wasn't moving. Another reason Lucas had picked this location. Anyone conducting surveillance would be sifted as the rest of the patrons walked through the aquarium, standing out like a rock against the water of a stream.

Lucas continued, not looking at the contact. "The mission for you is threefold, but simple. One, I need weapons. Nothing fancy. A pistol will do. Two, I need you to stake out a place in one of the Deira souks and alert me when a man leaves. Three, I need a van and you to drive it. Can you do this?"

"Yes. Yes, I can. In fact, I have a van right here at the mall. I would prefer to finish the discussion there."

Lucas agreed. He didn't mind giving specifics of the mission. If the contact was truly going to help, he would have to know who he was hunting. If he wasn't, he would be dead.

They walked to the parking-garage exit, near the entrance to the Burj Khalifa observation deck, the chubby man nowhere in sight.

They reached a dented white cargo van, no windows on the sides and enough dust on the rear to prevent anyone from seeing inside. As they approached, Lucas studied the surroundings. The van sat by itself, rows back from more convenient parking spots closer to the mall entrance. Looking at the walls and ceilings, Lucas realized the spot had been picked because it was outside of any surveillance cameras.

Strike two.

Appearing as if he sensed nothing amiss, he entered the passenger seat. The contact circled to the driver's seat, his eyes wide, a thin film of sweat on his upper lip. He attempted to smile, but failed. He said, "Show me on a map where you wish me to find your target."

He reached behind the seat, and Lucas considered killing him outright. He decided to wait. He needed the help and wasn't absolutely convinced the man intended harm. When the contact faced back around he held an ancient revolver.

Shit. Strike three.

Instead of fear, Lucas felt disappointment. His mission had just become much harder to accomplish.

He said, "I suppose we're now waiting on your friend."

The contact's face went white, his hand shaking so much the barrel of the revolver twitched. "I know about you. I was told of your skills. Get in the back. Now."

Lucas said, "They're lying. I had nothing to do with any Hezbollah deaths."

The man gripped the pistol with both hands, attempting to stop his tremors. "I didn't say anything about Hezbollah deaths. Get in back."

Lucas did so, before the man cocked the hammer to punctuate his request. As it was, the revolver was in double-action mode, which meant a heavy trigger pull and little chance the contact would accidentally fire the weapon in his nervous state. With the hammer back, the trigger became much, much lighter. Something Lucas didn't want as he waited for the gorilla friend. He needed to kill them both.

They waited in silence for thirty seconds, then the chubby man entered the back of the van, leading with a semiautomatic pistol. The contact exhaled his pent-up breath and said something in Arabic. The gorilla answered, then turned to Lucas.

"Abu Aziz wants you killed slowly, and after he told me what you did, I can't wait to get started."

Lucas took the sentence as a good omen, as he had assumed they meant to kill him right here. It would give him time to think. The gorilla pointed the pistol directly at his face and barked at the contact. Lucas heard the ignition turn over, focusing on the weapon inches from his nose. It was an old Colt 1911, and Lucas found it ironic that he was being threatened by the distinctly American armament.

The van began to move, and he noticed the hammer was down on this pistol as well. The opportunity popped in his head immediately. Unlike the revolver, the Colt was single-action. Meaning it couldn't be fired with the hammer down *at all*. It was nothing more than a paperweight.

Dumbass.

Lucas's hands struck like a snake, using the metal of the pistol itself to lock up the joints in the man's wrist. He rotated violently and heard the wrist crack, then lashed out with an elbow, crunching the Arab's nose.

The gorilla bellowed and wrapped his good arm around Lucas's neck, squeezing with all of his might. Lucas felt his eyes bulge and his windpipe begin to crush. He slammed his head back, but hit only air. He drummed both elbows into the man's gut, getting little response. He attempted to swim a hand between his neck and the man's arm, but it was as tight as a python and strong. Very, very strong.

Dimly, Lucas heard the contact shouting, attempting to drive and aim his revolver at the same time. The pain in his neck was blossoming out, strong enough to overshadow the lack of air. He threw a hammer fist between his legs, connecting with the man's genitals, the sweatpants providing no protection. The man jerked, and Lucas felt the air return.

He snaked his hand low again and closed his fingers

like a claw on the man's penis and testicles, attempting to rip his genitals from his body. He heard a high-pitched shriek, and the arm loosened enough to allow him to snake his other hand underneath it.

Maintaining his grip on the prized possessions, Lucas rotated under and out of the arm. Like a thing possessed, he used his free hand to pound the man's face, not stopping until he was on top of the prostrate body and the head was bouncing lifeless with each blow.

He was rocked forward as the van slammed to a stop. He rose up on his knees and saw the contact scrambling to rotate around, the revolver in one hand. He snatched the driver-side seatbelt, attempting to wrap it around the contact's neck while he was still in the seat. He missed, catching him across the face. He jerked to the rear, and the contact's head whipped back over the headrest, forcing him to bow his body out to relieve the strain.

Lucas kicked the revolver out of his grip and jerked the belt with both hands, bending his spine backward. The contact began to scream, clawing at the belt.

Lucas leaned in, watching the man's chest rise and fall, seeing the long neck in front of him, the Adam's apple bobbing up and down. An easy target.

He cranked the belt a little tighter and leaned in to the contact's ear. "You said you knew about me. About my skills. And they sent your skinny ass to take me out?"

The victim's eyes were huge, wildly rolling around looking for help. Some miracle to salvage his life. His arms ineffectually batted the air, trying to connect with the devil behind. Lucas said, "Time to meet the virgins."

He hammered the Adam's apple with a closed fist. The contact thrashed, his destroyed throat desperately trying to gain life-giving air. Lucas hammered it again. Then again. The contact stopped moving, and Lucas took stock of his status.

The mission was more than likely screwed. He had no help to pinpoint the Ghost and had lord knows how many men now hunting him. On the other hand, he could probably hire a local to trigger. Pay him simply to tell when the Ghost left. He'd told the contact he had three requirements. He now had a weapon and a van.

Two out of three ain't bad.

47

The Ghost patted the briefcase and said, "Be very care-ful with this. The components are not shockproof."

Hamid nodded. "I will, don't worry. Are you sure you can find the maintenance door?"

"Yes. You said simply exit the mall and walk around the right side of the Burj Khalifa. Find the first stairwell, walk down it, and knock three times."

"Yes. I'll be there. With the detonators and the explo-sives. Don't forget your uniform."

After settling into Hamid's flat, the Ghost had spent the remainder of the previous day breaking out the explo-sives from the computer case and monitor, then con-structing the detonators. All that remained was sticking the blasting caps into the explosives, then dialing the det-onators into the Burj Khalifa's Wi-Fi network.

He'd removed the *hawaladar* money from the brief-case and built a makeshift nest to protect the delicate electronics of the detonators. The explosives themselves were in a different duffel bag, separated from the blasting caps to prevent a catastrophic event.

The Ghost said, "I'll meet you at eleven."

"Okay. Are you sure you don't want my car?"

"Yes. I want the ability to use multiple methods of travel. I had some issues in Yemen, and there might be someone trying to find me. I don't want to make it easy on them."

He picked up the knapsack containing his money and Hamid's uniform and left the flat. He reached the ground level and surveyed around him, trying to see if anyone paid undue attention. He saw nothing but men, young and old, hawking their spices. He exited the souk and walked northwest on Al Kabeer Street, paralleling the Dubai Creek, headed to a section of town that sold electronics. He still needed an initiation device, and hoped to find it there. Hitting the first street outside the souk, he moved slowly, as if to get his bearings, but really to take a snapshot of the vehicles parked near the exit. He saw nothing suspicious.

The coolness of the morning was quickly burning off. In short order, he was sweating from the walk. He missed his turn in the congested maze of roads and was forced to backtrack until he reached Al Sabkha Road. Turning north, he walked for two blocks, until the stores on his left and right began advertising cameras, watches, and cell phones. He saw a sign for electronic security and entered a tiny mall, seeing the store in the back corner.

The shop seemed to specialize in alarms and surveillance cameras, but might have what he needed. He looked around the aisles for a few minutes, and then simply asked a clerk.

"I wish to purchase an IMSI grabber for cell phones. Do you sell them?"

"Yes, but only to government or the police. I can't sell them to people off the street."

"I need one that operates on batteries. It must have a life span of at least four hours, but doesn't need to do anything fancy. It must simply register the cell phone numbers and hold the phone. The only thing I need is an alarm when an identified number appears."

"I just told you I can't sell you the device. Sorry."

The Ghost leaned closer and opened his knapsack, showing the clerk a large wad of dinars. "I will pay you handsomely. Both for the device and for the service you provide in selling it to me."

The clerk glanced to the front door, then back at the knapsack.

"It will cost you a lot of money. I'm supposed to register the sale, and I will be taking a risk."

The Ghost simply nodded. The clerk made up his mind and locked the front door, turning around the "open" sign.

He went in the back and came out with a container a little bigger than a shoebox. He opened it, showing the Ghost the device.

"This has a range of about one hundred meters in the open. Of course, it will be much less with walls or other things in the way."

He spent the next few minutes demonstrating the workings of the device, showing him the battery indicator, the alarm settings, and the basic operations. The Ghost listened for a little bit, then said, "I can get the rest from the manual. I need two more."

"Three? Why on earth do you need three?"

"I have three locations. It isn't your concern."

The clerk hesitated, weighing the risk. The Ghost dropped the bundle of dinars on the counter.

"Get them."

Twenty minutes later he was back on the street, looking for a dry-goods store. He found one and bought four scrub brushes, the metal bristles three inches long and mated to a steel handle. He stepped out and caught a cab.

When he arrived at the Dubai Mall, he immediately searched for a restroom. He changed into Hamid's Burj Khalifa maintenance uniform and exited the mall on the south side, walking around the manmade lake until he reached the parking garage. The sidewalk ended, putting him in the drive for the mall itself. Following Hamid's directions, he continued around, keeping the Burj Khalifa to his left, towering over him like a giant metal obelisk.

He reached the stairwell just as a white-panel van came up the drive, forcing him to hop on the curb. He turned into the stairwell and did a double take. He couldn't be sure, but he believed the van driving toward the garage was the same one that had been outside the souk when he initially left. After Yemen, his survival instincts had become hyperaware, and the van sent a subconscious alarm into his primal core.

He watched it disappear, seeing a Caucasian male in the passenger seat. He continued down to the door, reflecting on its importance. Odds were it was nothing, but he didn't like playing the odds. He hadn't seen the driver, but if it *was* following him, it would be from Hezbollah. He couldn't afford to discount it even if it was a Westerner.

He banged the door three times and stepped back. Hamid opened and smiled.

"The building is yours. The observation deck elevators are at the hundred and twenty-fourth floor, like you asked."

"How long before they are used?"

"The first tour is at one p.m., so you have two hours."

"Perfect. Let's go."

They took a service elevator with the first button marked 100. It took a full minute to reach that level. From there, they took the stairs to the 125th floor, and the maintenance room for the observation deck elevators. The Ghost left Hamid outside for early warning and entered alone.

He had done quite a bit of research on elevators in the past twenty-four hours and knew exactly what he was looking for. He needed to intercept two things—the cables holding up the elevator and the brake system that would cause it to stop if the cables failed. The bank of elevators to the observation deck consisted of two double-deck Otis systems. Two targets that the envoy would have to use, a chokepoint that would cause his death. The only other way up to the observation deck was the stairs.

He immediately moved to the roof of the first, nestled at the top with the edge of the elevator level to the shelf left and right. The cables from the elevator roof attached to the pulley above with a space of a few feet between them. He broke out the explosives, already configured to cut steel.

Both elevators had five cables, all able to support the suspended weight of the cars by themselves. He would have to cut all five. He affixed two small charges to each cable, slightly offset, one high, one low. When detonated, the opposite charges would cause a cutting effect and sever the cable. The trick was ensuring that the subsequent explosions to the cables left and right didn't counteract the very cutting he sought to achieve. Fortunately, he had plenty of cable to work with to ensure success.

Within ten minutes, he had the basics of destruction in place. He then attached the Wi-Fi detonator, but did not attach the blasting caps, leaving them dangling from the detonator like the legs of a spider. The detonators themselves were inert, waiting on a wireless signal to arm. Dropping to the top of the elevator, he pulled out the brushes he had purchased. He affixed one to the roof of the elevator, hanging out into the four-inch gap between the elevator and the well. He placed the second brush to the shelf of the well itself, until the bristles touched across the gap.

He then pulled out the IMSI grabber and set it on the roof of the elevator. Before he forgot, he turned off his cell phone. He attached a micro USB cable from the download hub of the grabber, then cut off the female end, exposing bare wire. He attached the wire to the steel of the brush on the elevator. He then jumped across the well, placed the Wi-Fi transmitter for the detonators on the shelf, and cut the USB cable for it as well, splicing it into the brush on the far side.

When he was complete, he typed his cell phone number into the IMSI grabber alarm function and powered it up, waiting a minute until it was operational. He saw it sucking in numbers from all over the building.

Having been on the receiving end of cell phone compromises in Lebanon, he'd made a concerted effort to understand their function. He knew that all cell phones constantly look for the tower with the greatest signal strength, switching back and forth seamlessly to the user. It was a distinctly modern weakness that he intended to exploit.

The IMSI grabber acted like a miniature cell tower, causing any cell phones in range to register with it. Used by law enforcement—and other, unsavory types—to collate data and potentially listen in to cell conversations, it would lock up any cell phone in range, rendering the phone useless. In this case, it would also trigger the explosives. All the Ghost had to do was input the envoy's number into the grabber, once he found it.

He turned on his cell phone. Within seconds, his number appeared in the IMSI grabber, the phone duped into thinking it was the closest tower. A red LED lit up, signaling the alarm. He looked at the Wi-Fi transmitter and saw a green LED. The detonator on the cables lit up as well, calmly blinking on and off. The connection worked.

Now, had he inserted the blasting caps, the system would be armed. When the elevator began to lower again, the connection between the brushes would be broken, and the explosives would go off—sending the envoy to his demise in a terrifying free fall.

He smiled at the thought. At the ingenuity of the plan. The grisly death would be perfect for propaganda. To show the world the might of the Palestinian people, no matter the ridiculous attempts at peace going on.

He reset the IMSI grabber, zeroing out his phone number. He saw the green LEDs shut off and inserted the blasting caps.

In twenty-four minutes the second elevator was rigged exactly like the first. He had no idea which elevator the envoy would be in and wanted to ensure both fell to their doom.

Finished with the primary, he searched for the brake cable of both elevators. Unless the cable was cut, the elevator would fall for about a floor, then be gradually slowed by friction applied to the rails through specially constructed shoes. The brake itself was triggered by the speed of the elevator. If the cable attached to it reached a certain velocity, a flywheel was engaged, causing the brakes to be applied.

For the first time, he noticed no other cable. The brake should have been on the side, away from the main cables holding the weight of the elevator itself, but there was nothing. He made a concerted search and came up dry.

He exited the room, finding Hamid nervously talking to a businessman from one of the upper-floor suites. He waited until the man walked away, then approached. Hamid was sweating profusely, his skin sickly white.

"What was that about?"

"Nothing. He simply wanted to report a faulty bathroom."

The Ghost realized Hamid had no stomach for the work. He regretted showing his hand with the elevators, knowing Hamid would spill his guts if captured. *He's not a fighter. I shouldn't have placed so much on him.* It sank home that he needed to eliminate the weakness. Get rid of the link that would cause failure. He looked at Hamid's wilted face, slightly panting, and knew he wouldn't. Couldn't. What was to come was to come. He didn't have it in him to kill his friend and wished he had not drawn on him for help. Wished he'd used Hezbollah contacts instead, even given the risk.

"Where is the brake cable for the elevators? I can't find it."

"There is no cable. It's a new system that works on radar. It's computer controlled and constantly monitored. A network continuously assesses the speed of the elevator, and if it reaches a certain velocity, it shunts the brakes."

"Where is this system?"

"In the basement we entered."

In short order, they were back where they started, with Hamid showing the braking architecture. It consisted of a radar array aimed up into each elevator shaft, reading the speed of the cars, not unlike the radar guns used in a police speed trap.

The Ghost said, "Can we just shut it off? Disable it?"

"No. The elevators go through a computerized self-test. If the brake system isn't in operation, neither is the elevator."

The Ghost opened his cell phone, enabled the Wi-Fi feature, and saw he had no signal. Which meant there was no way to initiate explosives down here. He couldn't slave into the main on the elevators.

"Where is the last Wi-Fi node? How far does it extend?"

"I honestly don't know, but I do know the lobby for the Armani Hotel is right above us, and it has Wi-Fi."

The Ghost considered. He would have to return to the electronics souk and buy a Wi-Fi repeater, but it should work. If he placed one in the shaft of the elevator, it should be able to expand the signal from the lobby and allow his system to talk. He had to come back here tomorrow to input the American's cell phone number anyway. The problem was he would have little time, risking the envoy setting off the trap while he was still constructing it.

It was the best he could do.

48

My cell phone vibrated with a single word: *JACKPOT*. I dialed Decoy's phone. "Hey, man, you can't simply send a text like that. What do you have?"

"The phone grid was right on. It's his. He's sitting in a white-panel van outside a small indoor shopping area. No movement. Doesn't appear to be doing anything in the van. Just sitting."

I thought about what Lucas could be doing. "What's in the shopping center? Can you tell?"

"Looks like electronics. Cell phones, cameras, that sort of thing. He's got a local in the driver's seat, but they're not talking."

So he has help. I didn't want to talk too much on an open cell phone, and let the rest of my questions drift away. We'd left our concealed radios and other kit in Lebanon, and until we could get more, I was stuck with a standard cell phone. Knuckles, Decoy, and Brett had their Taskforce phones, which allowed them to communicate together in real time, but I could only go point-to-point, which was going to be a pain in the ass as surveillance chief.

We'd gotten the go-ahead to launch to Dubai last night. It was a little bit of good news/bad news for me. I'd told Kurt we had a lead, then how we'd found it. Saying he was a little pissed was putting it mildly. He'd about ripped the computer apart in front of him. In the end, I'd convinced him that I'd used my judgment, just like I was paid to do, and we'd found a solid anchor for Lucas. I knew he'd calm down, because he was smart enough to know there was no sense yelling about it now. What's done is done.

He'd spent a little more time chewing my ass, then ran out of steam, turning back to the operation. He almost grudgingly ran the cell number we'd located, and it had pinged as active in Dubai. Even better, he'd already launched our equipment bundle to Europe the day before, and it was due to hit a drop zone in the desert south of Dubai later this afternoon.

We'd landed midmorning and established a base of operations in a local hotel, getting connectivity with the Taskforce via a VPN. We got a current grid to the cell phone and had immediately established a surveillance box to start tracking Lucas.

My phone vibrated with another call. "He's moving. Headed north to the Sheikh Zayed Road."

"Did he ever get out?"

"Not that we saw. He could have earlier."

"Okay. Remember, loose follow. Lose him instead of compromise."

I was a little bit hamstrung because Lucas knew what

Jennifer and I looked like—we were both targets he had tried very hard to kill in the past—which really left me with a three-man surveillance element. Even that was sketchy, because Knuckles had been with me when we captured Lucas the first time. Lucas would have seen him only briefly, if at all, because bullets and fists had been flying. I was willing to risk using him mainly because even a three-man surveillance effort was not nearly enough manpower to conduct a proper follow. Two men would be a bigger risk, and if it came down to it, we could afford to lose him instead of getting compromised because we had his phone to fall back on. The problem was the phone would show us a location on a map, but not what Lucas was doing. We needed eyes on for that.

I got both Knuckles and Brett moving ahead of the van on the other side of the creek on Sheikh Zayed Road, positioned to pick it up and allow Decoy to roll off.

I decided to cross the creek myself, staying far back from the pack, not wanting to accidentally run into Lucas. Acting as the surveillance controller with just a cell phone was proving to be a challenge, since I couldn't hear what was going on with the team. I knew Knuckles, Decoy, and Brett were talking because they had Taskforce phones, but they wouldn't call me unless it was necessary, so I had no situational awareness.

My phone buzzed, and I snatched it up, seeing it was Jennifer. I felt a prick of disappointment and a flood of relief at the same time.

When we'd gotten the grid to the drop zone, I'd decided to send Jennifer on the recovery mission. I didn't want to send one of the clean guys, depleting my already small surveillance capability, since Lucas knew Jennifer on sight. I was a little worried about launching her out into the desert by herself, not because she was a woman, but because nobody should go out in such a harsh environment as a singleton. If she got stuck in the sand, or had any other issues, there wouldn't be anyone to rescue her.

She'd seemed pretty confident, and I'd given her plenty of four-wheel-drive training last year. She was no slouch at vehicle recovery. I'd decided to let her go after she'd given a pretty thorough brief-back on her route in and out. She'd rented a Nissan 4×4 from one of the adventure travel services that dotted Dubai and headed out. Hearing her voice meant she was back in cell range and safe.

"No issues with the equipment. Got everything we asked for."

"No issues with the drop?"

"Well . . . no, not really."

I smiled. Something had happened. "What's that mean?"

"The drop was off by about a thousand meters. Idiots never waited for me to initiate before tossing it out of the plane. No signals, no commo, nothing. Like they had someplace else more important to be."

"And?"

"And I got stuck in the sand. Okay? I'm still sweating like a hog from digging out."

I started to rib her just for fun when my phone buzzed from an incoming call. "Gotta go. Brett's on the other line. Go take a shower. See you tonight."

Brett said, "He was just dropped off at the Financial Centre metro station. I'm on him, Knuckles is off."

"Okay. See if he's meeting anyone on the train and give us a call when he gets off. We'll parallel on Sheikh Zayed Road."

I confirmed instructions to Decoy and Knuckles, trying to piece together what Lucas was doing. Why leave his vehicle on a major thoroughfare and take the metro? *What's he up to?*

Brett called twenty minutes later. "He's off at the Internet City stop. Talking on a cell phone. He did nothing but ride. I see his van approaching. Knuckles is coming to get me."

What the hell?

"Stay on him. Something's up."

We lost him for about ten minutes, forced to conduct a lost-contact drill of trolling the neighborhood he had last been seen entering. The next call came from Decoy and did nothing but muddy the waters even more.

"I got him. He's parked in a section of hardware stores, just sitting still. Like he was at the electronics store. Isn't getting out."

He gave his location, and I asked, "How long was he unsighted? Could he have gone inside?"

"I don't know. I suppose he had time to get out and purchase something."

It was Brett who broke the code on the strange activities. "I see him. Got him from the north. He's looking through binos at a store entrance."

He's following someone else.

49

The Ghost exited the taxi outside a hardware store and slowly turned around, as if to get his bearings. In reality, he was looking for the white-panel van. He was now sure he had seen the same van at both the Burj Khalifa and the electronics store, and while it might have simply been a coincidence, he had decided to run a surveillance detection route to see if he could flush out anybody on him.

He'd entered the metro, hoping to see the white van disgorge a passenger, knowing if he was under surveillance that's what would have to happen or they would risk losing him. The van didn't appear, and he had ridden for a few stops before getting off again, spotting nothing suspicious. Nobody on the train paid him any undue attention. He'd attempted to memorize anyone getting off with him, but none had spiked or done anything that indicated they were interested in what he was doing.

He entered a rustic hardware store with a large front window. Perusing a shelf of tools, he maintained observation on the front door, waiting to see if anyone entered.

After five minutes, he began to believe he was imagining things. He dropped a hammer back on a shelf and proceeded toward the exit. Before he opened the door, he saw a car directly across the street, a long scratch in the paint on the passenger side. The damage held no interest to him, but the man in the passenger seat sure did.

The black man from the metro.

He stared hard through the window, trying to convince himself he was wrong, but the more he studied, the more he was sure the man had been in his metro car and had exited with him. Now he was in his own vehicle, driven by someone else.

Why take the metro for two or three stops if you have a car?

But the man hadn't entered the metro with him. He'd come on at the next stop and hadn't given him a second glance. And he wasn't giving him or the store any attention now. He was looking down the street. *If he were following me, why would he be so stupid as to park out front?*

He decided to find out once and for all. And take the fight to them if it proved true. He had a small wad of explosives left, and one detonator. He'd thought about simply cramming it all on the final radar-array in the elevator shaft and was now glad he hadn't.

He walked the aisles until he found a small spool of soft soldering wire, rated to melt at three hundred degrees. He continued and purchased a roll of electrical tape, a metal funnel, and a package of magnets. Moving to the checkout counter, he glanced again at the front door. He saw the vehicle was gone.

He exited the store and hailed a cab. He told the driver to head downtown, rapidly assessing a plan of action. He needed to separate the followers from their vehicles, which meant he would need to dismount in an area that contained at least some Westerners. He knew they wouldn't risk raising attention by trying to penetrate a locals-only area.

He also needed the ability to wash himself. To lose the surveillance and let him execute his plan. He gave the driver directions to the Bastakia Quarter, an ancient Persian merchant center that was now a pseudo café/art area. It would have both tourists and locals and was big enough, with winding walkways between two-story buildings, that the surveillance would be forced to follow on foot. It also had limited parking areas. Few choices for them to leave their car, and few areas he would have to survey. Most important, it was anchored on the west end by a mosque. A place no Westerner would dare enter.

The cab dropped him off in one of the two parking areas, and he rapidly moved into the labyrinth of ancient buildings, weaving through swarms of tourists and locals alike. He saw an open double-wood door and entered, finding himself in a courtyard with men smoking water pipes and women drinking coffee. He ran to the east wall and peered out, seeing the parking lot and the roundabout that led to it. Within a minute, he saw the white-panel van coming through the roundabout. He had been right.

The van didn't stop at the parking area, but kept going until it was headed south on the eastern edge of the village. The Ghost saw brake lights flash, then lost sight of it.

Dropping off his man.

He didn't want the surveillance to think they'd lost him. He wanted all of the men out and tracking him.

He left the building and headed south, cutting toward the eastern edge. He could recognize only two of the surveillance team who were on him, but that didn't cause any concern. He was fairly sure the rest would find him and pick up a follow. Especially since he planned on being very visible.

He traversed back and forth, entering cafés and galleries and stopping at various historical sights, acting like a tourist, all the while giving anyone the best opportunity to spot him without acting in any way that said he believed he was under surveillance.

He finally began moving west with a purpose. He reached the front steps of the mosque and hesitated, giving the surveillance a final opportunity to see him enter. Climbing the steps, he took off his shoes, but instead of placing them on the floor, he carried them with him, walking at almost a trot to the back.

He went to the nearest men's restroom, glad the time was in between prayers, leaving the room deserted. He swiftly pulled out the metal funnel and began cramming a baseball-size lump of explosive into it. He formed it in the same shape as the funnel, using the metal as a guide, building up an inch-thick layer around the circumference and leaving a cone-shaped space in the center. When he was done, it looked like the funnel simply had a smaller capacity. His hope was to create an improvised shaped charge. He knew it wouldn't be perfect, but it should create enough of an explosive jet to accomplish what he wanted.

He placed the electric blasting cap into the small end of the funnel, seating it in the explosives. He then flipped a switch on his final detonator, turning off the Wi-Fi function and making it work manually with a closed-loop electric circuit. He attached both wires from the blasting cap to the detonator and taped it to the bottom of the funnel.

Satisfied with the device, he exited the mosque and immediately entered a government building on the right side, threading his way north until he exited on the Dubai Creek. Now, the walls and fence of the mosque itself would screen him as he went back to the parking area.

Speed-walking back east down the brick walkway paralleling the Dubai Creek, he hit the end of the mosque wall. He wanted to remain undetected, so he swerved into a large group of swarthy men waiting on a water taxi to take them across the river. Once through them, he could see the parking area and had to assume he'd left all surveillance staked out on the mosque.

He quickened his pace, scanning for the white-panel

van. He was sure it had dropped off a passenger, then parked to await further instructions.

He reached the parking area and saw no vans, white or otherwise. He walked between the cars, giving the area one more glance, then began moving swiftly toward the eastern road that bordered the village, intent on checking out the second parking area. If he saw nothing there, he'd simply leave the surveillance behind and consider his options.

Two rows from the traffic circle he saw the black man's car. Sitting empty. He went to the passenger side to be sure and recognized the scrape on the passenger door. He glanced left and right, then scuttled underneath the back bumper.

He found where the gas tank came closest to the exhaust pipe and placed two magnets on the tank. He affixed the metal funnel to the magnets, knowing the gap created enhanced the shaped-charge effect. Satisfied, he attached one end of the soldering wire to the electronic trigger. He wound the wire around the exhaust pipe in a single loop, then attached the other end to the second lead of the trigger. He ended by pushing the arming switch.

It would take some time, but the soldering wire would eventually melt from the heat of the exhaust. When that happened, the flow of electricity in the trigger would be interrupted, and the charge would go off, penetrating the gas tank and destroying both the car and its occupants.

In the end, it didn't really matter how much destruction he caused. The explosives alone would cause a police response, and anyone associated with the man would be investigated. It would tie them up for at least twenty-four hours, and that's all the time he would need.

He rolled out from underneath the car, surveyed the area from his knees, then joined the flow of pedestrian traffic back to the water-taxi stand. He glanced back at the car and could see the tip of the funnel hanging beneath. It was definitely out of place, but wouldn't draw any undue attention. Especially if the driver simply entered the car from the front without circling the trunk. He bought a ticket on a water taxi and sat with a group of day laborers all waiting to cross the creek.

50

I got the third "no change" call from Brett and realized that Lucas was going to wait outside the mosque for whoever he was tracking. I knew I was missing some type of opportunity and hated sitting there on my ass. I should be using the time for something else.

We'd confirmed that Lucas was a one-man surveillance effort, with the local acting as driver to simply pick him up and drop him off, which meant he had no one at the rear of the mosque. I thought about it, toying with the idea of trying to locate his target.

Initially, I'd restricted our surveillance box on Lucas to trailing behind, which also restricted our ability to react. In a perfect world, you'd have operators around him in a bubble, so that no matter which way he turned, if the eye lost him, he'd run into someone else in the bubble. Once we'd confirmed he was conducting surveillance as well, we didn't want to spook the very target he was after, and since we didn't know who that was, we couldn't prevent him from identifying us over time and distance. Simply staying with Lucas would inadvertently confirm to the target that he was under surveillance—in effect, blowing the operation. In truth, we'd been on Lucas for more than three hours, and there wasn't any way to determine if we hadn't already compromised him.

I decided to press someone to the far side of the mosque and get a snapshot of anyone who exited. Might get us nothing, but sometimes little things like this ended up paying off big-time. I'd leave Brett and Decoy on Lucas and send Knuckles, since he was the easiest one for Lucas to identify. I could always pull him back around if it came to it.

I gave him a call, telling him the plan and asking him to relay it through his Taskforce phone to everyone else. He rogered, and said he was going to reposition to the western parking lot. Out of nowhere I experienced a deep sense of déjà vu, the feeling bringing with it a tendril of dread.

A year ago, almost to the day, I had repositioned Knuckles and another team member for this exact same purpose, and they had run into a vehicle-borne IED. Knuckles had been ripped apart. The other team member had been killed.

Before I realized it, I had unconsciously hit redial on my phone to cancel the mission. I hung up before Knuckles could answer, physically shaking my head to clear the ghost feelings. *Get a grip. Dubai is not Cairo. No Arab Spring here.*

I inched my vehicle out of the alley I was hiding in anyway, wanting to see the route Knuckles would take. I reached the intersection and scanned left and right. Parking wasn't allowed along this road, so if I saw a stationary vehicle, it might be a threat.

I exhaled. There was nothing but moving traffic. I put the car in reverse just as Knuckles passed me, heading west. He kept his eyes to the front, but gave me a one-finger wave from the steering wheel. As he passed I caught a glimpse of something hanging from underneath his left rear quarter panel, just behind the tire.

I leaned forward, trying to identify if it was my imagination or real. He kept going, but it wasn't a trick of my déjà vu. Some small piece of metal was sticking out from underneath his car.

I hit redial, and it went straight to voice mail. *Shit*. I dialed Brett. When he answered, he was whispering.

"Pike, I can't talk. Lucas is moving my way."

"Fuck him. Dial Knuckles right now. Tell him to stop his car. *Now*."

"What?"

My phone buzzed with an incoming call from Knuckles. I hung up on Brett without another word and switched over.

"Knuckles, stop your car. Get out of your car. I think it's rigged with something."

"Huh?"

"Get the hell out of your car!"

"Okay. Next intersection I'll pull into an alley. I can't stop on this road."

"No! Get out now! It might be an IED."

"Jesus Christ! I thought you meant a beacon."

I heard a car door slam, then the sounds of him breathing as he moved away.

"I'm in an alley now. Vehicle's shut down. I'm out. Now tell me what the fuck's going on."

I told him about the left rear quarter panel, leaving out the premonition that had made me look. He'd think I was nuts. While he checked it out, I called Decoy.

"You near your car?"

"No."

"When you get to it, do a thorough scrub for IEDs. Knuckles has something he's checking out now. Whatever you do, don't just get in and crank it up."

My other line buzzed with Brett.

"What's up?"

"Lucas is on the move and I can't stick with him. My heat state's getting bad."

"Forget him. Let him go. Link up with Decoy, but don't start the car."

"Why?"

"He'll let you know. Lucas may have set us up."

I hung up, thinking of the implications of an IED placed on Knuckles's car. If it was real, then this whole day had been a charade. We thought we were the predators when we'd been the prey. And Lucas had much more help than a simple driver. I prayed it was just my overactive imagination, with the biggest cost being my getting reamed at the after-action review and owing a case of beer for stopping the operation.

Knuckles called, and I found out I wouldn't be driving all over Dubai searching for alcohol.

"It was an improvised shaped charge. Pretty ingenious. Most of it is homemade parts, but the detonator's pretty damn sophisticated. No anti-tampering on it, though. A couple of snips, and it was rendered safe."

"You got a plastic bag or something you can put it in?"

"Yeah, why?"

"We should have a biometrics kit in the equipment bundle. I want to print it and see if it's Lucas who built the thing."

"And?"

"And if it is, I'm done pussyfooting around. I'm putting a bullet in his head."

51

Decoy looked over my shoulder at the computer screen and said, "Who the hell is that guy?"

"I have no idea."

It had taken about an hour, but eventually we'd determined that all cars were clean, with me scrubbing mine just to be on the safe side. On my command, we'd let Lucas go, intending to find his bed-down site through his phone. After coming back to the hotel and helping Jennifer smuggle in the kit, we'd printed the funnel, sending everything we could back to the Taskforce. There ended up being four sets of fingerprints: two complete unknowns, Knuckles, and this guy, who had pinged in the database.

I unmuted the VOIP, with the entire team hovering around me. "Okay, one of you fifty-pound heads tell me what this is. Give me his history. Is he Hezbollah or what?"

"Well . . . uhhh . . . he's a complete mystery. He came up in a BATTS sweep in Yemen three days ago. He was in an AQAP torture house getting brutalized, along with fourteen or fifteen other guys. The house was hit by an

American-trained CT force looking for Khalid al-Asiri. It was a dry hole, and they scanned him just as routine SOP. He wasn't the target, and he didn't pop after the scan as anyone of interest."

"Is he Yemeni? Or Lebanese?"

"Saudi. And we ran an airline data search. Nobody by this name and nationality has left Yemen since the hit."

Saudi? What in the hell is going on?

"Any chance of a mistake?"

"Zero."

I glanced at my Timex and saw it was closing in on four p.m. So it would be almost seven a.m. there. Kurt would be working out right now, and I needed some guidance before I did something that caused serious heartburn.

"Go to the gym and find Colonel Hale. I need to speak to him ASAP."

I heard nothing but silence. I switched windows on the computer, hiding the picture of the Saudi and bringing up the camera. I saw two analysts looking at each other, neither of whom I recognized. New hires since I had left operational status.

"What are you doing? Did you hear me?"

One said, "Yes, but the section chief told us we had to go through him before seeing Colonel Hale. We aren't allowed to hit up the boss directly."

Behind me, Decoy said, "Who hired that ass-clown?"

"I don't know," I said, "but he's working on a short career."

I knew Kurt very well, and there was no way he would want to be cut out of the loop like that. Filters were fine, and even necessary, but a blanket edict was stupid. That's how bad things slip through the cracks, because decision makers don't have the information they needed.

"One of you go to the damn section chief and the other one get Colonel Hale."

"He's not at work yet. He'll be here in a couple of hours. Eight thirty, along with the dayshift guys."

"Look, I know that most of your stuff is slow-burn, but I have a crisis going on. I realize I'm far away from you right now, but I'm a much bigger threat than your stupid-ass section sergeant. Now go get Colonel Hale or I'm going to rip off your fucking head."

The threat of violence seemed to do the trick. One of them scurried off while the other looked sick. I blacked the camera and microphone on our side, grinning at the results. I turned around and saw everyone else grinning too. Until I got to Jennifer. She was scowling at me, shaking her head.

"What? Come on. That was a little bit funny, wasn't it?"

"Nobody likes a bully, Pike."

That comment hurt a little bit, because I really did get along great with all the support folks. I just didn't like little Napoleons preventing me from doing my job. I started to say something back to her when the computer squawked.

"Pike, you there?"

I saw Kurt and opened the mike and camera.

"Yes, sir. And I have a little issue I need some guidance on."

"Yeah, I got the rundown from the analysts. So you think Lucas has a posse over there?"

"What else could it be? And not an amateur one either. That IED was well constructed. He's had training."

"What do you want to do?"

"It's not what I want, it's more what you'll let me do. I've got Omega authority for Lucas, but I'm not sure he's the primary threat. He could just be the handler, and taking him out only cuts the leash on this Saudi guy."

"So you want Omega for an unknown? A target we can't identify? I agree on the threat, but I don't think that'll fly. The Oversight Council will see right through this request to the next one, worried about the precedent."

"Yeah, that's my point. I hope they do. Remember when we set up the Taskforce? Your initial take was for a primary target and the authority to flex to a secondary target on any perishable intel we got from the first hit. That thought was right then, and it's right now. No telling how many unknown bad guys Knuckles could have rolled up once he had Crusty, but he had to send all that bullshit back to the rear, then go through this huge vetting process. It's not the best way to run a railroad. Especially after you've put all the time and effort into developing the cover to get in-country."

"Yeah, yeah, but that's all water under the bridge. I

didn't get what I wanted, and now we operate within a different framework."

"That's what I mean. This is the perfect opportunity to show them you were right. The perfect justification."

"Well, maybe perfect on the enemy side because of the envoy's visit, but they're not going to be keen on turning you loose to dig around. *Especially* you."

"What the hell does that mean? Me? I've put more terrorists away than anyone—without *any* compromises."

Kurt laughed. "Calm down. You just tend to scare people."

"Bullshit. If they think my operations are scary, they can sit on their hands and see what's really frightening: a YouTube video of this unknown terrorist standing over the body of a dead American envoy."

52

The director of the CIA started the rock-throwing first. "Colonel Hale, do you really expect us to give you a blank check? You brief that you 'think' there's a bad guy in Dubai in addition to Lucas, and you 'think' he's working with Lucas, and that's enough? I've seen no evidence at all to indicate that, either in your brief or through my station assets in UAE."

This was stupid. No way am I going to win this fight.

He'd called the emergency session right after hanging up with Pike—only the third time he'd ever done so. He knew he had little chance of getting a quorum, but he had hoped the president would override the veto. Unfortunately, the president was unable to break away from a previous engagement.

Before he could respond, the secretary of defense cut in. "Last time we met, you said I knew you and that you never cried wolf. That may have been true a year ago, but lately it seems you do that every few days."

"Sir, I can't control the threat. I don't make this stuff up. It's real, and it's in Dubai. I understand the need for vetting so we don't go off half-cocked. I'm the one that asked the president to create this body for that very reason, but sometimes you need to throw out the rules. I'm not talking about setting a precedent. I'm talking about saving the envoy's life."

"Get Lucas, and I think you'll be doing that. Get him into interrogation, find a new thread, then come back to us to assess whether we want to go Omega again."

"Sir, the envoy's going to be in Dubai in less than twenty-four hours. There's no way we can do that swiftly enough to protect him."

The D/CIA addressed the secretary of state. "John, what're your thoughts? It'll be your mess to clean up if this goes to shit."

The secretary of state leaned forward. "I talked to McMasters last night, and he's completely comfortable continuing to Dubai. He said he didn't even care if we let Lucas run free. He's sure that the Dubai authorities can protect him, and I tend to agree."

Kurt said, "With all due respect, I don't think he's got the same information we do. He's not the man that should be making judgments on whether Dubai can protect him. He has no idea how dangerous Lucas is."

"Not the man to make judgments on Dubai? He spent four years there as the ambassador. If anyone should know, it's him. Anyway, Dubai's not Yemen or some other country going through a volcano. They're wired pretty tight."

Kurt started to say something else, and the SEC-

STATE held up his hand. "Look, Lucas I'm still okay with. If there's any fallout from taking him down, I'm sure we can contain it. I'm not so sure about this unknown. We have no idea who he's connected with or how it will unravel. I'm not willing to risk it."

I AWOKE BEFORE DAWN, having gotten little sleep. The impending operation against Lucas had run continuously in my mind, with my subconscious trying to assess where the curveballs would come from. When we'd have to flex.

Lucas was no ordinary target. He was a predator at the top of the food chain and deserved respect. He'd come close to killing me a couple of years ago, something that few men could claim. I'd decided to keep the plan simple, assuming risk on compromise instead of risk on his turning the tables on us. It wasn't the usual way an Omega operation went down, because we ordinarily placed Taskforce exposure above all else, but in this case we were pressed for time, and I could only leverage the few facts we had.

We knew two solid things about him: the make and model of his vehicle, and, thanks to his phone, his beddown location. Which is where we would take him down.

Not much of a surprise, he was staying in the same hotel as the envoy. I'd sent Brett and Decoy out on a recce, and they said the place was now a fortress, leading me to believe he wouldn't strike there. He just wanted to get close for surveillance purposes. The hotel gave him a perfect staging point, complete with a parking garage that, as a registered guest, he could use without raising a signature.

The plan was a template we used as an in-extremis solution. A battle drill we called a mugging. Basically, we'd simply hide in the shadows waiting for our prey. When he arrived, we'd thump his ass, giving him a little wood shampoo with some clubs like a couple of muggers from New York. It wasn't imaginative and was usually used as a last-resort, snap-decision thing when the original plan went to pieces. In this case I liked the simplicity. Fewer things to control, like the variables on Samir's rescue, so fewer things Lucas could manipulate.

The key to the template was getting him to come to us. I didn't want to crouch in a corner like a Peeping Tom, only to have him head the other way. In this case, I figured we had an ace in the hole with Jennifer.

Lucas had tried very hard to kill her a couple of years ago and would recognize her on sight. An irresistible lure. She would position in the lobby, with eyes on the elevators. When he appeared, she'd simply get up and walk through his cone of vision. I had no doubt whatsoever that her appearance would cause a reaction.

He'd either beeline to his vehicle or try to follow Jennifer, assuming she had something to do with the envoy's visit. I was betting on the follow-Jennifer option. He'd want to know what the hell she was doing there, a complete wrench thrown into his operation. He'd want to interrogate her, then plug the holes in whatever plan he had created.

Decoy and Brett would position in the lobby to give early warning of his intentions, since Jennifer couldn't look behind her. She had to act like she didn't know he was there. Knuckles and I would take him down.

The choice wasn't random. We hadn't drawn straws. Lucas had come close to killing both Knuckles and me and had tortured and killed a friend of ours, along with his entire family. His capture was a little personal, to put it mildly.

I rolled out of bed and turned on my laptop, logging into the hotel's Internet. Lucas was the twenty-five-meter target, but he wasn't the endgame. We still had the Saudi to contend with, a threat that would have to be removed as well, like stomping out all the embers in a fire to prevent a flare-up.

I pulled up our encrypted "company" e-mail and saw a message from Kurt. The first part was something I should have expected, especially since Kurt had said my running around loose gave the Oversight Council irritable bowel syndrome.

Blaine and support package on the way. ETA eighteen hours.

LTC Blaine Alexander, the element leader for Omega operations, was a pretty good man. He'd been working Omega for a few years, and we got along fine, although I hadn't done anything with him since I'd left the Taskforce. He'd probably wonder how I would act, since the last time he'd seen me I was literally a catatonic mess. He was the one who had the job of telling me my wife and daughter had been murdered. The one who brought the stalker to my dreams.

The second part of the message I had to read twice before the words sank in.

No Omega for the Saudi. Lucas only. Work it, then send back status. I'll re-engage for further operations with what you find out.

I couldn't believe it, wondering if they got the SIT-REP about the shaped-charge IED. If they understood the implications of that little device. Whoever made it was imaginative and ruthless. The fact that he hadn't pinged in any databases until now told me he had been very, very successful. He didn't wake up with the knowledge of how to create that IED. He'd done it before. Probably many times, and in such a manner that he hadn't ever come up as a threat. The Council was playing checkers against a man who was a wizard at chess.

And they were betting the envoy's life on the out-come.

53

The room's mounting heat caused the Ghost's thin veil of sleep to dissipate. He fought it, knowing he needed the rest. He threw off the threadbare sheet in a final attempt, but it did little to help. The seedy hotel had no air-conditioning, and the fan in the room was doing nothing to overcome the swelter of the rising sun.

Yesterday afternoon, after getting across the river on a dhow, he had returned to his friend's flat and waited to hear the news of the car bomb. After four hours, he'd heard nothing, either on the television or on the streets outside. He'd decided to relocate. He knew that simply because he hadn't heard anything didn't mean there wasn't an explosion, but he was taking no chances. If he *had* been under surveillance, they probably knew where he'd been sleeping. He'd found a small hotel nearby and urged his friend to move as well for the next forty-eight hours. Hamid had said he'd think about it, then had gone to work, apparently unconcerned, showing the Ghost how little experience he really had.

He padded barefoot to the small sink in the corner of

the room and splashed water on his face, then peeked out between the shutters of the window. He could see an alley below him, with various wholesale stores selling dry goods. Nothing appeared to be out of place. No one standing around without a purpose.

He placed the batteries in his final IMSI grabber and turned it on. Within seconds, it began registering dozens of numbers. He shut it off immediately, knowing he'd just disconnected quite a few phone calls. He was pleased that it worked as advertised, but didn't need any anomalies in the cell system to generate suspicion.

He placed it and the Wi-Fi booster he'd purchased yesterday into his knapsack and glanced at his watch. In two hours the envoy would be landing. If all went well, in five he would be dead.

GETTING JENNIFER IN PLACE inside the lobby of the Al Bustan Rotana turned out to be the easy part. Dressed nicely, she blended in well, drinking coffee at a small table next to an espresso bar that afforded a view of the entrance and both banks of elevators.

Finding a place to conduct the ambush had been damn near impossible. The hotel itself looked more like a high-end prison, with metal detectors on all doors and roving men in suits wearing sunglasses and wired earbuds. This, in addition to the cameras all over the place.

Initially, I had planned for Jennifer to walk to the parking garage, getting inside to some corner that was dark and scary, where we could thump Lucas unimpeded. When we arrived, we saw the garage entrance had been converted into a search-and-quarantine section, with every vehicle getting inspected bumper-to-bumper. I was pretty sure they wouldn't be very pleased with the armament we had brought.

This, coupled with the fact that Lucas's phone had been stationary outside a spice souk in Deira for the entire morning, had almost caused me to change my mind and simply execute the mugging using the vehicle. Just follow and rip him off the street at the first opportunity.

I really didn't want to do that given the variables of location and time. I wanted—needed—to control the kill zone, so we kept looking. Eventually, we ended up behind the hotel at a back entrance that led to several attached restaurants. The restaurants were open only for dinner, and the hallway between them ultimately ended up back in the hotel lobby. Even better, the hallway had a single camera at the lobby entrance for the hotel and a single camera at the exit, outside the door. The kicker had been that instead of a metal detector at the exit, it was simply locked. The hotel had decided to shut it down for the duration of the envoy's visit.

Sitting next to me in the van, staring at his Taskforce smartphone, Knuckles said, "Target's on the move." I looked at my own phone, brought over in the support package Jennifer had received, and saw Lucas was crossing the Dubai Creek and headed to us. Or the airport.

Moment of truth.

The envoy's party was due to land in about thirty minutes. If Lucas bypassed the hotel and made any indication that he was headed to the airport, we would be forced to take him down with the vehicle whether we liked it or not. I was betting he wouldn't, though. He'd had the time to come up with something ingenious, and with the Saudi unknown helping him, I didn't think he'd do some ghetto drive-by. He'd want to get away clean.

I keyed the push-to-talk on my radio. "Everyone set?"

Brett said, "Roger. I got the line of sight down the hallway."

Decoy said, "Yeah. I got the front door and the roundabout outside."

Jennifer said, "I'm still good. No change."

"Remember," I said, "he doesn't bite on the way in, we recock and try again on the way out."

Knuckles did a functions check on the new EMP gun we'd received in the drop, making sure it was ready to take out the camera above the door. I busied myself with my electric lockpick gun, mentally rehearsing in my mind the sequence I would go through.

Our part of the mission was the one big risk to discovery. I had to get the door open before Jennifer reached it, which meant Knuckles would have to kill the camera before Lucas committed to the trap. If he didn't, we'd have to cross our fingers that someone wouldn't come out and investigate why the camera wasn't working while we waited on round two.

Knuckles said, "He's made the turn on the road to the hotel."

I felt the adrenaline rise, knowing we were about two minutes out. Knuckles shut off the phone, slid open the door to the van, and said, "Decoy, your target."

"Roger."

Decoy was the trigger. The minute he saw Lucas, we'd be in motion.

Sooner than expected, I heard, "Target at entrance. Held up with security. They're searching his backpack."

That was one good thing about this location. We'd know positively that Lucas had no firearms. Knuckles handed me his radio and cell phone, then exited the vehicle, me right behind him. We slid down the wall of the hotel, doing whatever we could to stay out of the camera's field of view.

He reached within forty feet of the ball hanging above the door and began sighting. I backed up a few yards to prevent any backsplash from destroying our electronics. Especially my lock gun.

The EMP hummed and Knuckles said, "Go."

I raced to the lock, taking a knee and sliding in the thin needle. I inserted the tension wrench, then began pulsing the lock gun. It rattled like crazy, much louder than I remembered.

Decoy said, "Target's passed. Jennifer, your show."

I continued to work the lock and told Decoy to give me a play-by-play. Jennifer had done a timing run, and I knew the hallway was two minutes from the lobby to the door. Unfortunately, the last bend, right in front of a Chinese restaurant, was only one minute and thirty seconds away. From it someone would have a view of the door and me behind it through the plate glass.

"Jennifer's up and looking sexy, giving Lucas an eyeful. Come on, baby, show him some skin."

Asshole. I grinned in spite of the seriousness of what we were doing. Decoy was busting my balls because of a fight we'd had last year in a similar situation involving Jennifer. He'd made some inappropriate comments, and I'd about taken his head off. Now, he was poking me in the eye for the fun of it.

"Okay, Lucas has lock-on, and he definitely recognized her. He stopped for a second. He's now staring at her back, but headed to the elevator. Target unsighted. Brett, it's your ball."

Shit. Come on. Follow her.

Brett said, "I got him. He's at the elevator. Jennifer's about fifty feet from the hallway. He's still looking."

I continued working the lock, having trouble getting the pins to the shear line. One seated, then another, but slower than my rehearsal earlier in the van.

"Bingo. He's coming her way, walking fast. Jennifer, pick it up or he's going to catch you."

I heard Jennifer acknowledge, and I started to sweat. "Time?" I asked Knuckles.

Knuckles said, "Easy. You still got over a minute. Slow and smooth."

I felt another pin reach the shear line, realizing I was going to make it with half a minute to spare. The next call popped that illusion.

"Shit, he just started running. Jennifer, get moving! He's not going to follow. He's coming hard to take you out. Jennifer, you copy?"

I heard silence for a second, then, "Target unsighted. I say again, target unsighted."

I looked through the window, but saw nothing. At a sprint my time went from a minute and a half to about twenty seconds. I returned to the lock, the tension wrench having moved about forty-five degrees, which meant I had about two or three pins to go.

I seated another pin and heard Knuckles say in a monotone, "Got her in sight. You're out of time." I looked up to see Lucas right behind her, bearing down like a bull in full charge, both running flat out. Jennifer caught my eye, and I shook my head left and right in an exaggerated motion.

She glanced over her shoulder and Lucas struck, attempting to wrap his arms around her in a full-body tackle. She rotated and drove her foot straight into his stomach, his forward momentum increasing the power of the strike.

I heard his grunt and exhale of breath all the way outside as I frantically stroked the remaining pin.

"Come on, Pike!" Knuckles shouted. "He's getting back up!"

Jennifer was in a fighting crouch, dancing out of his way, slowly using up her remaining space to the door, attempting to give me time.

He swung a roundhouse at her head, hard enough to

knock her out completely. She parried and redirected the energy away from her, then slipped inside his reach and gave him a palm strike to his nose, snapping her hip and driving her body behind it. His head popped back like he'd run into an unseen pole, and she danced back out of his reach. I could see the look of shock on his face, her skill completely taking him by surprise.

He bellowed and rushed, wrapping her in a bear hug and trapping her arms. He slammed her full-force into a wall, and the last pin broke free.

I ripped open the door, Knuckles flying through and running straight at the pair. Lucas heard the movement and turned, still holding Jennifer. Knuckles hit him full-force on the side of his head with a closed fist, rattling him enough to lose control of Jennifer. She rotated out and kicked him hard in the genitals. He shrieked and fell to his knees, attempting to control the pain and continue to fight. He started to rise, and Knuckles gave him an uppercut to his face, knocking him back into me. I put him in a rear naked choke, and in ten seconds his arms quit windmilling. He was out.

Panting, I said, "What the hell happened to using the Taser?"

"I didn't have a clean shot with him holding Jennifer. And he deserved a little punishment."

"Jennifer, you all right?"

Leaning against a wall and breathing heavily, she said, "Yeah. Yeah, I'm okay."

"Let's get the hell out of here."

54

Staring down at Lucas's battered face, I radioed Brett in the follow car. "Any activity?"

"None. We're clean so far."

I'd left him and Decoy within sight of the rear door to give me a feel on whether we'd been compromised or not, while Knuckles, Jennifer, and I had tossed Lucas in our van and driven a couple of alleys away from the hotel, giving Blaine in our makeshift hotel tactical operations center a SITREP. Satisfied we were good to go, I addressed Lucas for the first time.

"Been a while. I'll bet seeing me walking around was a big fucking surprise."

He said nothing, his face a blank canvas showing neither fear nor anger.

"Look, I appreciate how tough you are, so I'm not going to go through a bunch of threats. Here's the deal: The United States Middle East envoy is landing in minutes. I can afford to talk right now, but once that envoy hits the ground, I'll be out of time. I know you're out to kill him, I just don't know how. Tell me that and you'll spare yourself some pain later, I promise."

I expected all sorts of stalling tactics. What I got completely surprised me.

Looking relieved, he said, "Pike, I'm on your side. That's what *I'm* doing here. I know there's a hit planned on the envoy, but it's not me. It's another guy from Lebanon called the Ghost. *He's* the one targeting the envoy. I'm trying to stop him."

Surprised or no, I lightly slapped his face twice, saying, "Cut the crap. What's the plan? The clock's ticking and I'd rather not destroy the envoy's itinerary by putting him back on a plane."

Which, of course, was a lie. I had no control over Mc-Masters's activities, but I didn't want Lucas to know that.

"I have no idea. That's the truth. I was tracking the assassin, but I haven't been able to figure out what he's up to. I have a bed-down site I was using as an anchor, but he didn't sleep there last night. Or if he did, he found another way out of the souk. If you guys can stop him, so much the better."

He saw me starting to get pissed and said, "Look, I don't expect you to believe me, but I'll tell you everything I know. I work for pay, but I don't kill U.S. government officials. I have my limits, and that's one. Up until a few days ago I was working for a group in Lebanon. I found out about this hit and we parted ways. Ever since then, I've been trying to track this guy down. He went to Yemen, then came here."

Despite myself, I found his words credible. I could confirm everything he had just said, to include the slaughter of the Hezbollah guys.

Bullshit. This guy's nothing but snake oil.

"Why the hell did you try to blow me up then? In Lebanon with that computer bomb? If you were so fired up about protecting the envoy, you had to know I was doing the same thing."

"Blow you up? I didn't even know you were in Lebanon! I gave an IED to a Hezbollah contact. They thought it was a camera to record a planning meeting about this hit, but I intended for it to kill the assassin. Somehow it missed, and he's still running around loose."

I took that in and said, "So I suppose you thought Jennifer was part of the assassin's master plan as well? That why you were about to kick her ass?"

"I wasn't going to hurt her. I recognized her and was trying to make contact. I was just going to talk to her. Yeah, I had to subdue her to do it because I know you guys want to kill me. It wasn't like I trusted her for a nice sit-down conversation. I'll admit I was going to prevent her from getting me in the crosshairs, but if I'd have hurt her, I wouldn't have been able to get any help on protecting the envoy. Shit, *she's* the one who kicked *me* first."

"What about the vehicle IED you emplaced yesterday? On a member of my team's car?"

"I have no idea what you're talking about. I spent all of yesterday following the Ghost, trying to figure out his plan. I lost him at a mosque. There's no way I could do that *and* go around building car bombs."

He looked genuinely puzzled by the question, as if he thought we were testing him and he knew his answer would fail. *This is sounding too crazy.* I put a double pillowcase on his head and motioned Jennifer and Knuckles out of the van. I positioned myself so I could see his body in the back and spoke over my shoulder.

"What do you think?"

Knuckles said, "I don't know. He's a slimy bastard, but everything he's saying makes sense. It answers the question of why there'd be a bomb from Hezbollah targeting the very assassin they were looking to hire, and we did see him kill the Hezbollah leadership cell. As insane as it sounds, he might be telling the truth."

"Jennifer?" I said.

"I don't trust him. This could just be a stalling tactic. He's pure evil. I find it hard to believe he'd do something that was morally just if no money were involved. He's not built that way."

"Yeah, I'm with you. But distrusting him doesn't solve our current problem. That Saudi is still running around."

Knuckles said, "Well, see what he can tell us about that guy. The minute he says something we can refute, we start getting rough."

Back in the van, I pulled his hood off. "Tell me about the Ghost. What's he look like? Where was he bedding down? What was your plan to remove him?"

"I need my tablet."

I dug the computer out of his backpack and handed it to him. He held out his hands and said, "This would be quicker if you cut these flex-ties."

I cuffed the back of his head. "Nice try. Get to work or I'm going to assume you're stalling."

In seconds, I was looking at a passport photo of the same guy from the Yemen biometric scan. The one who'd built the improvised shaped charge. The lighting was different in each, and in the passport photo he was wearing thick glasses, but there was no mistaking him. The name on the passport was the same as well. A citizen of Saudi Arabia.

Lucas said, "This is the guy. I don't know his true name, but he's called the Ghost for other killings he's done. He's been here for a few days, but I haven't been able to get a handle on his plan. I followed him most of the day yesterday, then, like I said, I lost him at a mosque. He went to electronic and hardware stores, but didn't develop any pattern, as if he was rehearsing a vehicle hit or anything. I also never saw him conduct a recce of anything else I would consider a kill zone. The only thing out of place was a visit to the Dubai Mall and the Burj Khalifa. By the time I parked, I had lost him, so I'm not sure what he was doing."

"That's not a whole lot. What can you give us to work with?"

He manipulated his tablet, pulling up a map with icons embedded. Most were of the locations we'd already seen the previous day. He pointed at a new one.

"I had a beacon installed into a briefcase he used. It hasn't been much help, but it did go to these two locations. The first is the bed-down site he used until last night. The second is inside the Burj Khalifa. Those are the only two anchors I have, which, since the briefcase only moved once during this entire time, I'm assuming are important. He's going to do something at the Burj Khalifa."

"What were you going to do to prevent it?"

"I was going to hit the bed-down site and see what I could find out. From there, if I got nothing, I was simply going to stage at the Burj to intercept him. He's going back there, I'm sure of it."

That sounded like as good of a plan as I could come up with right now. I went through his pockets and pulled out his hotel key.

"Jennifer, head up to his room and search it. See if Mister Goody Two-shoes here is feeding us horseshit. Let us know what you find."

"Where are you going?"

"The bed-down site."

Knuckles squinted and motioned me outside of the van. I bagged Lucas again and exited.

"Pike, you need to let Blaine know what's up before we do anything else."

Shit. I had forgotten Kurt had sent me some personal oversight. I had grown used to operating on my own. I liked and trusted LTC Alexander, but I was sure he'd simply side with his orders and the Council. *Well, it's*

worth the call. Worst case, you're going to ignore him any-
way. Best case, we get barbecued together when we get home.

I got him on my secure Taskforce phone and relayed
the situation. As expected, he balked.

"Pike, we're at Jackpot. We've accomplished our mission. Let's get Lucas on the Skyhook and call it a day. We
don't have Omega authority for anything else."

"Are you kidding me, sir? His information changes
everything. He's confirmed another assassin, and the
Omega was predicated on the hit being stopped with the
capture of Lucas. Shit, taking him down didn't alter anything at all."

"You're assuming he's telling the truth."

"No, I'm worst-casing it. If he's not telling the truth,
then we have nothing to fear because the assassin's in the
back of our van. If he is, we can't afford to ignore it."

"Let me get this information to Kurt and the Taskforce. He'll get Omega and make this whole thing legal."

I looked at my watch, feeling a chill. "Too late. Envoy's on the ground. We either go unilateral, or he dies."

55

The Ghost watched an attractive Westerner walk by him to the elevators. She had come from the back, and he wondered if they would bring the envoy's party in that way. He hadn't seen any metal detectors and assumed it was blocked off.

No matter. They'll still have to pass within range to reach the elevators themselves.

The itinerary he'd been given showed that the envoy should already be on the ground. The Ghost knew they would check into the hotel prior to going to Sheikh Mohammed bin Rashid's palace for a personal visit. After that, the royal tour of the town, to include the Burj Khalifa.

A flurry of activity out front attracted his attention. Three Mercedes limousines wheeled up, and out sprang eight men, five in Western suits, three in traditional Gulf Arabic attire. He surreptitiously snaked a hand into his knapsack and turned on the IMSI grabber.

The men were met at the front door by a receptionist and led around the security in place to the northern elevators, manned by two large security guards. In seconds, they were lost from sight. The Ghost killed the power to his device.

He had to wait less than fifteen minutes before the elevators opened and the entourage spilled out again, walking at a fast clip. Caught off guard, he dropped the coffee he was holding and powered up the grabber again. The men were out the front door in a flash, and he wondered if he'd managed to catch any of the numbers the second time around.

He waited until the limousines were out of sight before exiting himself and flagging a cab. He went back to his hotel and examined the clutch of numbers inside the grabber. Each cycle was stored by date and time, allowing him to filter the results.

Since the grabber drew in every cell phone within range, he had collected over three dozen numbers in the short span of time he had powered it up. No way could he tell which number was the envoy's by simply looking at the list. Which is why he had cycled the grabber twice. All he had to do was identify the cell numbers that were in both cycles. Those phones would have been within range of the grabber each time the envoy passed by, and thus would more than likely be part of the entourage.

He found twelve that were duplicated in each cycle. Undoubtedly, one or two were from the receptionist or even security, but that didn't matter. He needed only one number associated with the entourage. One cell phone to seek out his IMSI grabber in the elevator and

trigger the alarm. He'd simply plug in all twelve, knowing that somewhere in the batch lay the envoy's own
phone. The only way it would fail was if the receptionist
or some other false number took a trip to the Burj Khalifa observation deck before the envoy, and that was a
small chance.

He packed the grabber, seating it next to the Wi-Fi
repeater, then changed into his borrowed Burj Khalifa
maintenance uniform. He patted the pocket to ensure he
hadn't lost the key card for the basement entrance. Now
that he was at an endgame, he didn't want to rely on
anyone else, even his close friend Hamid.

He checked himself in the mirror, seeing the same frail
man that others discounted, his thick glasses adding to
the disarming effect. The reflection brought the start of
a smile.

He was invisible to most people looking, a person not
worth a second glance. A wisp of a man who others ignored, he had found his calling in not existing at all. In
becoming a wraith without substance. The talent had allowed him unprecedented success in the past.

And so it would be here.

As KNUCKLES AND I WALKED into the spice souk, I could
see we were going to have a tough time trying to get
anyone out of there in flex-cuffs. Especially since it would
more than likely be a brown guy carried by a bunch of
white guys. Well, three white guys and a black guy who
spoke English.

Decoy came through my earpiece. "Got the bed-down, and you're not going to like it. Third-floor room, only entrance is a very narrow stairwell. Rooms on each landing with people selling fake Rolexes and Coach bags on the first floor."

"So we can't get in without being seen?"

"No way. We can't get in without being accosted to buy something."

Figures.

After exhausting every option he could think of, Blaine had finally blessed off on letting us crack the bed-down site. I have to admit, I was impressed, because he would eventually have to brief Kurt, and it would cost him his job, if not something more permanent. He had, of course, demanded a SITREP after the fact before giving authority for anything else.

We'd flex-cuffed Lucas to an anchor point in the van, purchased a set of noise cancelation headphones and taped them to his ears, gagged him, then put the hood back on. Finally, Knuckles had used a rear naked choke to render him unconscious. I didn't want to leave him alone, but I had only four people and needed everyone for the bed-down site.

While Knuckles and I came up with a half-baked plan, I'd sent Brett and Decoy to pinpoint the location using the beacon Lucas had emplaced, which was still pinging strongly.

I said, "Give me a grid."

Seconds later, a text message came with a photo attached. I loaded it into the GPS software of my phone and started walking in the direction of the arrow. After winding through the souk for a couple of minutes, I spotted the stairwell from the photo Decoy had sent. He was right—it was very narrow and sandwiched between two different shops selling handmade tourist crap.

I pulled up short and called him back, looking at Knuckles as I spoke.

"Got any ideas?"

Decoy said, "Not really. I'm thinking we blow off the clandestine side of things and just go on up there like we own the place."

"Yeah, but if the guy hawking the Rolexes is friends with whoever lives there, he'll know we don't belong."

Knuckles interjected, "Send Brett up first. He engages the Rolex guy and gets inside the apartment where they're selling the stuff. Once we have that guy out of the way, then we walk up like we own the place."

Even though he was standing right next to me, he had said it on the radio. I nodded my head, liking the plan. "You guys copy that?"

"Yeah, we got it."

"Let's execute. Decoy, you got the lock, Knuckles, first in. Brett, when you're done, take up early warning at the bottom."

"This is Brett. Roger all. I'm moving. I'll key the mike when I'm inside."

I saw him turn the corner, then advance up the stairs. We waited for about thirty seconds, then heard Brett saying "Do you have a gold Submariner?" followed by a muffled response.

Knuckles and I walked straight to the stairwell, meeting Decoy at the entrance. We sprinted lightly up the stairs, taking them two at a time, no weapons drawn yet. The landing to the apartment was just as narrow as the stairwell, with room for only one person. Decoy took a knee and began working the lock manually to prevent anyone from hearing the noise of the electric gun.

Three minutes later he looked over his shoulder and gave an exaggerated nod. Knuckles and I pulled our Glocks from their concealed holsters and nodded back. Decoy turned the tension wrench, then pulled down on the door handle, swinging it open. He leaned over backward and we went by him into the room.

The first room was tiny, about ten feet by twenty feet, with a desk holding a thirteen-inch television and a make-shift pallet on the floor. It was empty. Knuckles continued on into the second room, and I followed, bumping into him because the room was even smaller than the first. It contained a bed and a sliding-door closet, but no human beings.

I backed out and found Decoy.

He said, "Bathroom's behind the entrance door. Clear."

"Start searching. See what you can find."

Five minutes later we had all we were going to get. There was very little to exploit—no computers, cell phones, or other electronic devices—but we found enough evidence to say that Lucas hadn't been lying about the bed-down location.

Knuckles had discovered several maintenance uniforms for the Burj Khalifa building, and Decoy, spraying an aerosol can on various items in the room, had turned a backpack splotchy pink. The can held an explosive residue reagent, and the color meant the backpack had contained plastique of some type.

I was coming up with how I could use what little evidence we had to convince Blaine to let us continue fishing when Brett called.

"Man entered stairwell. Unknown on the way up."

56

The radio call caused everyone to perk up.

I remembered where the tenant worked and said, "What's he wearing? Traditional dress?"

"No. He's wearing some sort of maintenance uniform."

The words hung in the air as we each stared around the tiny room for a place to hide in ambush, looking like we were in a seventies sitcom. There wasn't even a lampshade to put on our heads.

"Decoy, bathroom. Let the door open, then close it behind him. Knuckles, other room. When he enters, let's get on him quickly. No Tasers. The threat is him screaming. Don't let him make any noise."

Just as we got situated, with Knuckles facing me on the opposite side of the bedroom entrance, I remembered a potential giveaway and whispered into my radio, "Decoy, lock the door. I say again, lock the door."

I heard a whispered "Roger," then the distinct click of the old lock, hoping the man in the stairwell was either deaf or too stupid to recognize the sound.

Thirty seconds later the lock snicked again, then I heard the door creak open. What I didn't hear were any footsteps entering the room. No shuffle, no keys thrown on a desk, nothing. I gave Knuckles a quizzical look. He just shrugged, both hands on his weapon.

The man spoke up in Arabic. I didn't understand the words, but it wasn't too hard to figure out what he was saying. *Anyone in there?*

We'd left the room a mess, and he'd seen evidence of our search. I held my breath. All we needed were three small steps. Just enough to clear the door.

I strained my ears, trying to determine if he'd entered or not. He said the same thing in Arabic again, clearly suspicious. Then I heard what sounded like a piece of lumber hitting a wall.

I breached the doorway and saw Decoy dragging an unconscious Arab into the room from the landing.

He said, "He was about to leave. I clocked him with the door. I didn't think it would knock him out, but it did. Lucky he didn't fall down the damn stairs."

I closed the entrance door while Knuckles and Decoy searched him, finding key cards and identification for the Burj Khalifa but little else. I radioed Brett and gave him a status, asking him to check out any reaction on the lower landings.

He came back moments later. "You're good to go, but I'm claiming this fake watch. Had to buy it to support my reason for being in the stairwell a second time."

"Let me guess. You got the gold Submariner."

"Hell no. Omega Seamaster. That's what James Bond wears."

Chuckling, Decoy and Knuckles tied up then gagged the unconscious man. I filled a glass with water from the bathroom sink and splashed it in his face. He woke up instantly, whipping his head left and right. Seeing white boys, he attempted to leap to his feet and found he was trussed like a pig for slaughter. His eyes grew wide, the terror clearly evident. His hands began to tremble in the flex-cuffs like a man with Parkinson's disease. It wasn't the reaction of a master terrorist.

He's never been in the arena. Never done any operational acts.

It changed my approach. I had planned on using the information we knew to try to elicit more data from him, tripping him up with my supposed omniscience. I figured there was no way he would freely give me anything, and I would have to outwit him using trickery. He had no idea what I did or didn't know, and I hoped for him to give me something new because he thought I already had it, as a stalling tactic.

That interrogation plan had been based on a hardened terrorist. Someone who understood the risks and the pain that would come if he were captured. A terrorist like that could resist pressure for a great while. We had only about an hour to figure out what was going on, not nearly enough time for any sort of physical threat or action to sway a man who's prepared and has the strength of will to resist. Now, seeing the man cower, I decided to go full bore as the mean guy, see if he would crack.

I put on my best Shrek face and leaned in close. "Tell me you don't speak English and I'll rip out your tongue. Understand?"

He nodded his head vigorously.

"We've been hired by Sheikh Mohammed bin Rashid to track a man called the Ghost. He's here to kill an American. We know he's using the Burj Khalifa for the attack. We've watched you for days and know you are also involved."

Hell, might as well throw a little omniscience in there as well.

He shook his head violently. *Time for the bad guy.*

"Hand me the pliers." Knuckles gave me a pair of vise grips he'd found in the back. I held them up to his nose, so close he could smell the grease on them.

"Don't shake your head again. What I told you is fact. Denying it doesn't make it go away. I'm first going to crush your toes with these pliers. Then your fingers. Eventually, I'll work my way to your genitals. The duration is up to you, but I assure you that you have enough appendages to keep me busy for quite a while. Do you understand?"

His eyes grew wet, and a single tear tracked down his cheek. He squeezed them shut and nodded. *Success.*

To solidify it, I went to good cop. "Tell me what I want to know, and I won't harm you at all. I have no desire for that. I simply want to stop the attack. You work with me, and you walk away with your life, your limbs intact. Understand?"

He opened his eyes, wanting to believe what I said, but unsure. I could see the walls breaking inside him. He nodded again, with more force.

I returned to bad cop. "Lie to me, even once, and the pain will be immediate. I know quite a bit of what's been planned. You people have been sloppy. You say something wrong, and I might start with your penis."

Decoy removed his gag, and the man began talking. A fountain of information that we couldn't have shut off if we tried. Within six minutes I was sure we had everything the man knew, and the information wasn't pretty.

After he grew quiet, I said, "You've done well. I'm going to untie you now. You'll be coming with us."

He looked confused and said, "I thought you would leave if I told you everything?"

"I'll leave when your information pans out. If it doesn't, I'll be your personal nightmare. Hold out your wrists."

He did so, and I saw his brain working. Wondering why we would uncuff him if we really worked for the sheikh of Dubai.

"I'm setting your hands free because I can't have anyone talking about this in the souk. I don't want word to spread that you've been taken. You must act naturally all the way to our vehicle. If you don't, you will disappear. Understand?"

He nodded, I cut his wrist ties, and Decoy pushed him to the door. I said, "Get him to the van. I'm calling Blaine."

Bundling him out the door, Knuckles said, "You had *me* convinced he was in for some pain. What were you going to do if he clammed up?"

"Nothing. Just bag him."

I let them get down the stairs, then dialed the TOC.

"Sir, I've got most of what's going on. The attack's at the Burj Khalifa, like we thought, but it isn't any frontal assault. They're using the elevators. The guy doesn't know how—he's really a maintenance man—but he helped the Ghost get access to the elevator shafts. I'm headed there now."

"Can you defeat it before they get there?"

"I don't know. I don't have an accurate itinerary. Just call Kurt and tell him to relay not to use the elevators in the Burj Khalifa."

"Doing it now. Get your ass moving. According to what I have, he's either there or en route."

I made it to the van without issues, seeing all three of my teammates outside arguing.

"What's the problem? We need to move."

They all looked at me sheepishly, then Knuckles cracked open the sliding door, allowing me to see inside. One man was trussed on the floor, a bag on his head. It was the guy we had just captured.

"Where the fuck is Lucas?"

I knew the answer even before I asked the question.

Knuckles held up a carbon-fiber knife with a broken blade. "Gone. Like the last time we had him. I knew we shouldn't have left him alone."

Jesus Christ. That guy is Houdini. I remembered Jennifer was in his hotel room and immediately dialed her phone. It went to voice mail.

Decoy said, "We already called her. No joy."

Every fiber in my body was screaming to get back to the Bustan Rotana, to get her to safety. The men were all waiting for a decision, wondering which way I would go after my call in Lebanon.

McMasters was on the way to the Burj Khalifa, and the Ghost was already there. But Jennifer was in real danger. Lucas, while he had apparently told us the truth about his mission, was a psychopath. A threat on the loose.

The mistake in Lebanon surfaced in my mind, when I'd almost compromised the mission because I'd been afraid for her welfare.

She's trained. She can handle herself. He's probably not even going back to his hotel.

"Load up. We're going to the Burj Khalifa. Keep trying to call her while we drive."

57

Seeing that Lucas had wiped the history of his Internet usage, Jennifer powered down the laptop and inserted a thumb drive into a USB port. Turning it back on, the forensics device began to troll for random bits of data in the BIOS and hard drive of the computer. Within minutes, she had a list of Web sites used in the past twenty-four hours. Four were for hotels around the main train station in Frankfurt, Germany. Three were for different travel Web sites.

She clicked on one, bringing up a search for airlines and flights to Frankfurt, Germany, from Dubai, all for the following day.

She minimized Explorer and began searching his hard drive, looking for anything related to the envoy's visit. She found the envoy's itinerary, then the same passport information for the Ghost that she'd already seen.

Looking at her watch, she decided to simply image the hard drive and study it later, in the TOC. She pulled out the original thumb drive and inserted the same type system she had used in Lebanon. Two clicks later she had a bar saying ten minutes until download complete.

She moved to his luggage and began sorting through his clothes. She found nothing of interest. Lucas apparently had very good operational security, leaving little to be found by a snooping maid.

She found a leather satchel and zipped it open. Inside were small knickknacks that she found odd. A kitchen magnet with the picture of a couple embossed inside. Two separate key chains, one with a bottle opener from a hotel in Reno, the other with the name "Dani" dangling from it. And three driver's licenses.

Finally. His alias documents.

She looked at the first, seeing it was for a woman of about sixty. *No way could he use that.*

She looked at the second and felt a shock so great it made her knees weak. She made the connection with Lucas and sat heavily on the bed. She stared at the picture, then the name, making sure she wasn't wrong. She wasn't. She slipped the license into her pocket behind her phone and stood up, thinking through the ramifications. She didn't realize someone had entered the bedroom until he spoke.

"Well, well. Looks like my day isn't going to be all bad after all."

She whirled around and saw Lucas between her and the door to the living room of the suite, a flex-cuff still attached to one wrist, the other wrist raw and bleeding. She eyed him warily, but he remained where he was.

"Come on. I'm not going to do anything. You can leave. Right through the door there."

She said nothing, keeping her distance. He shuffled to the left and glanced at the closet. She followed his gaze, and he struck, closing his hands on each of her wrists in a steel grip.

Reacting instantly, she windmilled both arms in a circle, breaking his hold. She slid into his body and hooked her right leg behind the one bearing his weight. She jerked upward with her leg and pushed as hard as she could against his chest, slamming him to the ground.

She turned to run to the door, only to have him kick it closed from the ground. She whirled around and moved into a fighting crouch as he leapt to his feet. He grinned at the stance, then swung a slap at her face. She parried it with her left arm and lashed out in a jab, popping his head back.

When he returned her gaze, he was no longer grinning. He touched his nose, wiping a wisp of blood with his finger. "A fighter. I like that in a woman."

He launched into her, throwing a flurry of combinations in an attempt to knock her down. For several seconds, the only noises were the slapping of skin and the panting of the combatants, Jennifer furiously protecting herself against every blow. Lucas backed off, having failed to harm her.

Jennifer reached behind her, blindly trying to find the door handle. Lucas saw the move and came in again. This time, having gotten a feel for his technique, Jennifer not only stopped his attack, but she landed two more jabs to his face.

Lucas backed off again, breathing hard. "You fucking bitch. You're just making this hard on yourself."

She said nothing, reaching behind her again for the door handle. Lucas feinted in, and she returned to a crouch. Instead of closing the distance, he grabbed a lamp and hurled it at her head. She ducked, feeling the porcelain shatter against the door above her. Lucas was on her before she could recover, slamming his shin into her thigh, drawing a cry.

He followed the kick with a left cross to her head. She raised her arms and took the blow harmlessly, but opened up her left side in the process. He shot a right hook to her kidney, causing a blinding pain to radiate beneath her rib cage. She felt him close his hands around the back of her neck, controlling her head, and knew she was in trouble. She threw her arms down low to ward off what was coming, but it had little effect.

Lucas speared his knee through her feeble attempts at protection, hitting her in the solar plexus and driving the air from her lungs. She threw jabs at a body she couldn't see, connecting in one way or another, but doing little damage.

Maintaining control of her head, Lucas placed her back against the wall and drove his knee into her stomach two more times, the wall itself increasing the force of each blow. She screamed, the pain causing her to double over.

Lucas let go of her neck and she fell to the ground, gasping in a shallow pant in an attempt to draw in air.

She felt Lucas loop the lamp cord over her wrists and jerk it tight, her strength to resist gone.

"That little bit of work is going to cost you some foreplay," he said.

58

Jeff McMasters pasted on an interested smile and ignored the man droning on and on about all of the wonders of the Burj Khalifa.

Could you cram one more record in there? Tallest building, highest observation deck, longest elevator, highest swimming pool . . . My God, give it a rest.

He'd relinquished his ambassadorship in 2009, at the crest of Dubai's heady days of expansion. Months later, the world financial crisis had left Dubai facing epic debts that threatened the very stability of the state. Its neighbor, the oil-rich state of Abu Dhabi, had ridden to the rescue, providing an infusion of much-needed cash. The very building he was standing in highlighted Dubai's meteoric rise and subsequent rapid descent: An architectural marvel unrivaled in the world, its name had been changed from Burj Dubai to Burj Khalifa after the bailout, in deference to the ruling sheikh of Abu Dhabi, Khalifa bin Zayed Al Nahyan.

Following the tour guide around the eight-foot plastic scale model in the anteroom, he thought the rattling off of statistics and record-breaking feats sounded a little desperate, as if the tour guide was trying to convince him of the building's greatness—and by extension Dubai's worth.

McMasters let the voice fade into the background, the ever-present mission in Qatar creeping forward to his conscious mind. He was due to arrive at the peace conference the following day, and the closer it got, the more he thought about what could go wrong.

He'd agreed to become the new Middle East envoy before they'd told him what that entailed, namely a covert action involving passing money to the Palestinian Authority. As an ambassador, he'd been privy to various covert actions conducted by the CIA, but none had involved his embassy, and he'd certainly never participated in one as a player. In truth, as a diplomat, he found the whole notion of covert action distasteful. Lying and sneaking around simply wasn't in his makeup. Or so he had thought.

Now that he was a primary actor, he found it exciting. True, he was just the catalyst and not the agent who would actually transfer the money, but it was still a thrill. When first told of the mission, he had balked, asking how he was going to travel from country to country toting around a suitcase full of cash. He'd been told that the money would be coming separately, brought by two members of the CIA during the conference, and that it wouldn't be dollar bills, but diamonds. Much smaller to haul around.

The actual transfer plan had been withheld from him, using sources and methods known only to the CIA. He'd toyed with the idea of demanding the information, since it would be his head on the chopping block if something went wrong. He knew it was simply because he wanted to satisfy his curiosity. Wanted to feel more a part of the mission.

He was brought out of his thoughts by the tour guide walking toward a long hallway, past an incongruous picture of Tom Cruise hanging on the outside of the Burj Khalifa for some movie.

He nodded at the aides with him and followed, finally reaching two double-decker elevators after several minutes. Sheikh Mohammed bin Rashid pointed at the one to the right, leaving the remainder of the straphangers to ride up in the elevator to the left.

THE GHOST EXITED THE ELEVATOR'S MAINTENANCE ROOM on the 125th floor and saw two females dressed in Burj Khalifa uniforms scurrying down the hallway, animatedly talking. When they were abreast, he asked what the excitement was about.

"They're here. His Highness is here with the American. They'll be on top shortly."

He thanked them and headed in the opposite direction, toward the service elevator. Four minutes later, he exited in the basement. He paused for a second, listening for anyone else working. Hearing nothing, he jogged to the radar brake array for the observation elevators.

He used a stepladder to place the Wi-Fi repeater as high as possible into the left elevator shaft, giving it the greatest possible chance of hitting the network. He turned it on, watched the lights go from red to green, and returned to the bottom.

He placed a Wi-Fi sniffer he'd purchased near the detonator. He smiled when he saw four out of six bars. He turned on the detonator, holding his breath. The light flashed red, then went to green. It was armed.

He moved to the right elevator shaft and powered its detonator. It flashed red, then began to blink red and green over and over again. He was unsure what that meant, but knew it wasn't good. He placed the sniffer next to the detonator and saw he had no Wi-Fi signal.

So much for the advertisement on the box about the repeater range. The shaft itself was blocking the signal.

He held the sniffer at eye level and walked slowly toward the repeater, feeling the press of time. In three steps he had a single bar. Five more steps and it went to three bars. When he reached the wall between the two elevators he saw four bars. *Good enough to trigger.* He somehow needed to get the detonator to this wall.

He glanced around the room, looking for loose wire. He saw paint buckets, spare pieces of crown molding, and a tarp, but nothing remotely close to something he could use. Frustrated, he ran to the keypad for the door leading outside. It was encased in metal, with the wiring running up the wall inside a pipe.

No good. He wondered where the entourage was located. If they were already on the observation deck. If they weren't about to trigger the explosives, with him standing next to them.

To the left of the keypad was a speaker. Presumably an intercom that allowed communication to other maintenance personnel inside the building. It had no apparent wiring leading to it, meaning the wiring was behind the speaker and ran inside the wall. He found a flat piece of scrap metal and jammed it under the plate. He levered the speaker away from the wall, pulling out a mess of spaghetti.

Not wanting to shock himself, he identified the power line, then the wire used to transmit from the speaker. He separated the two, then gave a hard yank to the speaker wire, drawing out three feet. He began pulling hand over hand until he had no slack.

He glanced back at the elevator shaft. *Still not enough.*

He looped the wire around his hands and jerked with all of his might, the wire slicing into the fleshy part of his palm. He tried a second time and fell backward as the anchor gave way.

Several minutes later, he had the detonator separated from the explosives by about thirty meters of speaker wire. He affixed the detonator to the wall between the elevators and powered it up. He saw the flash of red, then a steady green. He wiped his brow and hurried to the exit door.

He swiped Hamid's key card, opened the door, and took the stairs up two at a time. He slowed as his head crested the top of the stairwell. He surveyed the drive to the mall parking garage and froze, his stomach clenching.

The black man he had tried to kill was walking toward him, another man at his side.

59

Knuckles shut off the van and pointed at the hooded man from the souk. "We going to leave him behind like we did Lucas?"

Getting Jennifer's voice mail one more time, I stabbed the keypad and hung up. "No. You're going back to the hotel. I can't get Jennifer. Something's wrong. Get over to the hotel and find her."

He started to say something, and my phone rang. I stabbed the call button and heard Blaine. *Dammit. Where is she?* I listened, then said, "We're there now, and I can see limos roped off. What the hell's going on? Why did they come here?"

On the other end of the phone, Blaine said, "Pike, we didn't get to them in time. We had too many layers to go through to get the phone number. We have it now, but it goes straight to voice mail."

"Call someone else. There are three limousines here. Someone's got their phone on."

"They *all* go to voice mail. We don't know why. Maybe the building is shielding the signal or something, but the bottom line is we didn't get the warning to them."

So much for doing this slow and methodical.

"How long are they going to be in there?"

"Less than ten minutes on the upper deck. The clock's ticking right now. What're your courses of action?"

"Shit, sir, I have no idea what trap he's built. He's been all over the damn building planting explosives. It's going to take time to get to the maintenance room on the upper floors. It's above the observation deck. On top of that, he apparently placed explosives in the basement as well."

Blaine said, "What can I do? What do you need?"

"I need someone to tell them to stay out of the damn elevators!"

I calmed down and continued. "I'd like to target the Ghost because I'm sure he's going to command detonate whatever he's got, but we don't know where he is. I have no doubt he's around here, but I can't waste the time looking. Second COA is to enter the building and see if we can render safe whatever trap he's laid, but it's the basement only. I have no idea if that'll be enough. Brett and Decoy are headed there right now."

"What's the risk to the force? Can you protect them?"

I watched Brett and Decoy cross the street, both carrying a small duffel bag full of tools. "No," I said, "there's no way I can mitigate the risk without the Ghost."

Blaine said something else, but I was no longer listening. A man with a Burj Khalifa maintenance uniform had just popped out of the bushes. Wearing thick glasses. Right next to the basement entrance.

THE GHOST DUCKED BACK INTO THE STAIRWELL, considering his options. Clearly, it was no coincidence that the black man was here. It was because of the envoy. The only mystery was how they'd penetrated his plan. They hadn't followed him here, or he would have been interrupted installing the phone numbers and arming the detonators.

It must be the building itself. They don't know I'm here.

They weren't looking for him. They were looking for his trap. He couldn't let them explore for any length of time. He hadn't placed any booby traps around his explosives, and they could be disarmed fairly easily.

He thought about hiding in the basement and attacking them, but didn't like the odds. Two on one would be hard to pull off. Somehow, he had to prevent them from entering the basement. But he had nothing. No way to distract them. No means of pulling them from their goal.

Except for myself.

It hit home that he would be irresistible bait. *They were following me earlier. They know what I look like.* He could prevent them from stopping the attack, but he would be caught. Chained and tortured, then killed. He wouldn't be able to utilize his false jihadi Web site group to claim credit. Wouldn't be able to put the Palestinian cause on the world stage. He would be walking to his death.

He peeked over the top and saw the men were less

than seventy meters away. If he waited any longer, he would be trapped anyway. He jumped up and grabbed the railing on the left side of the stairwell. Swiftly scrambling over it, he hid in the shrubbery beyond.

He thought again about his options, but came up blank. It was either him or failure. He felt a sadness seep inside. He steeled himself, shaking off the melancholy. He would need to remain out of their grasp for several minutes, leading them on a chase. From there, it would be up to Allah. Maybe he could get them to kill him here, before they started in on the torture.

He kept his eyes on the two men, waiting until just before they reached the stairwell. When he was certain they would sense his movement, he slipped over the side, walking behind them at a fast pace, purposely scuffling his shoes.

60

I dropped my phone and keyed the radio. "Brett, Decoy, turn around. The Ghost is behind you. Look behind you!"

I saw them whip around, then the man take off running. He circled around the back side of the building, running along a promenade that fronted a giant artificial lake.

Knuckles was already out of the van, waiting for me to give him the word, unleashing the hounds as it were. Instead, I said, "No, you go to Jennifer. Go get her. We'll handle this."

He gave me a sour look, not liking at all that he'd be sitting out the chase, but he nodded and moved back to the door.

I took off at a sprint, panting into my radio, "Hit him with the EMP gun. Take out any electronics on his body."

I was about seventy meters behind the target and forty meters behind Brett and Decoy. Brett was pulling away, running like a linebacker for the end zone. Moving at astonishing speed.

The Ghost flipped a glance over his shoulder, and I was close enough to see the shock on his face when he saw Brett closing the gap. He veered toward the water, and Decoy took a knee, aiming the EMP gun.

I saw him track the target all the way to the water's edge, presumably firing his body full of electromagnetic pulses. Hopefully scrambling whatever remote detonation mechanism he had.

The Ghost cleared the railing and dove into the lake right at the juncture of a false stream. He started swimming to the far side, looking like a child who had fallen out of a Disney ride, a dark cork in the impossibly blue water.

I saw a bridge crossing the stream, letting tourists continue their promenade along the false sea, and sprinted to it. I reached the far side, and we had a little bit of a "man-in-the-middle," with Brett and Decoy on one side, me on the other, and a bedraggled terrorist now treading water between us.

When he didn't move to either side, Decoy jumped in after him, forcing him to choose. He came my way, trying to climb up a maintenance box and jump back onto the promenade. It was easy to beat him to it.

I grabbed him by the lapels and swung him violently onto the ground, surprised at how light he was. His Coke-bottle glasses flew off, and he hit the ground hard, knocking the air out of him.

I ripped through every crevice and pocket of his body, trying to find whatever he had that would trigger the explosives in the building. I came up empty.

Brett reached me, saying, "Did we fry the device?"

"There isn't a fucking device."

I slapped the Ghost's face. "What's the threat? Where is it?"

He looked at me with a sense of calm and satisfaction, as if he'd just won a contest of skill.

"You're too late."

61

Jeff McMasters saw the end of the lap around the observation deck to his front and gave a silent thank-
you. The drone of the official tour guide had endlessly
echoed with bits of trivia of the city no matter which direction they looked.

He did have to admit they weren't kidding about the
height. They were so far up in the air that the "ordinary" skyscrapers of downtown Dubai looked like toys.
So far up that there had been no vertigo at all. It was
like looking out the window of an airplane, the earth so
distant that his mind couldn't compute the effect as being above it.

They reached the elevators, and the guide asked if he'd
like to go outside, to the tallest open-air observation deck
in the world. He, of course, expressed keen interest, wondering what else the man could blab about.

Blessedly, the tour guide simply said, "Enjoy yourself
and let me know when you're ready to return to the bottom."

He nodded as if he was having the time of his life and

pulled out his international BlackBerry. To his surprise, he had not a single e-mail or missed call. The damn thing rang endlessly, and he'd been out of contact for at least thirty minutes. He looked closer and saw he had no signal.

Must be something to do with this building.

Like a man addicted, he felt the need to get his phone back on the network. He nodded at Sheikh Mohammed bin Rashid and said, "Let's continue our tour of your fabulous city."

The sheikh smiled. "Of course. Today is your day."

As soon as the words came out of the Ghost's mouth, I knew he'd tricked us. Delayed us to execute his plan. I wanted to scream at my stupidity. I should have hit what I knew—the elevators in the building. I'd gotten tunnel vision when I'd seen him, and now it would cost us.

I wasted no more time on him, knowing there was no pressure on earth I could bring to bear in the short time I had to get him to talk. He was prepared to die. Unlike his accomplice—my ace in the hole.

I started snapping orders. "Brett, target's yours. Get him back to the van. Decoy, get the EMP gun recharged and ready. Knuckles, what's your status?"

"Still on the parking-garage road, about to enter the highway. What's up?"

"Turn around. Come back. Get that little weasel in the van to the basement door. He needs to lead us to the explosive set he saw the Ghost emplace."

"On the way. Ten seconds out. What about the shit on the hundred-twenty-fifth floor?"

"Nothing we can do about it. We're going to disable what we have."

"You think that'll be enough?"

"I have no idea, just get him moving."

Sprinting back the way I had come, I saw Knuckles leap out of the van, rushing our captive forward, holding the back of his neck, the man's feet barely touching the ground. We met up at the stairwell.

"Lead us directly to the location your friend placed the explosives. If you deceive us in any way, I swear to God I'm going to kill you."

His eyes bugging out of his head, he simply nodded. I swiped his card, and we entered in a rush. We stood inside for a millisecond before I slapped his stomach.

"Where, dammit? Where?"

His hands cuffed in front, he took off at a trot. "This way. To the shafts."

He led us through a maze, finally pointing at the gaping holes of two large elevator shafts. And the explosives inside each.

"Don't touch them. Find the detonators. They'll be electronic. Knock them out with the EMP gun."

We fanned out, and I saw a snake of wire leading from the explosives in the right shaft. I followed it with my eyes, winding and curving on the ground like a child's maze. Eventually, I ended up at the wall between the shafts themselves. And saw a blinking light.

"Decoy! There! Between the shafts! Hit it with the gun!"

He immediately took a knee, aiming the EMP. I heard a distinctive hum, then saw a blinding flash, followed by a shock wave that launched me backward.

I sat up, attempting to shake the ringing from my ears, looking to see if anyone on the team had been injured. Another sound penetrated the stillness. Something like a freight train loose on the tracks, coming from the shafts themselves.

The elevators.

I rolled backward as fast as I could, and another explosion rocked the basement, this one from the kinetic energy of a double-decker elevator hitting the earth from over ten thousand feet in the air.

62

Lucas began dressing himself and said, "Now Pike and I share something else in common."

Her wrists strapped to the top of the bed frame, Jennifer said nothing. Her panties and bra had been ripped off, but her pants remained wrapped around her lower legs, her shirt bunched up to her neck.

Lucas continued. "I'm sorry it has to end this way, but I've got a plane to catch, and I can't have you messing anything up. I mean that. You and Pike are the closest thing I have to friends, and it pains me to do this."

Jennifer tested the lamp wire around her wrists. During the assault she'd fought like a wild animal, to no avail, but had felt the wire loosen. It wasn't the best for holding knots, and she thought she could work it to her advantage, especially since Lucas hadn't bothered to tie her legs down. She continued to act catatonic. Defenseless. Simply staring at him with large eyes.

Lucas picked up a pillow from the floor. "I wish I could have simply talked to Pike. Let him know that it was all professional. Just like the targets he attacks.

There's nothing personal in it at all. In a way, I'm glad I missed him three years ago."

He held up the pillow. "Someday he'll come to grips with what he is, and he'll see that he's just like me. It's taking him a little longer, but it's true. He and I are the same."

He leaned over her. "I've heard that suffocation is the most painless way to go. Once you pass out, you feel nothing. Of course, I can't prove it, since no one I've done this to could give me an opinion when it was over. It's the best I can do, given the circumstances."

He brought the pillow to her face and hesitated, staring into her eyes. She rotated her body, bringing her legs into her stomach. She lashed out with all the strength she had in a mule kick, hitting him in his upper chest.

Caught off guard, Lucas flew across the room into the far wall. Jennifer yanked one arm free, then frantically began working her hand out of the second loop. Lucas sprang up and rushed her. She snapped out with a side kick, connecting again, and felt the hand slip out.

She jumped off the end of the bed, putting Lucas behind her, the door to the living room to her front. She yanked her pants up with one hand and clawed at the door with the other, getting it open. She almost made it out before he tackled her, bellowing in rage.

They bounced off the table in front of the anteroom television, then hit the floor. She rolled onto her back, Lucas straddling her body and trapping her left arm. She whipped her right elbow up and caught him on the chin, stunning him enough to allow her to snake out of his grasp. She leapt to her feet and he followed suit, slamming her into the wall. Rattled, the blow cutting her ability to think, she felt herself rotated around until her back was to the wall, her arms trapped in his grip.

He leaned into her face, the spittle flying out.

"You fucking bitch. Never want to make it easy. Always want the fucking pain. So be it."

He reached his hands up to the base of her neck to repeat the pummeling she'd endured earlier. She stared into his snarling visage and felt his hands close. She knew she was done. *No way out.*

She thought of Pike. Of how he wouldn't quit. Never, ever quit.

Never. Ever. Quit.

She whipped her head forward, catching him just above the bridge of his nose with the bony part of her forehead. He shrieked, and she did it again, feeling the nose crunch underneath the blow. Feeling him back up to escape.

She turned and ran, reaching the door to freedom a millisecond before him. She felt his breath on her neck, his hands grabbing her shirt. She launched a leg backward, felt it connect and heard him grunt, then she was outside.

She sprinted to the north elevator bank. The one with the envoy's security. She got within sight of it and started walking, checking her appearance. Her shirt was back in place, but she had abrasions on her wrists, and her hair, she knew, must look wild.

She glanced behind her and saw Lucas scowling from the entrance to his room. He pointed a finger at her like a weapon, then blew the tip as if he was clearing smoke before shutting the door. She continued past the elevators until she reached a stairwell, ignoring the stares of the security men. She sprinted down them and ran to her car. A minute later, she was out of the garage and pulled over to the side of the road, throwing up on the shoulder.

She collected herself, sitting in the front seat and panting, unable to fully come to grips with what had just happened. She felt a simmering rage. Pulling out her phone, she saw several missed calls from the team. *Out chasing a terrorist while I was raped.*

At that moment she decided to keep the attack a secret. To pretend the abomination was nothing more than a bad dream that had never happened. She'd help the team find and capture Lucas, then watch him get the Taskforce version of justice. For the first time, she understood fully what that meant. Embraced the reasons why. Wanted to be the one who dropped the hammer.

She texted Pike, telling him she was okay and on the way back. She put the phone away without calling, not caring what had transpired with the Ghost. She drove to their hotel and went to her room. She stripped out of her clothes and went straight to the shower, letting the hot water beat her body.

She began scrubbing furiously as if she was covered in poison, doing whatever it took to cleanse her skin of Lucas's touch. After an initial flurry, she stopped. She clinically surveyed the damage to keep her mind off the implications of the assault, wondering how she could keep it secret.

She had vicious bruises to her abdomen and a bite mark on one breast, but all of that could be hidden. Lucas had never struck her in the face, so nothing obvious would show. The biggest issue was the abrasions on her wrists. It would be hard to hide them. She thought of how she could bandage them, what she would say to the men of the team, when the enormity of the entire attack came crashing down, flooding her, drowning her.

She curled up in a ball in the bottom of the shower and wept.

63

The makeshift TOC was a flurry of activity, with all hands either deleting computer files, packing up equipment, or talking on the phone. I reached Jennifer's voice mail yet again and felt a trickle of dread. I'd received a text from her saying she was inbound, but all I really knew was that it had come from her phone. So far, the entire mission had been a debacle, like we had been painted with a curse, and the lack of contact with her was beginning to go beyond the "worried" stage and into the "screw the mission" stage.

Not that I could mess things up any worse. We had barely made it out of the Burj Khalifa intact, with seemingly every first responder in the country rolling in to the alarm calls. The bottom of the basement had looked like someone had detonated a car bomb in it, with the elevator shafts completely destroyed. I would have been happy with simple mechanical damage, but that wasn't the only thing left behind.

When I'd cleared my head enough to take stock, I'd seen the remains of quite a few people. Torn arms and legs, heads smashed beyond recognition; it was hard to tell how many people were dead. Not that it mattered. Only two counted: the sheikh of Dubai and McMasters. I was pretty sure they would be found in the pile and returned my focus on getting the hell out of the country. *Someone else's problem now.*

There'd been a rumor that someone had survived, and Blaine had raced out of the TOC to see if he could run anything to ground. I knew he was just wishing. I'd seen the damage. No way anyone lived through a fall like that.

A television in the back of the room, on an English-speaking channel, was going on and on about the disaster. I'd eventually tuned it out, focusing on getting everything sterilized, but Decoy hadn't. He got my attention.

"What?"

"They're saying an elevator has failed in the Burj."

"Okay. I don't need to watch the news for that. I saw it."

"No. They're saying *an* elevator. Not elevators, plural."

I stopped what I was doing, now paying attention.

"Did you see two elevators come down?" he asked.

Before I could answer, Blaine entered the room. Smiling. He should have been morose as hell, having given the order for a unilateral hit without Omega authority from the Oversight Council, then having it backfire in his face. He was done and should know it. I wondered if maybe he hadn't cracked.

"What?"

"We're okay. You did good work. Saved the day."

I flipped closed the computer in front of me and said, "Mind explaining?"

"The Ghost placed explosives on both the cables holding the cars and on the emergency brake systems designed to prevent a catastrophe if the cables failed. Your EMP stopped one single charge from going off. The brake system that contained the sheikh and the envoy. They got a wild ride for a few floors, but no permanent damage."

"So only one elevator came down?"

"Yeah. It's not pretty. Probably had ten to fifteen people in it, half American. Not good, but certainly not the worst we could be facing."

I sat back, no longer worried about packing up, letting the relief wash over me. Enjoying the small victory. And feeling a little guilty about calling this a victory when so many had died.

"Okay. I'll chalk this up as a win. What's Kurt saying? You going to jail?"

He grinned again. "No. The Council's okay with it because of the end result. If we hadn't executed, the envoy would be dead. Kurt's just a little pissed that I didn't call him beforehand. I'll get my ass chewed, but that's about it."

I was surprised. "You didn't call him at all? Even for a SITREP?"

"No. I figured he'd tell me to stand down and that it would be easier to ask for forgiveness than permission."

Now that *was a gutsy decision.*

"What if I'd screwed up? Turned this into an international incident?"

"Why ask the question? You didn't."

I couldn't believe he'd risked so much solely on my actions. It altered my opinion of him. Raised it exponentially.

I said, "Well, there's always next time."

He smiled and said, "We've got to get the detainees out to the desert. Skyhook's on the way. Kurt wants this wrapped up quickly, get us out of here before someone connects the dots. I'm flying home tomorrow with the support package. You guys switch hotels, stay for one more day, then head out."

The door opened, and Jennifer entered, sending a flutter to my stomach I wasn't used to feeling. I ignored Blaine.

"Jesus, what the hell have you been doing? I've been worried sick."

She gave me a wan smile and said, "I had some car trouble. A flat tire."

I noticed her hair was wet, and she was now wearing jeans and a long-sleeve shirt rolled down to her wrists. "You changed clothes. What's up? You took the time to take a shower before contacting us?"

She shifted back and forth and said, "I sent you a text. I sweated like crazy changing the tire. I just wanted to freshen up a little."

She looked around and said, "What's going on? Where do we stand?"

I explained the situation, then said, "As for where we stand, I was just asking that very thing."

Blaine said, "What else is there? I told you what's going to happen in the next twenty-four hours."

"What about Lucas?"

He held up his hands in a gesture of surrender. "Pike, hey, I get the guy tried to kill you, but he's not a security threat. His information panned out. He's gone, and the Taskforce isn't going to hunt him."

I saw Jennifer's jaw drop. I said, "Are you serious? He killed Ethan Meriweather, along with his entire family. He's still designated as a DOA target."

DOA stood for Dead Or Alive and was a Taskforce designation that was rarely used. Almost one hundred percent of the time, we wanted the information inside the terrorist's head. DOA meant the target was a distinct and urgent threat to national security, and we'd deemed the loss of information through interrogation less important than neutralizing him. Very few targets met that definition in our little world. Most terrorists like that were vaporized by a predator drone in areas within which we couldn't operate.

I'd never had a DOA target, but the teams that did jokingly said it stood for "Dead On Arrival," since nobody in their right mind would continue trying to capture a guy when it was authorized to kill him. Much, much easier to do. Lucas had earned the title when he'd murdered the family of a Taskforce member.

"Pike, I get that. If it was up to me, we'd go hunting

right now, but we've worn out our welcome on this op. Orders are to get everyone home and let things cool down. No more overt actions. Period."

Before I could answer, Jennifer blurted, "You can't let him go! He's a murderer. We need to catch him."

Both Blaine and I jerked our heads to her, startled at what she had said. An uncharacteristic outburst from someone who was as close to a bleeding heart as the Taskforce had.

Blaine said, "I hear you. I really do, and we'll get him eventually. He's just not a strategic threat. I have to agree with Kurt on this one. Yeah, he's a shithead, but he's not a Taskforce shithead. He's someone else's problem."

I saw Jennifer clenching her jaw so tight the muscles rippled in her cheek. She said nothing else, and honestly, I was good with it.

"So get these guys to the Skyhook and call it a day?"

"Yeah. Can you handle that?"

"No issues at all. We'll use the same DZ that the equipment came into. Jennifer can find it easy."

"Then get moving. I'll send the alert and the L-one-hundred will be here three hours after nightfall."

THIRTY MINUTES LATER we had two four-wheel-drive Nissan Pathfinders loaded up, Decoy and Brett in one with the two terrorists bundled in the back, and Jennifer and I leading the way to link up with the L100, the sun setting on the horizon.

The Skyhook was an extraction technique invented in

the late 1950s. Used operationally only a few times, it had remained in the U.S. inventory until the 1980s, when the Department of Defense decided it was easier to fly in a helicopter than risk the damage to a human using the extravagant system. I'd done a lot of borderline things in my career, but testing this capability was at the top of stupid, which is why we used it only for terrorists.

The system had actually been used by Hollywood more than by the CIA or DOD—appearing in multiple movies—and had eventually been phased out when helicopters began to do aerial refueling that gave them the ability to reach over great distances.

It still worked for us because our problem wasn't reach. It was explaining what the hell we were doing in the country. Thus, having a plane conduct an overflight on a registered flight plan, then dip for a span of seconds to intersect the package before returning to flight altitude, solved a lot of extraction problems for folks we couldn't get through immigration.

Bouncing across the desert, Jennifer did nothing but steer and navigate, never once asking me about anything that had happened. That and her demeanor told me something was different. She had an aura melting off of her that permeated the entire vehicle. Maybe something only I could sense, but it was there, filling the cab with its stench. I said nothing, waiting for her to open up.

Eventually, she said, "What do you think about Lucas? You going to let that go?"

"What do you mean? I don't really have a choice. He's

an asshole, but I'm not going to chase his butt all over the world."

She looked at me for a long pause, reading my face. When she returned to the road, she said, "What about Ethan's family? Isn't that enough?"

Where was this going?

"Yeah, that's definitely enough, but I don't have the team or the intel to chase him. He'll turn up."

"What if I told you I had the intel? That inside his room I found where he's going? Would that be enough?"

"What kind of game are you playing? Why are you asking?"

She looked at me again, and I saw a door slam closed. "Nothing. Just asking. It doesn't matter to me either."

64

We reached the pickup grid without speaking again. I knew something was wrong, but was genuinely unsure of what to say or how to act. I let it ride.

Decoy and Brett unloaded the two prisoners while I laid out the kit, consisting of nothing more than a specially constructed rope and a helium balloon. Jennifer attached the battery wires for what looked like an ordinary pocket calculator to the antenna lead of the radio, giving us the ability to hear the aircraft's encrypted transmissions through the stereo in the Pathfinder. It was a simple decryption device that translated the radio calls of the aircraft, transmitted using a standard FM frequency on the radio dial. The hitch was we couldn't speak back verbally. That didn't mean we couldn't communicate.

Both of the terrorists had been sedated with a special drug that was not unlike controlled substances used on every college campus in America. It gave a sense of euphoria while inhibiting conscious thought. They were coherent, but just barely, looking around with glazed eyes like they were trying to understand what was happening. They had enough coordination to put on the special jumpsuits for the ride, completely oblivious as to why they were doing it.

Ten minutes out, Jennifer fired up the Pathfinder and dialed the radio to the correct frequency. I stood by with an infrared pointer, barely able to make out the terrorists thirty feet away in the dark, sitting back-to-back in orange jumpsuits.

We heard nothing but static for four minutes, then a clear break.

"Prometheus, Prometheus, this is Stork. You got a baby for me to deliver?"

I fired up the IR pointer and began doing slow loops in the sky.

"Roger, Prometheus, got your rope. Stand by. Be on target in ten minutes."

That was the call to release the balloon. I attached two infrared ChemLights to the rope, separated by a hundred feet, then turned on the helium. Within seconds, the rope began to rise in the air.

Ordinarily, the plane would be able to see the line in daylight, driving right into it and capturing the rope with a special little "V" attachment in the nose. Since nothing was easy enough for the Taskforce, we did the capture at night, blacked out, which called for the pilot to literally find the two IR ChemLights while wearing night observation goggles and steer his nose toward them, keeping one high and one low, hoping to snag the line.

There was one other difference the Taskforce had to heighten the adventure. The old MC-130s used to have a cable running from the nose to the outside edge of the wings to protect the propellers if the pilot missed the rope, in effect preventing it from snarling in an engine. Since that setup would look decidedly strange on a "commercial" airplane, we didn't use it. Scary shit I would never do. Taskforce pilots were borderline insane.

We waited, getting no indication the plane was approaching, since all lights had been dashed and it was now diving from a commercial altitude to eight hundred feet. I kept my eye on the two passengers, making sure they didn't do anything stupid like try to jump up and run. We didn't flex-cuff them for the same reason we didn't give them a drug that would make them unconscious; if something went wrong, we wanted them to be at least somewhat capable of helping to save their lives.

Out of nowhere, I heard the four engines of the L100, a stretch, commercial version of the venerable C-130 cargo plane. It raced overhead, and I watched the terrorists, knowing what was coming.

Two seconds later, they were ripped from the ground and flying out of sight. It looked violent as hell, but I knew from experience it had less of a shock than a simple parachute opening.

I waited for the radio call, not wanting to go racing through the desert for a crashed airplane towing terrorists. The stereo crackled, and I relaxed from what came out.

"Prometheus, this is Stork. Baby's in the crib, and we're moving to delivery."

We high-fived for a moment, then packed up. Shortly, I was back in the tomb with Jennifer, only she was now in the passenger seat. We went for ten minutes, the silence getting so dense it was like cotton in the cab, surrounding us both and starting to smother. Eventually, she broke it.

"Do you think letting Lucas go is right?"

What is the damn fascination with him? She couldn't stand the way I acted in Bosnia when I captured him, now she wishes I'd smoked him when I had the chance?

I turned, seeing her face illuminated by the lights of the dash. "Jennifer, what's going on? Why do you keep asking about him?"

She paused, then said, "Nothing. I was just wondering."

"Bullshit. You remember on the boat, when you said you could read me? You were right, but it works both ways. Nobody else sees it, but I do. Tell me what's going on."

She stared at me for a moment, then snaked her hand over mine on the bench seat. "I have to tell you something."

"Okay . . . I'm ready. I think."

"It's personal. You can't tell anyone else. I mean that."

What the hell?

"Yeah, sure. You going to let me in on a big secret? I'm finally getting to see the real Jennifer or something?"

She said nothing, and I saw her eyes tear up. *Holy shit. What is going on?*

"Lucas . . . Lucas did something. Something I want you to know about."

I waited, only hearing sniffles, finally saying, "What?"

When she looked up, her eyes were still wet, but clear, and her voice was now firm. "You know what. He murdered Ethan. Slaughtered his whole family. We need to get him. We shouldn't let it go."

The change in tone raised a flag. She'd known about Ethan and his family when I had Lucas in Bosnia. *Why get bloodthirsty now?*

"Jennifer, you heard the boss. The Taskforce isn't going to do anything about it unless he becomes a threat to national security. We don't chase murderers."

"I'm not talking about the Taskforce. I'm talking about us."

"Huh? What do you mean?"

She reached into a pocket of her pants and brought out a card. An ID of some sort. She said, "Pull over."

"Why?"

"Please."

I did so, getting a radio call from Knuckles behind me. I told him we were fine and to continue on. He protested, and I barked at him. He slowly disappeared ahead of us. Jennifer turned on the dome light and handed me the card.

It was my friend's driver's license. Ethan, with that

same goofy grin. Now gone, tortured to death by Lucas. The picture caused a spike of anger at his loss.

She said, "I found that in Lucas's luggage, along with other things from people he's killed. I also found out where he's going and what hotel he'll be staying in. We can do this."

I wanted to. It felt right. But I knew it wouldn't work.

"Jennifer, I'm with you, but Lucas knows both you and me on sight. There's no way we can get this done. He's a hard target, not like some of the losers you've seen us take down. Shit, just look at what he did in Dubai."

She said, "So convince the team. They'll listen to you. They'll help."

"Why? Why do you want this so much now?"

She looked out the window at the stars, saying nothing. I was about to ask again when she said, "I realize this isn't like me, but I *knew* Ethan. I caused his death by showing up at his house. The ID made it real. And I need to make it right."

I looked at the license again, seeing Ethan alive in my mind's eye, then running through implications of a non-sanctioned hit. The logistics involved, and the repercussions. I thought we could do it, but only a DOA mission. There would be no way to exfiltrate a live prisoner, and no one to transfer him to if we could. I knew that would end the operation for Jennifer. Her sense of fair play wouldn't allow it, but I'd let her come to that conclusion.

"Okay. I'll talk to the team. See if they'll go along, but

we're going to be limited on our options. We'll have no support team to take custody."

"I get that. I understand."

"Well, what do you want to do with Lucas when we find him?"

She locked eyes with me, her teeth clenched together, the muscles in her jaw vibrating.

"I want you to fucking kill him."

65

Lucas Kane searched one more news story just to be sure and read the same results with a sense of relief. The peace conference in Qatar was going ahead as scheduled. Which meant the money transfer would go ahead as well.

When he'd arrived yesterday afternoon the news had been full of reports about the "failure" of one of the Burj Khalifa's elevators, with sensational stories about the excruciatingly protracted length of time the people floated inside, knowing they were going to die, screaming all the way down until they impacted at terminal velocity with the force of an out-of-control freight train.

The fact the sheikh of Dubai and the United States Middle East envoy were in the building made it that much more salacious, with newscasters breathlessly repeating what little they knew over and over again, adding nothing to the knowledge of what had occurred, but driving the story to a fever pitch. He'd assumed the worst, but finally, the Dubai government lifted its censorship blanket, and the news began reporting that both men had lived.

Not really caring about their corporeal status, Lucas focused on the political results of the attack, trying to find the standing of the envoy's mission in Qatar. He'd checked back online several times during the day until he had finally found the story in front of him.

It made him both relieved and a little jealous. While all news outlets were reporting a simple mechanical failure, he knew for a fact what had happened. *No wonder I had such trouble killing Pike. That guy's a fucking predator.* He couldn't help but be impressed with the operation, precisely because it hadn't made the news. With a pang of envy, Lucas realized that Pike and his team were better than anyone he had ever served with. He would have liked to recruit the man as a partner. *We could really clean up.*

He wondered if Pike had reflected on how he'd been able to prevent the deaths of the sheikh and the envoy. If he'd given a little thanks to Lucas for his help. *Probably not, after talking to Jennifer.*

He smiled at the memory, then reflexively moved his hand to his broken nose, the light touch bringing a stab of pain. *Serves that bitch right.*

Now sure his own mission hadn't been sabotaged, he typed a different address into the computer. After it loaded, he typed in an administrator's password, then began scrubbing the list.

He knew the envoy himself wouldn't be trudging around the Middle East carrying a suitcase full of cash. No matter how much VIP treatment he got, it just didn't make any sense. The risk of loss or discovery was simply too great, and he knew it wasn't coming from the State Department's budget in the first place.

If the envoy was truly transferring black cash, it would be coming from the CIA. Nobody else had the architecture or experience to bury a large sum of money from the scrutiny of Congress. Which meant a separate flight for the escorts, most likely ground branch case officers from the Special Activities Division.

Whoever was coming, he knew they'd be traveling as State Department employees. That being the case, they'd be using the State Department's travel Web site to book their tickets in an attempt to blend in with the myriad other moves State did on a daily basis.

Before he'd had to flee the United States, he'd developed a solid business solving problems for various people, including a man named Harold Standish on the National Security Council. Standish had passed him administrative rights to the State travel Web site, and they had proven useful on several different operations. In the end, Lucas had ended up killing Standish, but had kept the administrative privileges.

He sorted the listing of travelers by date, then location, working backward from Qatar. He came up empty. The site listed nobody as traveling to Qatar from the State Department in the next four days. *Probably because they're all on that private jet the envoy's using.* But that didn't explain the lack of the escorts. Surely they aren't on the plane as well, flying all over the Middle East protecting a suitcase of wealth?

Don't get panicked. Maybe they just haven't bought a ticket yet. The conference was due to last for five days, starting from today, so they could be flying at any time. He decided to simply wait here in Frankfurt, checking back each day. At the end of five days, he'd just have to figure out something else to do for a living. Maybe the Far East. In the meantime there was plenty of female companionship one block from his hotel, in the Frankfurt red-light district near the Hauptbahnhof.

66

I was finishing up in Lucas's hotel room when Decoy called to tell me no change.

"Still banging the keys in the Internet café."

"Can you see what he's working on?"

"Not without sitting next to him, but I'm close enough to see that someone really thrashed him. Both his eyes are black."

I placed Lucas's shirts back in the suitcase exactly as I had found them, then saw the leather satchel Jennifer had mentioned.

"Keep your distance. I'm almost done here. When he clears out, give us a call. Jennifer and I'll take a look. You guys stay on him. Where is it?"

"Underground at the Hauptbahnhof. There's a little shopping area here. Middle of the concourse, opposite the S-Bahn entrances. You can't miss it."

"Which box?"

"Third one from the left. Bank along the north wall."

"Got it."

Opening the satchel, I flipped through the trinkets until I found a keychain from Reno. A keychain I recognized. It was Ethan's wife's, who had been killed at the same time as Ethan. No way was the keychain a coincidence. Lucas had been there. Had murdered them. I dug around a little more and pulled out the other driver's license Jennifer had mentioned. *Someone else that bastard killed*. I wrote down the data, then zipped the satchel closed.

I hadn't found much about his future intentions, no receipts, ticket stubs, anything like that. But that was just gravy anyway, because I'd confirmed where he'd be sleeping tonight. Before exiting the room, I disabled the chain and the dead bolt, not wanting Lucas to be able to prevent my key card from working. Satisfied, I jogged down the stairs to join Jennifer in the lobby, wondering if what I was doing was just.

Out in the desert it had seemed right. Even easy. Jennifer agreeing that he should be killed had been the icing on the cake. It had to be the correct path if even *she* thought so. Now, I wasn't so sure. I would be the one pulling the trigger. Nobody else.

I'd lied to Blaine and let him fly on home, then broke the news to the team, attempting to convince them to assist. I'd told them it was strictly voluntary and strictly outside the Taskforce. This was personal, and I'd be the one doing the killing. Conducting surveillance was one thing, but there was no way I could ask the men to help me in the actual takedown of Lucas. When it came down to it, it would be a one-man operation, with the others long gone.

In the end, Jennifer had been right: They all came on board fairly easily. Knuckles was in immediately, even stating he didn't mind the killing part. Decoy came on board as well, but Brett balked. I understood his reluctance, especially since we hadn't ever been teammates. He didn't know Ethan or his family, couldn't understand the pain their loss had caused. Eventually the peer pressure got to him, and he agreed to conduct initial surveillance, but wanted nothing to do with the killing.

Now, after twenty-four hours and a night of rest, the feeling of righteousness had dissipated somewhat, and I was going through the motions of tracking Lucas mechanically, tamping down the passion of the act. I didn't like how it was affecting me. I thought killing him would be just like any other combat action I'd been forced into, but it wasn't, and the difference was starting to seep in.

I'd never taken a life in cold blood, purely for personal reasons, and a part of me was having a tough time coming to grips with the undertaking, even given the loss of Ethan's family. Not so much because of the killing, but because of the repercussions. Killing in combat, for the defense of the nation or simply self-preservation, was something I could do and had done. Killing in cold blood was something else entirely, and I was fearful of what it might do to my psyche. I wasn't guessing about the damage. I had a lot of experience in that arena.

I had lived in a cesspool of guilt and rage after my family died and knew intimately how powerful the subconscious mind was. I had no desire to return to that cancerous place and feared I was now freely volunteering to do so.

Another part of me, prehistoric and reptilian, relished the opportunity, the scar tissue that had covered it beginning to break down, giving it room to blossom. That part didn't give a rat's ass about the consequences. I could hear it chanting in the background, "Yes . . . yes . . . yes," and it was growing louder. The bloodlust was unsettling.

I found Jennifer in the lobby and said, "Your information was spot-on. It's his room."

We started walking across the lobby and she said, "So? What're you going to do?"

"Kill him tonight, when he's back in it." I said it like I was talking about getting takeout.

She nodded her head vaguely, coming to grips with the fact that the information she'd provided was now going to be used to take a life.

"I don't have time to go back and forth on this. We only have another day before we're missed by Kurt and the Taskforce."

We'd flown out right behind Blaine yesterday, him thinking we were going to hang around for one more day. After spending twenty-four hours in Frankfurt, we were now going to send a SITREP describing aircraft troubles—as if we'd just arrived from Dubai—and a subsequent layover. I'd bought us forty-eight hours, and that was it. I was just happy we'd managed to find Lucas in the city in such a short amount of time.

He'd thrown away the phone we'd originally tracked him with, so that was no help. Luckily, Jennifer had the four hotels she'd discovered from his Internet search in Dubai. Finding the one he was in, using his Canadian ID, had been easy. Finding his room without Taskforce hacking help, however, had been a different matter.

We had to do it the old-fashioned way, by distracting the guy behind the reception area. I'd first positioned Brett as a trigger for Lucas in the lobby, then had both him and Decoy begin the surveillance of him, using Knuckles as nothing more than a taxicab to drop them off and pick them up during the operation.

As soon as Lucas had cleared the building, I'd thrown Jennifer into the breach to use her wily female charms to get the reception guy to leave his counter. I don't know what she said, but off they went to the business center, leaving me with plenty of time to find Lucas's room and imprint a separate key card. She had come back glaring at me, with the young man in tow practically drooling.

Now, with everything in place, the operation became real. I was going to kill him. In cold blood. I was no longer going to *try* to kill him, and I wasn't looking for him in Frankfurt in the *hopes* of killing him. I'd found him, and he was dead just as surely as Ethan's family. Tonight.

Decoy called as we exited Lucas's hotel. "He's moving. Out of the café and up the stairs."

"Got it. We're headed that way now. Give me a call when he's clear."

"Roger."

I hung up my cell and said, "We have a little mini-mission. I need you to drop me off at the Hauptbahnhof, then circle the block until I call."

"What's up?"

"Apparently Lucas is using Internet cafés, and I want to see what he's up to. I need the forensics thumb drive you used in Lucas's room in Dubai."

She gave me a quizzical look, then I saw her brain make the connection of what I was asking, and she literally grew red in the face. "I . . . don't have it. I gave it to the support crew with the rest of our kit. I'm sorry. That was stupid of me."

Dammit. "Don't worry about it," I said. "I think Knuckles has one."

We'd given all of our overt kit like guns, beacons, and radios to the support crew to dispose of—minus one suppressed Glock I'd hidden in my luggage—but things like thumb drives and our Taskforce cell phones were ordinarily kept because they raised no suspicion. I was surprised that she'd given it up. *Not like her at all.*

Before I could even dial, she was on the phone with Knuckles, getting directions to meet him. In short order, I had the call from Brett saying Lucas was clear, and I was walking down the stairs to the Internet café. Luckily, the computer Decoy had described was still free.

I paid for five minutes, then pulled up Internet Explorer, finding the history empty. I plugged in the thumb drive and gathered the Web sites for the last hour. The most recent were for strip shows here in Frankfurt, which would make our follow a little bit easier tonight and might make it easier to kill Lucas since he'd probably be drunk.

Continuing, I found references to news stories about the Burj Khalifa, which confirmed that I was on the right box, then a site that confused me. It was a State Department travel agency, and the request had been for State Department personnel on all flights going from Germany to Qatar for the next few days.

Qatar? Why's he looking at that? What's he up to?

In the end, I decided it didn't matter. He only had a few more hours on this earth anyway.

67

Lucas returned to his room a little bored. He'd toured just about everything he could around the city, and with the lack of information about the couriers, he had nothing to really work on. He'd thought finding an RFID reader would be hard in Germany, but he'd managed to do that on the first attempt, even locating one that appeared like an ordinary computer, with inconspicuous antennae he could loop outside of his laptop bag when the time came.

With nothing else to do, he powered up the new reader and checked if he could dial into the device he had planted in Qatar. Once online, he inputted the ISP address and smiled when it connected. The improvised explosive device was in place and online. All it needed was a trigger, and he would get that soon.

Seeing it was four o'clock—past check-in time—he packed his bags and called the front desk. "Yes, this is Lucas Kane. I hate to be a bother, but this room is a bit stuffy. I'd like to switch."

"I'm sorry, sir, but we're completely full. I can offer you a discount."

Dammit.

"I don't want a discount. I want another room. Don't you have any open for late check-in? Give me theirs and they can have this one. I haven't been here all day, so the room's clean."

"Please hold."

While he didn't feel it necessary to switch out hotels every single day, on the days he wasn't leaving he liked to at least switch rooms, after the check-in time had passed. He did it out of habit. Practice. He felt no danger in Frankfurt, from Hezbollah or anyone else, but that didn't mean he needed to be sloppy.

The receptionist came back on. "Okay, sir. I do have a room. When would you like to switch?"

"Right now."

68

I leaned against the headboard of my small hotel bed, remote in one hand and a Glock 30 in the other, the compact gun overshadowed by the large can on the end of the barrel.

I stared at the television, the screen nothing but a bunch of jumbled images that didn't register in my conscious mind. Nothing was registering in my conscious mind. It was intentionally blank, like a Zen warrior guiding the arrow that is not aimed. At least that's what I was trying to achieve. In reality, I'd blanked my mind because I couldn't take the conflict raging between my good angel and my bad. It was easier just to sit, thinking of nothing.

And so I did, for hours, answering the phone occasionally to get an update on Lucas's night out. He was apparently a sexual dynamo, but he hadn't had a drop of liquor. At least he'd be sleepy from the workout. I hoped.

I was startled out of my reverie by a knock on the door. Shoving the Glock under a pillow, I opened it to find Jennifer outside.

"What's up? Is there an issue?"

"Not really. Just bored. I take it the call hasn't come in yet."

"Nope, but it's only ten p.m. He's probably not coming back until after midnight."

"Can I come in?"

I really didn't want her to. I didn't need the distraction. I needed to think. Or more precisely, I needed a still room so I wouldn't be forced to think.

She saw my reluctance and said, "Please? I need to ask you a favor."

I opened the door and pointed at the lone chair in the tiny room. I climbed back on the bed.

"You got a preference on channels?"

"An English one would be nice."

"I got *Doogie Howser* in German. Will that work?"

She smiled. "Sure."

I flipped the TV, turned down the sound of bad dubbing, and said, "What's up?"

"How are you getting to his hotel tonight?"

"Taxi."

"You think that's smart?"

"Well, it's smarter than walking. Trains have quit running this late."

"Yeah, that's my point. You'll be remembered when they find Lucas. I mean, you'll probably be one of two cabs who stop there tonight. You and Lucas himself."

"So, you have a better idea?"

"Yes. Let me drive you."

The offer surprised me, but it was out of the question.

"No way. Nobody else is getting involved. Especially you."

"Why? You need the help. Why 'especially me'?"

I hadn't meant for that to slip out, but I meant it. We'd never had our big talk on where we stood in our relationship, even though she'd threatened it a couple of times—scaring the hell out of me—so I'd never really told her how I felt about her. Truthfully, I was afraid of rejection and had tricked myself into believing that I was content with a lesser connection of being simple business partners. A little Jennifer was much better than none. But that didn't alter the fact that I would protect her from harm, whether she felt the same way about me or not. Especially since this harm was easily averted.

"Jennifer, you're not going with me. Period. Out of the question."

She came over and sat on the bed next to me, pulling up a pillow to place behind her back. And revealing the Glock.

She stared at it for a second, a look of regret on her face, as if she'd caused it to appear. She said, "Pike, I want to be a part of this. I feel responsible. I'm the one who told you. I want to help."

I waved my hand. "Quit it. It's not going to happen. Just drop it."

"It *is* going to happen, dammit! I *am* going to be a part of this operation!"

Whoa. Where's that coming from?

Before I could say anything, she continued. "Pike, it's my fault. *I'm* the reason you're doing this. I'm the one who brought it about. I know you don't understand. I don't expect you to, but I need this. I *need* to be a part of the operation. It can't be all you. We both suffer the consequences. I can't have you doing this alone based solely on what I told you."

What the hell was she talking about? Because she found the hotel rooms, she should be culpable for his death?

I decided to end this with a lie. "Okay, okay. Head on back to your room. I'll call you when I get the trigger he's back in bed."

She said, "Why don't I just stay here?"

"Because I want to be alone, all right?"

She squinted at me, catching the whiff of dishonesty, but walked to the door. She opened it and said, "You'd better call."

I said, "I will. Go."

I lay back on the bed, thinking again of what I was doing. More and more, it didn't seem right. Maybe it was simply disingenuous mental gymnastics, but Taskforce operations were sanctioned at the highest levels of government. When we went out on a hit, we did so after a thorough vetting, always because the target was a distinct threat to American lives. Doing this on my own, simply for revenge, was beginning to eat at my soul.

We operated with rules for a reason. I wondered if ignoring them made me no different than Lucas. Made me like the stalker of my dreams. A murderer.

Time passed quickly, and when I looked at the motel clock, I was surprised to see it was now past one a.m. The call would be coming at any moment. I made my decision and felt a measure of peace immediately.

Sorry, Ethan, but you know it's the right choice.

I reached for the phone to call surveillance when there was a knock on the door. Jennifer stood behind it, causing a little thread of anger.

"What are you doing here? I said I'd call."

"I couldn't sleep, and I figured it was getting close, so I came back."

She glanced away, refusing to look me in the eye. *She can't lie worth a damn. But apparently you can't either. She knew you weren't going to call.*

"Well, you can go to bed for good. The mission's off."

She said, "Why? Did he get on a train or something?"

"No. It's me. I'm not going to pull the trigger."

69

I t took a moment before the implications of his words settled into Jennifer's mind.

No, no, NO. He can't get a conscience now.

She said, "What do you mean? What happened?"

Pike turned away from the door, saying over his shoulder, "I can't do it. I'm going to call Kurt tomorrow, tell him everything we have and get him on board. Make it legal."

Jennifer said, "Pike, you know that won't work. Kurt will flip out that we're even in Germany. He'll order us home and then rip us apart. Even if he agrees, he'll want a support team here, and we don't have time for that."

He held up his hand. "Let it go. I've been thinking about it for two days. I'm not going to do the hit unsanctioned. Either Kurt facilitates or he doesn't, but I'm not going off on a vendetta like a Mafia hit man. It's eating me alive, and I don't like the damage."

Jennifer heard what he said and felt shame for what she was putting Pike through. She considered letting it go when that *day* sprang forth. Lucas's hot breath, the lamp cord cutting into her hands on the bed as she tried to keep him away, the beating she had taken.

That bastard deserves to die. And Pike deserves to kill him.

"Pike, I need to show you something."

"Jennifer, *forget* it. You didn't see me at my worst. It was a living hell, and this damn mission is bringing me back."

"Please sit down."

He did.

Jennifer said, "I found more than Ethan's driver's license in Lucas's room."

"What do you mean?"

Jennifer pulled out an ID card and handed it to him. She watched him recognize the face, then saw him begin to change before her very eyes. The resignation of only a moment ago disappeared, replaced by a rising tsunami of violence rippling just underneath the surface. A rage vibrating the very air around him. She felt the threat from across the room, and knew she'd made a mistake.

His face twisted toward her, almost unrecognizable, the scar on his cheek standing out stark white against the mottled red of his fury. "Where the fuck did you get this? What are you up to? Some parlor trick to get me to destroy myself? Why?"

He leapt to his feet, shouting now. "Jesus Christ, I can't believe you'd do this! I don't even know you! I don't want to know you. Get the fuck out!"

She began to backpedal, holding out her hands, getting out of the danger zone while she still could.

"Pike, it's real! I didn't want to tell you before. I didn't know what to do with it. I found Heather's license with Ethan's. Lucas killed your wife. And your daughter."

Pike stopped, the violence beginning to crack the surface. He stared through her, saying nothing, his body beginning to tremble. The phone rang, and he snatched it up. He listened for a moment, never saying a word. He ended the call, picked up the Glock, and racked the slide.

"Let's go."

She hesitated, frightened by the change. Unconsciously, she prepared to fight. To defend herself against what she'd created.

He didn't attack her. Just shoved her into the wall, stabbing his hands into her jacket pockets. She began to fight back when he found what he wanted, ripping the pocket open and removing the keys to her rental car.

"Fucking stay here then. I'm not going to beg you."

He slammed the door behind him, sucking the darkness out of the room. She collapsed into the chair.

What have I done?

70

I parked illegally on the street, right outside the front door of the hotel, the traffic light enough that I could do so without drawing attention. Not that I gave a damn anyway.

I stalked past the front desk, the woman behind it wishing me a good night. When I looked at her, she melted back, then glanced down quickly, pretending to become interested in something on her counter.

I sprinted up the stairs, taking them two and three at a time to the fifth floor. I glanced down the hallway, seeing it was deserted.

I walked until I reached the elevators, then took a left. Shortly, I was standing outside Lucas's door, the Glock now in my hand.

I felt the press of time, knowing someone could poke their head out at any moment and see me with the pistol. I gently slid in the key card, getting a green light. I popped open the door a crack and listened. I heard nothing, the room dark.

I snaked my way inside, leaving the door propped

open a crack with the damaged dead bolt to give me enough light from the hallway to see.

I made out Lucas in the bed, lying facedown. I walked up to the foot and placed the red dot from the Glock right at the base of the skull, holding it in a two-handed grip. I'd already decided not to do anything stupid like waking him up and telling him why he was about to die. No, it would be a quick double-tap and I would be gone, leaving the maids to clean up the mess and the devil to explain to him why he was now in hell.

The barrel trembled, wobbling up and down, left and right, refusing to settle. My little corner of darkness wanted more than a simple bullet. Wanted to slice his life away one cut at a time, drawing it out as long as his body could stand. I finally had a face to the stalker of my dreams. And the black corner of my soul wanted to kill him exactly the way he had murdered my family.

Get a grip. Get a grip. Can't do that and escape. Clock's ticking. Put a bullet in his head.

I took a deep, slow breath, the crime-scene photos shining in stark Technicolor in my mind. I felt the darkness swallow me and saw my hands steady, my arms becoming twin rails with a thin bloodred dot at the center. I tightened my finger, the slack from the trigger safety gone, the trigger beginning its journey smoothly to the rear. I saw movement under the covers next to Lucas. Someone groaned, a sleep-filled little exclamation.

A whore? He brought a whore up and Knuckles said nothing?

The covers snapped back, and a boy of about six flipped to the floor, walking to the bathroom with sleep-filled eyes, completely oblivious to the storm of death standing less than four feet from him. A boy the same age as my daughter when she had been murdered.

I waited until he closed the bathroom door, then backed slowly out of the room. I made it to the stairwell before the margin between life and death slammed home. A razor's edge that made me sick to my stomach, causing me to stop and hold on to the railing for support.

Two more pounds of trigger pull and you would have killed an innocent man.

71

The sun burned my eyes, even given the dark sunglasses I was wearing. The rays felt like sandpaper against the dryness. I hadn't gotten much sleep, then had awakened at the crack of dawn to control the surveillance effort for one final try. I handled the radio while Jennifer drove, trailing the surveillance box yet again. For her part, Jennifer was treating me with kid gloves. Unsure of what I would do, and I didn't blame her.

I had touched the face of the devil, gone further into the abyss than I had ever known, and almost became the personification of evil. Almost became the man in my dreams.

Now, we continued the hunt, but I knew it was futile. I had only one more night before Kurt began asking questions, and there was little chance we'd get lucky with the Jennifer distraction to find Lucas's room like last time. *Shit. You ended up* not *finding his room.*

Knuckles brought me out of my thoughts. "Still eating breakfast at the Burger King. Still got his bags with him."

Lucas had gone back under the Hauptbahnhof, wandering around doing nothing until a Burger King had opened up, and was now killing time eating a hamburger. In my mind, I half wondered if he wasn't going to get on a train this time instead of going to a new hotel. I almost wished he would. It would make my decision much easier. I wasn't going to follow him all over Europe.

I decided to pull the trigger anyway, not waiting to see what he did. "Knuckles, go ahead and back off. Let him go."

Jennifer whipped her head at me, and Knuckles said, "Come again? What was that?"

"Break down the box. Get the boys on the street and let Lucas go."

"What the hell are you talking about? Because you hit the wrong room last night? You want to quit?"

"We don't have the right equipment or manpower for this. Winging it isn't working. We're all leaving tomorrow anyway, and there's no way I'm going to crack into an unknown room again without intel. We've got no beacons, no tracking of him, no hacking capability, nothing. He can defeat us simply by changing rooms. On top of that, we've been conducting a full-up surveillance effort with the same two men. They're probably burned to a crisp, with Lucas planning some sort of ambush. It's over."

"Why don't I just keep the box until he's through eating? See what he does? You never know, he might go to the woods all by himself or something."

"Fucking let him go!"

There was a pause, then a "Roger." He hung up, and we sat in silence for a few minutes. Jennifer finally broke it.

"I'm sorry I gave you Heather's license."

I hadn't told anyone except her what had happened. I'd simply said that I'd entered, realized it was the wrong room, and left. I didn't want to relive it. Relive how close I'd come to slaughtering a complete stranger. A man who'd checked into a room, fully expecting to take his son to the zoo or something, only to have his son wake up with his father's brains all over the sheets.

She saw me lean back into the headrest and said, "Are you okay? I've never seen you like you were last night. I thought you were going to attack me. You acted just like . . . someone else. But I think I'm now more scared of leaving this unfinished. Of opening up your scars and leaving them bleeding. You sure you want to call it? Not that I'm pushing. If you're good with it, I'm good with it."

I spoke softly, feeling the blackness wanting back in control, not happy with my decision. "Jennifer, I almost killed an innocent man last night. In front of his child. I almost became Lucas. I'm not taking that chance again. Heather wouldn't want it, and I don't want it. I'll just have to wait for vengeance. Sooner or later, he'll cross Taskforce lines again. He's just not built any other way."

She put her hand on my arm. "Hey, in the end, you *weren't* someone else. You're better than that. You wouldn't have killed him." She smiled and patted me. "I think I've got you trained just about right. The only man who would have died is Lucas. But I'm glad you're worried. It means you're still the Pike I know. Last night I wasn't so sure."

I pulled off my sunglasses and looked into her eyes. "I was squeezing the trigger. If his son hadn't woken up, I would have killed him. I almost did anyway. When I entered, I wanted to pull Lucas's body apart with my bare hands. The crime-scene photos were in my head like an actual memory. Living and breathing as if I had been there. They were so clear. So . . . more than a memory. I could even smell the blood. There's one where Heather and Angie are lying on the floor, beaten almost beyond recognition. Tim in the background gutted. The room painted in red. Angie with her hand on Heather's leg . . ."

I stopped, the pictures springing back into my mind, causing a physical pain. I forced them away and continued. "The blackness came, and I almost couldn't turn it off. Even when I saw the boy. I swear to God, for a split second my brain was computing how best to kill them both . . . kill someone just for the fuck of it. Bring a little of the pain I had to endure to the world."

JENNIFER HEARD THE WORDS, the implications of what she had done sinking in. *My fault. My fault. Jesus. I'm destroying him.* She felt her eyes begin to water and quickly tried to wipe them before he noticed, but it was too late.

"What're you getting all teary for?"

"Nothing. I'm just sorry about this. Sorry I told you.

Let's go home. Forget about Lucas. It isn't worth your sanity."

Before he could answer, his phone vibrated. She only caught one half of the conversation, but it was enough.

"What the hell do you mean he's back in the Internet café? I told you to back off." Pike listened for a second, then said, "Don't give me that shit. Back. The. Fuck. Off. You copy?"

He hung up the phone and said, "Lucas is using the café again. Apparently, Decoy and Brett were stupid enough to break the box down and go get breakfast at the Hauptbahnhof. In view of the Internet café."

She said nothing, wanting to dial Knuckles and tell him to quit herself. Stop the torture she'd brought on for selfish reasons. Get Pike back to being Pike, away from the loss of his family, her need for vengeance overcome by her concern for Pike's welfare.

He continued. "Let's head back to the hotel and check on flights out of here. I'm exhausted, and this isn't helping my attitude. I want to go home. Forget about this place."

She said, "Me too. Let's get a seat in first class. Do nothing but watch movies for the next forty-eight hours. Go to some stupid bar you like. Forget about this whole damn mission."

He smiled for the first time and said, "Maybe go back to the Blind Tiger. If you can keep from kicking someone's ass."

"I could do that. If it would help you with this."

He stared at the ceiling, saying nothing for a moment. She wondered what she'd said. His next words caused her more pain.

"I was thinking it would help if we had that big talk you keep threatening. About where we stand. You know, last night I didn't want you to participate for different reasons than Knuckles. I protected him as a friend. Not the same way I think about you."

She heard the statement and felt immediate loathing mixed with fear. She didn't want to go there. Not so soon after what had happened to her. The thought of intimacy alone made her physically ill. The mission and vengeance against Lucas had kept her feelings at bay, but Pike's words scared her. Sickened her. If Pike found out what Lucas had done, he'd leave her for sure. She was now tainted goods. Polluted from the man who had slaughtered Pike's family. If they talked, she knew she would crush him instead of telling him why—something he didn't deserve. She felt tears again, hating herself, hating Lucas, hating what he had done, feeling the overpowering need for vengeance spring forth again.

It's not supposed to work like this. It isn't fair.

Pike said, "What the hell? Asking you out for a beer causes you to cry?"

Before she could answer, his phone rang.

He said, "You'd better tell me you're getting plane reservations."

He hung up without saying another word.

She said, "What?"

"He's out of the damn café, and they want me to check it out. Jesus. Stick a fork in this operation. It's over and done."

72

Jennifer dropped me off at the nearest stairwell to the underground, on Münchener Strasse. I trotted down the stairs, wondering what that conversation had been about. Something was going on with her, and I didn't know if I wanted to push to find out. Might not like the answer.

Knuckles called and said, "He's getting on the S-Nine. Headed west. You want us to pull off?"

Jesus. "What the hell difference does it make what I say? You'll just ignore me."

I hung up the phone and entered the café. I went to the box Knuckles had indicated, not wasting time with Internet Explorer. I shoved in the thumb drive and waited on the results.

The first hit was simply an IP address, with nothing showing other than that the computers had talked. The second was the State Department travel site again, only this time two names were highlighted. Both had entered Germany two days ago through Berlin. Now both were headed out on flights to Doha, Qatar, from Frankfurt in six hours.

What the hell is he doing?

I racked my brain trying to find connections. Nothing here indicated anything with the peace process he'd tried so valiantly to "protect," yet there was no way these two State personnel weren't involved in it. And the fact that he was even looking told me he was as well.

I brought up the final Web site and saw a plane reservation. For one Lucas Kane. To Qatar. I flipped to the State page and saw it was the same flight.

I thought about the implications and realized something else. *He's just entered into the Taskforce crosshairs again. Officially. That fucker is mine.*

I shut the computer down, dialing my phone. "Knuckles, get the men back to the hotel. Pull off Lucas now."

"Yeah, yeah. You sound like a broken record."

"No, dammit. Get them back before they get any more burned. We're going to need them. Lucas is going operational."

BACK IN THE HOTEL, I contacted the Taskforce through our company VPN. Before talking to Kurt, I needed additional evidence, so I had some analysts do a little research first. While they plugged away, I considered what I was going to say. How I could soften the blow of the team's location and current activities. I didn't come up with anything solid, and, after getting my research answers, decided to simply tell the truth.

Kurt was smiling on the screen, but I was fairly sure I would knock that grin off pretty quickly.

"Hey, Pike. Good work the other day. Your usual high-adventure, but the Council was impressed."

"Great. We're going to need the love. Where's Blaine and the support crew right now?"

"The Taskforce bird 'broke down' in Shannon, Ireland. I know it's BS, but let it go. Why?"

Here we go. "You need to get them to Qatar immediately. Lucas Kane is doing something operational. I don't know what, but he's headed there in six hours."

There goes the grin.

"What the hell are you talking about? How do you know anything about Lucas Kane?"

"I tracked him to Frankfurt. I'm on him now, and he's flying to Qatar on the same commercial flight as two State Department personnel."

"You did what? Jesus Christ, Pike! We have no authority for this. No Omega in Europe. What the hell are you doing? Trying to destroy the Taskforce?"

I didn't reply, letting him get some steam off. He finally said, "Well? You going to tell me why you've got a rogue Taskforce team running amok? Give me some incredible reason why you disobeyed direct orders from the president of the United States?"

"Lucas murdered my family. I came here to kill him."

His mouth opened, then closed without saying anything, so I continued. "Jennifer found Heather's driver's license in his room, along with Ethan Meriweather's. Lucas killed them both. She also found another license. I ran a check on the name through the Taskforce law enforcement section. It was Meredith Madison, the senator's wife. Remember she was killed in a hit-and-run? Never solved? And Senator Madison retired shortly thereafter? Lucas killed her as well, for God knows who."

Nothing came from the computer, Kurt's face stunned. Reflecting on my statements. Eventually, he focused back on me. "Pike, I honestly don't know what to say."

"Sir, that's water under the bridge now. I didn't kill him, and during the surveillance operation we found evidence that he's still got designs on the peace process. He's headed to Qatar, and I need to beat him there. Can you get me a plane?"

"What? Slow down. This is coming a little fast. What do you have?"

I gave him a rundown from start to finish. When I was done, I said, "I need to get to Qatar ahead of him. I'm sending Brett and Decoy on the flight, but I need to prep the terrain, and I need that support package with Blaine."

"It's nine hours from Ireland to Dubai. Lucas will be there in twelve. I don't have time to get them to you first. I don't even have Oversight approval to begin."

"Sir, no offense, but Lucas isn't going to wait on the Oversight Council to pull their head out of the sand. He's on the hunt, and someone's going to pay."

Kurt said nothing for a moment, coming to grips with the threat. Finally, he nodded and said, "Make sure it's him."

Yes. An evil grin slipped out. "Trust me, I fucking intend to."

73

Lucas arrived at the Qatar Airways counter a full three hours before the flight was due to depart, not knowing what time his targets would check in. He had no idea what they looked like, but he was confident he could pick them out when they approached the counter.

His plan was fairly simple: Like he had with the investigator, he would use an RFID tag to trigger an explosive device that would eliminate the targets, only this time it would be the men alone killed, leaving their luggage untouched. Unlike the other hit, he wouldn't be using the baggage tag. Instead, he'd use the electronic tag built into the passports the men used.

The idea came to him when he had tried to get another passport in Lebanon and had been told the modern ones were too hard to forge. Precisely because they were now embedded with an RFID tag that contained all of the information inside the passport. It was an electronic fingerprint that could be fed to his explosive device.

The plan posed some significant challenges, not the least being stealing the information in the first place. To allay security concerns, each U.S. passport had a mesh shield embedded in the cover, preventing anyone from gleaning data when the passport was closed. This was the primary problem Lucas would have to overcome; the targeted identities could only be stolen, and the explosive device could only be triggered, if the passports were opened in the respective RFID reader's presence.

He checked his watch and saw the flight was only an hour and a half from takeoff. *SAD boys like pushing it. Probably hungover.* A second later, he watched two men in suits glancing at the airline names displayed above each counter. They were both dressed like businessmen, but they couldn't hide a bluntness. An edge that didn't fit in with the attire.

When they walked past him, he saw both pulling ordinary suitcases and one toting a Zero Halliburton aluminum briefcase in his other hand. It was swathed in a tangerine colored fabric and had a self-locking zip-tie sealing the container closed. *Very smart.*

The consulate had prepared the money as a classified diplomatic pouch, and now these two muscleheads would pose as simple State Department couriers, delivering it to the destination. Given the peace summit, the pouch would appear completely natural.

Dip-pouches, by international convention, were inviolate. No security post or government official could inspect the contents, provided the couriers produced the correct paperwork. What puzzled Lucas was the size of the pouch. No way could there be a hell of a lot of money inside a briefcase. The largest denomination the United States currently issued was the hundred dollar bill, and that would fill the available space fairly rapidly.

This had better be fucking worth it. Go through all the trouble only to get a hundred grand and I'll be pissed.

The men finally committed to the Qatar Airways flight, and Lucas pulled his luggage up behind them, flipping the switch in his carry-on backpack. He watched each man present his passport, praying the lady behind the counter would hold it above the counter. She didn't.

He stuck with them, continuing the procedure through immigration and security, finally getting a chance to check the reader at the gate. He saw he had both identities.

He raised his head, a grin slipping out. He found himself looking into the eyes of a passenger across the room. The man glanced away, now studying a blank wall. The guy's demeanor triggered an alarm. He looked vaguely familiar, an indistinct tickle saying Lucas had seen him before. Lucas bent down and pretended to dig through his bag, giving no outward indication that the man had caught his attention, but he was now a person of interest.

An hour later, he was above ten thousand feet and allowed to use his computer, the two "State Department" personnel directly behind him, the unknown across the aisle and one row up.

He connected to the in-flight Internet and dialed the ISP of the device, holding his breath. He'd checked it at the Internet café, and it had worked, giving him a shot of confidence that his hotel contact had emplaced the device correctly, but now was the moment of truth. If he couldn't input the data, the IED might as well really be a flower vase.

The reader went through a self-test, connected to the Internet, then the ISP. He hit send and waited while the two readers talked. He saw the bar for the upload moving agonizingly slow, like an anchor pulled from the mud. He was about to reload, convinced the system had locked up, when it whipped to the end in the span of ten seconds. The data was gone.

He relaxed for the first time in days. It was out of his hands now. In six hours, the two men with the diplomatic pouch would either be vaporized, or he'd be flying to the Far East empty-handed, looking for a job.

74

Our aircraft pulled into the VIP terminal of Al Udeid Air Base, an hour southwest of Doha, and I wondered who would greet us. The entire coordination had been hastily done, and chances were high that someone on the tarmac was expecting a three-star general to march out and start handing out challenge coins. The only good thing about it was we were two hours ahead of Lucas. Just enough time to get set.

I'd given Brett and Decoy their marching orders to board Lucas's plane, getting them out the door, then had Knuckles and Jennifer pack up while we waited on Kurt. He'd eventually called and said he had a C-21 aircraft at Ramstein Air Base an hour away from us. The C-21 was the military version of the Learjet 35 business jet and was used to transport dignitaries and generals around the world. This one had been hauling a three-star around when it broke down. It was in maintenance and due to continue its journey today. Somehow, Kurt had managed to cloak that it was ready to fly, with the general thinking he had another day of TDY in Germany. In the meantime, we'd stolen the plane. It was a one-way trip, with the general getting his bird back tomorrow morning none the wiser.

Now was the tricky part: getting out of this aircraft and off a U.S. Air Force base in a foreign country without anyone remembering who we were. Which would be tough considering we didn't have any vehicles, and this base was treated as if it was in a war zone.

I looked out the window and saw two men in civilian safari clothes. The kind CIA office clerks wore whenever they went overseas. Zip-off cargo pants and multipocketed shirts. It was a good sign, especially since I didn't see anyone in uniform.

The stairs lowered, and I went out first. A man walked up, and I prepared to roll with whatever came out of his mouth. A skill perfected over years of lying about who I was or what I was doing.

He stuck his hand out and said, "Channing Gray. I understand you're here in support of security for State and need a vehicle."

Wow. This is going to be easy.

I shook his hand and said, "Pike Logan, and yes. We're behind schedule, so whatever you could do to expedite would be appreciated."

He pointed at a white SUV and said, "That's yours. I just need the fund cite to release it. My boss isn't willing to pay, so it's going on State's bill."

Dammit. It's all taxpayer money. I faked a number, adding in an occasional letter, and praying he knew less about fund cites than I did. He studied the number, and I began coming up with excuses as to why it didn't look right. A second later, he handed me the keys saying, "Inspect it for damage before you go. If it's not noted, we'll charge the fund cite when you return."

I nodded my head, then completely ignored the request. We loaded up the SUV and headed out, seeing the massive search of inbound vehicles at the entrance gate, but we were free to go as a vehicle leaving.

75

As soon as the wheels hit the ground, Lucas turned on his new cell phone and dialed the porter. If he wanted the remainder of his money, he'd be waiting outside. The phone began ringing, and he noticed the unknown two rows up dialing as well. That, in itself, wasn't suspicious, but Lucas really wished he could hear what the man was saying.

He hadn't shown Lucas any interest whatsoever on the entire six-hour flight, making him feel a little bit better about his paranoia, but Lucas had lived a long, long time precisely because he assumed everybody was out to get him, and he wasn't about to relax now.

The plane reached its designated parking area, and everyone stood up to retrieve their carry-ons. Lucas ignored the men behind him, knowing they would all be in the same bus in a matter of minutes. Better not to show any interest whatsoever.

They reached immigration and, as first class passengers, were all shuffled into the diplomatic line, with the two CIA men let through before anyone else. Lucas didn't mind that, since they still had to retrieve their luggage from baggage claim. Lucas was going to let his luggage spin around the carousel until someone picked it up and put it in storage. If all went as planned, he'd be back at the airport in under an hour. He'd retrieve his baggage and return to Europe, leaving while the officials here were still trying to sort out the disaster. He hadn't planned anything further than that. It all depended on what the dip-pouch contained.

He parted ways with the fake State Department escorts, heading straight for the exit and the porter he'd paid to pick him up. He saw the original person of interest from his flight was doing the same. No luggage. Another spike.

He decided to test it, swerving toward the bathroom. Inside, he dialed his contact, telling him he was on the ground. He exited the bathroom, looking to see if the unknown was waiting, knowing he would be if he was surveillance.

A quick survey told him the man was not in the immediate vicinity. He relaxed, then caught another guy from his flight. A black man who had been in first class with him. He was now hanging out next to the baggage carousel, the belt no longer moving, the only luggage on it Lucas's own. The man was leaning against the wall doing nothing, the crowd swirling around him.

No bags at his feet, no apparent reason to stay, but there he was. Another person to watch.

Lucas ignored him and went through the exit, seeing his porter, smiling like the Cheshire cat.

"Hello, sir. Luggage?"

"It's coming later. Just get me to my hotel."

They exited the airport, heading north on Ras Abu Abboud Street. Reaching the Doha port, the driver drove along the Corniche, passing by the Emiri Diwan presidential palace where the peace talks would be held. Lucas wondered how many of the Diplomatic Quartet, as the Palestinian/Israeli diplomacy group was known, were staying in the same hotel as the envoy. He hoped all of them, because his strike would generate that much more confusion as they tried to assess the political purposes behind it.

The porter continued north along the Corniche, heading toward the diplomatic quarter. When they stopped at a traffic light Lucas flipped his visor down, lowering the makeup mirror. And felt the adrenaline flow. The black man from the airport was directly behind him in a rented SUV.

He said, "Don't take me straight to the hotel. Take a left at the roundabout by the Sheraton and stop at the City Center mall. Drop me off quickly, then keep going."

"Why? It is too hot to walk."

"I need to buy phone minutes. I'll be okay. Once you drop me off, I need you to go back the way we came. Park at the Souk Waqif, then do some shopping."

He held out a wad of Qatari rials. The porter looked at the money with suspicion.

"Why? Why do you want me to do this?"

"Look, I'm a businessman from America. I told you

that. People over here don't like Americans, and I just want to make sure nobody is out to get me."

The porter smiled, like he'd heard a child telling a ghost story, and said, "You have nothing to worry about here. This isn't Iraq."

"Well, it's worth money to you if you'll do it."

Lucas saw him shrug. "Okay. Your money is fine with me. I tried to tell you it wasn't necessary."

They made the turn at the roundabout, and Lucas surprised the porter by bailing out of the door the minute the vehicle slowed to a safe speed. Lucas watched him continue on, then backed up into a pile of construction debris, squatting down and looking for the black man. What he saw was the Caucasian pass by, the one who'd glanced away in the airport hours ago. And he was following the porter.

Not paranoid after all. All he needed was the time it took the CIA men to reach his hotel. Forty minutes max. He hoped the porter could pull off a goose chase that long.

He took off at a sprint back toward the roundabout.

76

Decoy called me as soon as the plane had landed, saying they were on the ground and moving. Lucas had shown no interest in the State Department weenies on the flight, but that was to be expected. It wasn't like he was going to slap a bumper sticker on his luggage reading "I'm out to kill someone."

Need more information on what those boys are doing.

When his update was complete, I said, "Okay, both you and Brett have vehicles staged in the rental lot. Spots thirty-five and forty-six. Keys are in the ignition. We're staged out front and can trigger, but you need to hurry."

"Roger all. Moving."

"Put your phone in surveillance mode. I want to know what's going on."

Taskforce cell phones worked like every other phone in the world, but had the ability to do group conversations, like a conference call, something that I'd been missing for the initial surveillance of Lucas in Dubai. The problem was it ran the battery down that much quicker. If we had to go dismounted, away from the car chargers, we'd only get about two hours before we lost all comms. I hoped that would be enough. I could feel the endgame coming. Which was good, because Brett and Decoy had been conducting a two-man follow for days. Sooner or later, Lucas would pick them up. If he hadn't already.

I had both Jennifer and Knuckles with me in the small pay lot right out front of the baggage claim exit. I would have liked to use them constructively, but couldn't see how, since Lucas would spot them. At least we could see everyone who left. My bet was Lucas would flag a cab, and the make and model would be crucial to relay to Decoy and Brett for the follow. I told Jennifer to keep eyes on and dialed Kurt on my Taskforce phone.

"Sir, we're set, ready to go. Lucas has paid some interest on the two State guys. Can you find out what they're up to? They have a classified dip-pouch with them. I'm wondering if that's the target. If Lucas plans on nabbing the information they're bringing to embarrass the U.S. or maybe sell it. I need to know what's in the pouch."

I expected some delay, some further questions. All I got was, "They have a dip-pouch?"

I could almost hear the wheels turning in Kurt's head. "Yeah. A Halliburton case with the orange cover."

There was another pause, then, "Holy shit. Pull off Lucas. Get on the State guys. Get some protection on them."

"What? I can't do that. I'm already positioned to trigger Lucas. The couriers were met by diplomatic folks to transfer the pouch. I have no idea where they are, and I can't get through security at the airport with any speed. If I break down the trigger to find them, I'll lose Lucas. What's up?"

"The pouch contains diamonds. A shitload of diamonds for a covert transfer to the Palestinian Authority. This isn't about the peace conference. It's a fucking robbery."

Jennifer's comment in Dubai came full force: *He's pure evil. I find it hard to believe he'd do something that was morally just if no money were involved.*

"Sir, I can't get to the diamonds, but I'm on Lucas. I've got him."

"Pike, he's got a plan. Being on him may not be enough."

"Call the State guys. Get them to stay in the airport until I can resolve this."

"Working that now, but I doubt I can get their cell numbers soon enough. The best I'll be able to do is warn them, but they're going to leave the airport."

Jesus. Jennifer was right. There had *to be money involved. No way would Lucas have prevented the assassination of the envoy for any greater good. Should've dug.* The connection had been staring me in the face.

Jennifer tapped my arm, and I saw Lucas exit the airport, moving to a beat-up Ford instead of a taxi. *Great. He has help, too.*

"Sir, Lucas is on the move. I'll call you when I can."

"Pike, so you know, I didn't get Omega for Qatar. I didn't even try. I sent Blaine on my own authority."

"And?"

"And I'm giving you Omega. If you can't capture Lucas, kill him. If it comes down to it—if it goes bad—you followed orders. My orders. You thought the Council had approved. But I'd rather you didn't get compromised."

Wow. Talk about pressure. "Roger all. Gotta go. But you'd better get the president ready for some drama in Doha. Either from Lucas or from me."

I put the phone in surveillance mode and passed the make and model of Lucas's vehicle, getting a confirmation from Brett and Decoy that they were set. Knuckles asked, "What was that all about?"

"Kurt thinks those guys are carrying diamonds worth a shit-ton of cash, and Lucas is trying to take it."

Jennifer said, "What? This all happened over money? He's just trying to rob the U.S.?"

"Yeah, apparently."

Her jaw clenched, and she squeezed the steering wheel so hard her knuckles turned white. I pretended not to notice, feeling the same way.

I said, "Get out into traffic. He's far enough ahead that we can leave, and I don't want to be forced to play catch-up if we're needed."

We started shadowing the pathetic little two-man surveillance effort, monitoring the radio traffic between Decoy and Brett. We reached a roundabout, and Brett came on.

"My heat state just jumped. I was forced to get directly behind him or lose him, and he pulled the visor mirror down. He's looking at me now. I need to pull off."

Decoy said, "I got him. I'm at your seven o'clock. Let him go."

I could feel the surveillance breaking down. With Brett burned, Decoy had about two turns before he'd have to pull off too. Especially if Lucas was actively looking. I said nothing, letting them use their own judgment.

We continued down the Corniche, getting a play-by-play from Decoy, with Brett shadowing one road over. They made the roundabout next to the Sheraton and continued west. I looked at my map and saw they were paralleling the diplomatic quarter. *Here we go*.

I cut in to the net. "Keep your eyes out. Keep him in sight. He's next to the diplomatic quarter. This will be it."

A minute later, Decoy came on. "We got a problem. I'm still on the car, but there's only one man in it. The driver."

77

"You sure? Lucas is foxtrot now?" I couldn't believe we'd missed someone exiting the vehicle.

"Yeah. I was a couple of cars back, slowed down by the roundabout, and when I caught back up, he was gone. I didn't see him dismount, but he's no longer in the vehicle."

Dammit. "Break off, break off. Circle the block. Pick him back up. Go north into the diplomatic quarter. He's probably trying to intercept the dip-pouch."

"Pike, our embassy is hell and gone from here. The State guys aren't hauling money to the Australian Embassy."

"We don't know what the hell those guys are doing. How they're going to transfer the cash. Lucas does. Find him, now! We'll take up the slack on the vehicle."

Since Lucas was gone, we were fresh. The driver would have no idea who we were. Jennifer was already burning rubber to make up the ground, instinctively knowing what I would say and that we were in the game. I vectored Brett one road over and caught the Ford passing in front of us. Knuckles shouted, "There he is!" and Jennifer jerked the wheel, cutting off traffic to get behind him.

He said, "Whoa! Keep it steady. We're still in a follow here. Don't burn us."

Jennifer looked at me for guidance, understanding the situation even before Knuckles. Already knowing what I was going to say.

"Brett, we're headed north on Al Asmakh Street. Cut over to Grand Hammad and box him in. Get ready to take him down."

Knuckles realized the problem a split second after he'd opened his mouth. "Okay, okay. I got the right side. Passenger side."

This guy was the only anchor we had to Lucas, and we needed the information in his head. It would be quick and dirty.

I said, "I'll take the left. Brett, you pin him in. Don't let him escape to your front."

"Roger all."

The vehicle never made it to Grand Hammad, pulling into the parking lot for a shopping area. I looked at the moving map on my phone and saw it was the Souk Waqif. *Great. A rat maze.*

The vehicle stopped outside a hotel, and the man exited in a hurry, looking over his shoulder. He was wearing Western dress. A uniform of some kind. He saw us coming and took off running. Straight into the souk.

Brett parked at the far end of the lot and came sprinting our way. I said, "Jennifer, get this thing ready to roll out of here. Knuckles, go left. Block the left."

I knew it was a ridiculous order. The souk would have forty different exits, and there was no way Knuckles could block them all. I started to chase, pounding across the parking lot and watching the target disappear through a door. Then I remembered Dubai and Brett's track-star speed. "Brett! You got him?"

He was behind me, still catching up. "Yeah. I see him."

"Catch his ass."

I was running flat out toward the door he'd disappeared through when Brett passed me like I was standing still. I was able to see Brett jerk right and struggled to keep him in sight. The souk was narrow, using only natural light, making it hard to run full-bore for fear of slamming into something. I was knocking folks out of the way trying to keep up when I broke out into an alley that wasn't covered.

Brett was forty meters ahead and right on the guy's heels. He leapt through the air and hammered him just below the shoulder blades, slamming the guy into a stall full of parakeets. I caught up a split second later, hearing the stall owner screeching just like his birds. A crowd gathered, and the screeching grew louder. I looked around and saw birds all over the damn place. We'd caught him in some aviary zoo, with stalls left and right jammed with all manner of fowl, the owners now raising their arms and squawking louder than the goods they were selling.

By the time I'd reached them Brett had the guy in an arm bar, the man's teeth gritted in pain. I turned around and pointed at the gathering crowd, telling them to back off in English, but using my tone and stance to convey what the language barrier would not. They got the point and quieted down, content to watch the circus.

I knelt down next to Brett. "What's he saying?"

"Nothing. He was hired to drive Lucas. He dropped him off next to the City Center mall. Nothing we don't already know."

I leaned in close. "Crank his arm."

Brett did so, and the man shrieked. "Listen to me," I said. "The man you carried is going to kill someone. I'm trying to prevent it. If you don't want to help, you'll die as well. What was his plan?"

The man moaned, his eyes rolling, and I could tell he was making connections he hadn't before. He'd done something more than just drive for Lucas and he was now realizing it might be bad. He said, "I don't know about any plan. He said he was a businessman. Here on business. All I did was drive him from the airport. I don't know about any plan."

"Where is he staying? Where were you going to take him?"

"To the mall. I swear, he told me to take him to the mall. That's it."

Lying through his teeth. I jerked his collar tight, cutting into his throat. "Tell me more than that, you asshole. You didn't pick him up as a cab fare, and he didn't have you meet him at the airport to take him to the mall. Where was he going?"

The man's eyes flicked wildly left and right, and he shouted in broken Arabic to the crowd around us. They began to react, closing in. I jerked his lapel again and felt something cut into my hand. His name tag. From the Four Seasons Hotel.

I shook him hard and said, "Is he going to the Four Seasons? Is that it?"

He moaned again, and nodded. "He's trying to get special favors from the American delegation there. For his business. I'm not supposed to say anything. Don't tell him I told you. He owes me money."

I stood up, telling Brett to release him. When I turned around, we faced a hostile crowd, angry at the way we'd treated the man. I ignored them and continued to work the problem.

"Knuckles, call Kurt and find out what you can about the Four Seasons Hotel and the peace conference. See who's staying there. Jennifer, back the SUV right up to the door we entered."

Knuckles acknowledged, and Jennifer said, "I'm already there, what's up?"

The mob had gotten tight around us, allowing the driver to flee out the back of the bird souk. Two men closed on Brett and began shouting, inside his personal space.

"We'll be coming out hot. Keep the engine revving."

Brett pushed one back, and the other threw a pathetic

roundhouse. Brett dropped him with a straight punch, and the throng went wild.

I wasted no time trying to reason with any of them, even though most were still doing nothing but yelling. I hooked the legs of the nearest guy and jerked him to the ground, then popped the man behind him in the mouth, causing him to crumble. My intent was to open a path, not hurt anyone.

Someone grabbed my shoulder from the front and I clamped my hand over his, trapping it. I leaned forward, rotating down and away, and heard the wrist break. The guy screamed and dropped. Someone flew into the wall to my right, his head snapping back and making contact with the stone. He fell like a sack of wheat, and I saw Brett running back the way we had come. I took off after him, thinking of the old proverb about running from a grizzly.

I don't have to be faster than the bear. Just faster than you.

Brett apparently knew the proverb as well, running like a scalded cheetah and leaving me to the crowd. Luckily, while there was no way I could catch him, I could certainly outrun a bunch of wheezing souk-stall owners.

I jumped into the back of our SUV seconds after Brett. I glared at him and said, "Jennifer, get the hell out of here."

She hit the gas, driving to Brett's vehicle on the far side of the parking lot. I turned to Knuckles. "What did you find out from Kurt?"

"Nothing good. I've vectored Decoy, but we're probably already too late."

"What?"

"The Four Seasons is where the entire Quartet is staying for the peace summit. Lucas is at ground zero."

78

Lucas saw the line snaking out the door to the Four Seasons before he even began walking up the drive. The security had become extremely tight, with everyone waiting until each piece of luggage was checked and they themselves had been wanded by a security guard. It would have been more efficient to have two lines, one for people checking in and one for people already staying, but apparently that idea hadn't occurred to the management.

He took his place at the end and slowly shuffled forward. He glanced at his watch, knowing the two CIA escorts would be here at any time. Just as he reached the front and handed his backpack over, he saw a Westerner exit the hotel and speak in the ear of one of the security personnel. After that, he positioned himself at the head of the circle in front of the hotel.

He's going to meet the couriers to get them past security. A horrendous thought crossed his mind. *What if they bypass the check-in? He takes them straight to their room?* The plan would fail. They *had* to check in.

The security guard snapped him out of his thoughts by poking him in the shoulder. "Sir, raise your arms and spread your legs."

He did so, watching the Westerner as the wand ran up and down his body. A minute later, he was told he could enter the hotel. He walked into the lobby and took a left, toward the reception counter, glancing over his shoulder to the security at the door, trying to see the couriers' car pull up. What he saw instead caused him to freeze.

The Caucasian from the airplane was now in the security line. Patiently waiting to enter the hotel. *Jesus. How the hell did he know where to find me?* Options were flitting through his head when the receptionist said, "Sir? Sir? Can I help you?"

"Uhh . . . yeah. I'm checking in." He handed her his passport and turned to the right while she tapped on the computer. There, situated at chest height, was his vase. A large, expensive-looking vessel containing real, fresh flowers. The positioning was perfect. The men would leave their baggage on the ground, below the counter-top, where the marble would protect it, while their upper bodies would be shredded.

Provided they checked in at all.

He glanced back out the door and was shocked again to see the two CIA men coming through the lobby, led by the escort out front, bypassing the security line. *Jesus Christ.* If they checked in now, he'd be in the blast radius.

They did so, marching right up to the counter.

The lady helping him asked something else, but he

wasn't listening. He saw one of the couriers pull out his passport and hastily said, "Where's the bathroom? I have to go."

"Sir? Sign here and you can use the restroom in your room."

The clerk helping the CIA men took the first passport in her hand.

Dropping the subterfuge, Lucas snatched his key without signing and fled across the lobby to the far side. He reached the concierge desk, ignoring the stares and watching the receptionist desk.

The clerk opened the passport, and nothing happened for a split second. Then, a violent explosion erupted from the vase. The embedded ball bearings came searing out in a radial arc, decapitating both CIA men and the escort with them. The bodies toppled over, one on top of the other.

The receptionist helping the CIA men had fallen behind the counter. Lucas had no idea of her status. The one who had helped him was shredded from the pottery shards of the back-blast and was shrieking. The orange-covered briefcase was in pristine condition, still standing next to the fallen men. Lucas ran to the site of the blast, as if to aid the downed men. When he crossed back through the lobby, he saw the unknown from the plane, fighting his way through security. And staring right at Lucas.

Lucas had planned on simply taking the case to his room, using the confusion of the blast to cloak his activities. He'd been in many such situations and knew that the initial response was always fractured, and nobody would question him walking away with the bag. They'd all be either catatonic because of the attack or rendering first aid to the fallen. Now, though, there was one man who was neither and was slicing his way through the crowds like wind through a dandelion.

Need to get out of here. Into the city. Then back to the airport.

Lucas snatched the handle of the dip-pouch container and took off running, away from the elevators and toward the stairs at the back of the hotel.

79

We were at the roundabout a block from the hotel, within striking distance of ending this whole thing, when Decoy called.

"Explosive device just went off inside the lobby. I'm working my way through the usual hysteria and some tight-ass security. I'll give you a call when I get inside."

Dammit. That son of a bitch. "How bad? How many dead?"

"I can't see shit. I'm still outside the security barrier, and the place has definitely turned into—"

I heard nothing but shouting through the line. "Decoy, you still there?"

"I got Lucas. I can see him! I can see him through the door . . . get the fuck out of my way . . . he's got the case, and he's moving to the back of the hotel . . ."

I heard muffled cursing and the shuffling of bodies, then what sounded like someone slapping leather. Decoy came back on, a little out of breath. "He's going out the back. I can't get to him. Too much bullshit panic going on. There's a bunch of Barney Fife security guys, and I can't be sure someone doesn't have a gun. I can keep pushing, but I might get myself killed."

"We'll track him. Take your time and get inside. Give me an assessment of the damage. I need to know who he killed. What he's done to the peace summit."

I looked at the map. The Four Seasons was right up against the ocean. If Lucas headed out the back, he was pinned in. He could go either north or south, running parallel to the coast, but unless he started swimming, that was it. North led to the diplomatic area, which meant security. South led to the Sheraton resort, and beyond that, the Corniche promenade. *He's going south.*

I called Brett behind us. "Stop where you are and dismount. Lucas is probably on the grounds of the Sheraton by now. We're at the Trade Center Roundabout. Jennifer's going to let Knuckles and me off here. You take the south end of the resort. Get into the park. We'll box him in."

"What do you want me to do if I find him?"

"Just get eyes on and call. We'll get to you for the takedown, but if he starts heading into the city before we can close, he's your target. Keep him on the coast. If he gets across the Corniche road, we'll never find him again."

LUCAS SPRINTED DOWN THE CIRCULAR STEPS to the restaurant below, then plowed through the throng that had gathered, all staring at one another as if their neighbor could explain the explosion, the women holding their hands to their mouths. He reached the back door and burst out of it like a horse at the Preakness. He ran flat out for about a minute, then slowed when he realized he was not being chased.

He thought about his options. First and foremost, he needed to get into the city. He'd seen the Caucasian at the front door, but not the black man. There was at least one unaccounted for on the loose. Which meant there were probably more.

He racked his brain, trying to remember who else had been in first class with him. It was unlikely the men had forces already on the ground, so whoever was after him would have either been on the same plane or flying in behind them. It had been only about thirty minutes since he left the airport, so that left the plane he was on—at least for now.

Removing the couriers and taking into account the two men he knew were after him, he could come up with four other men. *Say just one at the front door right now, that leaves five on the loose.* Five. And he could recognize only one. But they would have to cover both avenues of escape, so he was facing three at most. *Which way?* North was the quickest route back into the city. If he went fast, he could probably beat whatever box they were setting up. But it was also the diplomatic quarter. He had no idea who the men chasing him were and didn't know if they had contacts with other government agencies. He didn't want to risk the proximity of the various embassies within the quarter, all stuffed with security. South was longer, but he could get inside the Sheraton resort and really move out.

He ripped the tangerine fabric off the briefcase, stuffed it in a trash can, and began jogging along the water toward the huge pyramid of the Sheraton Hotel. He entered the gardens surrounding the pool and hugged the shoreline, acting as if he were a guest.

He saw nothing out of the ordinary. No men speaking into their sleeves, moving rapidly, or other telltale signs. He reached the far side of the garden and was faced with a manmade lagoon. It had a single footpath extending out into the bay before rejoining the shore farther south at the base of the Sheraton park. It was a barren kill zone. If he got on it, they could block both ends and he'd be done.

His other option was to enter the hotel proper, something he didn't want to do. He had no idea if the Four Seasons and the Sheraton maintained communication with each other and didn't want to enter another security zone. *No choice.*

Before opening the door, he put his hand to the window to cut the glare, peeking inside. The hallway was packed with people streaming out of a ballroom. He caught a commotion deep in the interior. He placed his other hand next to his head and saw Pike Logan barreling toward him, knocking people out of the way like a thousand pounds of bull ripping loose in a rodeo.

He snapped his head back. *Jesus Christ. What the fuck is he doing here?* Without thought, he leapt onto the walkway for the artificial lagoon and started sprinting like his life depended on it. And he now knew it did.

80

I ran through the lobby of the Sheraton, looking for the quickest route to the back door. Some sort of convention had just taken a break, and a steady stream of people was flowing out from the main ballrooms, clogging up the hallway. Knuckles took a right and shouted, "This way."

I saw the pool area ahead and fought to keep up, pushing people out of the way. "Head to the gardens by the pool. We'll sweep toward Brett in the south."

We exited, and I took a quick glance around, seeing an expansive landscaped area with multiple paths meandering through it. *Jesus. He could hide anywhere in here.* Knuckles took the first path he saw and started moving at a light jog, peering into the bushes. I stopped at a map on a bulletin board. The quickest way around the hotel and into the city was the south, but that had a chokepoint of a lagoon. He'd have to go across a causeway with no cover, something Lucas wouldn't do unless he was driven to it. *No, he's in here.*

I looked at the map again and saw that the lagoon path ran right into a parking lot next to the tennis courts at the north end of the park. From there, it was a straight shot to the Corniche road. It was too big a risk.

"Knuckles, I'm headed to the lagoon for a quick look. Brett, what's your status?"

"I'm in the park to the south of the lagoon, moving north."

"Close in quickly. He hasn't had that much time, and if he's across the lagoon, we're about to lose him."

I broke out of the landscaping on the south side of the hotel, seeing the expanse of the artificial lagoon. I traced the pathway around it, focusing on every human I saw. Most were couples. None were running. I saw a threesome of two men and a woman at the apex of the path, right before it began to curve back to shore. One of the men was carrying a brushed aluminum briefcase.

LUCAS HAD STOPPED RUNNING as soon as he realized it was drawing attention from everyone else on the path. It would be a beacon attracting Pike when he got outside. He sidled up to a couple slowly walking down the promenade. When they stopped, he stopped. Eventually, the man glared at him, pulling his wife and walking at a faster pace. Lucas began walking again, a little farther back, but still close enough to irritate the man. Lucas glanced back and saw Pike at the edge of the lagoon.

Keep cool. He's not running. He hasn't seen you.

He turned his head around and walked right into the man, who'd stopped walking and now stood with legs spread, hands on his hips.

The man said something in French and poked Lucas in the shoulder. Lucas said, "Hey, look, I don't want any trouble. Sorry. Please move out of the way."

Speaking with a heavy accent, the man said, "Why don't you just stay here? Wait five minutes before you start following us again?"

Lucas looked back and saw Pike had now stepped onto the walkway, coming toward him and talking into a cell phone.

Shit. I'm going to get boxed.

Without a word, he punched the man hard in the stomach. When he bent over in pain, Lucas whipped the briefcase into his face, dropping him like a stone. The woman screamed, and Lucas hooked her legs, getting her off balance, then shoved her hard in the shoulder, throwing her into the lagoon.

Her splash caused several people to orient on the scuffle. Two came running toward him from the direction of the hotel. Right behind them was Pike. Now sprinting and no longer talking on the phone.

Lucas took off as well, scanning the far side of the lagoon for other men, knowing they were coming. He needed to beat them to shore or he was done.

He had fifty meters to go when he saw rapid movement deep in the park. It was the black man, coming on strong, but not yet seeing Lucas. He was running on the edge of the park, without orienting on the lagoon path.

Lucas redoubled his efforts, leapt off the path to the shore, and began sprinting to the tennis courts and the parking lot beyond. He saw salvation, a mere one hundred yards away.

A taxi. With its on-duty light illuminated.

"Brett, he's on the lagoon path. Get your ass north!"

Before I even put the phone down, I saw Lucas punch the man he was with, then toss the woman into the lagoon. *What the hell?*

At first, I'd thought Lucas had help and was glad to see the violence. I took off after him, rounding the apex and ignoring the pleas of the female treading water.

I saw him reach the shore and head to the road running parallel to the tennis courts. He was getting closer to making it into the city, but I was confident we'd catch him. Especially with Brett's speed.

Lucas left the road, running across a primarily empty parking lot. I followed his line of march and saw his intent.

"Brett, he's heading for a taxi. Get on him! Don't let him reach it."

I saw Brett round the corner to the tennis court road and knew he wasn't going to catch Lucas in time. "Jennifer! What's your location? Come south to the tennis courts, block in Lucas."

I got no response and kept running, now on the tennis road myself. I was thirty meters behind Brett and seventy behind Lucas. He ripped open the back door of the taxi and threw in the briefcase.

I saw the door close, and the cab began to roll. It circled around, getting onto the tennis court road. And freedom. I stopped running, disgusted. We'd need a miracle to catch him now. "Jennifer, what's your status? He's in a cab about to head north on the Corniche road. I need eyes on."

I received no response. Instead, an SUV jumped the curb from the Corniche road. It raced across the grass, chewing up the perfectly coiffed landscaping, and exploded into the parking lot, reaching a speed of forty miles an hour.

It veered right at the cab, homing in like a laser-guided missile. The cab swerved left to avoid an impact, to no avail. The SUV collided head-on into the rear passenger door, both vehicles grinding to a stop.

Through the rising smoke, I saw Lucas crawl out the far side and drop to the ground. He rose unsteadily, grabbed the briefcase, and began jogging across the parking lot. The SUV door opened, and Jennifer sprang out, moving much faster. She leapt across the hood of the cab, closed the gap to Lucas, and threw herself into his body, hitting him in the backs of his thighs and bringing him to the ground.

Sprinting as fast as I could, I saw Jennifer wrap her legs around his waist and her arms around his neck in a submission hold. I saw Lucas's arms swinging wildly at the demon on his back, to no avail. Brett reached them first, and I heard him shouting something. He then began to pull Jennifer's arms away from Lucas's neck.

I was close enough to see that Lucas was already unconscious, his tongue lolling to the side, eyes half open, and still Jennifer torqued her arms back, bending his neck farther and farther. Brett shouted again, and I realized what was happening.

Jesus. She's trying to kill him.

81

The doorknob to the conference room rattled, and we all snapped our heads toward it. Blaine Alexander entered and went from face to face until he saw me.

"He wants to talk to you."

"Me? What the hell for?"

"Don't know, and you don't have to do it."

I thought for a minute. About the costs and the rewards. "Would it help with the interrogation?"

"Yeah. We give him something, now he has to give back. He knows a ton about Hezbollah operations, but he's playing coy. We'll get it out of him eventually, but this would make it easier. So far it's his only demand."

I looked at Jennifer. She said, "I don't think you should do it. It's not worth the price. It'll eat you alive, and . . . and you might not be able to hold back."

"I'm okay with that. I won't kill him. I'm just not sure I want to hear what that fuck's got to say."

Blaine said, "I'll be there as well. I'll make sure Pike stays cool."

"You don't want to go, I'll take your place," Brett said. "Give Mr. Kane a little love."

Which was a damn sight different from what he was spouting in the SUV headed back to Al Udeid Air Base.

Decoy had rolled into the parking lot as Brett and I were wrestling Jennifer off of Lucas. He'd monitored the radio transmissions and had abandoned the bomb damage assessment to help us apprehend him. Jennifer had fought like a wildcat, but eventually given up. We'd thrown Lucas's rag doll body into the back and hauled ass out of there.

I'd called Blaine, giving him the situation as I knew it, and telling him we had the diamonds and Lucas. After I'd hung up, I'd given Jennifer a questioning look. Her wild eyes were gone, now filled with what looked like shame.

I said, "What was that?"

"I don't know. I didn't want you to get near him. To be forced to kill him. I was afraid of what it would do to you."

"So *you* were going to kill him?"

From the driver's seat, Knuckles said, "It's not too late."

Brett, in the back watching Lucas, said, "Nobody's going to kill him. Not with me in the vehicle. It's not what we do."

Knuckles said, "He's a DOA target. Doesn't matter."

"It sure as shit *does* matter. It's dead *or* alive. We got him alive, and that's how he's going to stay."

Knuckles looked at me, and I said, "Let it go."

Blaine had managed to set up a no-search entrance onto Al Udeid Air Base using a back gate. From there, we'd taken over a segment of the CIA station on the airfield and were now locked in a conference room until we could fly out. The first thing we'd learned was that the two "State Department" couriers were actually CIA operatives from Brett's old organization, the Special Activities Division, which had caused him to have a change of heart on the whole DOA thing.

Blaine said, "Nobody's going to give Mr. Kane any love. He's a detained asset like any other. Get your emotions out of it."

He looked at me. "Can you do that?"

"Yeah. I can do it."

Jennifer reached across the table and squeezed my hand. "Don't talk about your family. Don't go there."

I gave her what I hoped was a look of reassurance and left the room with Blaine. To keep my mind off of who I was facing, I asked him where we stood.

"So far, not too bad. The bombing at the Four Seasons has pretty much consumed the entire police force here. We've fed them the porter, and he's now in custody. Odds are he doesn't know anything, but he makes a pretty good scapegoat, since he worked at the hotel."

"What about the chase and the wrecked vehicles?"

"Well, luckily you were smart enough to rent them with Knuckles's ID. That thing's been no good since Beirut anyway. We'll pay for the damage through a cutout the ID's tagged to and burn that company as well. It's a hole, but given the mess going on with the bombing, and the peace conference, a hit-and-run isn't going to get a lot of police attention. I'll be here playing cleanup for a while, but I think we'll be good. The key is getting your party out of here and on U.S. soil. The sooner the better."

"When's that?"

"The bird I came in on is gassed up and ready to go. The trick is working it into the flow without drawing attention. CIA has two aircraft leaving in a couple of hours to Iraq. We'll insert into their package to confuse the issue, using false tail numbers until we get to Germany."

We reached a single steel door at the end of the hallway. Blaine said, "You sure about this?"

"Yeah. Let's get it over with."

He swung open the door, and I saw the back of a man sitting in a single chair. No other furniture in the room. No pictures on the walls, no windows, the room illuminated with harsh overhead fluorescent lights. The only thing in view besides the man was a digital video camera on a tripod to his front.

I circled and saw they had Lucas flex-tied tightly to the chair. Each wrist and ankle cuffed to the metal arms and legs with a thick plastic zip-tie. The chair itself was bolted down. *Looks like we've learned a lesson.*

Lucas saw me and said, "Well, well. Marshal Dillon finally gets his man."

"What do you want?"

"Just to talk. That's it. I've missed talking to someone

who knows what it's like. But I want to talk alone. That was the deal. No cameras and nobody else in the room."

Blaine said, "Tough shit. Here's Pike. You have five minutes."

I said, "I'm good with it. I'm okay. I can do this."

82

Blaine gave me a hard look, trying to determine if I was a loose cannon or not. I nodded, and he grudgingly left the room. I turned off the camera.

"Okay, Lucas. Here we are. Say whatever it is you have to say."

"Come on, Pike. Don't give me any sanctimonious bullshit. You and I are the same. Three years ago, it was almost you in this chair."

"Three years ago you murdered people all over the country trying to get to me. We are *not* the same."

"So what? You kill people all the time. You just think it's because of some bullshit patriotic reason. I used to be the same way. When I got out of the Navy, I hated the private sector, but after a while, I saw it wasn't any different. I say I'm doing it for money. You tell yourself you're doing it for the country. In the end we both do it because we like it."

I felt the first tickle of anger. "Bullshit. I don't run around murdering people."

He laughed. "Because the government doesn't call it murder? Killing's killing."

I decided to knock him back. "Why'd you murder the senator's wife?"

It worked. He grew quiet, then said, "You've been busy."

"Why?"

"Someone had a vote coming up, and the senator wasn't playing ball. I got in, and he retired. Simple as that."

"What about the military contractor, Tim?"

"How'd you know about him? Where's this information coming from?"

"Answer the question."

"He was competing for a contract with an overseas company. He had the edge as a U.S. firm. Getting rid of him made the overseas company a sole-source bid."

"And the woman and child that were with him?"

Don't go there. Stop right now. I had promised myself I wouldn't bring up their deaths, but I had walked right down the road to this point like I'd been hypnotized.

"They were just collateral damage. I didn't want to kill them, but they walked right into the middle of the operation. I had to make it look like something crazy had happened."

"Collateral damage? You fucking murdered two people and call it collateral damage?"

He scoffed. "Come on, Pike. You never called in an airstrike on a target and had women and kids inside staying with the terrorist? It's the same damn thing."

The rage started to grow, the blackness spreading. My hands began to shake. *Back off. Go somewhere else.*

"Who broke your nose? I'd like to shake that guy's hand, you piece of shit."

He looked confused. "Jennifer broke my nose. Right after . . ."

What the hell is he talking about?

"Right after what?"

He gave me a smug smile. "She didn't tell you? I guess maybe I was wrong. Maybe we're not the same. At least in the bedroom."

His words sank in, and a part of me was ripped out by the roots. I felt nauseated and dizzy, my vision tunneling into a tube. I leaned against the wall, afraid I was going to black out. I squatted down, breathing deeply. The feeling passed, and a coldness began to seep into my body, like water from the bottom of the ocean. It spread throughout, driving out the rage. Driving out the blackness. I felt nothing at all, and in that moment, I knew what it was like to be Lucas Kane.

I rose slowly, and he sensed something was wrong. Recognizing how mistaken he had been before. We hadn't been alike at all. Until now.

I went to the steel door and flipped the bolt lock. I pulled out my Spyderco knife. I needed to free him from his bonds, but could only do one arm at a time, so I had to make sure he couldn't attack while I freed the other.

I reached around him and sliced his right bicep at the juncture where it joined his humerus, the serrated blade going down until I had severed the tendons.

He screamed and thrashed, then began yelling, "What

the fuck are you doing? Have you lost your mind? Think of the intelligence I have. The help I can give!"

I said, "You're wrong about me. I'm not like you."

I cut the cuff of the arm I'd just damaged, then the cuff to his right ankle.

"I'm no murderer."

I bent down and cut the left ankle cuff. I heard Blaine pounding on the door outside. I ignored it and cut the cuff on his remaining good arm.

I looked into his eyes. "But I am a killer."

I tossed the knife onto the floor in front of him and stood to the side.

"I wish I could make this painless, but it's got to look like something crazy happened here. Like you escaped and attacked me."

He said, "Are you fucking nuts? I'm not going to fight you. You just destroyed my arm! I'll wait until they break that door down."

I swung a vicious right hook and snapped his head back.

"Then I guess you're going to die like a fucking weasel in that chair. Go for the knife. It's the last chance the U.S. government is going to give you."

He twisted his head until he could see me. "Why, man? I can help the United States. I have more operational data in my head than you'll ever get. I *penetrated* Hezbollah. Come on, Jennifer's just a piece of ass. Ask the man outside the door! She's not worth the damage you're going to do to United States security!"

I smiled with little warmth. I now knew I was going to enjoy this. "She's worth all I have to give. And for you, that's going to be considerable."

He said nothing. I flipped Heather's driver's license into his lap. "You never made the connection to the name, did you?"

He recognized the license, confusion in his eyes, wondering how I'd found it. Wondering where this was going. When he focused on the last name, his eyes narrowed to slits, and I knew I had won. Knew he would realize nothing remained but to fight. He dove out of the chair toward the knife. I waited a half second, until he got his good hand on it.

Then I went to work.

83

Looking expectantly around the room, Kurt waited for another question, but none came. *Well, this was a hell of a lot easier than I thought it would be.* Given the chaotic actions in Doha, including his unilateral order to launch a Taskforce team, every single member of the Oversight Council had come to hear the briefing, but none had blistered him like he thought they would.

He turned to President Warren and said, "Sir, subject to anything you have, this concludes the briefing."

"Nope," President Warren said. "That's it. Thanks for coming by. I'd blocked out two hours for this, but looks like we're done."

The room broke into a low buzz, and Kurt turned to pack his attaché case. The president leaned in and said, "I'd like to see you for a minute."

Kurt nodded, thinking, *Great. Knew it was too easy.*

Alexander Palmer, the national security advisor, began speaking to the president, and Kurt followed them both out of the room. They exited the Old Executive Office Building and entered the West Wing of the White House.

In short order, they reached the Oval Office. The president looked at his watch, then cut off the conversation. He motioned to Kurt, and all three began to enter the Oval Office. Before Kurt reached the door, he heard the president say, "Alex, I'd like to see Kurt in private, if that's okay."

Palmer looked peeved, but said nothing.

Kurt wondered if that was a good thing or a bad thing. *What the hell is this all about?*

The president took a seat behind his desk and got right to the point.

"So, Lucas escaped and attacked Pike, huh?"

"Yes, sir."

"This would be what, his third time to get out of Taskforce control? This time inside a facility full of Taskforce operators? You saying your boys are too stupid to learn from previous mistakes?"

Where's this going? How come he didn't dig into this in front of the Council?

"No, sir."

"Doesn't sound like the Lucas Kane you've been briefing. You said he'd sell his mother for money and did nothing on emotion. Why would he attack Pike instead of trying to simply get free?"

"I think we misread him. Pike was in the room with him. Apparently he knew he was done and wanted a little payback."

"So now he escaped *in front of* Pike? Is that what you're saying?"

"I don't have a complete report yet."

The president let that hang in the air for a moment, then said, "A little birdy told me his restraints had been cut."

Uh-oh.

"That little birdy's full of shit."

President Warren broke into a grin. "Come on. Nobody cares! You guys saved the day. Pike's a damn hero. The director of the CIA is happy Lucas got smoked because of the men he lost from SAD, and the secretary of state is jumping for joy because the peace process was saved. *I'm* jumping for joy because the peace process was saved. Shit, nobody batted an eye that you launched an entire Taskforce team without even *informing* the Council. You could have told us you'd had Lucas drawn and quartered on the square."

Kurt inwardly sighed, relieved. *He just wants some inside skinny. Too bad I can't give it to him.*

"Sir, I can't alter what happened. Lucas went crazy. He could have possibly escaped, but he chose to attack Pike. He went down hard. His choice."

"So I heard in the briefing. I thought Pike was better trained than that. What happened to all that kung-fu, martial arts shit? He couldn't subdue him? He had to beat him to death with his bare hands?"

"Lucas got some licks in. Hit Pike with a knife. He was just defending himself."

The president grinned again and turned his chair to the window. "Convenient that Pike was the one to kill him."

Kurt felt the edge return. *Surely he doesn't know about Pike's family.* If he did, the president would know he had been lying outright.

"Why?"

"Nothing. Just that Lucas tried to kill him and Jennifer three years ago, and now he ends up dying at Pike's hands. All neat and tied up in a bow. But, if that's what happened, that's what happened. Right?"

"That's what my after-action report will read."

The president spun back around. "All right, all right. I'll live with it. But when I'm out of this office, we're going for some beers."

Kurt said, "Yes, sir."

President Warren waited for something more. When none came, he sighed and said, "What about the two terrorists we have? You think we'll get anything out of them for future operations?"

Relieved to be away from the death of Lucas, Kurt said, "Hamid, the guy we got in the apartment in Dubai, is a nobody. He was helping the Ghost out of friendship. No other terrorism connections. We're going to turn him loose after making sure we're right. Run him through GITMO, then repatriate him."

"And the Ghost?"

"I don't know. He's not a global jihadist. He's just a nationalist for the Palestinian cause. He's not one of those guys frothing at the mouth about Muslims taking it to the capitalist pigs. He doesn't know much about any global movements, but he's one deadly dude. Pike's got an idea, though."

"What's that?"

"I'm not sure I should tell you so soon. It's just an idea at this stage. Ever hear of the Selous Scouts?"

"No."

"It was a Special Forces unit in the Rhodesian civil war. The government used 'turned terrorists' to infiltrate the insurgency movements. Teamed with Special Forces operators, it was extremely effective, with damage that far outweighed its size."

President Warren looked incredulous. "Yeah, you should have waited on that. Only Pike would like an idea that crazy. Where is he now, by the way?"

"On leave in Charleston. Getting some well-deserved rest."

84

Pike said, "The reservation's in my name. Order me a rum and Coke. I'll be up as soon as I park."

Jennifer said, "Here? You can't afford this."

"I can every once in a while. When it's a special occasion."

Jennifer exited the vehicle and entered Halls Chophouse, one of the finest steakhouses on the Charleston peninsula. And the cost on the menu reflected it. Not that she was complaining, because Pike was paying, and the service, food, and atmosphere were well worth the price.

Being led to their table on the second floor, she wondered what he'd meant by the comment "special occasion." She'd made it plain that she didn't want to talk about their relationship, and he'd taken that at face value, agreeing immediately. Which just raised more suspicion. *He's been hinting about the talk for weeks.*

She just couldn't do it. She knew if they had the "Big Talk," as Pike called it, she'd have to bring up Lucas. And what he had done to her. She cared deeply for Pike and knew she couldn't have a relationship that started out as a lie. He deserved to know, and she was petrified to tell him. She had been soiled by the man who'd taken everything he'd held dear. *There's no way he'll look at me the same.* No way he wouldn't be revolted in her presence. Even if he pretended, it would be there, she knew. She'd rather remain as a business partner. *Half of Pike is better than none.*

She felt the sadness coming again. Since they'd returned to Charleston, she'd continually fought the urge to cry and realized the attack itself wasn't the true punishment. It was the loss of Pike the attack had caused. Because of Lucas, she would never connect with him. Lucas had taken everything from her over nothing more than greed. She wished she could cause him pain even now.

Pike seemed to be oblivious to her mood swings. In fact, he seemed on top of the world. She wondered if that was an act, after what he had done to Lucas. If maybe he wasn't covering up the same type of scars she had. She was worried about him. Worried that he would explode from what he had done, letting the pent-up venom out in a rage and causing his downfall. She might not get to have him, but she could still protect him.

The waiter came, and she ordered two Bacardi Cuba Libres. When he returned, Pike was right behind him.

"Got lucky. Open spot on John Street."

She smiled and paused for the waiter to leave.

"So, what's the occasion?"

"Nothing big. Just that we made it home alive and in one piece."

She said, "Are you really in one piece? I mean, you sure are acting chipper, like every day's your birthday."

He grinned, and she saw it was genuine. "Yeah, I'm good. I'm better than good. I feel whole again."

She said nothing, reading his eyes to flush the lie. She sensed none, unlike she had in Beirut. No hidden pain. *Is he really whole? After what I saw in Frankfurt?*

"Pike, please don't hide it. Don't pretend. I've seen what that's like with you. I'll still be here." She smiled. "I've seen you at your worst. I don't want to see that again."

"Jennifer, I mean it. I had a couple of bad nights, but they were all based on Lucas. He tried to convince me we were the same, and I think I was wondering if he wasn't right. But I'm nothing like him."

She let that sit for a second, then said, "So killing him had no effect? I'm not poking, it's just that you were pretty adamant in Frankfurt. Afraid of the cost."

"Yeah, I was. But that's exactly what I mean. I almost killed an innocent man. Lucas would have done it and not lost a wink of sleep. I came close, and it tore me up." He paused, then said, "You ever see the movie *The Green Mile*?"

"Yeah, I think. That movie with Tom Hanks?"

"That's the one. Killing Lucas was like releasing the bees in that movie. Remember when John Coffey opened his mouth and all those bees flew out into the bad guy?

That's what it felt like to me. All of my hate and anger went straight into Lucas, and it hasn't come back."

She said nothing, happy for him and sad for herself. Lucas's demise had made her feel shameful because of the joy it had brought. But it hadn't brought closure. Only telling Pike would do that—and when she did, it would be closure for good between them.

He took her hand, surprising her. "Which is why I brought you here tonight. I said I'm whole, but I'm not. There's a piece missing."

She felt a panic rise. *You promised*.

He leaned in and kissed her on the lips. She didn't move, didn't respond, frozen in place. She felt the urge to run. To stall for time. To prevent this from being the last dinner she had with him.

"Pike, I can't do this. Don't make me do this tonight."

"I know. Don't worry, I know. That kiss was just a little Monkey's Blood."

She stared blankly at him, the confusion mounting.

He said, "I'm not whole because you're not whole."

He placed his other hand over hers and leaned across the table until they were inches apart. She saw the kindness in his eyes and felt the sadness blossom anew at the loss she was about to create.

"Pike. I have to tell you something."

He said, "Shhhh. You don't have to tell me anything. I just want you to know I'm here, just like you were for me. No commitments, no big talk until you're ready. I just want you to know I understand."

She felt the tears well up and said, "No, you *don't* understand—"

He cut her off. "Jennifer, I didn't kill Lucas because of what he did to my family. I killed him for what he did to you."

It took several seconds for the meaning to become clear. Then several more for the implications to sink in. *He already knows. And doesn't care.*

Pike leaned in farther and kissed her again. This time she hesitatingly returned it.

He said, "I hear Monkey's Blood can cure anything."

ACKNOWLEDGMENTS

Strangely enough, the first person I would like to thank provided help for something that ended up getting cut completely. A big part of the initial draft of *Enemy of Mine* was set in Syria. As fate would have it, Rob, my old college roommate, was the defense attaché for the U.S. Embassy in Damascus. We planned on a research trip to both Syria and Lebanon, with him as a tour guide, and he helped with initial plotting from tactical details such as the interior flow of the Damascus airport to strategic information about Hezbollah, President Assad, and the future of the Levant. Then, Syria went up in smoke and my trip fell apart, with Rob becoming preoccupied with cabinet-level visits and car bombs. Sorry all of that got cut, Rob, but rest assured the ethos is threaded throughout. The Ghost was born in our conversations. Glad you made it home safely.

With the Levant portion of my trip in shambles, I had to rely on old-fashioned research into Beirut. I've now read a ton of dry books on Hezbollah and the Palestinian problem, but only one really captured the atmosphere of

Lebanon. Michael Totten, a journalist who spent a great deal of time all over the Levant, wrote *The Road to Fatima Gate*, which I used relentlessly. If you have any interest, I'd recommend picking it up.

There are a couple of unnamed drivers in Qatar and Dubai who helped immensely, one from Bangladesh and one from Egypt. Want to know what's going on at the local level, beyond the tourist hype and the official government line? Hire an unregulated cabbie. They love to showcase their knowledge and are more than willing to do things that some would say are a little gray. My wife was convinced I was going to end up as a ransom demand, but it was the best money I have ever spent on any of my research.

Thanks to Axe, Slappy, and Sergeant Major "A" for helping with the dive scene. I'm not a combat diver, but I am PADI certified, so I figured how hard could it be to write an underwater scene? Turns out, diving with a rebreather is a little bit different than open-circuit diving, and luckily I had them to correct my mistakes. If any remain, rest assured, they're mine alone.

Stuck in a barracks with Axe, he also gave my complicated elevator ambush a sanity check on my explosives planning—along with catching a huge mistake on the IED the Ghost places on Knuckles's car.

I have to give a shout-out to J-Boy, who claims he invented a widget I used in the book. I'm fairly certain I'm the one who invented it, but he remembers it differently, so I'll give him his due. More importantly, he also confirmed my dim memory of diplomatic-pouch procedures.

The case officer in Beirut, code named Cedar Hill, is a real person. Well, at least a real name. Here in South Carolina there's a wonderful organization called the Barrier Island Free Medical Clinic that provides continuing primary health care to uninsured adults living at or below 200 percent of the federal poverty level. All of its doctors are volunteers, and all of its operating costs are donated or generated through fundraisers. One of the founding members enjoyed *One Rough Man* and contacted me out of the blue, asking if I would let them auction off a character name in this book at their annual charity golf tournament, with the proceeds benefiting the clinic. Completely flattered, I said yes, and Cedar Hill became Louis Britt. I haven't met him, but I hope he enjoys the character.

Seeing my name on the cover of a book is still a surreal experience, and I'm indebted to my agent, John Talbot; my editor, Ben Sevier; and the entire Dutton team. Thank you for keeping me on track and preventing me from making rookie mistakes, both on the page and in the publishing world, period. It amazes me when I'm out buying dinner and see my book in a grocery store, and I'm under no illusions about how it got there.

Finally, to my wife, for not only the usual rap-on-the-knuckles fifth grade grammar checks, but also for keeping the house together on my frequent absences. She had a lot of practice during my Army years, but it's looking like being a writer/security consultant is going to give those deployments a run for the money. I oogly moogly you.

Read on for an excerpt from the new
Pike Logan thriller from Brad Taylor,

The Polaris Protocol

Available in hardcover from Dutton

1

Sergeant Ronald Blackmar never heard the round before it hit, but registered the whine of a ricochet right next to his head and felt the sliver of rock slice into his cheek. He slammed lower behind the outcropping and felt his face, seeing blood on his assault gloves. His platoon leader, First Lieutenant Blake Alberty, threw himself into the prone and said with black humor, "You get our asses out of here, and I'll get you another Purple Heart."

Blackmar said, "I've got nothing else to work with. The eighty-ones won't reach and the Apaches are dry."

Another stream of incoming machine-gun rounds raked their position, and Alberty returned fire, saying, "We're in trouble. And I'm not going to be the next COP Keating."

Both from the Twenty-fifth Infantry Division, they were part of a string of combat outposts in the Kunar province of Afghanistan. Ostensibly designed to prevent the infiltration of Taliban fighters from the nearby border of Pakistan, in reality they were a giant bull's-eye for anyone wanting a scalp. Attacked at the COP on a daily basis, they still followed orders, continuing their patrols to the nearby villages in an effort to get the locals on the government's side.

The mountains of the Kunar province were extreme and afforded the Taliban an edge simply by putting the Americans on equal terms. Everything was done on foot, and the mountains negated artillery, leaving the troops reliant on helicopter gunship support. The same thing COP Keating had relied on when it was overrun two years before.

The incoming fire grew in strength, and Alberty began receiving reports of casualties. They were on their own and about to be overrun. A trophy for the Taliban. Blackmar heard the platoon's designated marksmen firing, their rifles' individual cracks distinctive among the rattle of automatic fire, and felt impotent.

As the forward observer, the purpose of his entire career had been to provide steel on-target for the infantry he supported. He was the man they turned to when they wanted American firepower, and now he had nothing to provide, his radio silent.

Alberty shouted, "They're flanking! They're flanking! We need the gunships."

Blackmar was about to reply when his radio squawked. "Kilo Seven-Nine, this is Texas Thirteen. You have targets?"

He said, "Yes, yes. What's your ordnance?"

"Five-hundred-pound GBU."

GBU? A fast mover with JDAMs?

He said, "What's your heading?"

The pilot said, "Don't worry about it. I'm a BUFF. Way above you."

Blackmar heard the words and couldn't believe it. He'd called in everything from eighty-one-millimeter mortars to F-15 strike aircraft, but he'd never called fire from a B-52 Stratofortress. Not that it mattered, as the five-hundred-pound JDAM was guided by GPS.

He lased the Taliban position for range, shacked up his coordinates, and sent the fire request. The pilot reported bombs out, asking for a splash. He kept his eyes on the enemy, waiting. Nothing happened.

Alberty screamed, "You hit the village! You hit the village! Shift, shift!"

The village? That damn thing is seven hundred meters away.

He checked his location and lased again, now plotting the impact danger close as the enemy advanced. He repeated the call with the new coordinates and waited for the splash.

Alberty shouted again, "You're pounding the fucking village! Get the rounds on-target, damn it!"

Blackmar frantically checked his map and his range, shouting back, "I'm right! I'm on-target. The bombs aren't tracking."

The volume of enemy fire increased, and Alberty began maneuvering his forces, forgetting about the firepower circling at thirty thousand feet. Blackmar called for another salvo, recalculating yet again. No ordnance impacted the enemy. Thirty minutes later, the Americans' superior firepower meant nothing, as the fight went hand-to-hand.

Captain "Tiny" Shackleford noticed the first glitch when the coordinates on his screen showed the RQ-107 unmanned aerial vehicle a hundred miles away from the designated flight path. Which, given his target area over Iran's nuclear facilities, was a significant problem.

Flying the drone from inside Tonopah airbase, Nevada, he felt a rush of adrenaline as if he were still in the cockpit of an F-16 over enemy airspace and his early-warning sensors had triggered a threat. He called an alert, saying he had an issue, then realized he'd lost the link with the UAV. He began working the problem, trying to prevent the drone from going into autopilot and landing, while the CIA owners went into overdrive.

The RQ-107 was a new stealth UAV, the latest and greatest evolution of unmanned reconnaissance, and as such, it was used out of Afghanistan to probe the nuclear ambitions of Iran. It had the proven ability to fly above the Persian state with impunity and was a major link to the intelligence community on Iranian intentions. Losing one inside Iranian airspace would be a disaster. An army of technicians went to work, a modern-day version of *Apollo 13*.

They failed.

*   *   *

MARK OGLETHORPE, THE UNITED STATES secretary of defense, said, "We've had forty-two confirmed GPS failures. We've identified the glitch, and it's repaired, but we lost a UAV inside Iran because of it."

Alexander Palmer, the national security advisor, said, "Glitch? I'd say it's more than a glitch. What happened?"

"The new AEP system of the GPS constellation had a software-hardware mating problem. It's something that the contractor couldn't see beforehand."

"Bullshit. It's something they *failed* to see. Did it affect the civilian systems? Am I going to hear about this from Transportation?"

"No. Only the military signal, but you're definitely going to hear about it from the Iranians. They're already claiming they brought our bird down."

Palmer rubbed his forehead, thinking about what to brief the president. "I don't give a damn about that. They got the drone, and that's going to be a fact on tomorrow's news. Let 'em crow."

"You want to allow them the propaganda of saying they can capture our most sophisticated UAV? We'll look like idiots."

"Someone *is* an idiot. But I'd rather the world wonder about the Iranian statements."

"As opposed to what?"

"The fucking truth, that's what."

2

Present Day

Joshua Bryant saw the seat belt light flash and knew they had just broken through ten thousand feet. Time to shut off his iPod, but more importantly, it was his turn in the window seat.

Only fifteen years old, his passion in life was airplanes and his singular goal was to become a pilot—unlike his younger sister, who wanted the window only to aggravate him. She'd complained as they had boarded, and his mother had split the difference. She got the window for takeoff, and he got it for landing.

"Mom, we're coming into final approach and it's my turn."

His sister immediately responded, "No, we're not! He's just talking like he knows what's going on."

Joshua started to reply when the pilot came over the intercom, telling them they had about ten more minutes before parking at their gate in Denver. Joshua smiled, just to annoy her. She grouched a little more but gave up her seat.

After buckling up, he pressed his face against the glass, looking toward the wing jutting out three rows up, watching the flaps getting manipulated by the pilot. The aircraft continued its approach and he saw the distinctive swastika shape of Denver International Airport.

A flight attendant came by, checking seat belts at a leisurely pace, and then another rushed up and whispered in her ear. They both speed-walked in the direction of the cockpit, the original flight attendant's face pale.

Joshua didn't give it much thought, returning his attention to the window. He placed his hands on either side of his face to block the glare and began scanning. On the ground below he saw a small private plane taxiing. With as much conscious thought as someone recognizing a vegetable, he knew it was a Cessna 182.

The Boeing 757 continued to descend and began to overtake the Cessna. Strangely, the Cessna continued taxiing. With a start, Joshua realized it had taken off, directly underneath them. He watched it rise in slow motion, closing the distance to their fragile airship.

He turned from the window and screamed, "Plane! An airplane!"

His mother said, "What?"

The Cessna collided with the left wing just outside the engine, a jarring bump as if the 757 had hit a pocket of turbulent air. Passengers began to whip their heads left and right, looking for someone to explain what had happened.

Twenty feet of wing sheared off as the Cessna chewed through the metal like a buzz saw, exploding in a spectacular spray of aluminum confetti, followed by a fuel-air ball of fire.

Joshua knew the wing would no longer provide lift. Knew they were all dead.

He was the first to scream.

The aircraft yawed to the left, seeming to hang in the air for the briefest of moments, then began to plummet to earth sideways. The rest of the passengers joined Joshua, screaming maniacally, as if that would have any effect on the outcome.

The fuselage picked up speed and began to spin, the centrifugal force slapping the passengers about, one minute right-side up, the next upside down, filling the cabin with flying debris.

Four seconds later, the screams of all one hundred and eighty-seven souls ceased at the exact same moment.

3

Three Days Before

"They're here. I just heard the door open and close."

Even though the door in question was to the adjacent hotel room, the man whispered as if they could hear him as clearly as he could them.

"Jack, for the last time, as your editor, this is crazy."

"You didn't say that when I began."

"That was before you started playing G. Gordon Liddy at the Watergate!"

Jack heard voices out of the small speaker on the desk and said, "I gotta go. Stay near your phone in case I need help."

He heard "Jack—" but ended the call without responding.

He checked to make sure the digital recorder was working, then leaned in, waiting for someone to appear on the small screen. The thin spy camera had slipped out of position just a bit, making the room look tilted.

A hefty Caucasian sat down in view, wearing jeans and a polo shirt that was a size too small. *The contact.*

Another man began speaking off-camera in flawless English with a slight Spanish accent which, given what Jack was investigating, was to be expected. The words, however, were not. Nothing the man said had anything to do with the drug cartels or America. It was all about technology.

Eventually, the contact spoke. Jack leaned in, willing him to say what he wanted to hear. Wanting to believe his insane risk had been worth it.

He, also, said not a word about drugs, but blathered on about the right of the masses to digital technology and the developed-world governments' undying interest in monopolizing information.

Jack rubbed his eyes. *What the hell is this all about? Who gives a shit about information flow?*

The guy sounded like an anarchist, not a connection for the expansion of the Sinaloa drug cartel into America. The contact droned on about his ability to free up information, then said something that caused Jack to perk up. He mentioned the U.S. Air Force in Colorado Springs.

Now we're getting somewhere.

Colorado Springs was just outside Denver and was the American crossroads for the Interstate 10 drug corridor leading out of El Paso, which passed right by the hotel he was now in. Running straight up until it connected with US Interstate 25, the corridor branched left and right at Colorado Springs, into the heartland of the United States.

The future battleground he was trying to prove was coming.

Jack leaned in, straining to catch every word, but most had nothing to do with drugs, or Mexico, or anything else he was investigating. He sat back, disgusted and angry that he'd paid the informant who led him to this meeting. Angry at the risk he had taken. Something bad was going on, but it wasn't anything he cared about.

Wasted money. Wasted time.

Through the speaker, he heard the door open again, not really listening anymore, cataloging how he could reconnect with his sources and informants. Trying to figure out how he could get back on the pulse of his story.

A voice in Spanish cried out, begging for mercy. The sound punctured his thoughts, not because of the words, but because of the terror, the cheap acoustics doing nothing to mask the dread. Jack stared at the screen, but the man remained outside the scope of the lens. He begged for his life, the fear seeping through like blood from a wound. On-camera, the American contact had his hands in the air, his mouth slack, clearly unsure what was going on. Jack heard his own name and felt terror wash over him like an acid bath.

Jesus Christ. It's the desk clerk. He's sold me out.

He slammed the lid to the digital recorder closed and shoved it under the bed, then grabbed the speaker and yanked it out of its connection to the wireless receiver. He threw it in the bathroom, then fumbled for his phone, his hands shaking, looking for a way out that wasn't the door. He realized there was none. Realized he'd made a catastrophic mistake.

He pulled up speed dial and hit a button. The phone went straight to voice mail. He shouted, "Andy, Andy, I'm in trouble. I'm in big trouble. Where the fuck are you?"

The door burst open and he remained standing, the phone trembling in his hand. Two men entered, both pointing pistols at him. He shouted, "No, no, no!" throwing his arms into the air. One snarled in Spanish, and he feigned ignorance. The other said in English, "Get on your knees. Now."

He did so, the fear so great he thought he would pass out. He'd studied the Mexican drug cartels for more than four years, seeing the savagery they would inflict on those who attempted to thwart them, and in no way did he want to provoke their ire any more than he had.

They handcuffed him with efficiency, no outward abuse, no punches or smacking just because they could, which did nothing but raise his alarm. They weren't local thugs. They were trained and had done this many times before. He began calculating what he could do. How long he had. He knew they wouldn't kill him here, in El Paso. The drug trade was vicious, violent beyond the average human's comprehension, but it still wasn't here. They'd move him, which meant some time. At least a day while they tried to get him across the border, to Ciudad Juárez, where they could torture him freely.

One day. Twenty-four hours. He looked at his watch and saw the seconds begin to disappear.

4

I opened the door and felt like I needed an oxygen mask from the smoke spilling out, the nightclub so full of fumes from cigarettes that I was having a hard time seeing five feet.

Guess this place hasn't heard of the secondhand dangers.

I felt Jennifer recoil and pulled her inside. Sometimes you get to play baccarat in Monte Carlo in a tuxedo, and sometimes you have to belly up to a smoke-infested bar in Turkmenistan. *Story of my life.*

The room reminded me of the bar at the beginning of *Raiders of the Lost Ark*, where Indiana Jones meets up with his ex-girlfriend. A bunch of burly men and raunchy woman yelling and shouting at one another. All I needed to do was get Jennifer to challenge some big-ass bear of a man to a vodka-drinking contest, and the image would be complete.

Sotto voce, Jennifer said, "This place looks like the cantina in *Star Wars*."

I chuckled and said, "Wrong movie. Come on. We've got thirty minutes before the meet. Let's see if we can blend in that long."

We found a table in the corner, and I checked my phone, seeing I had lost service yet again. The cellular infrastructure inside Ashgabat, the capital of Turkmenistan, was pathetic to say the least. It was making our surveillance effort very difficult, but in truth no harder than it had been for our commando forefathers who worked through the Cold War. It just meant we had to go old-school.

I keyed the radio strapped to my leg and leaned into Jennifer, as if I were talking to her. "Knuckles, you staged?"

"Yes. We got a box. You send the photo and trigger, and we'll do the rest."

"Roger all."

Jennifer glanced at her watch and said, "This guy is cutting it close."

"I know. He's not stupid. He's aware of the curfew, and he's going to use it."

Nobody was allowed to walk around after eleven at night in the capital, but really that was a crapshoot. A lot of people did, and the police then usually picked on the Westerners to fleece for bribes. Or other unsavory things. There had been reports of them arresting women, taking them to jail, then extorting sexual favors. It would make a surveillance effort after the witching hour very, very hard.

"What if he doesn't show? Are we going to push it and try again tomorrow or head to Gonur?"

"We still have forty-eight hours. One more night. If he doesn't show then, we're leaving for Gonur. We can't blow off the contract. This was just a freebie anyway."

Gonur was a four-thousand-year-old archeological site set in the middle of the Kara-Kum desert, and we, as the proud owners of a company called Grolier Recovery Services, had been hired to help a team of experts take a look at the dig. Well, at least that's what the government of Turkmenistan thought.

In reality, we were a cover corporation using counterterrorist operators as employees, all working for an organization so removed from the traditional U.S. defense and intelligence infrastructure it didn't even have a real name. We simply called it the Taskforce, and it had sent us to Turkmenistan to identify a wealthy Saudi Arabian who was funding the Islamic Movement of Uzbekistan. Unfortunately, our cover took precedence over the mission, so if we didn't locate the contact, we were looking at spending a few days sweating in the desert. Something Jennifer would love. She enjoyed anything and everything dealing with old crap.

She waved her hand in front of her face, trying to clear the smoke, while she surveyed the bar, looking for our linkage target. She said, "I can't believe Pedro would meet a rich Saudi in this dump. Why not in a mosque? Or any number of coffee shops? The intel seems off to me."

Pedro was our nickname for a terrorist affiliated with the IMU. He was all set to be removed from the playing field in Uzbekistan when the Taskforce learned he was meeting a contact in Ashgabat. They decided to see if we could identify the contact, implant a collection device in his personal effects, and try to swim upstream to the

Kingdom of Saudi Arabia with the end state being identification of the money man.

I said, "The mosques here are all owned by the government. In fact, the government monitors everything here, like it's still part of the Soviet Union. He'd need someplace noisy. Someplace that self-defeats the bugs all over this damn country."

Which was why we wouldn't be doing anything overt against Pedro. Much easier to take him down when he returned to Uzbekistan. Our mission was pure snoop and poop. No high adventure.

I went to the bar, happy to see a smattering of Europeans, including one old couple clearly forcing themselves to enjoy the "culture." Jennifer and I wouldn't stand out. I got a couple of glasses of hot tea, and by the time I had returned to the table, Jennifer said, "Pedro's at the door."

I casually glanced that way and saw him, our linkage target. He was swarthy, with a full head of chestnut hair and a red beard that looked like a briar patch. Dressed in a striped shirt, the sleeves rolled up to the elbows and the tail hanging out over a pair of black slacks made of rough cloth, he looked like every other regular. He glanced around, locked on something, then began walking toward our three o'clock. I followed his line of march and saw a single man sitting at a table smoking a cigarette. *Bingo*.

"Jennifer, you see where he's headed?"

"Yeah, yeah. I got him."

"It'll be your camera."

We each had a covert digital setup embedded in our clothing—me in the upper shoulder of my jacket, and Jennifer in a brooch on her chest, the battery pack, brains, and Bluetooth transmitter hidden in our clothing. We'd purposely sat at ninety degrees to each other to give us complete coverage of the room. If he had gone toward the nine o'clock, I'd have been getting the picture.

The cameras were digital marvels controlled by our smartphones. They had limited optical zoom but a very, very good digital zoom complete with digital stabilization. The hard part had been getting the things to line up naturally to what we wanted to see, as my jacket kept shifting when I sat down, and Jennifer, believe it or not, couldn't get the thing to aim level because of the swell of her breast. After screwing around with them for a while, we'd managed to figure it out.

Jennifer brought out her phone and began working it, the image from the camera fed to it via Bluetooth. I waited to confirm the man was Pedro's contact, then began relaying to Knuckles as a backup to the photo.

"Knuckles, Pike. Zulu One located. Prepare to copy description."

After a few seconds, I heard, "Send it."

"Dark top, black, possibly blue. Long-sleeve, button-front. No jacket. Sleeves rolled completely down. Young-ish, twenty-five to thirty. Hawklike face, long nose. Swarthy—looks Saudi. Long hair down to his collar, but well kept. Looks long on purpose, not because he can't afford a barber. Small mustache but clean chin. No outstanding identifying marks. Sort of looks like Jake Gyllenhaal in *Prince of Persia*."

Jennifer, working the digital zoom, looked up and said, "He doesn't look anything like Jake Gyllenhaal. What an insult."

I keyed my radio. "Correction. Apparently Jake is much, much more attractive. Stand by for photo."

Jennifer fiddled with her phone for a second longer, then nodded at me.

My radio crackled to life and I heard, "This guy doesn't look a damn thing like Jake Gyllenhaal, except for the hair."

Jennifer grinned, and I said, "Sue me. You guys collapse in?"

"Yeah, we're set."

I saw Jennifer scrunch her eyebrows, still looking at her phone. I glanced at Jake and Pedro, but they weren't doing anything suspicious.

"What's up?"

"My phone just picked up a signal. I have a missed call and a voice mail."

"Who in the world is calling you in Turkmenistan?"

"Jack. My brother Jack."